Co

PRINCE CLASSICS

THE MONSTER
AND OTHER STORIES
&
THE OPEN BOAT
AND OTHER STORIES

STEPHEN CRANE

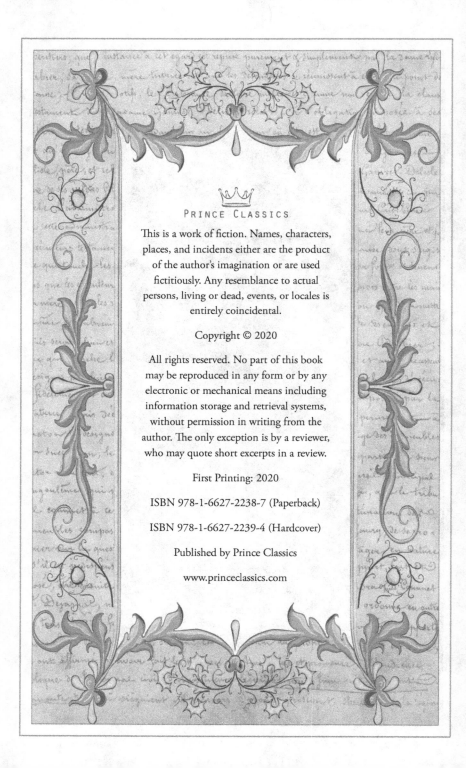

PRINCE CLASSICS

First Printing: 2020

ISBN 978-1-6627-2238-7 (Paperback)

ISBN 978-1-6627-2239-4 (Hardcover)

Published by Prince Classics

www.princeclassics.com

Stephen Crane (November 1, 1871 – June 5, 1900) was an American poet, novelist, and short story writer. Prolific throughout his short life, he wrote notable works in the Realist tradition as well as early examples of American Naturalism and Impressionism. He is recognized by modern critics as one of the most innovative writers of his generation. The ninth surviving child of Methodist parents, Crane began writing at the age of four and had published several articles by the age of 16. Having little interest in university studies though he was active in a fraternity, he left Syracuse University in 1891 to work as a reporter and writer. Crane's first novel was the 1893 Bowery tale Maggie: A Girl of the Streets, generally considered by critics to be the first work of American literary Naturalism. He won international acclaim in 1895 for his Civil War novel The Red Badge of Courage, which he wrote without having any battle experience. (Source: Wikipedia)

Literary works:
Maggie: A Girl of the Streets (1893)
The Red Badge of Courage (1895)
The Black Riders and Other Lines (1895)
George's Mother (1896)
The Third Violet (1897)
The Open Boat and Other Tales of Adventure (1898)
War is Kind (1899)
Active Service (1899)
The Monster and Other Stories (1899)
Wounds in the Rain (1900)
Great Battles of the World
The O'Ruddy (1903)
The Monster. London
Last Words. London
Whilomville Stories

THE MONSTER
AND OTHER STORIES
&
THE OPEN BOAT
AND OTHER STORIES

THE MONSTER AND
OTHER STORIES

THE MONSTER

I

Little Jim was, for the time, engine Number 36, and he was making the run between Syracuse and Rochester. He was fourteen minutes behind time, and the throttle was wide open. In consequence, when he swung around the curve at the flower-bed, a wheel of his cart destroyed a peony. Number 36 slowed down at once and looked guiltily at his father, who was mowing the lawn. The doctor had his back to this accident, and he continued to pace slowly to and fro, pushing the mower.

Jim dropped the tongue of the cart. He looked at his father and at the broken flower. Finally he went to the peony and tried to stand it on its pins, resuscitated, but the spine of it was hurt, and it would only hang limply from his hand. Jim could do no reparation. He looked again towards his father.

He went on to the lawn, very slowly, and kicking wretchedly at the turf. Presently his father came along with the whirring machine, while the sweet, new grass blades spun from the knives. In a low voice, Jim said, "Pa!"

The doctor was shaving this lawn as if it were a priest's chin. All during the season he had worked at it in the coolness and peace of the evenings after supper. Even in the shadow of the cherry-trees the grass was strong and healthy. Jim raised his voice a trifle. "Pa!"

The doctor paused, and with the howl of the machine no longer occupying the sense, one could hear the robins in the cherry-trees arranging their affairs. Jim's hands were behind his back, and sometimes his fingers clasped and unclasped. Again he said, "Pa!" The child's fresh and rosy lip was lowered.

The doctor stared down at his son, thrusting his head forward and frowning attentively. "What is it, Jimmie?"

"Pa!" repeated the child at length. Then he raised his finger and pointed at the flowerbed. "There!"

"What?" said the doctor, frowning more. "What is it, Jim?"

After a period of silence, during which the child may have undergone a severe mental tumult, he raised his finger and repeated his former word—"There!" The father had respected this silence with perfect courtesy. Afterwards his glance carefully followed the direction indicated by the child's finger, but he could see nothing which explained to him. "I don't understand what you mean, Jimmie," he said.

It seemed that the importance of the whole thing had taken away the boy's vocabulary, He could only reiterate, "There!"

The doctor mused upon the situation, but he could make nothing of it. At last he said, "Come, show me."

Together they crossed the lawn towards the flower-bed. At some yards from the broken peony Jimmie began to lag. "There!" The word came almost breathlessly.

"Where?" said the doctor.

Jimmie kicked at the grass. "There!" he replied.

The doctor was obliged to go forward alone. After some trouble he found the subject of the incident, the broken flower. Turning then, he saw the child lurking at the rear and scanning his countenance.

The father reflected. After a time he said, "Jimmie, come here." With an infinite modesty of demeanor the child came forward. "Jimmie, how did this happen?"

The child answered, "Now—I was playin' train—and—now—I runned over it."

"You were doing what?"

"I was playin' train."

14

The father reflected again. "Well, Jimmie," he said, slowly, "I guess you had better not play train any more to-day. Do you think you had better?"

"No, sir," said Jimmie.

During the delivery of the judgment the child had not faced his father, and afterwards he went away, with his head lowered, shuffling his feet.

II

It was apparent from Jimmie's manner that he felt some kind of desire to efface himself. He went down to the stable. Henry Johnson, the negro who cared for the doctor's horses, was sponging the buggy. He grinned fraternally when he saw Jimmie coming. These two were pals. In regard to almost everything in life they seemed to have minds precisely alike. Of course there were points of emphatic divergence. For instance, it was plain from Henry's talk that he was a very handsome negro, and he was known to be a light, a weight, and an eminence in the suburb of the town, where lived the larger number of the negroes, and obviously this glory was over Jimmie's horizon; but he vaguely appreciated it and paid deference to Henry for it mainly because Henry appreciated it and deferred to himself. However, on all points of conduct as related to the doctor, who was the moon, they were in complete but unexpressed understanding. Whenever Jimmie became the victim of an eclipse he went to the stable to solace himself with Henry's crimes. Henry, with the elasticity of his race, could usually provide a sin to place himself on a footing with the disgraced one. Perhaps he would remember that he had forgotten to put the hitching-strap in the back of the buggy on some recent occasion, and had been reprimanded by the doctor. Then these two would commune subtly and without words concerning their moon, holding themselves sympathetically as people who had committed similar treasons. On the other hand, Henry would sometimes choose to absolutely repudiate this idea, and when Jimmie appeared in his shame would bully him most virtuously, preaching with assurance the precepts of the doctor's creed, and pointing out to Jimmie all his abominations. Jimmie did not discover that this was odious in his comrade. He accepted it and lived in its shadow with humility, merely trying to conciliate the saintly Henry with acts of deference. Won by this attitude, Henry would sometimes allow the child to enjoy the felicity of squeezing the sponge over a buggy-wheel, even when Jimmie was still gory from unspeakable deeds.

Whenever Henry dwelt for a time in sackcloth, Jimmie did not patronize him at all. This was a justice of his age, his condition. He did not know. Besides, Henry could drive a horse, and Jimmie had a full sense of this sublimity. Henry personally conducted the moon during the splendid journeys through the country roads, where farms spread on all sides, with sheep, cows, and other marvels abounding.

"Hello, Jim!" said Henry, poising his sponge. Water was dripping from the buggy. Sometimes the horses in the stalls stamped thunderingly on the pine floor. There was an atmosphere of hay and of harness.

For a minute Jimmie refused to take an interest in anything. He was very downcast. He could not even feel the wonders of wagon washing. Henry, while at his work, narrowly observed him.

"Your pop done wallop yer, didn't he?" he said at last.

"No," said Jimmie, defensively; "he didn't."

After this casual remark Henry continued his labor, with a scowl of occupation. Presently he said: "I done tol' yer many's th' time not to go a-foolin' an' a-projjeckin' with them flowers. Yer pop don' like it nohow." As a matter of fact, Henry had never mentioned flowers to the boy.

Jimmie preserved a gloomy silence, so Henry began to use seductive wiles in this affair of washing a wagon. It was not until he began to spin a wheel on the tree, and the sprinkling water flew everywhere, that the boy was visibly moved. He had been seated on the sill of the carriage-house door, but at the beginning of this ceremony he arose and circled towards the buggy, with an interest that slowly consumed the remembrance of a late disgrace.

Johnson could then display all the dignity of a man whose duty it was to protect Jimmie from a splashing. "Look out, boy! look out! You done gwi' spile yer pants. I raikon your mommer don't 'low this foolishness, she know it. I ain't gwi' have you round yere spilin' yer pants, an' have Mis' Trescott light on me pressen'ly. 'Deed I ain't." He spoke with an air of great irritation, but he was not annoyed at all. This tone was merely a part of his importance. In reality he was always delighted to have the child there to witness the business of the stable. For one thing, Jimmie was invariably overcome with reverence when he was told how beautifully a harness was polished or a horse groomed. Henry explained each detail of this kind with unction, procuring great joy from the child's admiration.

III

After Johnson had taken his supper in the kitchen, he went to his loft in the carriage house and dressed himself with much care. No belle of a court circle could bestow more mind on a toilet than did Johnson. On second thought, he was more like a priest arraying himself for some parade of the church. As he emerged from his room and sauntered down the carriage-drive, no one would have suspected him of ever having washed a buggy.

It was not altogether a matter of the lavender trousers, nor yet the straw hat with its bright silk band. The change was somewhere, far in the interior of Henry. But there was no cake-walk hyperbole in it. He was simply a quiet, well-bred gentleman of position, wealth, and other necessary achievements out for an evening stroll, and he had never washed a wagon in his life.

In the morning, when in his working-clothes, he had met a friend—"Hello, Pete!" "Hello, Henry!" Now, in his effulgence, he encountered this same friend. His bow was not at all haughty. If it expressed anything, it expressed consummate generosity—"Good-evenin', Misteh Washington." Pete, who was very dirty, being at work in a potato-patch, responded in a mixture of abasement and appreciation—Good-evenin', Misteh Johnsing."

The shimmering blue of the electric arc lamps was strong in the main street of the town. At numerous points it was conquered by the orange glare of the outnumbering gaslights in the windows of shops. Through this radiant lane moved a crowd, which culminated in a throng before the post-office, awaiting the distribution of the evening mails. Occasionally there came into it a shrill electric street-car, the motor singing like a cageful of grasshoppers, and possessing a great gong that clanged forth both warnings and simple noise. At the little theatre, which was a varnish and red plush miniature of one of the famous New York theatres, a company of strollers was to play "East Lynne." The young men of the town were mainly gathered at the corners, in distinctive groups, which expressed various shades and lines of chumship, and had little to do with any social gradations. There they discussed everything with critical insight, passing the whole town in review as it swarmed in the street. When the gongs of the electric cars ceased for a moment to harry the ears, there could be heard the sound of the feet of the leisurely crowd on the bluestone pavement, and it was like the peaceful evening lashing at the shore of a lake. At the foot of the hill, where two lines of maples sentinelled the way, an electric lamp glowed high among the embowering branches, and made most wonderful shadow-etchings on the road below it.

When Johnson appeared amid the throng a member of one of the profane groups at a corner instantly telegraphed news of this extraordinary arrival to his companions. They hailed him. "Hello, Henry! Going to walk for a cake to-night?"

"Ain't he smooth?"

"Why, you've got that cake right in your pocket, Henry!"

"Throw out your chest a little more."

Henry was not ruffled in any way by these quiet admonitions and compliments. In reply he laughed a supremely good-natured, chuckling laugh, which nevertheless expressed an underground complacency of superior metal.

Young Griscom, the lawyer, was just emerging from Reifsnyder's barber shop, rubbing his chin contentedly. On the steps he dropped his hand and looked with wide eyes into the crowd. Suddenly he bolted back into the shop. "Wow!" he cried to the parliament; "you ought to see the coon that's coming!"

Reifsnyder and his assistant instantly poised their razors high and turned towards the window. Two belathered heads reared from the chairs. The electric shine in the street caused an effect like water to them who looked through the glass from the yellow glamour of Reifsnyder's shop. In fact, the people without resembled the inhabitants of a great aquarium that here had a square pane in it. Presently into this frame swam the graceful form of Henry Johnson.

"Chee!" said Reifsnyder. He and his assistant with one accord threw their obligations to the winds, and leaving their lathered victims helpless, advanced to the window. "Ain't he a taisy?" said Reifsnyder, marvelling.

But the man in the first chair, with a grievance in his mind, had found a weapon. "Why, that's only Henry Johnson, you blamed idiots! Come on now, Reif, and shave me. What do you think I am—a mummy?"

Reifsnyder turned, in a great excitement. "I bait you any money that vas not Henry Johnson! Henry Johnson! Rats!" The scorn put into this last word made it an explosion. "That man was a Pullman-car porter or someding. How could that be Henry Johnson?" he demanded, turbulently. "You vas crazy."

The man in the first chair faced the barber in a storm of indignation. "Didn't I give him those lavender trousers?" he roared.

And young Griscom, who had remained attentively at the window, said: "Yes, I guess that was Henry. It looked like him."

"Oh, vell," said Reifsnyder, returning to his business, "if you think so! Oh, vell!" He implied that he was submitting for the sake of amiability.

Finally the man in the second chair, mumbling from a mouth made timid by adjacent lather, said: "That was Henry Johnson all right. Why, he always dresses like that when he wants to make a front! He's the biggest dude in town—anybody knows that."

"Chinger!" said Reifsnyder.

Henry was not at all oblivious of the wake of wondering ejaculation that streamed out behind him. On other occasions he had reaped this same joy, and he always had an eye for the demonstration. With a face beaming with happiness he turned away from the scene of his victories into a narrow side street, where the electric light still hung high, but only to exhibit a row of tumble-down houses leaning together like paralytics.

The saffron Miss Bella Farragut, in a calico frock, had been crouched on the front stoop, gossiping at long range, but she espied her approaching caller at a distance. She dashed around the corner of the house, galloping like a horse. Henry saw it all, but he preserved the polite demeanor of a guest when a waiter spills claret down his cuff. In this awkward situation he was simply perfect.

The duty of receiving Mr. Johnson fell upon Mrs. Farragut, because Bella, in another room, was scrambling wildly into her best gown. The fat old woman met him with a great ivory smile, sweeping back with the door, and bowing low. "Walk in, Misteh Johnson, walk in. How is you dis ebenin', Misteh Johnson—how is you?"

Henry's face showed like a reflector as he bowed and bowed, bending almost from his head to his ankles, "Good-evenin', Mis' Fa'gut; good-evenin'. How is you dis evenin'? Is all you' folks well, Mis' Fa'gut?"

After a great deal of kowtow, they were planted in two chairs opposite each other in the living-room. Here they exchanged the most tremendous civilities, until Miss Bella swept into the room, when there was more kowtow on all sides, and a smiling show of teeth that was like an illumination.

The cooking-stove was of course in this drawing-room, and on the fire was some kind of a long-winded stew. Mrs. Farragut was obliged to arise and attend to it from time to time. Also young Sim came in and went to bed on his pallet in the corner. But to all these domesticities the three maintained an absolute dumbness. They bowed and smiled and ignored and imitated until a late hour, and if they had been the occupants of the most gorgeous salon in the world they could not have been more like three monkeys.

After Henry had gone, Bella, who encouraged herself in the appropriation of phrases, said, "Oh, ma, isn't he divine?"

IV

A Saturday evening was a sign always for a larger crowd to parade the thoroughfare. In summer the band played until ten o'clock in the little park. Most of the young men of the town affected to be superior to this band, even to despise it; but in the still and fragrant evenings they invariably turned out in force, because the girls were sure to attend this concert, strolling slowly over the grass, linked closely in pairs, or preferably in threes, in the curious public dependence upon one another which was their inheritance. There was no particular social aspect to this gathering, save that group regarded group with interest, but mainly in silence. Perhaps one girl would nudge another girl and suddenly say, "Look! there goes Gertie Hodgson and her sister!" And they would appear to regard this as an event of importance.

On a particular evening a rather large company of young men were gathered on the sidewalk that edged the park. They remained thus beyond the borders of the festivities because of their dignity, which would not exactly allow them to appear in anything which was so much fun for the younger lads. These latter were careering madly through the crowd, precipitating minor accidents from time to time, but usually fleeing like mist swept by the wind before retribution could lay hands upon them.

The band played a waltz which involved a gift of prominence to the bass horn, and one of the young men on the sidewalk said that the music reminded him of the new engines on the hill pumping water into the reservoir. A similarity of this kind was not inconceivable, but the young man did not say it because he disliked the band's playing. He said it because it was fashionable to say that manner of thing concerning the band. However, over in the stand, Billie Harris, who played the snare-drum, was always surrounded by a throng of boys, who adored his every whack.

After the mails from New York and Rochester had been finally distributed, the crowd from the post-office added to the mass already in the park. The wind waved the leaves of the maples, and, high in the air, the blue-burning globes of the arc lamps caused the wonderful traceries of leaf shadows on the ground. When the light fell upon the upturned face of a girl, it caused it to glow with a wonderful pallor. A policeman came suddenly from the darkness and chased a gang of obstreperous little boys. They hooted him from a distance. The leader of the band had some of the mannerisms of the great musicians, and during a period of silence the crowd smiled when they saw him raise his hand to his brow, stroke it sentimentally, and glance upward with a look of poetic anguish. In the shivering light, which gave to the park an effect like a great vaulted hall, the throng swarmed, with a gentle murmur of dresses switching the turf, and with a steady hum of voices.

Suddenly, without preliminary bars, there arose from afar the great hoarse roar of a factory whistle. It raised and swelled to a sinister note, and then it sang on the night wind one long call that held the crowd in the park immovable, speechless. The band-master had been about to vehemently let fall his hand to start the band on a thundering career through a popular march, but, smitten by this giant voice from the night, his hand dropped slowly to his knee, and, his mouth agape, he looked at his men in silence. The cry died away to a wail and then to stillness. It released the muscles of the company of young men on the sidewalk, who had been like statues, posed eagerly, lithely, their ears turned. And then they wheeled upon each other simultaneously, and, in a single explosion, they shouted, "One!"

Again the sound swelled in the night and roared its long ominous cry, and as it died away the crowd of young men wheeled upon each other and, in chorus, yelled, "Two!"

There was a moment of breathless waiting. Then they bawled, "Second district!" In a flash the company of indolent and cynical young men had vanished like a snowball disrupted by dynamite.

V

Jake Rogers was the first man to reach the home of Tuscarora Hose Company Number Six. He had wrenched his key from his pocket as he tore down the street, and he jumped at the spring-lock like a demon. As the doors flew back before his hands he leaped and kicked the wedges from a pair of wheels, loosened a tongue from its clasp, and in the glare of the electric light which the town placed before each of its hose-houses the next comers beheld the spectacle of Jake Rogers bent like hickory in the manfulness of his pulling, and the heavy cart was moving slowly towards the doors. Four men joined him at the time, and as they swung with the cart out into the street, dark figures sped towards them from the ponderous shadows back of the electric lamps. Some set up the inevitable question, "What district?"

"Second," was replied to them in a compact howl. Tuscarora Hose Company Number Six swept on a perilous wheel into Niagara Avenue, and as the men, attached to the cart by the rope which had been paid out from the windlass under the tongue, pulled madly in their fervor and abandon, the gong under the axle clanged incitingly. And sometimes the same cry was heard, "What district?"

"Second."

On a grade Johnnie Thorpe fell, and exercising a singular muscular ability, rolled out in time from the track of the on-coming wheel, and arose, dishevelled and aggrieved, casting a look of mournful disenchantment upon the black crowd that poured after the machine. The cart seemed to be the apex of a dark wave that was whirling as if it had been a broken dam. Back of the lad were stretches of lawn, and in that direction front-doors were banged by men who hoarsely shouted out into the clamorous avenue, "What district?"

At one of these houses a woman came to the door bearing a lamp, shielding her face from its rays with her hands. Across the cropped grass the avenue represented to her a kind of black torrent, upon which, nevertheless, fled numerous miraculous figures upon bicycles. She did not know that the towering light at the corner was continuing its nightly whine.

Suddenly a little boy somersaulted around the corner of the house as if he had been projected down a flight of stairs by a catapultian boot. He halted himself in front of the house by dint of a rather extraordinary evolution with his legs. "Oh, ma," he gasped, "can I go? Can I, ma?"

She straightened with the coldness of the exterior mother-judgment, although the hand that held the lamp trembled slightly. "No, Willie; you had better come to bed."

Instantly he began to buck and fume like a mustang. "Oh, ma," he cried, contorting himself—"oh, ma, can't I go? Please, ma, can't I go? Can't I go, ma?"

"It's half-past nine now, Willie."

He ended by wailing out a compromise: "Well, just down to the corner, ma? Just down to the corner?"

From the avenue came the sound of rushing men who wildly shouted. Somebody had grappled the bell-rope in the Methodist church, and now over the town rang this solemn and terrible voice, speaking from the clouds. Moved from its peaceful business, this bell gained a new spirit in the portentous night, and it swung the heart to and fro, up and down, with each peal of it.

"Just down to the corner, ma?"

"Willie, it's half-past nine now."

VI

The outlines of the house of Dr. Trescott had faded quietly into the evening, hiding a shape such as we call Queen Anne against the pall of the blackened sky. The neighborhood was at this time so quiet, and seemed so devoid of obstructions, that Hannigan's dog thought it a good opportunity to prowl in forbidden precincts, and so came and pawed Trescott's lawn, growling, and considering himself a formidable beast. Later, Peter Washington strolled past the house and whistled, but there was no dim light shining from Henry's loft, and presently Peter went his way. The rays from the street, creeping in silvery waves over the grass, caused the row of shrubs along the drive to throw a clear, bold shade.

A wisp of smoke came from one of the windows at the end of the house and drifted quietly into the branches of a cherry-tree. Its companions followed it in slowly increasing numbers, and finally there was a current controlled by invisible banks which poured into the fruit-laden boughs of the cherry-tree. It was no more to be noted than if a troop of dim and silent gray monkeys had been climbing a grapevine into the clouds.

24

After a moment the window brightened as if the four panes of it had been stained with blood, and a quick ear might have been led to imagine the fire-imps calling and calling, clan joining clan, gathering to the colors. From the street, however, the house maintained its dark quiet, insisting to a passer-by that it was the safe dwelling of people who chose to retire early to tranquil dreams. No one could have heard this low droning of the gathering clans.

Suddenly the panes of the red window tinkled and crashed to the ground, and at other windows there suddenly reared other flames, like bloody spectres at the apertures of a haunted house. This outbreak had been well planned, as if by professional revolutionists.

A man's voice suddenly shouted: "Fire! Fire! Fire!" Hannigan had flung his pipe frenziedly from him because his lungs demanded room. He tumbled down from his perch, swung over the fence, and ran shouting towards the front-door of the Trescotts'. Then he hammered on the door, using his fists as if they were mallets. Mrs. Trescott instantly came to one of the windows on the second floor. Afterwards she knew she had been about to say, "The doctor is not at home, but if you will leave your name, I will let him know as soon as he comes."

Hannigan's bawling was for a minute incoherent, but she understood that it was not about croup.

"What?" she said, raising the window swiftly.

"Your house is on fire! You're all ablaze! Move quick if—" His cries were resounding, in the street as if it were a cave of echoes. Many feet pattered swiftly on the stones. There was one man who ran with an almost fabulous speed. He wore lavender trousers. A straw hat with a bright silk band was held half crumpled in his hand.

As Henry reached the front-door, Hannigan had just broken the lock with a kick. A thick cloud of smoke poured over them, and Henry, ducking his head, rushed into it. From Hannigan's clamor he knew only one thing, but it turned him blue with horror. In the hall a lick of flame had found the cord that supported "Signing the Declaration." The engraving slumped suddenly down at one end, and then dropped to the floor, where it burst with the sound of a bomb. The fire was already roaring like a winter wind among the pines.

At the head of the stairs Mrs. Trescott was waving her arms as if they were two reeds.

"Jimmie! Save Jimmie!" she screamed in Henry's face. He plunged past her and disappeared, taking the long-familiar routes among these upper chambers, where he had once held office as a sort of second assistant house-maid.

Hannigan had followed him up the stairs, and grappled the arm of the maniacal woman there. His face was black with rage. "You must come down," he bellowed.

She would only scream at him in reply: "Jimmie! Jimmie! Save Jimmie!" But he dragged her forth while she babbled at him.

As they swung out into the open air a man ran across the lawn, and seizing a shutter, pulled it from its hinges and flung it far out upon the grass. Then he frantically attacked the other shutters one by one. It was a kind of temporary insanity.

"Here, you," howled Hannigan, "hold Mrs. Trescott—And stop—"

The news had been telegraphed by a twist of the wrist of a neighbor who had gone to the fire-box at the corner, and the time when Hannigan and his charge struggled out of the house was the time when the whistle roared its hoarse night call, smiting the crowd in the park, causing the leader of the band, who was about to order the first triumphal clang of a military march, to let his hand drop slowly to his knees.

VII

Henry pawed awkwardly through the smoke in the upper halls. He had attempted to guide himself by the walls, but they were too hot. The paper was crimpling, and he expected at any moment to have a flame burst from under his hands.

"Jimmie!"

He did not call very loud, as if in fear that the humming flames below would overhear him.

"Jimmie! Oh, Jimmie!"

Stumbling and panting, he speedily reached the entrance to Jimmie's room and flung open the door. The little chamber had no smoke in it at all. It was faintly illuminated by a beautiful rosy light reflected circuitously from the flames that were consuming the house. The boy had apparently just been aroused by the noise. He sat in his bed, his lips apart, his eyes wide, while upon his little white-robed figure played caressingly the light from the fire. As the door flew open he had before him this apparition of his pal, a terror-stricken negro, all tousled and with wool scorching, who leaped upon him and bore him up in a blanket as if the whole affair were a case of kidnapping by a dreadful robber chief. Without waiting to go through the usual short but complete process of wrinkling up his face, Jimmie let out a gorgeous bawl, which resembled the expression of a calf's deepest terror. As Johnson, bearing him, reeled into the smoke of the hall, he flung his arms about his neck and buried his face in the blanket. He called twice in muffled tones: "Mam-ma! Mam-ma!" When Johnson came to the top of the stairs with his burden, he took a quick step backward. Through the smoke that rolled to him he could see that the lower hall was all ablaze. He cried out then in a howl that resembled Jimmie's former achievement. His legs gained a frightful faculty of bending sideways. Swinging about precariously on these reedy legs, he made his way back slowly, back along the upper hall. From the way of him then, he had given up almost all idea of escaping from the burning house, and with it the desire. He was submitting, submitting because of his fathers, bending his mind in a most perfect slavery to this conflagration.

He now clutched Jimmie as unconsciously as when, running toward the house, he had clutched the hat with the bright silk band.

Suddenly he remembered a little private staircase which led from a bedroom to an apartment which the doctor had fitted up as a laboratory and work-house, where he used some of his leisure, and also hours when he might have been sleeping, in devoting himself to experiments which came in the way of his study and interest.

When Johnson recalled this stairway the submission to the blaze departed instantly. He had been perfectly familiar with it, but his confusion had destroyed the memory of it.

In his sudden momentary apathy there had been little that resembled fear, but now, as a way of safety came to him, the old frantic terror caught him. He was no longer creature to the flames, and he was afraid of the battle with them. It was a singular and swift set of alternations in which he feared twice without submission, and submitted once without fear.

"Jimmie!" he wailed, as he staggered on his way. He wished this little inanimate body at his breast to participate in his tremblings. But the child had lain limp and still during these headlong charges and countercharges, and no sign came from him.

Johnson passed through two rooms and came to the head of the stairs. As he opened the door great billows of smoke poured out, but gripping Jimmie closer, he plunged down through them. All manner of odors assailed him during this flight. They seemed to be alive with envy, hatred, and malice. At the entrance to the laboratory he confronted a strange spectacle. The room was like a garden in the region where might be burning flowers. Flames of violet, crimson, green, blue, orange, and purple were blooming everywhere. There was one blaze that was precisely the hue of a delicate coral. In another place was a mass that lay merely in phosphorescent inaction like a pile of emeralds. But all these marvels were to be seen dimly through clouds of heaving, turning, deadly smoke.

Johnson halted for a moment on the threshold. He cried out again in the negro wail that had in it the sadness of the swamps. Then he rushed across the room. An orange-colored flame leaped like a panther at the lavender trousers. This animal bit deeply into Johnson. There was an explosion at one side, and suddenly before him there reared a delicate, trembling sapphire shape like a fairy lady. With a quiet smile she blocked his path and doomed him and Jimmie. Johnson shrieked, and then ducked in the manner of his race in fights. He aimed to pass under the left guard of the sapphire lady. But she was swifter than eagles, and her talons caught in him as he plunged past her. Bowing his head as if his neck had been struck, Johnson lurched forward, twisting this way and that way. He fell on his back. The still form in the blanket flung from his arms, rolled to the edge of the floor and beneath the window.

Johnson had fallen with his head at the base of an old-fashioned desk. There was a row of jars upon the top of this desk. For the most part, they were silent amid this rioting, but there was one which seemed to hold a scintillant and writhing serpent.

Suddenly the glass splintered, and a ruby-red snakelike thing poured its thick length out upon the top of the old desk. It coiled and hesitated, and then began to swim a languorous way down the mahogany slant. At the angle it waved its sizzling molten head to and fro over the closed eyes of the man beneath it. Then, in a moment, with a mystic impulse, it moved again, and the red snake flowed directly down into Johnson's upturned face.

Afterwards the trail of this creature seemed to reek, and amid flames and low explosions drops like red-hot jewels pattered softly down it at leisurely intervals.

VIII

Suddenly all roads led to Dr. Trescott's. The whole town flowed towards one point. Chippeway Hose Company Number One toiled desperately up Bridge Street Hill even as the Tuscaroras came in an impetuous sweep down Niagara Avenue. Meanwhile the machine of the hook-and-ladder experts from across the creek was spinning on its way. The chief of the fire department had been playing poker in the rear room of Whiteley's cigar-store, but at the first breath of the alarm he sprang through the door like a man escaping with the kitty.

In Whilomville, on these occasions, there was always a number of people who instantly turned their attention to the bells in the churches and school-houses. The bells not only emphasized the alarm, but it was the habit to send these sounds rolling across the sky in a stirring brazen uproar until the flames were practically vanquished. There was also a kind of rivalry as to which bell should be made to produce the greatest din. Even the Valley Church, four miles away among the farms, had heard the voices of its brethren, and immediately added a quaint little yelp.

Dr. Trescott had been driving homeward, slowly smoking a cigar, and feeling glad that this last case was now in complete obedience to him, like a wild animal that he had subdued, when he heard the long whistle, and chirped to his horse under the unlicensed but perfectly distinct impression that a fire had broken out in Oakhurst, a new and rather high-flying suburb of the town which was at least two miles from his own home. But in the second blast and in the ensuing silence he read the designation of his own district. He was then only a few blocks from his house. He took out the whip and laid it lightly on the mare. Surprised and frightened at this extraordinary action, she leaped forward, and as the reins straightened like steel bands, the doctor leaned backward a trifle. When the mare whirled him up to the closed gate he was wondering whose house could be afire. The man who had rung the signal-box yelled something at him, but he already knew. He left the mare to her will.

In front of his door was a maniacal woman in a wrapper. "Ned!" she screamed at sight of him. "Jimmie! Save Jimmie!"

Trescott had grown hard and chill. "Where?" he said. "Where?"

Mrs. Trescott's voice began to bubble. "Up—up—up—" She pointed at the second-story windows.

Hannigan was already shouting: "Don't go in that way! You can't go in that way!"

Trescott ran around the corner of the house and disappeared from them. He knew from the view he had taken of the main hall that it would be impossible to ascend from there. His hopes were fastened now to the stairway which led from the laboratory. The door which opened from this room out upon the lawn was fastened with a bolt and lock, but he kicked close to the lock and then close to the bolt. The door with a loud crash flew back. The doctor recoiled from the roll of smoke, and then bending low, he stepped into the garden of burning flowers. On the floor his stinging eyes could make out a form in a smouldering blanket near the window. Then, as he carried his son towards the door, he saw that the whole lawn seemed now alive with men and boys, the leaders in the great charge that the whole town was making. They seized him and his burden, and overpowered him in wet blankets and water.

But Hannigan was howling: "Johnson is in there yet! Henry Johnson is in there yet! He went in after the kid! Johnson is in there yet!"

These cries penetrated to the sleepy senses of Trescott, and he struggled with his captors, swearing, unknown to him and to them, all the deep blasphemies of his medical-student days. He rose to his feet and went again towards the door of the laboratory. They endeavored to restrain him, although they were much affrighted at him.

But a young man who was a brakeman on the railway, and lived in one of the rear streets near the Trescotts, had gone into the laboratory and brought forth a thing which he laid on the grass.

IX

There were hoarse commands from in front of the house. "Turn on your water, Five!" "Let 'er go, One!" The gathering crowd swayed this way and that way. The flames, towering high, cast a wild red light on their faces. There came the clangor of a gong from along some adjacent street. The crowd exclaimed at it. "Here comes Number Three!" "That's Three a-comin'!" A panting and irregular mob dashed into view, dragging a hose-cart. A cry of exultation arose from the little boys. "Here's Three!" The lads welcomed Never-Die Hose Company Number Three as if it was composed of a chariot dragged by a band of gods. The perspiring citizens flung themselves into the fray. The boys danced in impish joy at the displays of prowess. They acclaimed the approach of Number Two. They welcomed Number Four with cheers. They were so deeply moved by this whole affair that they bitterly guyed the late appearance of the hook and ladder company, whose heavy apparatus had almost stalled them on the Bridge Street hill. The lads hated and feared a fire, of course. They did not particularly want to have anybody's house burn, but still it was fine to see the gathering of the companies, and amid a great noise to watch their heroes perform all manner of prodigies.

They were divided into parties over the worth of different companies, and supported their creeds with no small violence. For instance, in that part of the little city where Number Four had its home it would be most daring for a boy to contend the superiority of any other company. Likewise, in another quarter, where a strange boy was asked which fire company was the best in Whilomville, he was expected to answer "Number One." Feuds, which the boys forgot and remembered according to chance or the importance of some recent event, existed all through the town.

They did not care much for John Shipley, the chief of the department. It was true that he went to a fire with the speed of a falling angel, but when there he invariably lapsed into a certain still mood, which was almost a preoccupation, moving leisurely around the burning structure and surveying it, putting meanwhile at a cigar. This quiet man, who even when life was in danger seldom raised his voice, was not much to their fancy. Now old Sykes Huntington, when he was chief, used to bellow continually like a bull and gesticulate in a sort of delirium. He was much finer as a spectacle than this Shipley, who viewed a fire with the same steadiness that he viewed a raise in a large jack-pot. The greater number of the boys could never understand why the members of these companies persisted in re-electing Shipley, although they often pretended to understand it, because "My father says" was a very formidable phrase in argument, and the fathers seemed almost unanimous in advocating Shipley.

At this time there was considerable discussion as to which company had gotten the first stream of water on the fire. Most of the boys claimed that Number Five owned that distinction, but there was a determined minority who contended for Number One. Boys who were the blood adherents of other companies were obliged to choose between the two on this occasion, and the talk waxed warm.

But a great rumor went among the crowds. It was told with hushed voices. Afterwards a reverent silence fell even upon the boys. Jimmie Trescott and Henry Johnson had been burned to death, and Dr. Trescott himself had been most savagely hurt. The crowd did not even feel the police pushing at them. They raised their eyes, shining now with awe, towards the high flames.

The man who had information was at his best. In low tones he described the whole affair. "That was the kid's room—in the corner there. He had measles or somethin', and this coon—Johnson—was a-settin' up with 'im, and Johnson got sleepy or somethin' and upset the lamp, and the doctor he was down in his office, and he came running up, and they all got burned together till they dragged 'em out."

Another man, always preserved for the deliverance of the final judgment, was saying: "Oh, they'll die sure. Burned to flinders. No chance. Hull lot of 'em. Anybody can see." The crowd concentrated its gaze still more closely upon these flags of fire which waved joyfully against the black sky. The bells of the town were clashing unceasingly.

A little procession moved across the lawn and towards the street. There were three cots, borne by twelve of the firemen. The police moved sternly, but it needed no effort of theirs to open a lane for this slow cortege. The men who bore the cots were well known to the crowd, but in this solemn parade during the ringing of the bells and the shouting, and with the red glare upon the sky, they seemed utterly foreign, and Whilomville paid them a deep respect. Each man in this stretcher party had gained a reflected majesty. They were footmen to death, and the crowd made subtle obeisance to this august dignity derived from three prospective graves. One woman turned away with a shriek at sight of the covered body on the first stretcher, and people faced her suddenly in silent and mournful indignation. Otherwise there was barely a sound as these twelve important men with measured tread carried their burdens through the throng.

The little boys no longer discussed the merits of the different fire companies. For the greater part they had been routed. Only the more courageous viewed closely the three figures veiled in yellow blankets.

X

Old Judge Denning Hagenthorpe, who lived nearly opposite the Trescotts, had thrown his door wide open to receive the afflicted family. When it was publicly learned that the doctor and his son and the negro were still alive, it required a specially detailed policeman to prevent people from scaling the front porch and interviewing these sorely wounded. One old lady appeared with a miraculous poultice, and she quoted most damning Scripture to the officer when he said that she could not pass him. Throughout the night some lads old enough to be given privileges or to compel them from their mothers remained vigilantly upon the kerb in anticipation of a death or some such event. The reporter of the Morning Tribune rode thither on his bicycle every hour until three o'clock.

Six of the ten doctors in Whilomville attended at Judge Hagenthorpe's house.

Almost at once they were able to know that Trescott's burns were not vitally important. The child would possibly be scarred badly, but his life was undoubtedly safe. As for the negro Henry Johnson, he could not live. His body was frightfully seared, but more than that, he now had no face. His face had simply been burned away.

Trescott was always asking news of the two other patients. In the morning he seemed fresh and strong, so they told him that Johnson was doomed. They then saw him stir on the bed, and sprang quickly to see if the bandages needed readjusting. In the sudden glance he threw from one to another he impressed them as being both leonine and impracticable.

The morning paper announced the death of Henry Johnson. It contained a long interview with Edward J. Hannigan, in which the latter described in full the performance of Johnson at the fire. There was also an editorial built from all the best words in the vocabulary of the staff. The town halted in its accustomed road of thought, and turned a reverent attention to the memory of this hostler. In the breasts of many people was the regret that they had not known enough to give him a hand and a lift when he was alive, and they judged themselves stupid and ungenerous for this failure.

The name of Henry Johnson became suddenly the title of a saint to the little boys. The one who thought of it first could, by quoting it in an argument, at once overthrow his antagonist, whether it applied to the subject or whether it did not.

"Nigger, nigger, never die.

Black face and shiny eye."

Boys who had called this odious couplet in the rear of Johnson's march buried the fact at the bottom of their hearts.

Later in the day Miss Bella Farragut, of No. 7 Watermelon Alley, announced that she had been engaged to marry Mr. Henry Johnson.

XI

The old judge had a cane with an ivory head. He could never think at his best until he was leaning slightly on this stick and smoothing the white top with slow movements of his hands. It was also to him a kind of narcotic. If by any chance he mislaid it, he grew at once very irritable, and was likely to speak sharply to his sister, whose mental incapacity he had patiently endured for thirty years in the old mansion on Ontario Street. She was not at all aware of her brother's opinion of her endowments, and so it might be said that the judge had successfully dissembled for more than a quarter of a century, only risking the truth at the times when his cane was lost.

On a particular day the judge sat in his armchair on the porch. The sunshine sprinkled through the lilac-bushes and poured great coins on the boards. The sparrows disputed in the trees that lined the pavements. The judge mused deeply, while his hands gently caressed the ivory head of his cane.

Finally he arose and entered the house, his brow still furrowed in a thoughtful frown. His stick thumped solemnly in regular beats. On the second floor he entered a room where Dr. Trescott was working about the bedside of Henry Johnson. The bandages on the negro's head allowed only one thing to appear, an eye, which unwinkingly stared at the judge. The later spoke to Trescott on the condition of the patient. Afterward he evidently had something further to say, but he seemed to be kept from it by the scrutiny of the unwinking eye, at which he furtively glanced from time to time.

When Jimmie Trescott was sufficiently recovered, his mother had taken him to pay a visit to his grandparents in Connecticut. The doctor had remained to take care of his patients, but as a matter of truth he spent most of his time at Judge Hagenthorpe's house, where lay Henry Johnson. Here he slept and ate almost every meal in the long nights and days of his vigil.

At dinner, and away from the magic of the unwinking eye, the judge said, suddenly, "Trescott, do you think it is—" As Trescott paused expectantly, the judge fingered his knife. He said, thoughtfully, "No one wants to advance such ideas, but somehow I think that that poor fellow ought to die."

There was in Trescott's face at once a look of recognition, as if in this tangent of the judge he saw an old problem. He merely sighed and answered, "Who knows?" The words were spoken in a deep tone that gave them an elusive kind of significance.

The judge retreated to the cold manner of the bench. "Perhaps we may not talk with propriety of this kind of action, but I am induced to say that you are performing a questionable charity in preserving this negro's life. As near as I can understand, he will hereafter be a monster, a perfect monster, and probably with an affected brain. No man can observe you as I have observed you and not know that it was a matter of conscience with you, but I am afraid, my friend, that it is one of the blunders of virtue." The judge had delivered his views with his habitual oratory. The last three words he spoke with a particular emphasis, as if the phrase was his discovery.

The doctor made a weary gesture. "He saved my boy's life."

"Yes," said the judge, swiftly—"yes, I know!"

"And what am I to do?" said Trescott, his eyes suddenly lighting like an outburst from smouldering peat. "What am I to do? He gave himself for—for Jimmie. What am I to do for him?"

The judge abased himself completely before these words. He lowered his eyes for a moment. He picked at his cucumbers.

Presently he braced himself straightly in his chair. "He will be your creation, you understand. He is purely your creation. Nature has very evidently given him up. He is dead. You are restoring him to life. You are making him, and he will be a monster, and with no mind.

"He will be what you like, judge," cried Trescott, in sudden, polite fury. "He will be anything, but, by God! he saved my boy."

The judge interrupted in a voice trembling with emotion: "Trescott! Trescott! Don't I know?"

Trescott had subsided to a sullen mood. "Yes, you know," he answered, acidly; "but you don't know all about your own boy being saved from death." This was a perfectly childish allusion to the judge's bachelorhood. Trescott knew that the remark was infantile, but he seemed to take desperate delight in it.

But it passed the judge completely. It was not his spot.

"I am puzzled," said he, in profound thought. "I don't know what to say."

Trescott had become repentant. "Don't think I don't appreciate what you say, judge. But—"

"Of course!" responded the judge, quickly. "Of course."

"It—" began Trescott.

"Of course," said the judge.

In silence they resumed their dinner.

"Well," said the judge, ultimately, "it is hard for a man to know what to do."

"It is," said the doctor, fervidly.

There was another silence. It was broken by the judge:

"Look here, Trescott; I don't want you to think—"

"No, certainly not," answered the doctor, earnestly.

"Well, I don't want you to think I would say anything to—It was only that I thought that I might be able to suggest to you that—perhaps—the affair was a little dubious."

With an appearance of suddenly disclosing his real mental perturbation, the doctor said: "Well, what would you do? Would you kill him?" he asked, abruptly and sternly.

"Trescott, you fool," said the old man, gently.

"Oh, well, I know, judge, but then—" He turned red, and spoke with new violence: "Say, he saved my boy—do you see? He saved my boy."

"You bet he did," cried the judge, with enthusiasm. "You bet he did." And they remained for a time gazing at each other, their faces illuminated with memories of a certain deed.

After another silence, the judge said, "It is hard for a man to know what to do."

XII

Late one evening Trescott, returning from a professional call, paused his buggy at the Hagenthorpe gate. He tied the mare to the old tin-covered post, and entered the house. Ultimately he appeared with a companion—a man who walked slowly and carefully, as if he were learning. He was wrapped to the heels in an old-fashioned ulster. They entered the buggy and drove away.

After a silence only broken by the swift and musical humming of the wheels on the smooth road, Trescott spoke. "Henry," he said, "I've got you a home here with old Alek Williams. You will have everything you want to eat and a good place to sleep, and I hope you will get along there all right. I will pay all your expenses, and come to see you as often as I can. If you don't get along, I want you to let me know as soon as possible, and then we will do what we can to make it better."

The dark figure at the doctor's side answered with a cheerful laugh. "These buggy wheels don' look like I washed 'em yesterday, docteh," he said.

Trescott hesitated for a moment, and then went on insistently, "I am taking you to Alek Williams, Henry, and I—"

The figure chuckled again. "No, 'deed! No, seh! Alek Williams don' know a hoss! 'Deed he don't. He don' know a hoss from a pig." The laugh that followed was like the rattle of pebbles.

Trescott turned and looked sternly and coldly at the dim form in the gloom from the buggy-top. "Henry," he said, "I didn't say anything about horses. I was saying—"

"Hoss? Hoss?" said the quavering voice from these near shadows. "Hoss? 'Deed I don' know all erbout a boss! 'Deed I don't." There was a satirical chuckle.

At the end of three miles the mare slackened and the doctor leaned forward, peering, while holding tight reins. The wheels of the buggy bumped often over out-cropping bowlders. A window shone forth, a simple square of topaz on a great black hill-side. Four dogs charged the buggy with ferocity, and when it did not promptly retreat, they circled courageously around the flanks, baying. A door opened near the window in the hill-side, and a man came and stood on a beach of yellow light.

"Yah! yah! You Roveh! You Susie! Come yah! Come yah this minit!"

Trescott called across the dark sea of grass, "Hello, Alek!"

"Hello!"

"Come down here and show me where to drive."

The man plunged from the beach into the surf, and Trescott could then only trace his course by the fervid and polite ejaculations of a host who was somewhere approaching. Presently Williams took the mare by the head, and uttering cries of welcome and scolding the swarming dogs, led the equipage towards the lights. When they halted at the door and Trescott was climbing out, Williams cried, "Will she stand, docteh?"

"She'll stand all right, but you better hold her for a minute. Now, Henry." The doctor turned and held both arms to the dark figure. It crawled to him painfully like a man going down a ladder. Williams took the mare away to be tied to a little tree, and when he returned he found them awaiting him in the gloom beyond the rays from the door.

He burst out then like a siphon pressed by a nervous thumb. "Hennery! Hennery, ma ol' frien'. Well, if I ain' glade. If I ain' glade!"

Trescott had taken the silent shape by the arm and led it forward into the full revelation of the light. "Well, now, Alek, you can take Henry and put him to bed, and in the morning I will—"

Near the end of this sentence old Williams had come front to front with Johnson. He gasped for a second, and then yelled the yell of a man stabbed in the heart.

For a fraction of a moment Trescott seemed to be looking for epithets. Then he roared: "You old black chump! You old black—Shut up! Shut up! Do you hear?"

Williams obeyed instantly in the matter of his screams, but he continued in a lowered voice: "Ma Lode amassy! Who'd ever think? Ma Lode amassy!"

Trescott spoke again in the manner of a commander of a battalion. "Alek!"

The old negro again surrendered, but to himself he repeated in a whisper, "Ma Lode!" He was aghast and trembling.

As these three points of widening shadows approached the golden doorway a hale old negress appeared there, bowing. "Good-evenin', docteh! Good-evenin'! Come in! come in!" She had evidently just retired from a tempestuous struggle to place the room in order, but she was now bowing rapidly. She made the effort of a person swimming.

"Don't trouble yourself, Mary," said Trescott, entering. "I've brought Henry for you to take care of, and all you've got to do is to carry out what I tell you." Learning that he was not followed, he faced the door, and said, "Come in, Henry."

Johnson entered. "Whee!" shrieked Mrs. Williams. She almost achieved a back somersault. Six young members of the tribe of Williams made a simultaneous plunge for a position behind the stove, and formed a wailing heap.

XIII

"You know very well that you and your family lived usually on less than three dollars a week, and now that Dr. Trescott pays you five dollars a week for Johnson's board, you live like millionaires. You haven't done a stroke of work since Johnson began to board with you—everybody knows that—and so what are you kicking about?"

The judge sat in his chair on the porch, fondling his cane, and gazing down at old Williams, who stood under the lilac-bushes. "Yes, I know, jedge," said the negro, wagging his head in a puzzled manner. "Tain't like as if I didn't 'preciate what the docteh done, but—but—well, yeh see, jedge," he added, gaining a new impetus, "it's—it's hard wuk. This ol' man nev' did wuk so hard. Lode, no."

"Don't talk such nonsense, Alek," spoke the judge, sharply. "You have never really worked in your life—anyhow, enough to support a family of sparrows, and now when you are in a more prosperous condition than ever before, you come around talking like an old fool."

The negro began to scratch his head. "Yeh see, jedge," he said at last, "my ol' 'ooman she cain't 'ceive no lady callahs, nohow."

"Hang lady callers'" said the judge, irascibly. "If you have flour in the barrel and meat in the pot, your wife can get along without receiving lady callers, can't she?"

"But they won't come ainyhow, jedge," replied Williams, with an air of still deeper stupefaction. "Noner ma wife's frien's ner noner ma frien's 'll come near ma res'dence."

"Well, let them stay home if they are such silly people."

The old negro seemed to be seeking a way to elude this argument, but evidently finding none, he was about to shuffle meekly off. He halted, however. "Jedge," said he, "ma ol' 'ooman's near driv' abstracted.'"

"Your old woman is an idiot," responded the judge.

Williams came very close and peered solemnly through a branch of lilac. "Judge," he whispered, "the chillens."

"What about them?"

Dropping his voice to funereal depths, Williams said, "They—they cain't eat."

"Can't eat!" scoffed the judge, loudly. "Can't eat! You must think I am as big an old fool as you are. Can't eat—the little rascals! What's to prevent them from eating?"

In answer, Williams said, with mournful emphasis, "Hennery." Moved with a kind of satisfaction at his tragic use of the name, he remained staring at the judge for a sign of its effect.

The judge made a gesture of irritation. "Come, now, you old scoundrel, don't beat around the bush any more. What are you up to? What do you want? Speak out like a man, and don't give me any more of this tiresome rigamarole."

"I ain't er-beatin' round 'bout nuffin, jedge," replied Williams, indignantly. "No, seh; I say whatter got to say right out. 'Deed I do."

"Well, say it, then."

"Jedge," began the negro, taking off his hat and switching his knee with it, "Lode knows I'd do jes 'bout as much fer five dollehs er week as ainy cul'd man, but—but this yere business is awful, jedge. I raikon 'ain't been no sleep in—in my house sence docteh done fetch 'im."

"Well, what do you propose to do about it?"

Williams lifted his eyes from the ground and gazed off through the trees. "Raikon I got good appetite, an' sleep jes like er dog, but he—he's done broke me all up. 'Tain't no good, nohow. I wake up in the night; I hear 'im, mebbe, er-whimperin' an' er-whimperin', an' I sneak an' I sneak until I try th' do' to see if he locked in. An' he keep me er-puzzlin' an' er-quakin' all night long. Don't know how'll do in th' winter. Can't let 'im out where th' chillen is. He'll done freeze where he is now." Williams spoke these sentences as if he were talking to himself. After a silence of deep reflection he continued: "Folks go round sayin' he ain't Hennery Johnson at all. They say he's er devil!"

"What?" cried the judge.

"Yesseh," repeated Williams, in tones of injury, as if his veracity had been challenged. "Yesseh. I'm er-tellin' it to yeh straight, jedge. Plenty cul'd people folks up my way say it is a devil."

"Well, you don't think so yourself, do you?"

"No. 'Tain't no devil. It's Hennery Johnson."

"Well, then, what is the matter with you? You don't care what a lot of foolish people say. Go on 'tending to your business, and pay no attention to such idle nonsense."

"'Tis nonsense, jedge; but he *looks* like er devil."

"What do you care what he looks like?" demanded the judge.

"Ma rent is two dollehs and er half er month," said Williams, slowly.

"It might just as well be ten thousand dollars a month," responded the judge. "You never pay it, anyhow."

"Then, anoth' thing," continued Williams, in his reflective tone. "If he was all right in his haid I could stan' it; but, jedge, he's crazier 'n er loon. Then when he looks like er devil, an' done skears all ma frien's away, an' ma chillens cain't eat, an' ma ole 'ooman jes raisin' Cain all the time, an' ma rent two dollehs an' er half er month, an' him not right in his haid, it seems like five dollehs er week—"

The judge's stick came down sharply and suddenly upon the floor of the porch. "There," he said, "I thought that was what you were driving at."

Williams began swinging his head from side to side in the strange racial mannerism. "Now hol' on a minnet, jedge," he said, defensively. "'Tain't like as if I didn't 'preciate what the docteh done. 'Tain't that. Docteh Trescott is er kind man, an' 'tain't like as if I didn't 'preciate what he done; but—but—"

"But what? You are getting painful, Alek. Now tell me this: did you ever have five dollars a week regularly before in your life?"

Williams at once drew himself up with great dignity, but in the pause after that question he drooped gradually to another attitude. In the end he answered, heroically: "No, jedge, I 'ain't. An' 'tain't like as if I was er-sayin' five dollehs wasn't er lot er money for a man like me. But, jedge, what er man oughter git fer this kinder wuk is er salary. Yesseh, jedge," he repeated, with a great impressive gesture; "fer this kinder wuk er man oughter git er Salary." He laid a terrible emphasis upon the final word.

The judge laughed. "I know Dr. Trescott's mind concerning this affair, Alek; and if you are dissatisfied with your boarder, he is quite ready to move him to some other place; so, if you care to leave word with me that you are tired of the arrangement and wish it changed, he will come and take Johnson away."

Williams scratched his head again in deep perplexity. "Five dollehs is er big price fer bo'd, but 'tain't no big price fer the bo'd of er crazy man," he said, finally.

"What do you think you ought to get?" asked the judge.

"Well," answered Alek, in the manner of one deep in a balancing of the scales, "he looks like er devil, an' done skears e'rybody, an' ma chillens cain't eat, an' I cain't sleep, an' he ain't right in his haid, an'—"

"You told me all those things."

After scratching his wool, and beating his knee with his hat, and gazing off through the trees and down at the ground, Williams said, as he kicked nervously at the gravel, "Well, jedge, I think it is wuth—" He stuttered.

"Worth what?"

"Six dollehs," answered Williams, in a desperate outburst.

The judge lay back in his great arm-chair and went through all the motions of a man laughing heartily, but he made no sound save a slight cough. Williams had been watching him with apprehension.

"Well," said the judge, "do you call six dollars a salary?"

"No, seh," promptly responded Williams. "'Tain't a salary. No, 'deed! 'Tain't a salary." He looked with some anger upon the man who questioned his intelligence in this way.

"Well, supposing your children can't eat?"

"I—"

"And supposing he looks like a devil? And supposing all those things continue? Would you be satisfied with six dollars a week?"

Recollections seemed to throng in Williams's mind at these interrogations, and he answered dubiously. "Of co'se a man who ain't right in his haid, an' looks like er devil—But six dollehs—" After these two attempts at a sentence Williams suddenly appeared as an orator, with a great shiny palm waving in the air. "I tell yeh, jedge, six dollehs is six dollehs, but if I git six dollehs for bo'ding Hennery Johnson, I uhns it! I uhns it!"

"I don't doubt that you earn six dollars for every week's work you do," said the judge.

"Well, if I bo'd Hennery Johnson fer six dollehs er week, I uhns it! I uhns it!" cried Williams, wildly.

XIV

Reifsnyder's assistant had gone to his supper, and the owner of the shop was trying to placate four men who wished to be shaved at once. Reifsnyder was very garrulous—a fact which made him rather remarkable among barbers, who, as a class, are austerely speechless, having been taught silence by the hammering reiteration of a tradition. It is the customers who talk in the ordinary event.

As Reifsnyder waved his razor down the cheek of a man in the chair, he turned often to cool the impatience of the others with pleasant talk, which they did not particularly heed.

"Oh, he should have let him die," said Bainbridge, a railway engineer, finally replying to one of the barber's orations. "Shut up, Reif, and go on with your business!"

Instead, Reifsnyder paused shaving entirely, and turned to front the speaker. "Let him die?" he demanded. "How vas that? How can you let a man die?"

"By letting him die, you chump," said the engineer. The others laughed a little, and Reifsnyder turned at once to his work, sullenly, as a man overwhelmed by the derision of numbers.

"How vas that?" he grumbled later. "How can you let a man die when he vas done so much for you?"

"'When he vas done so much for you?'" repeated Bainbridge. "You better shave some people. How vas that? Maybe this ain't a barber shop?"

A man hitherto silent now said, "If I had been the doctor, I would have done the same thing."

"Of course," said Reifsnyder. "Any man could do it. Any man that vas not like you, you—old—flint-hearted—fish." He had sought the final words with painful care, and he delivered the collection triumphantly at Bainbridge. The engineer laughed.

The man in the chair now lifted himself higher, while Reifsnyder began an elaborate ceremony of anointing and combing his hair. Now free to join comfortably in the talk, the man said: "They say he is the most terrible thing in the world. Young Johnnie Bernard—that drives the grocery wagon—saw him up at Alek Williams's shanty, and he says he couldn't eat anything for two days."

"Chee!" said Reifsnyder.

"Well, what makes him so terrible?" asked another.

"Because he hasn't got any face," replied the barber and the engineer in duct.

"Hasn't got any face!" repeated the man. "How can he do without any face?"

> "He has no face in the front of his head.
>
> In the place where his face ought to grow."

Bainbridge sang these lines pathetically as he arose and hung his hat on a hook. The man in the chair was about to abdicate in his favor. "Get a gait on you now," he said to Reifsnyder. "I go out at 7.31."

As the barber foamed the lather on the cheeks of the engineer he seemed to be thinking heavily. Then suddenly he burst out. "How would you like to be with no face?" he cried to the assemblage.

"Oh, if I had to have a face like yours—" answered one customer.

Bainbridge's voice came from a sea of lather. "You're kicking because if losing faces became popular, you'd have to go out of business."

"I don't think it will become so much popular," said Reifsnyder.

"Not if it's got to be taken off in the way his was taken off," said another man. "I'd rather keep mine, if you don't mind."

"I guess so!" cried the barber. "Just think!"

The shaving of Bainbridge had arrived at a time of comparative liberty for him. "I wonder what the doctor says to himself?" he observed. "He may be sorry he made him live."

"It was the only thing he could do," replied a man. The others seemed to agree with him.

"Supposing you were in his place," said one, "and Johnson had saved your kid. What would you do?"

"Certainly!"

"Of course! You would do anything on earth for him. You'd take all the trouble in the world for him. And spend your last dollar on him. Well, then?"

"I wonder how it feels to be without any face?" said Reifsnyder, musingly.

The man who had previously spoken, feeling that he had expressed himself well, repeated the whole thing. "You would do anything on earth for him. You'd take all the trouble in the world for him. And spend your last dollar on him. Well, then?"

"No, but look," said Reifsnyder; "supposing you don't got a face!"

XV

As soon as Williams was hidden from the view of the old judge he began to gesture and talk to himself. An elation had evidently penetrated to his vitals, and caused him to dilate as if he had been filled with gas. He snapped his fingers in the air, and whistled fragments of triumphal music. At times, in his progress towards his shanty, he indulged in a shuffling movement that was really a dance. It was to be learned from the intermediate monologue that he had emerged from his trials laurelled and proud. He was the unconquerable Alexander Williams. Nothing could exceed the bold self-reliance of his manner. His kingly stride, his heroic song, the derisive flourish of his hands—all betokened a man who had successfully defied the world.

On his way he saw Zeke Paterson coming to town. They hailed each other at a distance of fifty yards.

"How do, Broth' Paterson?"

"How do, Broth' Williams?"

They were both deacons.

"Is you' folks well, Broth' Paterson?"

"Middlin', middlin'. How's you' folks, Broth' Williams?"

Neither of them had slowed his pace in the smallest degree. They had simply begun this talk when a considerable space separated them, continued it as they passed, and added polite questions as they drifted steadily apart. Williams's mind seemed to be a balloon. He had been so inflated that he had not noticed that Paterson had definitely shied into the dry ditch as they came to the point of ordinary contact.

Afterwards, as he went a lonely way, he burst out again in song and pantomimic celebration of his estate. His feet moved in prancing steps.

When he came in sight of his cabin, the fields were bathed in a blue dusk, and the light in the window was pale. Cavorting and gesticulating, he gazed joyfully for some moments upon this light. Then suddenly another idea seemed to attack his mind, and he stopped, with an air of being suddenly dampened. In the end he approached his home as if it were the fortress of an enemy.

Some dogs disputed his advance for a loud moment, and then discovering their lord, slunk away embarrassed. His reproaches were addressed to them in muffled tones.

Arriving at the door, he pushed it open with the timidity of a new thief. He thrust his head cautiously sideways, and his eyes met the eyes of his wife, who sat by the table, the lamp-light defining a half of her face. "'Sh!" he said, uselessly. His glance travelled swiftly to the inner door which shielded the one bed-chamber. The pickaninnies, strewn upon the floor of the living-room, were softly snoring. After a hearty meal they had promptly dispersed themselves about the place and gone to sleep. "'Sh!" said Williams again to his motionless and silent wife. He had allowed only his head to appear. His wife, with one hand upon the edge of the table and the other at her knee, was regarding him with wide eyes and parted lips as if he were a spectre. She looked to be one who was living in terror, and even the familiar face at the door had thrilled her because it had come suddenly.

Williams broke the tense silence. "Is he all right?" he whispered, waving his eyes towards the inner door. Following his glance timorously, his wife nodded, and in a low tone answered:

"I raikon he's done gone t' sleep."

Williams then slunk noiselessly across his threshold.

He lifted a chair, and with infinite care placed it so that it faced the dreaded inner door. His wife moved slightly, so as to also squarely face it. A silence came upon them in which they seemed to be waiting for a calamity, pealing and deadly.

Williams finally coughed behind his hand. His wife started, and looked upon him in alarm. "Pears like he done gwine keep quiet ternight," he breathed. They continually pointed their speech and their looks at the inner door, paying it the homage due to a corpse or a phantom. Another long stillness followed this sentence. Their eyes shone white and wide. A wagon rattled down the distant road. From their chairs they looked at the window, and the effect of the light in the cabin was a presentation of an intensely black and solemn night. The old woman adopted the attitude used always in church at funerals. At times she seemed to be upon the point of breaking out in prayer.

"He mighty quiet ter-night," whispered Williams. "Was he good ter-day?" For answer his wife raised her eyes to the ceiling in the supplication of Job. Williams moved restlessly. Finally he tiptoed to the door. He knelt slowly and without a sound, and placed his ear near the key-hole. Hearing a noise behind him, he turned quickly. His wife was staring at him aghast. She stood in front of the stove, and her arms were spread out in the natural movement to protect all her sleeping ducklings.

But Williams arose without having touched the door. "I raikon he er-sleep," he said, fingering his wool. He debated with himself for some time. During this interval his wife remained, a great fat statue of a mother shielding her children.

It was plain that his mind was swept suddenly by a wave of temerity. With a sounding step he moved towards the door. His fingers were almost upon the knob when he swiftly ducked and dodged away, clapping his hands to the back of his head. It was as if the portal had threatened him. There was a little tumult near the stove, where Mrs. Williams's desperate retreat had involved her feet with the prostrate children.

After the panic Williams bore traces of a feeling of shame. He returned to the charge. He firmly grasped the knob with his left hand, and with his other hand turned the key in the lock. He pushed the door, and as it swung portentously open he sprang nimbly to one side like the fearful slave liberating the lion. Near the stove a group had formed, the terror stricken mother, with her arms stretched, and the aroused children clinging frenziedly to her skirts.

The light streamed after the swinging door, and disclosed a room six feet one way and six feet the other way. It was small enough to enable the radiance to lay it plain. Williams peered warily around the corner made by the door-post.

Suddenly he advanced, retired, and advanced again with a howl. His palsied family had expected him to spring backward, and at his howl they heaped themselves wondrously. But Williams simply stood in the little room emitting his howls before an open window. "He's gone! He's gone! He's gone!" His eye and his hand had speedily proved the fact. He had even thrown open a little cupboard.

Presently he came flying out. He grabbed his hat, and hurled the outer door back upon its hinges. Then he tumbled headlong into the night. He was yelling: "Docteh Trescott! Docteh Trescott!" He ran wildly through the fields, and galloped in the direction of town. He continued to call to Trescott, as if the latter was within easy hearing. It was as if Trescott was poised in the contemplative sky over the running negro, and could heed this reaching voice—"Docteh Trescott!"

In the cabin, Mrs. Williams, supported by relays from the battalion of children, stood quaking watch until the truth of daylight came as a reinforcement and made the arrogant, strutting, swashbuckler children, and a mother who proclaimed her illimitable courage.

XVI

Theresa Page was giving a party. It was the outcome of a long series of arguments addressed to her mother, which had been overheard in part by her father. He had at last said five words, "Oh, let her have it." The mother had then gladly capitulated.

Theresa had written nineteen invitations, and distributed them at recess to her schoolmates. Later her mother had composed five large cakes, and still later a vast amount of lemonade.

So the nine little girls and the ten little boys sat quite primly in the dining-room, while Theresa and her mother plied them with cake and lemonade, and also with ice-cream. This primness sat now quite strangely upon them. It was owing to the presence of Mrs. Page. Previously in the parlor alone with their games they had overturned a chair; the boys had let more or less of their hoodlum spirit shine forth. But when circumstances could be possibly magnified to warrant it, the girls made the boys victims of an insufferable pride, snubbing them mercilessly. So in the dining-room they resembled a class at Sunday-school, if it were not for the subterranean smiles, gestures, rebuffs, and poutings which stamped the affair as a children's party.

Two little girls of this subdued gathering were planted in a settle with their backs to the broad window. They were beaming lovingly upon each other with an effect of scorning the boys.

Hearing a noise behind her at the window, one little girl turned to face it. Instantly she screamed and sprang away, covering her face with her hands. "What was it? What was it?" cried every one in a roar. Some slight movement of the eyes of the weeping and shuddering child informed the company that she had been frightened by an appearance at the window. At once they all faced the imperturbable window, and for a moment there was a silence. An astute lad made an immediate census of the other lads. The prank of slipping out and looming spectrally at a window was too venerable. But the little boys were all present and astonished.

As they recovered their minds they uttered warlike cries, and through a side door sallied rapidly out against the terror. They vied with each other in daring.

None wished particularly to encounter a dragon in the darkness of the garden, but there could be no faltering when the fair ones in the dining-room were present. Calling to each other in stern voices, they went dragooning over the lawn, attacking the shadows with ferocity, but still with the caution of reasonable beings. They found, however, nothing new to the peace of the night. Of course there was a lad who told a great lie. He described a grim figure, bending low and slinking off along the fence. He gave a number of details, rendering his lie more splendid by a repetition of certain forms which he recalled from romances. For instance, he insisted that he had heard the creature emit a hollow laugh.

Inside the house the little girl who had raised the alarm was still shuddering and weeping. With the utmost difficulty was she brought to a state approximating calmness by Mrs. Page. Then she wanted to go home at once.

Page entered the house at this time. He had exiled himself until he concluded that this children's party was finished and gone. He was obliged to escort the little girl home because she screamed again when they opened the door and she saw the night.

She was not coherent even to her mother. Was it a man? She didn't know. It was simply a thing, a dreadful thing.

XVII

In Watermelon Alley the Farraguts were spending their evening as usual on the little rickety porch. Sometimes they howled gossip to other people on other rickety porches. The thin wail of a baby arose from a near house. A man had a terrific altercation with his wife, to which the alley paid no attention at all.

There appeared suddenly before the Farraguts a monster making a low and sweeping bow. There was an instant's pause, and then occurred something that resembled the effect of an upheaval of the earth's surface. The old woman hurled herself backward with a dreadful cry. Young Sim had been perched gracefully on a railing. At sight of the monster he simply fell over it to the ground. He made no sound, his eyes stuck out, his nerveless hands tried to grapple the rail to prevent a tumble, and then he vanished. Bella, blubbering, and with her hair suddenly and mysteriously dishevelled, was crawling on her hands and knees fearsomely up the steps.

Standing before this wreck of a family gathering, the monster continued to bow. It even raised a deprecatory claw. "Doh' make no botheration 'bout me, Miss Fa'gut," it said, politely. "No, 'deed. I jes drap in ter ax if yer well this evenin', Miss Fa'gut. Don' make no botheration. No, 'deed. I gwine ax you to go to er daince with me, Miss Fa'gut. I ax you if I can have the magnifercent gratitude of you' company on that 'casion, Miss Fa'gut."

The girl cast a miserable glance behind her. She was still crawling away. On the ground beside the porch young Sim raised a strange bleat, which expressed both his fright and his lack of wind. Presently the monster, with a fashionable amble, ascended the steps after the girl.

She grovelled in a corner of the room as the creature took a chair. It seated itself very elegantly on the edge. It held an old cap in both hands. "Don' make no botheration, Miss Fa'gut. Don' make no botherations. No, 'deed. I jes drap in ter ax you if you won' do me the proud of acceptin' ma humble invitation to er daince, Miss Fa'gut."

She shielded her eyes with her arms and tried to crawl past it, but the genial monster blocked the way. "I jes drap in ter ax you 'bout er daince, Miss Fa'gut. I ax you if I kin have the magnifercent gratitude of you' company on that 'casion, Miss Fa'gut."

In a last outbreak of despair, the girl, shuddering and wailing, threw herself face downward on the floor, while the monster sat on the edge of the chair gabbling courteous invitations, and holding the old hat daintily to his stomach.

At the back of the house, Mrs. Farragut, who was of enormous weight, and who for eight years had done little more than sit in an armchair and describe her various ailments, had with speed and agility scaled a high board fence.

XVIII

The black mass in the middle of Trescott's property was hardly allowed to cool before the builders were at work on another house. It had sprung upward at a fabulous rate. It was like a magical composition born of the ashes. The doctor's office was the first part to be completed, and he had already moved in his new books and instruments and medicines.

Trescott sat before his desk when the chief of police arrived. "Well, we found him," said the latter.

"Did you?" cried the doctor. "Where?"

"Shambling around the streets at daylight this morning. I'll be blamed if I can figure on where he passed the night."

"Where is he now?"

"Oh, we jugged him. I didn't know what else to do with him. That's what I want you to tell me. Of course we can't keep him. No charge could be made, you know."

"I'll come down and get him."

The official grinned retrospectively. "Must say he had a fine career while he was out. First thing he did was to break up a children's party at Page's. Then he went to Watermelon Alley. Whoo! He stampeded the whole outfit. Men, women, and children running pell-mell, and yelling. They say one old woman broke her leg, or something, shinning over a fence. Then he went right out on the main street, and an Irish girl threw a fit, and there was a sort of a riot. He began to run, and a big crowd chased him, firing rocks. But he gave them the slip somehow down there by the foundry and in the railroad yard. We looked for him all night, but couldn't find him."

"Was he hurt any? Did anybody hit him with a stone?"

"Guess there isn't much of him to hurt any more, is there? Guess he's been hurt up to the limit. No. They never touched him. Of course nobody really wanted to hit him, but you know how a crowd gets. It's like—it's like—"

"Yes, I know."

For a moment the chief of the police looked reflectively at the floor. Then he spoke hesitatingly. "You know Jake Winter's little girl was the one that he scared at the party. She is pretty sick, they say."

"Is she? Why, they didn't call me. I always attend the Winter family."

"No? Didn't they?" asked the chief, slowly. "Well—you know—Winter is—well, Winter has gone clean crazy over this business. He wanted—he wanted to have you arrested."

"Have me arrested? The idiot! What in the name of wonder could he have me arrested for?"

"Of course. He is a fool. I told him to keep his trap shut. But then you know how he'll go all over town yapping about the thing. I thought I'd better tip you."

"Oh, he is of no consequence; but then, of course, I'm obliged to you, Sam."

"That's all right. Well, you'll be down tonight and take him out, eh? You'll get a good welcome from the jailer. He don't like his job for a cent. He says you can have your man whenever you want him. He's got no use for him."

"But what is this business of Winter's about having me arrested?"

"Oh, it's a lot of chin about your having no right to allow this—this—this man to be at large. But I told him to tend to his own business. Only I thought I'd better let you know. And I might as well say right now, doctor, that there is a good deal of talk about this thing. If I were you, I'd come to the jail pretty late at night, because there is likely to be a crowd around the door, and I'd bring a—er—mask, or some kind of a veil, anyhow."

XIX

Martha Goodwin was single, and well along into the thin years. She lived with her married sister in Whilomville. She performed nearly all the housework in exchange for the privilege of existence. Every one tacitly recognized her labor as a form of penance for the early end of her betrothed, who had died of small-pox, which he had not caught from her.

But despite the strenuous and unceasing workaday of her life, she was a woman of great mind. She had adamantine opinions upon the situation in Armenia, the condition of women in China, the flirtation between Mrs. Minster of Niagara Avenue and young Griscom, the conflict in the Bible class of the Baptist Sunday-school, the duty of the United States towards the Cuban insurgents, and many other colossal matters. Her fullest experience of violence was gained on an occasion when she had seen a hound clubbed, but in the plan which she had made for the reform of the world she advocated drastic measures. For instance, she contended that all the Turks should be pushed into the sea and drowned, and that Mrs. Minster and young Griscom should be hanged side by side on twin gallows. In fact, this woman of peace, who had seen only peace, argued constantly for a creed of illimitable ferocity. She was invulnerable on these questions, because eventually she overrode all opponents with a sniff. This sniff was an active force. It was to her antagonists like a bang over the head, and none was known to recover from this expression of exalted contempt. It left them windless and conquered. They never again came forward as candidates for suppression. And Martha walked her kitchen with a stern brow, an invincible being like Napoleon.

Nevertheless her acquaintances, from the pain of their defeats, had been long in secret revolt. It was in no wise a conspiracy, because they did not care to state their open rebellion, but nevertheless it was understood that any woman who could not coincide with one of Martha's contentions was entitled to the support of others in the small circle. It amounted to an arrangement by which all were required to disbelieve any theory for which Martha fought. This, however, did not prevent them from speaking of her mind with profound respect.

Two people bore the brunt of her ability. Her sister Kate was visibly afraid of her, while Carrie Dungen sailed across from her kitchen to sit respectfully at Martha's feet and learn the business of the world. To be sure, afterwards, under another sun, she always laughed at Martha and pretended to deride her ideas, but in the presence of the sovereign she always remained silent or admiring. Kate, the sister, was of no consequence at all. Her principal delusion was that she did all the work in the up-stairs rooms of the house, while Martha did it down-stairs. The truth was seen only by the husband, who treated Martha with a kindness that was half banter, half deference. Martha herself had no suspicion that she was the only pillar of the domestic edifice. The situation was without definitions. Martha made definitions, but she devoted them entirely to the Armenians and Griscom and the Chinese and other subjects. Her dreams, which in early days had been of love of meadows and the shade of trees, of the face of a man, were now involved otherwise, and they were companioned in the kitchen curiously, Cuba, the hot-water kettle, Armenia, the washing of the dishes, and the whole thing being jumbled. In regard to social misdemeanors, she who was simply the mausoleum of a dead passion was probably the most savage critic in town. This unknown woman, hidden in a kitchen as in a well, was sure to have a considerable effect of the one kind or the other in the life of the town. Every time it moved a yard, she had personally contributed an inch. She could hammer so stoutly upon the door of a proposition that it would break from its hinges and fall upon her, but at any rate it moved. She was an engine, and the fact that she did not know that she was an engine contributed largely to the effect. One reason that she was formidable was that she did not even imagine that she was formidable. She remained a weak, innocent, and pig-headed creature, who alone would defy the universe if she thought the universe merited this proceeding.

One day Carrie Dungen came across from her kitchen with speed. She had a great deal of grist. "Oh," she cried, "Henry Johnson got away from where they was keeping him, and came to town last night, and scared everybody almost to death."

Martha was shining a dish-pan, polishing madly. No reasonable person could see cause for this operation, because the pan already glistened like silver. "Well!" she ejaculated. She imparted to the word a deep meaning. "This, my prophecy, has come to pass." It was a habit.

The overplus of information was choking Carrie. Before she could go on she was obliged to struggle for a moment. "And, oh, little Sadie Winter is awful sick, and they say Jake Winter was around this morning trying to get Doctor Trescott arrested. And poor old Mrs. Farragut sprained her ankle in trying to climb a fence. And there's a crowd around the jail all the time. They put Henry in jail because they didn't know what else to do with him, I guess. They say he is perfectly terrible."

Martha finally released the dish-pan and confronted the headlong speaker. "Well!" she said again, poising a great brown rag. Kate had heard the excited new-comer, and drifted down from the novel in her room. She was a shivery little woman. Her shoulder-blades seemed to be two panes of ice, for she was constantly shrugging and shrugging. "Serves him right if he was to lose all his patients," she said suddenly, in blood-thirsty tones. She snipped her words out as if her lips were scissors.

"Well, he's likely to," shouted Carrie Dungen. "Don't a lot of people say that they won't have him any more? If you're sick and nervous, Doctor Trescott would scare the life out of you, wouldn't he? He would me. I'd keep thinking."

Martha, stalking to and fro, sometimes surveyed the two other women with a contemplative frown.

XX

After the return from Connecticut, little Jimmie was at first much afraid of the monster who lived in the room over the carriage-house. He could not identify it in any way. Gradually, however, his fear dwindled under the influence of a weird fascination. He sidled into closer and closer relations with it.

One time the monster was seated on a box behind the stable basking in the rays of the afternoon sun. A heavy crepe veil was swathed about its head.

Little Jimmie and many companions came around the corner of the stable. They were all in what was popularly known as the baby class, and consequently escaped from school a half-hour before the other children. They halted abruptly at sight of the figure on the box. Jimmie waved his hand with the air of a proprietor.

"There he is," he said.

"O-o-o!" murmured all the little boys—"o-o-o!" They shrank back, and grouped according to courage or experience, as at the sound the monster slowly turned its head. Jimmie had remained in the van alone. "Don't be afraid! I won't let him hurt you," he said, delighted.

"Huh!" they replied, contemptuously. "We ain't afraid."

Jimmie seemed to reap all the joys of the owner and exhibitor of one of the world's marvels, while his audience remained at a distance—awed and entranced, fearful and envious.

One of them addressed Jimmie gloomily. "Bet you dassent walk right up to him." He was an older boy than Jimmie, and habitually oppressed him to a small degree. This new social elevation of the smaller lad probably seemed revolutionary to him.

"Huh!" said Jimmie, with deep scorn. "Dassent I? Dassent I, hey? Dassent I?"

The group was immensely excited. It turned its eyes upon the boy that Jimmie addressed. "No, you dassent," he said, stolidly, facing a moral defeat. He could see that Jimmie was resolved. "No, you dassent," he repeated, doggedly.

"Ho?" cried Jimmie. "You just watch!—you just watch!"

Amid a silence he turned and marched towards the monster. But possibly the palpable wariness of his companions had an effect upon him that weighed more than his previous experience, for suddenly, when near to the monster, he halted dubiously. But his playmates immediately uttered a derisive shout, and it seemed to force him forward. He went to the monster and laid his hand delicately on its shoulder. "Hello, Henry," he said, in a voice that trembled a trifle. The monster was crooning a weird line of negro melody that was scarcely more than a thread of sound, and it paid no heed to the boy.

Jimmie: strutted back to his companions. They acclaimed him and hooted his opponent. Amid this clamor the larger boy with difficulty preserved a dignified attitude.

"I dassent, dassent I?" said Jimmie to him.

"Now, you're so smart, let's see you do it!"

This challenge brought forth renewed taunts from the others. The larger boy puffed out his checks. "Well, I ain't afraid," he explained, sullenly. He had made a mistake in diplomacy, and now his small enemies were tumbling his prestige all about his ears. They crowed like roosters and bleated like lambs, and made many other noises which were supposed to bury him in ridicule and dishonor. "Well, I ain't afraid," he continued to explain through the din.

Jimmie, the hero of the mob, was pitiless. "You ain't afraid, hey?" he sneered. "If you ain't afraid, go do it, then."

"Well, I would if I wanted to," the other retorted. His eyes wore an expression of profound misery, but he preserved steadily other portions of a pot-valiant air. He suddenly faced one of his persecutors. "If you're so smart, why don't you go do it?" This persecutor sank promptly through the group to the rear. The incident gave the badgered one a breathing-spell, and for a moment even turned the derision in another direction. He took advantage of his interval. "I'll do it if anybody else will," he announced, swaggering to and fro.

Candidates for the adventure did not come forward. To defend themselves from this counter-charge, the other boys again set up their crowing and bleating. For a while they would hear nothing from him. Each time he opened his lips their chorus of noises made oratory impossible. But at last he was able to repeat that he would volunteer to dare as much in the affair as any other boy.

"Well, you go first," they shouted.

But Jimmie intervened to once more lead the populace against the large boy. "You're mighty brave, ain't you?" he said to him. "You dared me to do it, and I did—didn't I? Now who's afraid?" The others cheered this view loudly, and they instantly resumed the baiting of the large boy.

He shamefacedly scratched his left shin with his right foot. "Well, I ain't afraid." He cast an eye at the monster. "Well, I ain't afraid." With a glare of hatred at his squalling tormentors, he finally announced a grim intention. "Well, I'll do it, then, since you're so fresh. Now!"

The mob subsided as with a formidable countenance he turned towards the impassive figure on the box. The advance was also a regular progression from high daring to craven hesitation. At last, when some yards from the monster, the lad came to a full halt, as if he had encountered a stone wall. The observant little boys in the distance promptly hooted. Stung again by these cries, the lad sneaked two yards forward. He was crouched like a young cat ready for a backward spring. The crowd at the rear, beginning to respect this display, uttered some encouraging cries. Suddenly the lad gathered himself together, made a white and desperate rush forward, touched the monster's shoulder with a far-outstretched finger, and sped away, while his laughter rang out wild, shrill, and exultant.

The crowd of boys reverenced him at once, and began to throng into his camp, and look at him, and be his admirers. Jimmie was discomfited for a moment, but he and the larger boy, without agreement or word of any kind, seemed to recognize a truce, and they swiftly combined and began to parade before the others.

"Why, it's just as easy as nothing," puffed the larger boy. "Ain't it, Jim?"

"Course," blew Jimmie. "Why, it's as e-e-easy."

They were people of another class. If they had been decorated for courage on twelve battle-fields, they could not have made the other boys more ashamed of the situation.

Meanwhile they condescended to explain the emotions of the excursion, expressing unqualified contempt for any one who could hang back. "Why, it ain't nothin'. He won't do nothin' to you," they told the others, in tones of exasperation.

One of the very smallest boys in the party showed signs of a wistful desire to distinguish himself, and they turned their attention to him, pushing at his shoulders while he swung away from them, and hesitated dreamily. He was eventually induced to make furtive expedition, but it was only for a few yards. Then he paused, motionless, gazing with open mouth. The vociferous entreaties of Jimmie and the large boy had no power over him.

Mrs. Hannigan had come out on her back porch with a pail of water. From this coign she had a view of the secluded portion of the Trescott grounds that was behind the stable. She perceived the group of boys, and the monster on the box. She shaded her eyes with her hand to benefit her vision. She screeched then as if she was being murdered. "Eddie! Eddie! You come home this minute!"

Her son querulously demanded, "Aw, what for?"

"You come home this minute. Do you hear?"

The other boys seemed to think this visitation upon one of their number required them to preserve for a time the hang-dog air of a collection of culprits, and they remained in guilty silence until the little Hannigan, wrathfully protesting, was pushed through the door of his home. Mrs. Hannigan cast a piercing glance over the group, stared with a bitter face at the Trescott house, as if this new and handsome edifice was insulting her, and then followed her son.

There was wavering in the party. An inroad by one mother always caused them to carefully sweep the horizon to see if there were more coming. "This is my yard," said Jimmie, proudly. "We don't have to go home."

The monster on the box had turned its black crepe countenance towards the sky, and was waving its arms in time to a religious chant. "Look at him now," cried a little boy. They turned, and were transfixed by the solemnity and mystery of the indefinable gestures. The wail of the melody was mournful and slow. They drew back. It seemed to spellbind them with the power of a funeral. They were so absorbed that they did not hear the doctor's buggy drive up to the stable. Trescott got out, tied his horse, and approached the group. Jimmie saw him first, and at his look of dismay the others wheeled.

"What's all this, Jimmie?" asked Trescott, in surprise.

The lad advanced to the front of his companions, halted, and said nothing. Trescott's face gloomed slightly as he scanned the scene.

"What were you doing, Jimmie?"

"We was playin'," answered Jimmie, huskily.

"Playing at what?"

"Just playin'."

Trescott looked gravely at the other boys, and asked them to please go home. They proceeded to the street much in the manner of frustrated and revealed assassins. The crime of trespass on another boy's place was still a crime when they had only accepted the other boy's cordial invitation, and they were used to being sent out of all manner of gardens upon the sudden appearance of a father or a mother. Jimmie had wretchedly watched the departure of his companions. It involved the loss of his position as a lad who controlled the privileges of his father's grounds, but then he knew that in the beginning he had no right to ask so many boys to be his guests.

Once on the sidewalk, however, they speedily forgot their shame as trespassers, and the large boy launched forth in a description of his success in the late trial of courage. As they went rapidly up the street, the little boy who had made the furtive expedition cried out confidently from the rear, "Yes, and I went almost up to him, didn't I, Willie?"

The large boy crushed him in a few words. "Huh!" he scoffed. "You only went a little way. I went clear up to him."

The pace of the other boys was so manly that the tiny thing had to trot, and he remained at the rear, getting entangled in their legs in his attempts to reach the front rank and become of some importance, dodging this way and that way, and always piping out his little claim to glory.

<u>XXI</u>

"By-the-way, Grace," said Trescott, looking into the dining-room from his office door, "I wish you would send Jimmie to me before school-time."

When Jimmie came, he advanced so quietly that Trescott did not at first note him. "Oh," he said, wheeling from a cabinet, "here you are, young man."

"Yes, sir."

Trescott dropped into his chair and tapped the desk with a thoughtful finger. "Jimmie, what were you doing in the back garden yesterday—you and the other boys—to Henry?"

"We weren't doing anything, pa."

Trescott looked sternly into the raised eyes of his son. "Are you sure you were not annoying him in any way? Now what were you doing, exactly?"

"Why, we—why, we—now—Willie Dalzel said I dassent go right up to him, and I did; and then he did; and then—the other boys were 'fraid; and then—you comed."

Trescott groaned deeply. His countenance was so clouded in sorrow that the lad, bewildered by the mystery of it, burst suddenly forth in dismal lamentations. "There, there. Don't cry, Jim," said Trescott, going round the desk. "Only—" He sat in a great leather reading-chair, and took the boy on his knee. "Only I want to explain to you—"

After Jimmie had gone to school, and as Trescott was about to start on his round of morning calls, a message arrived from Doctor Moser. It set forth that the latter's sister was dying in the old homestead, twenty miles away up the valley, and asked Trescott to care for his patients for the day at least. There was also in the envelope a little history of each case and of what had already been done. Trescott replied to the messenger that he would gladly assent to the arrangement.

He noted that the first name on Moser's list was Winter, but this did not seem to strike him as an important fact. When its turn came, he rang the Winter bell. "Good-morning, Mrs. Winter," he said, cheerfully, as the door was opened. "Doctor Moser has been obliged to leave town to-day, and he has asked me to come in his stead. How is the little girl this morning?"

Mrs. Winter had regarded him in stony surprise. At last she said: "Come in! I'll see my husband." She bolted into the house. Trescott entered the hall, and turned to the left into the sitting-room.

Presently Winter shuffled through the door. His eyes flashed towards Trescott. He did not betray any desire to advance far into the room. "What do you want?" he said.

"What do I want? What do I want?" repeated Trescott, lifting his head suddenly. He had heard an utterly new challenge in the night of the jungle.

"Yes, that's what I want to know," snapped Winter. "What do you want?"

Trescott was silent for a moment. He consulted Moser's memoranda. "I see that your little girl's case is a trifle serious," he remarked. "I would advise you to call a physician soon. I will leave you a copy of Dr. Moser's record to give to any one you may call." He paused to transcribe the record on a page of his note-book. Tearing out the leaf, he extended it to Winter as he moved towards the door. The latter shrunk against the wall. His head was hanging as he reached for the paper. This caused him to grasp air, and so Trescott simply let the paper flutter to the feet of the other man.

"Good-morning," said Trescott from the hall. This placid retreat seemed to suddenly arouse Winter to ferocity. It was as if he had then recalled all the truths which he had formulated to hurl at Trescott. So he followed him into the hall, and down the hall to the door, and through the door to the porch, barking in fiery rage from a respectful distance. As Trescott imperturbably turned the mare's head down the road, Winter stood on the porch, still yelping. He was like a little dog.

XXII

"Have you heard the news?" cried Carrie Dungen as she sped towards Martha's kitchen. "Have you heard the news?" Her eyes were shining with delight.

"No," answered Martha's sister Kate, bending forward eagerly. "What was it? What was it?"

Carrie appeared triumphantly in the open door. "Oh, there's been an awful scene between Doctor Trescott and Jake Winter. I never thought that Jake Winter had any pluck at all, but this morning he told the doctor just what he thought of him."

"Well, what did he think of him?" asked Martha.

"Oh, he called him everything. Mrs. Howarth heard it through her front blinds. It was terrible, she says. It's all over town now. Everybody knows it."

"Didn't the doctor answer back?"

"No! Mrs. Howarth—she says he never said a word. He just walked down to his buggy and got in, and drove off as co-o-o-l. But Jake gave him jinks, by all accounts."

"But what did he say?" cried Kate, shrill and excited. She was evidently at some kind of a feast.

"Oh, he told him that Sadie had never been well since that night Henry Johnson frightened her at Theresa Page's party, and he held him responsible, and how dared he cross his threshold—and—and—and—"

"And what?" said Martha.

"Did he swear at him?" said Kate, in fearsome glee.

"No—not much. He did swear at him a little, but not more than a man does anyhow when he is real mad, Mrs. Howarth says."

"O-oh!" breathed Kate. "And did he call him any names?"

Martha, at her work, had been for a time in deep thought. She now interrupted the others. "It don't seem as if Sadie Winter had been sick since that time Henry Johnson got loose. She's been to school almost the whole time since then, hasn't she?"

They combined upon her in immediate indignation. "School? School? I should say not. Don't think for a moment. School!"

Martha wheeled from the sink. She held an iron spoon, and it seemed as if she was going to attack them. "Sadie Winter has passed here many a morning since then carrying her schoolbag. Where was she going? To a wedding?"

The others, long accustomed to a mental tyranny, speedily surrendered.

"Did she?" stammered Kate. "I never saw her."

Carrie Dungen made a weak gesture.

"If I had been Doctor Trescott," exclaimed Martha, loudly, "I'd have knocked that miserable Jake Winter's head off."

Kate and Carrie, exchanging glances, made an alliance in the air. "I don't see why you say that, Martha," replied Carrie, with considerable boldness, gaining support and sympathy from Kate's smile. "I don't see how anybody can be blamed for getting angry when their little girl gets almost scared to death and gets sick from it, and all that. Besides, everybody says—"

"Oh, I don't care what everybody says," said Martha.

"Well, you can't go against the whole town," answered Carrie, in sudden sharp defiance.

"No, Martha, you can't go against the whole town," piped Kate, following her leader rapidly.

"'The whole town,'" cried Martha. "I'd like to know what you call 'the whole town.' Do you call these silly people who are scared of Henry Johnson 'the whole town'?"

"Why, Martha," said Carrie, in a reasoning tone, "you talk as if you wouldn't be scared of him!"

"No more would I," retorted Martha.

"O-oh, Martha, how you talk!" said Kate. "Why, the idea! Everybody's afraid of him."

Carrie was grinning. "You've never seen him, have you?" she asked, seductively.

"No," admitted Martha.

"Well, then, how do you know that you wouldn't be scared?"

Martha confronted her. "Have you ever seen him? No? Well, then, how do you know you *would* be scared?"

The allied forces broke out in chorus: "But, Martha, everybody says so. Everybody says so."

"Everybody says what?"

"Everybody that's seen him say they were frightened almost to death. Tisn't only women, but it's men too. It's awful."

Martha wagged her head solemnly. "I'd try not to be afraid of him."

"But supposing you could not help it?" said Kate.

"Yes, and look here," cried Carrie. "I'll tell you another thing. The Hannigans are going to move out of the house next door."

"On account of him?" demanded Martha.

Carrie nodded. "Mrs. Hannigan says so herself."

"Well, of all things!" ejaculated Martha. "Going to move, eh? You don't say so! Where they going to move to?"

"Down on Orchard Avenue."

"Well, of all things! Nice house?"

"I don't know about that. I haven't heard. But there's lots of nice houses on Orchard."

"Yes, but they're all taken," said Kate. "There isn't a vacant house on Orchard Avenue."

"Oh yes, there is," said Martha. "The old Hampstead house is vacant."

"Oh, of course," said Kate. "But then I don't believe Mrs. Hannigan would like it there. I wonder where they can be going to move to?"

"I'm sure I don't know," sighed Martha. "It must be to some place we don't know about."

"Well." said Carrie Dungen, after a general reflective silence, "it's easy enough to find out, anyhow."

"Who knows—around here?" asked Kate.

"Why, Mrs. Smith, and there she is in her garden," said Carrie, jumping to her feet. As she dashed out of the door, Kate and Martha crowded at the window. Carrie's voice rang out from near the steps. "Mrs. Smith! Mrs. Smith! Do you know where the Hannigans are going to move to?"

XXIII

The autumn smote the leaves, and the trees of Whilomville were panoplied in crimson and yellow. The winds grew stronger, and in the melancholy purple of the nights the home shine of a window became a finer thing. The little boys, watching the sear and sorrowful leaves drifting down from the maples, dreamed of the near time when they could heap bushels in the streets and burn them during the abrupt evenings.

Three men walked down the Niagara Avenue. As they approached Judge Hagenthorpe's house he came down his walk to meet them in the manner of one who has been waiting.

"Are you ready, judge?" one said.

"All ready," he answered.

The four then walked to Trescott's house. He received them in his office, where he had been reading. He seemed surprised at this visit of four very active and influential citizens, but he had nothing to say of it.

After they were all seated, Trescott looked expectantly from one face to another. There was a little silence. It was broken by John Twelve, the wholesale grocer, who was worth $400,000, and reported to be worth over a million.

"Well, doctor," he said, with a short laugh, "I suppose we might as well admit at once that we've come to interfere in something which is none of our business."

"Why, what is it?" asked Trescott, again looking from one face to another. He seemed to appeal particularly to Judge Hagenthorpe, but the old man had his chin lowered musingly to his cane, and would not look at him.

"It's about what nobody talks of—much," said Twelve. "It's about Henry Johnson."

Trescott squared himself in his chair. "Yes?" he said.

Having delivered himself of the title, Twelve seemed to become more easy. "Yes," he answered, blandly, "we wanted to talk to you about it."

"Yes?" said Trescott.

Twelve abruptly advanced on the main attack. "Now see here, Trescott, we like you, and we have come to talk right out about this business. It may be none of our affairs and all that, and as for me, I don't mind if you tell me so; but I am not going to keep quiet and see you ruin yourself. And that's how we all feel."

"I am not ruining myself," answered Trescott.

"No, maybe you are not exactly ruining yourself," said Twelve, slowly, "but you are doing yourself a great deal of harm. You have changed from being the leading doctor in town to about the last one. It is mainly because there are always a large number of people who are very thoughtless fools, of course, but then that doesn't change the condition."

A man who had not heretofore spoken said, solemnly, "It's the women."

"Well, what I want to say is this," resumed Twelve: "Even if there are a lot of fools in the world, we can't see any reason why you should ruin yourself by opposing them. You can't teach them anything, you know."

"I am not trying to teach them anything." Trescott smiled wearily. "I— It is a matter of—well—"

"And there are a good many of us that admire you for it immensely," interrupted Twelve; "but that isn't going to change the minds of all those ninnies."

"It's the women," stated the advocate of this view again.

"Well, what I want to say is this," said Twelve. "We want you to get out of this trouble and strike your old gait again. You are simply killing your practice through your infernal pigheadedness. Now this thing is out of the ordinary, but there must be ways to—to beat the game somehow, you see. So we've talked it over—about a dozen of us—and, as I say, if you want to tell us to mind our own business, why, go ahead; but we've talked it over, and we've come to the conclusion that the only way to do is to get Johnson a place somewhere off up the valley, and—"

Trescott wearily gestured. "You don't know, my friend. Everybody is so afraid of him, they can't even give him good care. Nobody can attend to him as I do myself."

"But I have a little no-good farm up beyond Clarence Mountain that I was going to give to Henry," cried Twelve, aggrieved. "And if you—and if you—if you—through your house burning down, or anything—why, all the boys were prepared to take him right off your hands, and—and—"

Trescott arose and went to the window. He turned his back upon them. They sat waiting in silence. When he returned he kept his face in the shadow. "No, John Twelve," he said, "it can't be done."

There was another stillness. Suddenly a man stirred on his chair.

"Well, then, a public institution—" he began.

"No," said Trescott; "public institutions are all very good, but he is not going to one."

In the background of the group old Judge Hagenthorpe was thoughtfully smoothing the polished ivory head of his cane.

XXIV

Trescott loudly stamped the snow from his feet and shook the flakes from his shoulders. When he entered the house he went at once to the dining-room, and then to the sitting-room. Jimmie was there, reading painfully in a large book concerning giraffes and tigers and crocodiles.

"Where is your mother, Jimmie?" asked Trescott.

"I don't know, pa," answered the boy. "I think she is up-stairs."

Trescott went to the foot of the stairs and called, but there came no answer. Seeing that the door of the little drawing-room was open, he entered. The room was bathed in the half-light that came from the four dull panes of mica in the front of the great stove. As his eyes grew used to the shadows he saw his wife curled in an arm-chair. He went to her. "Why, Grace." he said, "didn't you hear me calling you?"

She made no answer, and as he bent over the chair he heard her trying to smother a sob in the cushion.

"Grace!" he cried. "You're crying!"

She raised her face. "I've got a headache, a dreadful headache, Ned."

"A headache?" he repeated, in surprise and incredulity.

He pulled a chair close to hers. Later, as he cast his eye over the zone of light shed by the dull red panes, he saw that a low table had been drawn close to the stove, and that it was burdened with many small cups and plates of uncut tea-cake. He remembered that the day was Wednesday, and that his wife received on Wednesdays.

"Who was here to-day, Gracie?" he asked.

From his shoulder there came a mumble, "Mrs. Twelve."

"Was she—um," he said. "Why—didn't Anna Hagenthorpe come over?"

The mumble from his shoulder continued, "She wasn't well enough."

Glancing down at the cups, Trescott mechanically counted them. There were fifteen of them. "There, there," he said. "Don't cry, Grace. Don't cry."

The wind was whining round the house, and the snow beat aslant upon the windows. Sometimes the coal in the stove settled with a crumbling sound, and the four panes of mica flashed a sudden new crimson. As he sat holding her head on his shoulder, Trescott found himself occasionally trying to count the cups. There were fifteen of them.

THE BLUE HOTEL

I

The Palace Hotel at Fort Romper was painted a light blue, a shade that is on the legs of a kind of heron, causing the bird to declare its position against any background. The Palace Hotel, then, was always screaming and howling in a way that made the dazzling winter landscape of Nebraska seem only a gray swampish hush. It stood alone on the prairie, and when the snow was falling the town two hundred yards away was not visible. But when the traveller alighted at the railway station he was obliged to pass the Palace Hotel before he could come upon the company of low clapboard houses which composed Fort Romper, and it was not to be thought that any traveller could pass the Palace Hotel without looking at it. Pat Scully, the proprietor, had proved himself a master of strategy when he chose his paints. It is true that on clear days, when the great trans-continental expresses, long lines of swaying Pullmans, swept through Fort Romper, passengers were overcome at the sight, and the cult that knows the brown-reds and the subdivisions of the dark greens of the East expressed shame, pity, horror, in a laugh. But to the citizens of this prairie town and to the people who would naturally stop there, Pat Scully had performed a feat. With this opulence and splendor, these creeds, classes, egotisms, that streamed through Romper on the rails day after day, they had no color in common.

As if the displayed delights of such a blue hotel were not sufficiently enticing, it was Scully's habit to go every morning and evening to meet the leisurely trains that stopped at Romper and work his seductions upon any man that he might see wavering, gripsack in hand.

One morning, when a snow-crusted engine dragged its long string of freight cars and its one passenger coach to the station, Scully performed the marvel of catching three men. One was a shaky and quick-eyed Swede, with a great shining cheap valise; one was a tall bronzed cowboy, who was on his way to a ranch near the Dakota line; one was a little silent man from the East, who didn't look it, and didn't announce it. Scully practically made them prisoners. He was so nimble and merry and kindly that each probably felt it would be the height of brutality to try to escape. They trudged off over the creaking board sidewalks in the wake of the eager little Irishman. He wore a heavy fur cap squeezed tightly down on his head. It caused his two red ears to stick out stiffly, as if they were made of tin.

At last, Scully, elaborately, with boisterous hospitality, conducted them through the portals of the blue hotel. The room which they entered was small. It seemed to be merely a proper temple for an enormous stove, which, in the centre, was humming with godlike violence. At various points on its surface the iron had become luminous and glowed yellow from the heat. Beside the stove Scully's son Johnnie was playing High-Five with an old farmer who had whiskers both gray and sandy. They were quarrelling. Frequently the old farmer turned his face towards a box of sawdust—colored brown from tobacco juice—that was behind the stove, and spat with an air of great impatience and irritation. With a loud flourish of words Scully destroyed the game of cards, and bustled his son up-stairs with part of the baggage of the new guests. He himself conducted them to three basins of the coldest water in the world. The cowboy and the Easterner burnished themselves fiery-red with this water, until it seemed to be some kind of a metal polish. The Swede, however, merely dipped his fingers gingerly and with trepidation. It was notable that throughout this series of small ceremonies the three travellers were made to feel that Scully was very benevolent. He was conferring great favors upon them. He handed the towel from one to the other with an air of philanthropic impulse.

Afterwards they went to the first room, and, sitting about the stove, listened to Scully's officious clamor at his daughters, who were preparing the mid-day meal. They reflected in the silence of experienced men who tread carefully amid new people. Nevertheless, the old farmer, stationary, invincible in his chair near the warmest part of the stove, turned his face from the sawdust box frequently and addressed a glowing commonplace to the strangers. Usually he was answered in short but adequate sentences by either the cowboy or the Easterner. The Swede said nothing. He seemed to be occupied in making furtive estimates of each man in the room. One might have thought that he had the sense of silly suspicion which comes to guilt. He resembled a badly frightened man.

Later, at dinner, he spoke a little, addressing his conversation entirely to Scully. He volunteered that he had come from New York, where for ten years he had worked as a tailor. These facts seemed to strike Scully as fascinating, and afterwards he volunteered that he had lived at Romper for fourteen years. The Swede asked about the crops and the price of labor. He seemed barely to listen to Scully's extended replies. His eyes continued to rove from man to man.

Finally, with a laugh and a wink, he said that some of these Western communities were very dangerous; and after his statement he straightened his legs under the table, tilted his head, and laughed again, loudly. It was plain that the demonstration had no meaning to the others. They looked at him wondering and in silence.

II

As the men trooped heavily back into the front-room, the two little windows presented views of a turmoiling sea of snow. The huge arms of the wind were making attempts—mighty, circular, futile—to embrace the flakes as they sped. A gate-post like a still man with a blanched face stood aghast amid this profligate fury. In a hearty voice Scully announced the presence of a blizzard. The guests of the blue hotel, lighting their pipes, assented with grunts of lazy masculine contentment. No island of the sea could be exempt in the degree of this little room with its humming stove. Johnnie, son of Scully, in a tone which defined his opinion of his ability as a card-player, challenged the old farmer of both gray and sandy whiskers to a game of High-Five. The farmer agreed with a contemptuous and bitter scoff. They sat close to the stove, and squared their knees under a wide board. The cowboy and the Easterner watched the game with interest. The Swede remained near the window, aloof, but with a countenance that showed signs of an inexplicable excitement.

The play of Johnnie and the gray-beard was suddenly ended by another quarrel. The old man arose while casting a look of heated scorn at his adversary. He slowly buttoned his coat, and then stalked with fabulous dignity from the room. In the discreet silence of all other men the Swede laughed. His laughter rang somehow childish. Men by this time had begun to look at him askance, as if they wished to inquire what ailed him.

A new game was formed jocosely. The cowboy volunteered to become the partner of Johnnie, and they all then turned to ask the Swede to throw in his lot with the little Easterner, He asked some questions about the game, and, learning that it wore many names, and that he had played it when it was under an alias, he accepted the invitation. He strode towards the men nervously, as if he expected to be assaulted. Finally, seated, he gazed from face to face and laughed shrilly. This laugh was so strange that the Easterner looked up quickly, the cowboy sat intent and with his mouth open, and Johnnie paused, holding the cards with still fingers.

Afterwards there was a short silence. Then Johnnie said, "Well, let's get at it. Come on now!" They pulled their chairs forward until their knees were bunched under the board. They began to play, and their interest in the game caused the others to forget the manner of the Swede.

The cowboy was a board-whacker. Each time that he held superior cards he whanged them, one by one, with exceeding force, down upon the improvised table, and took the tricks with a glowing air of prowess and pride that sent thrills of indignation into the hearts of his opponents. A game with a board-whacker in it is sure to become intense. The countenances of the Easterner and the Swede were miserable whenever the cowboy thundered down his aces and kings, while Johnnie, his eyes gleaming with joy, chuckled and chuckled.

Because of the absorbing play none considered the strange ways of the Swede. They paid strict heed to the game. Finally, during a lull caused by a new deal, the Swede suddenly addressed Johnnie: "I suppose there have been a good many men killed in this room." The jaws of the others dropped and they looked at him.

"What in hell are you talking about?" said Johnnie.

The Swede laughed again his blatant laugh, full of a kind of false courage and defiance. "Oh, you know what I mean all right," he answered.

"I'm a liar if I do!" Johnnie protested. The card was halted, and the men stared at the Swede. Johnnie evidently felt that as the son of the proprietor he should make a direct inquiry. "Now, what might you be drivin' at, mister?" he asked. The Swede winked at him. It was a wink full of cunning. His fingers shook on the edge of the board. "Oh, maybe you think I have been to nowheres. Maybe you think I'm a tenderfoot?"

"I don't know nothin' about you," answered Johnnie, "and I don't give a damn where you've been. All I got to say is that I don't know what you're driving at. There hain't never been nobody killed in this room."

The cowboy, who had been steadily gazing at the Swede, then spoke: "What's wrong with you, mister?"

Apparently it seemed to the Swede that he was formidably menaced. He shivered and turned white near the corners of his mouth. He sent an appealing glance in the direction of the little Easterner. During these moments he did not forget to wear his air of advanced pot-valor. "They say they don't know what I mean," he remarked mockingly to the Easterner.

The latter answered after prolonged and cautious reflection. "I don't understand you," he said, impassively.

The Swede made a movement then which announced that he thought he had encountered treachery from the only quarter where he had expected sympathy, if not help. "Oh, I see you are all against me. I see—"

The cowboy was in a state of deep stupefaction. "Say." he cried, as he tumbled the deck violently down upon the board "—say, what are you gittin' at, hey?"

The Swede sprang up with the celerity of a man escaping from a snake on the floor. "I don't want to fight!" he shouted. "I don't want to fight!"

The cowboy stretched his long legs indolently and deliberately. His hands were in his pockets. He spat into the sawdust box. "Well, who the hell thought you did?" he inquired.

The Swede backed rapidly towards a corner of the room. His hands were out protectingly in front of his chest, but he was making an obvious struggle to control his fright. "Gentlemen," he quavered, "I suppose I am going to be killed before I can leave this house! I suppose I am going to be killed before I can leave this house!" In his eyes was the dying-swan look. Through the windows could be seen the snow turning blue in the shadow of dusk. The wind tore at the house and some loose thing beat regularly against the clapboards like a spirit tapping.

A door opened, and Scully himself entered. He paused in surprise as he noted the tragic attitude of the Swede. Then he said, "What's the matter here?"

The Swede answered him swiftly and eagerly: "These men are going to kill me."

"Kill you!" ejaculated Scully. "Kill you! What are you talkin'?"

The Swede made the gesture of a martyr.

Scully wheeled sternly upon his son. "What is this, Johnnie?"

The lad had grown sullen. "Damned if I know," he answered. "I can't make no sense to it." He began to shuffle the cards, fluttering them together with an angry snap. "He says a good many men have been killed in this room, or something like that. And he says he's goin' to be killed here too. I don't know what ails him. He's crazy, I shouldn't wonder."

Scully then looked for explanation to the cowboy, but the cowboy simply shrugged his shoulders.

"Kill you?" said Scully again to the Swede. "Kill you? Man, you're off your nut."

"Oh, I know." burst out the Swede. "I know what will happen. Yes, I'm crazy—yes. Yes, of course, I'm crazy—yes. But I know one thing—" There was a sort of sweat of misery and terror upon his face. "I know I won't get out of here alive."

The cowboy drew a deep breath, as if his mind was passing into the last stages of dissolution. "Well, I'm dog-goned," he whispered to himself.

Scully wheeled suddenly and faced his son. "You've been troublin' this man!"

Johnnie's voice was loud with its burden of grievance. "Why, good Gawd, I ain't done nothin' to 'im."

The Swede broke in. "Gentlemen, do not disturb yourselves. I will leave this house. I will go away because"—he accused them dramatically with his glance—"because I do not want to be killed."

Scully was furious with his son. "Will you tell me what is the matter, you young divil? What's the matter, anyhow? Speak out!"

"Blame it!" cried Johnnie in despair, "don't I tell you I don't know. He—he says we want to kill him, and that's all I know. I can't tell what ails him."

The Swede continued to repeat: "Never mind, Mr. Scully; nevermind. I will leave this house. I will go away, because I do not wish to be killed. Yes, of course, I am crazy—yes. But I know one thing! I will go away. I will leave this house. Never mind, Mr. Scully; never mind. I will go away."

"You will not go 'way," said Scully. "You will not go 'way until I hear the reason of this business. If anybody has troubled you I will take care of him. This is my house. You are under my roof, and I will not allow any peaceable man to be troubled here." He cast a terrible eye upon Johnnie, the cowboy, and the Easterner.

"Never mind, Mr. Scully; never mind. I will go away. I do not wish to be killed." The Swede moved towards the door, which opened upon the stairs. It was evidently his intention to go at once for his baggage.

"No, no," shouted Scully peremptorily; but the white-faced man slid by him and disappeared. "Now," said Scully severely, "what does this mane?"

Johnnie and the cowboy cried together: "Why, we didn't do nothin' to 'im!"

Scully's eyes were cold. "No," he said, "you didn't?"

Johnnie swore a deep oath. "Why this is the wildest loon I ever see. We didn't do nothin' at all. We were jest sittin' here play in' cards, and he—"

The father suddenly spoke to the Easterner. "Mr. Blanc," he asked, "what has these boys been doin'?"

The Easterner reflected again. "I didn't see anything wrong at all," he said at last, slowly.

Scully began to howl. "But what does it mane?" He stared ferociously at his son. "I have a mind to lather you for this, me boy."

Johnnie was frantic. "Well, what have I done?" he bawled at his father.

III

"I think you are tongue-tied," said Scully finally to his son, the cowboy, and the Easterner; and at the end of this scornful sentence he left the room.

Up-stairs the Swede was swiftly fastening the straps of his great valise. Once his back happened to be half turned towards the door, and, hearing a noise there, he wheeled and sprang up, uttering a loud cry. Scully's wrinkled visage showed grimly in the light of the small lamp he carried. This yellow effulgence, streaming upward, colored only his prominent features, and left his eyes, for instance, in mysterious shadow. He resembled a murderer.

"Man! man!" he exclaimed, "have you gone daffy?"

"Oh, no! Oh, no!" rejoined the other. "There are people in this world who know pretty nearly as much as you do—understand?"

For a moment they stood gazing at each other. Upon the Swede's deathly pale checks were two spots brightly crimson and sharply edged, as if they had been carefully painted. Scully placed the light on the table and sat himself on the edge of the bed. He spoke ruminatively. "By cracky, I never heard of such a thing in my life. It's a complete muddle. I can't, for the soul of me, think how you ever got this idea into your head." Presently he lifted his eyes and asked: "And did you sure think they were going to kill you?"

The Swede scanned the old man as if he wished to see into his mind. "I did," he said at last. He obviously suspected that this answer might precipitate an outbreak. As he pulled on a strap his whole arm shook, the elbow wavering like a bit of paper.

Scully banged his hand impressively on the foot-board of the bed. "Why, man, we're goin' to have a line of ilictric street-cars in this town next spring."

"'A line of electric street-cars,'" repeated the Swede, stupidly.

"And," said Scully, "there's a new railroad goin' to be built down from Broken Arm to here. Not to mention the four churches and the smashin' big brick school-house. Then there's the big factory, too. Why, in two years Romper 'll be a *metropolis*."

Having finished the preparation of his baggage, the Swede straightened himself. "Mr. Scully," he said, with sudden hardihood, "how much do I owe you?"

"You don't owe me anythin'," said the old man, angrily.

"Yes, I do," retorted the Swede. He took seventy-five cents from his pocket and tendered it to Scully; but the latter snapped his fingers in disdainful refusal. However, it happened that they both stood gazing in a strange fashion at three silver pieces on the Swede's open palm.

"I'll not take your money," said Scully at last. "Not after what's been goin' on here." Then a plan seemed to strike him. "Here," he cried, picking up his lamp and moving towards the door. "Here! Come with me a minute."

"No," said the Swede, in overwhelming alarm.

"Yes," urged the old man. "Come on! I want you to come and see a picter—just across the hall—in my room."

The Swede must have concluded that his hour was come. His jaw dropped and his teeth showed like a dead man's. He ultimately followed Scully across the corridor, but he had the step of one hung in chains.

Scully flashed the light high on the wall of his own chamber. There was revealed a ridiculous photograph of a little girl. She was leaning against a balustrade of gorgeous decoration, and the formidable bang to her hair was prominent. The figure was as graceful as an upright sled-stake, and, withal, it was of the hue of lead. "There," said Scully, tenderly, "that's the picter of my little girl that died. Her name was Carrie. She had the purtiest hair you ever saw! I was that fond of her, she—"

Turning then, he saw that the Swede was not contemplating the picture at all, but, instead, was keeping keen watch on the gloom in the rear.

"Look, man!" cried Scully, heartily. "That's the picter of my little gal that died. Her name was Carrie. And then here's the picter of my oldest boy, Michael. He's a lawyer in Lincoln, an' doin' well. I gave that boy a grand eddycation, and I'm glad for it now. He's a fine boy. Look at 'im now. Ain't he bold as blazes, him there in Lincoln, an honored an' respicted gintleman. An honored an' respicted gintleman," concluded Scully with a flourish. And, so saying, he smote the Swede jovially on the back.

The Swede faintly smiled.

"Now," said the old man, "there's only one more thing." He dropped suddenly to the floor and thrust his head beneath the bed. The Swede could hear his muffled voice. "I'd keep it under me piller if it wasn't for that boy Johnnie. Then there's the old woman—Where is it now? I never put it twice in the same place. Ah, now come out with you!"

Presently he backed clumsily from under the bed, dragging with him an old coat rolled into a bundle. "I've fetched him," he muttered. Kneeling on the floor, he unrolled the coat and extracted from its heart a large yellow-brown whiskey bottle.

His first maneuver was to hold the bottle up to the light. Reassured, apparently, that nobody had been tampering with it, he thrust it with a generous movement towards the Swede.

The weak-kneed Swede was about to eagerly clutch this element of strength, but he suddenly jerked his hand away and cast a look of horror upon Scully.

"Drink," said the old man affectionately. He had risen to his feet, and now stood facing the Swede.

There was a silence. Then again Scully said: "Drink!"

The Swede laughed wildly. He grabbed the bottle, put it to his mouth, and as his lips curled absurdly around the opening and his throat worked, he kept his glance, burning with hatred, upon the old man's face.

IV

After the departure of Scully the three men, with the card-board still upon their knees, preserved for a long time an astounded silence. Then Johnnie said: "That's the dod-dangest Swede I ever see."

"He ain't no Swede," said the cowboy, scornfully.

"Well, what is he then?" cried Johnnie. "What is he then?"

"It's my opinion," replied the cowboy deliberately, "he's some kind of a Dutchman." It was a venerable custom of the country to entitle as Swedes all light-haired men who spoke with a heavy tongue. In consequence the idea of the cowboy was not without its daring. "Yes, sir," he repeated. "It's my opinion this feller is some kind of a Dutchman."

"Well, he says he's a Swede, anyhow," muttered Johnnie, sulkily. He turned to the Easterner: "What do you think, Mr. Blanc?"

"Oh, I don't know," replied the Easterner.

"Well, what do you think makes him act that way?" asked the cowboy.

"Why, he's frightened." The Easterner knocked his pipe against a rim of the stove. "He's clear frightened out of his boots."

"What at?" cried Johnnie and cowboy together.

The Easterner reflected over his answer.

"What at?" cried the others again.

"Oh, I don't know, but it seems to me this man has been reading dime-novels, and he thinks he's right out in the middle of it—the shootin' and stabbin' and all."

"But," said the cowboy, deeply scandalized, "this ain't Wyoming, ner none of them places. This is Nebrasker."

"Yes," added Johnnie, "an' why don't he wait till he gits *out West?*"

The travelled Easterner laughed. "It isn't different there even—not in these days. But he thinks he's right in the middle of hell."

Johnnie and the cowboy mused long.

"It's awful funny," remarked Johnnie at last.

"Yes," said the cowboy. "This is a queer game. I hope we don't git snowed in, because then we'd have to stand this here man bein' around with us all the time. That wouldn't be no good."

"I wish pop would throw him out," said Johnnie.

Presently they heard a loud stamping on the stairs, accompanied by ringing jokes in the voice of old Scully, and laughter, evidently from the Swede. The men around the stove stared vacantly at each other. "Gosh!" said the cowboy. The door flew open, and old Scully, flushed and anecdotal, came into the room. He was jabbering at the Swede, who followed him, laughing bravely. It was the entry of two roisterers from a banquet-hall.

"Come now," said Scully sharply to the three seated men, "move up and give us a chance at the stove." The cowboy and the Easterner obediently sidled their chairs to make room for the new-comers. Johnnie, however, simply arranged himself in a more indolent attitude, and then remained motionless.

"Come! Git over, there," said Scully.

"Plenty of room on the other side of the stove," said Johnnie.

"Do you think we want to sit in the draught?" roared the father.

But the Swede here interposed with a grandeur of confidence. "No, no. Let the boy sit where he likes," he cried in a bullying voice to the father.

"All right! All right!" said Scully, deferentially. The cowboy and the Easterner exchanged glances of wonder.

The five chairs were formed in a crescent about one side of the stove. The Swede began to talk; he talked arrogantly, profanely, angrily. Johnnie, the cowboy, and the Easterner maintained a morose silence, while old Scully appeared to be receptive and eager, breaking in constantly with sympathetic ejaculations.

Finally the Swede announced that he was thirsty. He moved in his chair, and said that he would go for a drink of water.

"I'll git it for you," cried Scully at once.

"No," said the Swede, contemptuously. "I'll get it for myself." He arose and stalked with the air of an owner off into the executive parts of the hotel.

As soon as the Swede was out of hearing Scully sprang to his feet and whispered intensely to the others: "Up-stairs he thought I was tryin' to poison 'im."

"Say," said Johnnie, "this makes me sick. Why don't you throw 'im out in the snow?"

"Why, he's all right now," declared Scully. "It was only that he was from the East, and he thought this was a tough place. That's all. He's all right now."

The cowboy looked with admiration upon the Easterner. "You were straight," he said. "You were on to that there Dutchman."

"Well," said Johnnie to his father, "he may be all right now, but I don't see it. Other time he was scared, but now he's too fresh."

Scully's speech was always a combination of Irish brogue and idiom, Western twang and idiom, and scraps of curiously formal diction taken from the story-books and newspapers, He now hurled a strange mass of language at the head of his son. "What do I keep? What do I keep? What do I keep?" he demanded, in a voice of thunder. He slapped his knee impressively, to indicate that he himself was going to make reply, and that all should heed. "I keep a hotel," he shouted. "A hotel, do you mind? A guest under my roof has sacred privileges. He is to be intimidated by none. Not one word shall he hear that would prejudice him in favor of goin' away. I'll not have it. There's no place in this here town where they can say they iver took in a guest of mine because he was afraid to stay here." He wheeled suddenly upon the cowboy and the Easterner. "Am I right?"

"Yes, Mr. Scully," said the cowboy, "I think you're right."

"Yes, Mr. Scully," said the Easterner, "I think you're right."

V

At six-o'clock supper, the Swede fizzed like a fire-wheel. He sometimes seemed on the point of bursting into riotous song, and in all his madness he was encouraged by old Scully. The Easterner was incased in reserve; the cowboy sat in wide-mouthed amazement, forgetting to eat, while Johnnie wrathily demolished great plates of food. The daughters of the house, when they were obliged to replenish the biscuits, approached as warily as Indians, and, having succeeded in their purpose, fled with ill-concealed trepidation. The Swede domineered the whole feast, and he gave it the appearance of a cruel bacchanal. He seemed to have grown suddenly taller; he gazed, brutally disdainful, into every face. His voice rang through the room. Once when he jabbed out harpoon-fashion with his fork to pinion a biscuit, the weapon nearly impaled the hand of the Easterner which had been stretched quietly out for the same biscuit.

After supper, as the men filed towards the other room, the Swede smote Scully ruthlessly on the shoulder. "Well, old boy, that was a good, square meal." Johnnie looked hopefully at his father; he knew that shoulder was tender from an old fall; and, indeed, it appeared for a moment as if Scully was going to flame out over the matter, but in the end he smiled a sickly smile and remained silent. The others understood from his manner that he was admitting his responsibility for the Swede's new view-point.

Johnnie, however, addressed his parent in an aside. "Why don't you license somebody to kick you down-stairs?" Scully scowled darkly by way of reply.

When they were gathered about the stove, the Swede insisted on another game of High Five. Scully gently deprecated the plan at first, but the Swede turned a wolfish glare upon him. The old man subsided, and the Swede canvassed the others. In his tone there was always a great threat. The cowboy and the Easterner both remarked indifferently that they would play. Scully said that he would presently have to go to meet the 6.58 train, and so the Swede turned menacingly upon Johnnie. For a moment their glances crossed like blades, and then Johnnie smiled and said, "Yes, I'll play."

They formed a square, with the little board on their knees. The Easterner and the Swede were again partners. As the play went on, it was noticeable that the cowboy was not board-whacking as usual. Meanwhile, Scully, near the lamp, had put on his spectacles and, with an appearance curiously like an old priest, was reading a newspaper. In time he went out to meet the 6.58 train, and, despite his precautions, a gust of polar wind whirled into the room as he opened the door. Besides scattering the cards, it dulled the players to the marrow. The Swede cursed frightfully. When Scully returned, his entrance disturbed a cosey and friendly scene. The Swede again cursed. But presently they were once more intent, their heads bent forward and their hands moving swiftly. The Swede had adopted the fashion of board-whacking.

Scully took up his paper and for a long time remained immersed in matters which were extraordinarily remote from him. The lamp burned badly, and once he stopped to adjust the wick. The newspaper, as he turned from page to page, rustled with a slow and comfortable sound. Then suddenly he heard three terrible words: "You are cheatin'!"

Such scenes often prove that there can be little of dramatic import in environment. Any room can present a tragic front; any room can be comic. This little den was now hideous as a torture-chamber. The new faces of the men themselves had changed it upon the instant. The Swede held a huge fist in front of Johnnie's face, while the latter looked steadily over it into the blazing orbs of his accuser. The Easterner had grown pallid; the cowboy's jaw had dropped in that expression of bovine amazement which was one of his important mannerisms. After the three words, the first sound in the room was made by Scully's paper as it floated forgotten to his feet. His spectacles had also fallen from his nose, but by a clutch he had saved them in air. His hand, grasping the spectacles, now remained poised awkwardly and near his shoulder. He stared at the card-players.

Probably the silence was while a second elapsed. Then, if the floor had been suddenly twitched out from under the men they could not have moved quicker. The five had projected themselves headlong towards a common point. It happened that Johnnie, in rising to hurl himself upon the Swede, had stumbled slightly because of his curiously instinctive care for the cards and the board. The loss of the moment allowed time for the arrival of Scully, and also allowed the cowboy time to give the Swede a great push which sent him staggering back. The men found tongue together, and hoarse shouts of rage, appeal, or fear burst from every throat. The cowboy pushed and jostled feverishly at the Swede, and the Easterner and Scully clung wildly to Johnnie; but, through the smoky air, above the swaying bodies of the peace-compellers, the eyes of the two warriors ever sought each other in glances of challenge that were at once hot and steely.

Of course the board had been overturned, and now the whole company of cards was scattered over the floor, where the boots of the men trampled the fat and painted kings and queens as they gazed with their silly eyes at the war that was waging above them.

Scully's voice was dominating the yells. "Stop now? Stop, I say! Stop, now—"

Johnnie, as he struggled to burst through the rank formed by Scully and the Easterner, was crying, "Well, he says I cheated! He says I cheated! I won't allow no man to say I cheated! If he says I cheated, he's a ——— ———!"

The cowboy was telling the Swede, "Quit, now! Quit, d'ye hear—"

The screams of the Swede never ceased: "He did cheat! I saw him! I saw him—"

As for the Easterner, he was importuning in a voice that was not heeded: "Wait a moment, can't you? Oh, wait a moment. What's the good of a fight over a game of cards? Wait a moment—"

In this tumult no complete sentences were clear. "Cheat"—"Quit"—"He says"—these fragments pierced the uproar and rang out sharply. It was remarkable that, whereas Scully undoubtedly made the most noise, he was the least heard of any of the riotous band.

Then suddenly there was a great cessation. It was as if each man had paused for breath; and although the room was still lighted with the anger of men, it could be seen that there was no danger of immediate conflict, and at once Johnnie, shouldering his way forward, almost succeeded in confronting the Swede. "What did you say I cheated for? What did you say I cheated for? I don't cheat, and I won't let no man say I do!"

The Swede said, "I saw you! I saw you!"

"Well," cried Johnnie, "I'll fight any man what says I cheat!"

"No, you won't," said the cowboy. "Not here."

"Ah, be still, can't you?" said Scully, coming between them.

The quiet was sufficient to allow the Easterner's voice to be heard. He was repealing, "Oh, wait a moment, can't you? What's the good of a fight over a game of cards? Wait a moment!"

Johnnie, his red face appearing above his father's shoulder, hailed the Swede again. "Did you say I cheated?"

The Swede showed his teeth. "Yes."

"Then," said Johnnie, "we must fight."

"Yes, fight," roared the Swede. He was like a demoniac. "Yes, fight! I'll show you what kind of a man I am! I'll show you who you want to fight!

Maybe you think I can't fight! Maybe you think I can't! I'll show you, you skin, you card-sharp! Yes, you cheated! You cheated! You cheated!"

"Well, let's go at it, then, mister," said Johnnie, coolly.

The cowboy's brow was beaded with sweat from his efforts in intercepting all sorts of raids. He turned in despair to Scully. "What are you goin' to do now?"

A change had come over the Celtic visage of the old man. He now seemed all eagerness; his eyes glowed.

"We'll let them fight," he answered, stalwartly. "I can't put up with it any longer. I've stood this damned Swede till I'm sick. We'll let them fight."

VI

The men prepared to go out-of-doors. The Easterner was so nervous that he had great difficulty in getting his arms into the sleeves of his new leather coat. As the cowboy drew his fur cap down over his ears his hands trembled. In fact, Johnnie and old Scully were the only ones who displayed no agitation. These preliminaries were conducted without words.

Scully threw open the door. "Well, come on," he said. Instantly a terrific wind caused the flame of the lamp to struggle at its wick, while a puff of black smoke sprang from the chimney-top. The stove was in mid-current of the blast, and its voice swelled to equal the roar of the storm. Some of the scarred and bedabbled cards were caught up from the floor and dashed helplessly against the farther wall. The men lowered their heads and plunged into the tempest as into a sea.

No snow was falling, but great whirls and clouds of flakes, swept up from the ground by the frantic winds, were streaming southward with the speed of bullets. The covered land was blue with the sheen of an unearthly satin, and there was no other hue save where, at the low, black railway station—which seemed incredibly distant—one light gleamed like a tiny jewel. As the men floundered into a thigh deep drift, it was known that the Swede was bawling out something. Scully went to him, put a hand on his shoulder and projected an ear. "What's that you say?" he shouted.

"I say," bawled the Swede again, "I won't stand much show against this gang. I know you'll all pitch on me."

Scully smote him reproachfully on the arm. "Tut, man!" he yelled. The wind tore the words from Scully's lips and scattered them far alee.

"You are all a gang of—" boomed the Swede, but the storm also seized the remainder of this sentence.

Immediately turning their backs upon the wind, the men had swung around a corner to the sheltered side of the hotel. It was the function of the little house to preserve here, amid this great devastation of snow, an irregular V-shape of heavily incrusted grass, which crackled beneath the feet. One could imagine the great drifts piled against the windward side. When the party reached the comparative peace of this spot it was found that the Swede was still bellowing.

"Oh, I know what kind of a thing this is! I know you'll all pitch on me. I can't lick you all!"

Scully turned upon him panther fashion. "You'll not have to whip all of us. You'll have to whip my son Johnnie. An' the man what troubles you durin' that time will have me to dale with."

The arrangements were swiftly made. The two men faced each other, obedient to the harsh commands of Scully, whose face, in the subtly luminous gloom, could be seen set in the austere impersonal lines that are pictured on the countenances of the Roman veterans. The Easterner's teeth were chattering, and he was hopping up and down like a mechanical toy. The cowboy stood rock-like.

The contestants had not stripped off any clothing. Each was in his ordinary attire. Their fists were up, and they eyed each other in a calm that had the elements of leonine cruelty in it.

During this pause, the Easterner's mind, like a film, took lasting impressions of three men—the iron-nerved master of the ceremony; the Swede, pale, motionless, terrible; and Johnnie, serene yet ferocious, brutish yet heroic. The entire prelude had in it a tragedy greater than the tragedy of action, and this aspect was accentuated by the long, mellow cry of the blizzard, as it sped the tumbling and wailing flakes into the black abyss of the south.

"Now!" said Scully.

The two combatants leaped forward and crashed together like bullocks. There was heard the cushioned sound of blows, and of a curse squeezing out from between the tight teeth of one.

As for the spectators, the Easterner's pent-up breath exploded from him with a pop of relief, absolute relief from the tension of the preliminaries. The cowboy bounded into the air with a yowl. Scully was immovable as from supreme amazement and fear at the fury of the fight which he himself had permitted and arranged.

For a time the encounter in the darkness was such a perplexity of flying arms that it presented no more detail than would a swiftly revolving wheel. Occasionally a face, as if illumined by a flash of light, would shine out, ghastly and marked with pink spots. A moment later, the men might have been known as shadows, if it were not for the involuntary utterance of oaths that came from them in whispers.

Suddenly a holocaust of warlike desire caught the cowboy, and he bolted forward with the speed of a broncho. "Go it, Johnnie! go it! Kill him! Kill him!"

Scully confronted him. "Kape back," he said; and by his glance the cowboy could tell that this man was Johnnie's father.

To the Easterner there was a monotony of unchangeable fighting that was an abomination. This confused mingling was eternal to his sense, which was concentrated in a longing for the end, the priceless end. Once the fighters lurched near him, and as he scrambled hastily backward he heard them breathe like men on the rack.

"Kill him, Johnnie! Kill him! Kill him! Kill him!" The cowboy's face was contorted like one of those agony masks in museums.

"Keep still," said Scully, icily.

Then there was a sudden loud grunt, incomplete, cut short, and Johnnie's body swung away from the Swede and fell with sickening heaviness to the grass. The cowboy was barely in time to prevent the mad Swede from flinging himself upon his prone adversary. "No, you don't," said the cowboy, interposing an arm. "Wait a second."

Scully was at his son's side. "Johnnie! Johnnie, me boy!" His voice had a quality of melancholy tenderness. "Johnnie! Can you go on with it?" He looked anxiously down into the bloody, pulpy face of his son.

There was a moment of silence, and then Johnnie answered in his ordinary voice, "Yes, I—it—yes."

Assisted by his father he struggled to his feet. "Wait a bit now till you git your wind," said the old man.

A few paces away the cowboy was lecturing the Swede. "No, you don't! Wait a second!"

The Easterner was plucking at Scully's sleeve. "Oh, this is enough," he pleaded. "This is enough! Let it go as it stands. This is enough!"

"Bill," said Scully, "git out of the road." The cowboy stepped aside. "Now." The combatants were actuated by a new caution as they advanced towards collision. They glared at each other, and then the Swede aimed a lightning blow that carried with it his entire weight. Johnnie was evidently half stupid from weakness, but he miraculously dodged, and his fist sent the over-balanced Swede sprawling.

The cowboy, Scully, and the Easterner burst into a cheer that was like a chorus of triumphant soldiery, but before its conclusion the Swede had scuffled agilely to his feet and come in berserk abandon at his foe. There was another perplexity of flying arms, and Johnnie's body again swung away and fell, even as a bundle might fall from a roof. The Swede instantly staggered to a little wind-waved tree and leaned upon it, breathing like an engine, while his savage and flame-lit eyes roamed from face to face as the men bent over Johnnie. There was a splendor of isolation in his situation at this time which the Easterner felt once when, lifting his eyes from the man on the ground, he beheld that mysterious and lonely figure, waiting.

"Arc you any good yet, Johnnie?" asked Scully in a broken voice.

The son gasped and opened his eyes languidly. After a moment he answered, "No—I ain't—any good—any—more." Then, from shame and bodily ill he began to weep, the tears furrowing down through the blood-stains on his face. "He was too—too—too heavy for me."

Scully straightened and addressed the waiting figure. "Stranger," he said, evenly, "it's all up with our side." Then his voice changed into that vibrant huskiness which is commonly the tone of the most simple and deadly announcements. "Johnnie is whipped."

Without replying, the victor moved off on the route to the front door of the hotel.

The cowboy was formulating new and un-spellable blasphemies. The Easterner was startled to find that they were out in a wind that seemed to come direct from the shadowed arctic floes. He heard again the wail of the snow as it was flung to its grave in the south. He knew now that all this time the cold had been sinking into him deeper and deeper, and he wondered that he had not perished. He felt indifferent to the condition of the vanquished man.

"Johnnie, can you walk?" asked Scully.

"Did I hurt—hurt him any?" asked the son.

"Can you walk, boy? Can you walk?"

Johnnie's voice was suddenly strong. There was a robust impatience in it. "I asked you whether I hurt him any!"

"Yes, yes, Johnnie," answered the cowboy, consolingly; "he's hurt a good deal."

96

They raised him from the ground, and as soon as he was on his feet he went tottering off, rebuffing all attempts at assistance. When the party rounded the corner they were fairly blinded by the pelting of the snow. It burned their faces like fire. The cowboy carried Johnnie through the drift to the door. As they entered some cards again rose from the floor and beat against the wall.

The Easterner rushed to the stove. He was so profoundly chilled that he almost dared to embrace the glowing iron. The Swede was not in the room. Johnnie sank into a chair, and, folding his arms on his knees, buried his face in them. Scully, warming one foot and then the other at a rim of the stove, muttered to himself with Celtic mournfulness. The cowboy had removed his fur cap, and with a dazed and rueful air he was running one hand through his tousled locks. From overhead they could hear the creaking of boards, as the Swede tramped here and there in his room.

The sad quiet was broken by the sudden flinging open of a door that led towards the kitchen. It was instantly followed by an inrush of women. They precipitated themselves upon Johnnie amid a chorus of lamentation. Before they carried their prey off to the kitchen, there to be bathed and harangued with that mixture of sympathy and abuse which is a feat of their sex, the mother straightened herself and fixed old Scully with an eye of stern reproach. "Shame be upon you, Patrick Scully!" she cried. "Your own son, too. Shame be upon you!"

"There, now! Be quiet, now!" said the old man, weakly.

"Shame be upon you, Patrick Scully!" The girls, rallying to this slogan, sniffed disdainfully in the direction of those trembling accomplices, the cowboy and the Easterner. Presently they bore Johnnie away, and left the three men to dismal reflection.

VII

"I'd like to fight this here Dutchman myself," said the cowboy, breaking a long silence.

Scully wagged his head sadly. "No, that wouldn't do. It wouldn't be right. It wouldn't be right."

"Well, why wouldn't it?" argued the cowboy. "I don't see no harm in it."

"No," answered Scully, with mournful heroism. "It wouldn't be right. It was Johnnie's fight, and now we mustn't whip the man just because he whipped Johnnie."

"Yes, that's true enough," said the cowboy; "but—he better not get fresh with me, because I couldn't stand no more of it."

"You'll not say a word to him," commanded Scully, and even then they heard the tread of the Swede on the stairs. His entrance was made theatric. He swept the door back with a bang and swaggered to the middle of the room. No one looked at him. "Well," he cried, insolently, at Scully, "I s'pose you'll tell me now how much I owe you?"

The old man remained stolid. "You don't owe me nothin'."

"Huh!" said the Swede, "huh! Don't owe 'im nothin'."

The cowboy addressed the Swede. "Stranger, I don't see how you come to be so gay around here."

Old Scully was instantly alert. "Stop!" he shouted, holding his hand forth, fingers upward. "Bill, you shut up!"

The cowboy spat carelessly into the sawdust box. "I didn't say a word, did I?" he asked.

"Mr. Scully," called the Swede, "how much do I owe you?" It was seen that he was attired for departure, and that he had his valise in his hand.

"You don't owe me nothin'," repeated Scully in his same imperturbable way.

"Huh!" said the Swede. "I guess you're right. I guess if it was any way at all, you'd owe me somethin'. That's what I guess." He turned to the cowboy. "'Kill him! Kill him! Kill him!'" he mimicked, and then guffawed victoriously.

"'Kill him!'" He was convulsed with ironical humor.

But he might have been jeering the dead. The three men were immovable and silent, staring with glassy eyes at the stove.

The Swede opened the door and passed into the storm, giving one derisive glance backward at the still group.

As soon as the door was closed, Scully and the cowboy leaped to their feet and began to curse. They trampled to and fro, waving their arms and smashing into the air with their fists. "Oh, but that was a hard minute!" wailed Scully. "That was a hard minute! Him there leerin' and scoffin'! One bang at his nose was worth forty dollars to me that minute! How did you stand it, Bill?"

"How did I stand it?" cried the cowboy in a quivering voice. "How did I stand it? Oh!"

The old man burst into sudden brogue. "I'd loike to take that Swade," he wailed, "and hould 'im down on a shtone flure and bate 'im to a jelly wid a shtick!"

The cowboy groaned in sympathy. "I'd like to git him by the neck and ha-ammer him "—he brought his hand down on a chair with a noise like a pistol-shot—"hammer that there Dutchman until he couldn't tell himself from a dead coyote!"

"I'd bate 'im until he—"

"I'd show *him* some things—"

And then together they raised a yearning, fanatic cry—"Oh-o-oh! if we only could—"

"Yes!"

"Yes!"

"And then I'd—"

"O-o-oh!"

VIII

The Swede, tightly gripping his valise, tacked across the face of the storm as if he carried sails. He was following a line of little naked, gasping trees, which he knew must mark the way of the road. His face, fresh from the pounding of Johnnie's fists, felt more pleasure than pain in the wind and the driving snow. A number of square shapes loomed upon him finally, and he knew them as the houses of the main body of the town. He found a street and made travel along it, leaning heavily upon the wind whenever, at a corner, a terrific blast caught him.

He might have been in a deserted village. We picture the world as thick with conquering and elate humanity, but here, with the bugles of the tempest pealing, it was hard to imagine a peopled earth. One viewed the existence of man then as a marvel, and conceded a glamour of wonder to these lice which were caused to cling to a whirling, fire-smote, ice-locked, disease-stricken, space-lost bulb. The conceit of man was explained by this storm to be the very engine of life. One was a coxcomb not to die in it. However, the Swede found a saloon.

In front of it an indomitable red light was burning, and the snow-flakes were made blood color as they flew through the circumscribed territory of the lamp's shining. The Swede pushed open the door of the saloon and entered. A sanded expanse was before him, and at the end of it four men sat about a table drinking. Down one side of the room extended a radiant bar, and its guardian was leaning upon his elbows listening to the talk of the men at the table. The Swede dropped his valise upon the floor, and, smiling fraternally upon the barkeeper, said, "Gimme some whiskey, will you?" The man placed a bottle, a whiskey-glass, and a glass of ice-thick water upon the bar. The Swede poured himself an abnormal portion of whiskey and drank it in three gulps. "Pretty bad night," remarked the bartender, indifferently. He was making the pretension of blindness which is usually a distinction of his class; but it could have been seen that he was furtively studying the half-erased blood-stains on the face of the Swede. "Bad night," he said again.

"Oh, it's good enough for me," replied the Swede, hardily, as he poured himself some more whiskey. The barkeeper took his coin and maneuvered it through its reception by the highly nickelled cash-machine. A bell rang; a card labelled "20 cts." had appeared.

"No," continued the Swede, "this isn't too bad weather. It's good enough for me."

"So?" murmured the barkeeper, languidly.

The copious drams made the Swede's eyes swim, and he breathed a trifle heavier. "Yes, I like this weather. I like it. It suits me." It was apparently his design to impart a deep significance to these words.

"So?" murmured the bartender again. He turned to gaze dreamily at the scroll-like birds and bird-like scrolls which had been drawn with soap upon the mirrors back of the bar.

"Well, I guess I'll take another drink," said the Swede, presently. "Have something?"

"No, thanks; I'm not drinkin'," answered the bartender. Afterwards he asked, "How did you hurt your face?"

The Swede immediately began to boast loudly. "Why, in a fight. I thumped the soul out of a man down here at Scully's hotel."

The interest of the four men at the table was at last aroused.

"Who was it?" said one.

"Johnnie Scully," blustered the Swede. "Son of the man what runs it. He will be pretty near dead for some weeks, I can tell you. I made a nice thing of him, I did. He couldn't get up. They carried him in the house. Have a drink?"

Instantly the men in some subtle way incased themselves in reserve. "No, thanks," said one. The group was of curious formation. Two were prominent local business men; one was the district-attorney; and one was a professional gambler of the kind known as "square." But a scrutiny of the group would not have enabled an observer to pick the gambler from the men of more reputable pursuits. He was, in fact, a man so delicate in manner, when among people of fair class, and so judicious in his choice of victims, that in the strictly masculine part of the town's life he had come to be explicitly trusted and admired. People called him a thoroughbred. The fear and contempt with which his craft was regarded was undoubtedly the reason that his quiet dignity shone conspicuous above the quiet dignity of men who might be merely hatters, billiard markers, or grocery-clerks. Beyond an occasional unwary traveller, who came by rail, this gambler was supposed to prey solely upon reckless and senile farmers, who, when flush with good crops, drove into town in all the pride and confidence of an absolutely invulnerable stupidity. Hearing at times in circuitous fashion of the despoilment of such a farmer, the important men of Romper invariably laughed in contempt of the victim, and, if they thought of the wolf at all, it was with a kind of pride at the knowledge that he would never dare think of attacking their wisdom and courage. Besides, it was popular that this gambler had a real wife and two real children in a neat cottage in a suburb, where he led an exemplary home life; and when any one even suggested a discrepancy in his character, the crowd immediately vociferated descriptions of this virtuous family circle. Then men who led exemplary home lives, and men who did not lead exemplary home lives, all subsided in a bunch, remarking that there was nothing more to be said.

However, when a restriction was placed upon him—as, for instance, when a strong clique of members of the new Pollywog Club refused to permit him, even as a spectator, to appear in the rooms of the organization—the candor and gentleness with which he accepted the judgment disarmed many of his foes and made his friends more desperately partisan. He invariably distinguished between himself and a respectable Romper man so quickly and frankly that his manner actually appeared to be a continual broadcast compliment.

And one must not forget to declare the fundamental fact of his entire position in Romper. It is irrefutable that in all affairs outside of his business, in all matters that occur eternally and commonly between man and man, this thieving card-player was so generous, so just, so moral, that, in a contest, he could have put to flight the consciences of nine-tenths of the citizens of Romper.

And so it happened that he was seated in this saloon with the two prominent local merchants and the district-attorney.

The Swede continued to drink raw whiskey, meanwhile babbling at the barkeeper and trying to induce him to indulge in potations. "Come on. Have a drink. Come on. What—no? Well, have a little one, then. By gawd, I've whipped a man to-night, and I want to celebrate. I whipped him good, too. Gentlemen," the Swede cried to the men at the table, "have a drink?"

"Ssh!" said the barkeeper.

The group at the table, although furtively attentive, had been pretending to be deep in talk, but now a man lifted his eyes towards the Swede and said, shortly, "Thanks. We don't want any more."

At this reply the Swede ruffled out his chest like a rooster. "Well," he exploded, "it seems I can't get anybody to drink with me in this town. Seems so, don't it? Well!"

"Ssh!" said the barkeeper.

"Say," snarled the Swede, "don't you try to shut me up. I won't have it. I'm a gentleman, and I want people to drink with me. And I want 'em to drink with me now. *Now*—do you understand?" He rapped the bar with his knuckles.

Years of experience had calloused the bartender. He merely grew sulky. "I hear you," he answered.

"Well," cried the Swede, "listen hard then. See those men over there? Well, they're going to drink with me, and don't you forget it. Now you watch."

"Hi!" yelled the barkeeper, "this won't do!"

"Why won't it?" demanded the Swede. He stalked over to the table, and by chance laid his hand upon the shoulder of the gambler. "How about this?" he asked, wrathfully. "I asked you to drink with me."

The gambler simply twisted his head and spoke over his shoulder. "My friend, I don't know you."

"Oh, hell!" answered the Swede, "come and have a drink."

"Now, my boy," advised the gambler, kindly, "take your hand off my shoulder and go 'way and mind your own business." He was a little, slim man, and it seemed strange to hear him use this tone of heroic patronage to the burly Swede. The other men at the table said nothing.

"What! You won't drink with me, you little dude? I'll make you then! I'll make you!" The Swede had grasped the gambler frenziedly at the throat, and was dragging him from his chair. The other men sprang up. The barkeeper dashed around the corner of his bar. There was a great tumult, and then was seen a long blade in the hand of the gambler. It shot forward, and a human body, this citadel of virtue, wisdom, power, was pierced as easily as if it had been a melon. The Swede fell with a cry of supreme astonishment.

The prominent merchants and the district attorney must have at once tumbled out of the place backward. The bartender found himself hanging limply to the arm of a chair and gazing into the eyes of a murderer.

"Henry," said the latter, as he wiped his knife on one of the towels that hung beneath the bar-rail, "you tell 'em where to find me. I'll be home, waiting for 'em." Then he vanished. A moment afterwards the barkeeper was in the street dinning through the storm for help, and, moreover, companionship.

The corpse of the Swede, alone in the saloon, had its eyes fixed upon a dreadful legend that dwelt atop of the cash-machine: "This registers the amount of your purchase."

IX

Months later, the cowboy was frying pork over the stove of a little ranch near the Dakota line, when there was a quick thud of hoofs outside, and presently the Easterner entered with the letters and the papers.

"Well," said the Easterner at once, "the chap that killed the Swede has got three years. Wasn't much, was it?"

"He has? Three years?" The cowboy poised his pan of pork, while he ruminated upon the news. "Three years. That ain't much."

"No. It was a light sentence," replied the Easterner as he unbuckled his spurs. "Seems there was a good deal of sympathy for him in Romper."

"If the bartender had been any good," observed the cowboy, thoughtfully, "he would have gone in and cracked that there Dutchman on the head with a bottle in the beginnin' of it and stopped all this here murderin'."

"Yes, a thousand things might have happened," said the Easterner, tartly.

The cowboy returned his pan of pork to the fire, but his philosophy continued. "It's funny, ain't it? If he hadn't said Johnnie was cheatin' he'd be alive this minute. He was an awful fool. Game played for fun, too. Not for money. I believe he was crazy."

"I feel sorry for that gambler," said the Easterner.

"Oh, so do I," said the cowboy. "He don't deserve none of it for killin' who he did."

"The Swede might not have been killed if everything had been square."

"Might not have been killed?" exclaimed the cowboy. "Everythin' square? Why, when he said that Johnnie was cheatin' and acted like such a jackass? And then in the saloon he fairly walked up to git hurt?" With these arguments the cowboy browbeat the Easterner and reduced him to rage.

"You're a fool!" cried the Easterner, viciously. "You're a bigger jackass than the Swede by a million majority. Now let me tell you one thing. Let me tell you something. Listen! Johnnie *was* cheating!"

"'Johnnie,'" said the cowboy, blankly. There was a minute of silence, and then he said, robustly, "Why, no. The game was only for fun."

"Fun or not," said the Easterner, "Johnnie was cheating. I saw him. I know it. I saw him. And I refused to stand up and be a man. I let the Swede fight it out alone. And you—you were simply puffing around the place and wanting to fight. And then old Scully himself! We are all in it! This poor gambler isn't even a noun. He is kind of an adverb. Every sin is the result of a collaboration. We, five of us, have collaborated in the murder of this Swede. Usually there are from a dozen to forty women really involved in every murder, but in this case it seems to be only five men—you, I, Johnnie, old Scully, and that fool of an unfortunate gambler came merely as a culmination, the apex of a human movement, and gets all the punishment."

The cowboy, injured and rebellious, cried out blindly into this fog of mysterious theory: "Well, I didn't do anythin', did I?"

HIS NEW MITTENS

I

Little Horace was walking home from school, brilliantly decorated by a pair of new red mittens. A number of boys were snowballing gleefully in a field. They hailed him. "Come on, Horace! We're having a battle."

Horace was sad. "No," he said, "I can't. I've got to go home." At noon his mother had admonished him: "Now, Horace, you come straight home as soon as school is out. Do you hear? And don't you get them nice new mittens all wet, either. Do you hear?" Also his aunt had said: "I declare, Emily, it's a shame the way you allow that child to ruin his things." She had meant mittens. To his mother, Horace had dutifully replied, "Yes'm." But he now loitered in the vicinity of the group of uproarious boys, who were yelling like hawks as the white balls flew.

Some of them immediately analyzed this extraordinary hesitancy. "Hah!" they paused to scoff, "afraid of your new mittens, ain't you?" Some smaller boys, who were not yet so wise in discerning motives, applauded this attack with unreasonable vehemence. "A-fray-ed of his mit-tens! A-fray-ed of his mit-tens." They sang these lines to cruel and monotonous music which is as old perhaps as American childhood, and which it is the privilege of the emancipated adult to completely forget. "Afray-ed of his mit-tens!"

Horace cast a tortured glance towards his playmates, and then dropped his eyes to the snow at his feet. Presently he turned to the trunk of one of the great maple-trees that lined the curb. He made a pretence of closely examining the rough and virile bark. To his mind, this familiar street of Whilomville seemed to grow dark in the thick shadow of shame. The trees and the houses were now palled in purple.

"A-fray-ed of his mit-tens!" The terrible music had in it a meaning from the moonlit war-drums of chanting cannibals.

At last Horace, with supreme effort, raised his head. "'Tain't them I care about," he said, gruffly. "I've got to go home. That's all."

Whereupon each boy held his left forefinger as if it were a pencil and began to sharpen it derisively with his right forefinger. They came closer, and sang like a trained chorus, "A-fray-ed of his mittens!"

When he raised his voice to deny the charge it was simply lost in the screams of the mob. He was alone, fronting all the traditions of boyhood held before him by inexorable representatives. To such a low state had he fallen that one lad, a mere baby, outflanked him and then struck him in the cheek with a heavy snowball. The act was acclaimed with loud jeers. Horace turned to dart at his assailant, but there was an immediate demonstration on the other flank, and he found himself obliged to keep his face towards the hilarious crew of tormentors. The baby retreated in safety to the rear of the crowd, where he was received with fulsome compliments upon his daring. Horace retreated slowly up the walk. He continually tried to make them heed him, but the only sound was the chant, "A-fray-ed of his mit-tens!" In this desperate withdrawal the beset and haggard boy suffered more than is the common lot of man.

Being a boy himself, he did not understand boys at all. He had, of course, the dismal conviction that they were going to dog him to his grave. But near the corner of the field they suddenly seemed to forget all about it. Indeed, they possessed only the malevolence of so many flitter-headed sparrows. The interest had swung capriciously to some other matter. In a moment they were off in the field again, carousing amid the snow. Some authoritative boy had probably said, "Aw, come on!"

As the pursuit ceased, Horace ceased his retreat. He spent some time in what was evidently an attempt to adjust his self respect, and then began to wander furtively down towards the group. He, too, had undergone an important change. Perhaps his sharp agony was only as durable as the malevolence of the others. In this boyish life obedience to some unformulated creed of manners was enforced with capricious but merciless rigor. However, they were, after all, his comrades, his friends.

They did not heed his return. They were engaged in an altercation. It had evidently been planned that this battle was between Indians and soldiers. The smaller and weaker boys had been induced to appear as Indians in the initial skirmish, but they were now very sick of it, and were reluctantly but steadfastly, affirming their desire for a change of caste. The larger boys had all won great distinction, devastating Indians materially, and they wished the war to go on as planned. They explained vociferously that it was proper for the soldiers always to thrash the Indians. The little boys did not pretend to deny the truth of this argument; they confined themselves to the simple statement that, in that case, they wished to be soldiers. Each little boy willingly appealed to the others to remain Indians, but as for himself he reiterated his desire to enlist as a soldier. The larger boys were in despair over this dearth of enthusiasm in the small Indians. They alternately wheedled and bullied, but they could not persuade the little boys, who were really suffering dreadful humiliation rather than submit to another onslaught of soldiers. They were called all the baby names that had the power of stinging deep into their pride, but they remained firm.

Then a formidable lad, a leader of reputation, one who could whip many boys that wore long trousers, suddenly blew out his checks and shouted, "Well, all right then. I'll be an Indian myself. Now." The little boys greeted with cheers this addition to their wearied ranks, and seemed then content. But matters were not mended in the least, because all of the personal following of the formidable lad, with the addition of every outsider, spontaneously forsook the flag and declared themselves Indians. There were now no soldiers. The Indians had carried everything unanimously. The formidable lad used his influence, but his influence could not shake the loyalty of his friends, who refused to fight under any colors but his colors.

Plainly there was nothing for it but to coerce the little ones. The formidable lad again became a soldier, and then graciously permitted to join him all the real fighting strength of the crowd, leaving behind a most forlorn band of little Indians. Then the soldiers attacked the Indians, exhorting them to opposition at the same time.

The Indians at first adopted a policy of hurried surrender, but this had no success, as none of the surrenders were accepted. They then turned to flee, bawling out protests. The ferocious soldiers pursued them amid shouts. The battle widened, developing all manner of marvellous detail.

Horace had turned towards home several times, but, as a matter of fact, this scene held him in a spell. It was fascinating beyond anything which the grown man understands. He had always in the back of his head a sense of guilt, even a sense of impending punishment for disobedience, but they could not weigh with the delirium of this snow-battle.

II

One of the raiding soldiers, espying Horace, called out in passing, "A-fray-ed of his mit-tens!" Horace flinched at this renewal, and the other lad paused to taunt him again. Horace scooped some snow, moulded it into a ball, and flung it at the other. "Ho!" cried the boy, "you're an Indian, are you? Hey, fellers, here's an Indian that ain't been killed yet." He and Horace engaged in a duel in which both were in such haste to mould snowballs that they had little time for aiming.

Horace once struck his opponent squarely in the chest. "Hey," he shouted, "you're dead. You can't fight any more, Pete. I killed you. You're dead."

The other boy flushed red, but he continued frantically to make ammunition. "You never touched me!" he retorted, glowering. "You never touched me! Where, now?" he added, defiantly. "Where did you hit me?"

"On the coat! Right on your breast! You can't fight any more! You're dead!"

"You never!"

"I did, too! Hey, fellers, ain't he dead? I hit 'im square!"

"He never!"

Nobody had seen the affair, but some of the boys took sides in absolute

110

accordance with their friendship for one of the concerned parties. Horace's opponent went about contending, "He never touched me! He never came near me! He never came near me!"

The formidable leader now came forward and accosted Horace. "What was you? An Indian? Well, then, you're dead—that's all. He hit you. I saw him."

"Me?" shrieked Horace. "He never came within a mile of me——"

At that moment he heard his name called in a certain familiar tune of two notes, with the last note shrill and prolonged. He looked towards the sidewalk, and saw his mother standing there in her widow's weeds, with two brown paper parcels under her arm. A silence had fallen upon all the boys. Horace moved slowly towards his mother. She did not seem to note his approach; she was gazing austerely off through the naked branches of the maples where two crimson sunset bars lay on the deep blue sky.

At a distance of ten paces Horace made a desperate venture. "Oh, ma," he whined, "can't I stay out for a while?"

"No," she answered solemnly, "you come with me." Horace knew that profile; it was the inexorable profile. But he continued to plead, because it was not beyond his mind that a great show of suffering now might diminish his suffering later.

He did not dare to look back at his playmates. It was already a public scandal that he could not stay out as late as other boys, and he could imagine his standing now that he had been again dragged off by his mother in sight of the whole world. He was a profoundly miserable human being.

Aunt Martha opened the door for them. Light streamed about her straight skirt. "Oh," she said, "so you found him on the road, eh? Well, I declare! It was about time!"

Horace slunk into the kitchen. The stove, straddling out on its four iron legs, was gently humming. Aunt Martha had evidently just lighted the lamp, for she went to it and began to twist the wick experimentally.

"Now," said the mother, "let's see them mittens."

Horace's chin sank. The aspiration of the criminal, the passionate desire for an asylum from retribution, from justice, was aflame in his heart. "I—I—don't—don't know where they are." he gasped finally, as he passed his hand over his pockets.

"Horace," intoned his mother, "you are tellin' me a story!"

"'Tain't a story," he answered, just above his breath. He looked like a sheep-stealer.

His mother held him by the arm, and began to search his pockets. Almost at once she was able to bring forth a pair of very wet mittens. "Well, I declare!" cried Aunt Martha. The two women went close to the lamp, and minutely examined the mittens, turning them over and over. Afterwards, when Horace looked up, his mother's sad-lined, homely face was turned towards him. He burst into tears.

His mother drew a chair near the stove. "Just you sit there now, until I tell you to git off." He sidled meekly into the chair. His mother and his aunt went briskly about the business of preparing supper. They did not display a knowledge of his existence; they carried an effect of oblivion so far that they even did not speak to each other. Presently they went into the dining and living room; Horace could hear the dishes rattling. His Aunt Martha brought a plate of food, placed it on a chair near him, and went away without a word.

Horace instantly decided that he would not touch a morsel of the food. He had often used this ruse in dealing with his mother. He did not know why it brought her to terms, but certainly it sometimes did.

The mother looked up when the aunt returned to the other room. "Is he eatin' his supper?" she asked.

The maiden aunt, fortified in ignorance, gazed with pity and contempt upon this interest. "Well, now, Emily, how do I know?" she queried. "Was I goin' to stand over 'im? Of all the worryin' you do about that child! It's a shame the way you're bringin' up that child."

"Well, he ought to eat somethin'. It won't do fer him to go without eatin'," the mother retorted, weakly.

Aunt Martha, profoundly scorning the policy of concession which these words meant, uttered a long, contemptuous sigh.

III

Alone in the kitchen, Horace stared with sombre eyes at the plate of food. For a long time he betrayed no sign of yielding. His mood was adamantine. He was resolved not to sell his vengeance for bread, cold ham, and a pickle, and yet it must be known that the sight of them affected him powerfully. The pickle in particular was notable for its seductive charm. He surveyed it darkly.

But at last, unable to longer endure his state, his attitude in the presence of the pickle, he put out an inquisitive finger and touched it, and it was cool and green and plump. Then a full conception of the cruel woe of his situation swept upon him suddenly, and his eyes filled with tears, which began to move down his cheeks. He sniffled. His heart was black with hatred. He painted in his mind scenes of deadly retribution. His mother would be taught that he was not one to endure persecution meekly, without raising an arm in his defence. And so his dreams were of a slaughter of feelings, and near the end of them his mother was pictured as coming, bowed with pain, to his feet. Weeping, she implored his charity. Would he forgive her? No; his once tender heart had been turned to stone by her injustice. He could not forgive her. She must pay the inexorable penalty.

The first item in this horrible plan was the refusal of the food. This he knew by experience would work havoc in his mother's heart. And so he grimly waited.

But suddenly it occurred to him that the first part of his revenge was in danger of failing. The thought struck him that his mother might not capitulate in the usual way. According to his recollection, the time was more than due when she should come in, worried, sadly affectionate, and ask him if he was ill. It had then been his custom to hint in a resigned voice that he was the victim of secret disease, but that he preferred to suffer in silence and alone. If she was obdurate in her anxiety, he always asked her in a gloomy, low voice to go away and leave him to suffer in silence and alone in the darkness without food. He had known this maneuvering to result even in pie.

But what was the meaning of the long pause and the stillness? Had his old and valued ruse betrayed him? As the truth sank into his mind, he supremely loathed life, the world, his mother. Her heart was beating back the besiegers; he was a defeated child.

He wept for a time before deciding upon the final stroke. He would run away. In a remote corner of the world he would become some sort of bloody-handed person driven to a life of crime by the barbarity of his mother. She should never know his fate. He would torture her for years with doubts and doubts, and drive her implacably to a repentant grave. Nor would Aunt Martha escape. Some day, a century hence, when his mother was dead, he would write to his Aunt Martha, and point out her part in the blighting of his life. For one blow against him now he would, in time, deal back a thousand— aye, ten thousand.

He arose and took his coat and cap. As he moved stealthily towards the door he cast a glance backward at the pickle. He was tempted to take it, but he knew that if he left the plate inviolate his mother would feel even worse.

A blue snow was falling. People, bowed forward, were moving briskly along the walks. The electric lamps hummed amid showers of flakes. As Horace emerged from the kitchen, a shrill squall drove the flakes around the corner of the house. He cowered away from it, and its violence illumined his mind vaguely in new directions. He deliberated upon a choice of remote corners of the globe. He found that he had no plans which were definite enough in a geographical way, but without much loss of time he decided upon California. He moved briskly as far as his mother's front gate on the road to California. He was off at last. His success was a trifle dreadful; his throat choked.

But at the gate he paused. He did not know if his journey to California would be shorter if he went down Niagara Avenue or off through Hogan

Street. As the storm was very cold and the point was very important, he decided to withdraw for reflection to the wood-shed. He entered the dark shanty, and took seat upon the old chopping-block upon which he was supposed to perform for a few minutes every afternoon when he returned from school. The wind screamed and shouted at the loose boards, and there was a rift of snow on the floor to leeward of a crack.

Here the idea of starting for California on such a night departed from his mind, leaving him ruminating miserably upon his martyrdom. He saw nothing for it but to sleep all night in the wood-shed and start for California in the morning bright and early. Thinking of his bed, he kicked over the floor and found that the innumerable chips were all frozen tightly, bedded in ice.

Later he viewed with joy some signs of excitement in the house. The flare of a lamp moved rapidly from window to window. Then the kitchen door slammed loudly and a shawled figure sped towards the gate. At last he was making them feel his power. The shivering child's face was lit with saturnine glee as in the darkness of the wood-shed he gloated over the evidences of consternation in his home. The shawled figure had been his Aunt Martha dashing with the alarm to the neighbors.

The cold of the wood-shed was tormenting him. He endured only because of the terror he was causing. But then it occurred to him that, if they instituted a search for him, they would probably examine the wood-shed. He knew that it would not be manful to be caught so soon. He was not positive now that he was going to remain away forever, but at any rate he was bound to inflict some more damage before allowing himself to be captured. If he merely succeeded in making his mother angry, she would thrash him on sight. He must prolong the time in order to be safe. If he held out properly, he was sure of a welcome of love, even though he should drip with crimes.

Evidently the storm had increased, for when he went out it swung him violently with its rough and merciless strength. Panting, stung, half blinded with the driving flakes, he was now a waif, exiled, friendless, and poor. With a bursting heart, he thought of his home and his mother. To his forlorn vision they were as far away as heaven.

IV

Horace was undergoing changes of feeling so rapidly that he was merely moved hither and then thither like a kite. He was now aghast at the merciless ferocity of his mother. It was she who had thrust him into this wild storm, and she was perfectly indifferent to his fate, perfectly indifferent. The forlorn wanderer could no longer weep. The strong sobs caught at his throat, making his breath come in short, quick snuffles. All in him was conquered save the enigmatical childish ideal of form, manner. This principle still held out, and it was the only thing between him and submission. When he surrendered, he must surrender in a way that deferred to the undefined code. He longed simply to go to the kitchen and stumble in, but his unfathomable sense of fitness forbade him.

Presently he found himself at the head of Niagara Avenue, staring through the snow into the blazing windows of Stickney's butcher-shop. Stickney was the family butcher, not so much because of a superiority to other Whilomville butchers as because he lived next door and had been an intimate friend of the father of Horace. Rows of glowing pigs hung head downward back of the tables, which bore huge pieces of red beef. Clumps of attenuated turkeys were suspended here and there. Stickney, hale and smiling, was bantering with a woman in a cloak, who, with a monster basket on her arm, was dickering for eight cents' worth of some thing. Horace watched them through a crusted pane. When the woman came out and passed him, he went towards the door. He touched the latch with his finger, but withdrew again suddenly to the sidewalk. Inside Stickney was whistling cheerily and assorting his knives.

Finally Horace went desperately forward, opened the door, and entered the shop. His head hung low. Stickney stopped whistling. "Hello, young man," he cried, "what brings you here?"

Horace halted, but said nothing. He swung one foot to and fro over the saw-dust floor.

116

Stickney had placed his two fat hands palms downward and wide apart on the table, in the attitude of a butcher facing a customer, but now he straightened.

"Here," he said, "what's wrong? What's wrong, kid?"

"Nothin'," answered Horace, huskily. He labored for a moment with something in his throat, and afterwards added, "O'ny——I've——I've run away, and—"

"Run away!" shouted Stickney. "Run away from what? Who?"

"From——home," answered Horace. "I don't like it there any more. I——" He had arranged an oration to win the sympathy of the butcher; he had prepared a table setting forth the merits of his case in the most logical fashion, but it was as if the wind had been knocked out of his mind. "I've run away. I——"

Stickney reached an enormous hand over the array of beef, and firmly grappled the emigrant. Then he swung himself to Horace's side. His face was stretched with laughter, and he playfully shook his prisoner. "Come—come—come. What dashed nonsense is this? Run away, hey? Run away?" Whereupon the child's long-tried spirit found vent in howls.

"Come, come," said Stickney, busily. "Never mind now, never mind. You just come along with me. It'll be all right. I'll fix it. Never you mind."

Five minutes later the butcher, with a great ulster over his apron, was leading the boy homeward.

At the very threshold, Horace raised his last flag of pride. "No——no," he sobbed. "I don't want to. I don't want to go in there." He braced his foot against the step and made a very respectable resistance.

"Now, Horace," cried the butcher. He thrust open the door with a bang. "Hello there!" Across the dark kitchen the door to the living-room opened and Aunt Martha appeared. "You've found him!" she screamed.

"We've come to make a call," roared the butcher. At the entrance to the living-room a silence fell upon them all. Upon a couch Horace saw his mother lying limp, pale as death, her eyes gleaming with pain. There was an electric pause before she swung a waxen hand towards Horace. "My child," she murmured, tremulously. Whereupon the sinister person addressed, with a prolonged wail of grief and joy, ran to her with speed. "Mam-ma! Mam-ma! Oh, mam-ma!" She was not able to speak in a known tongue as she folded him in her weak arms.

Aunt Martha turned defiantly upon the butcher because her face betrayed her. She was crying. She made a gesture half military, half feminine. "Won't you have a glass of our root-beer, Mr. Stickney? We make it ourselves."

THE OPEN BOAT AND
OTHER STORIES

To the Memory of

THE LATE WILLIAM HIGGINS

and to

CAPTAIN EDWARD MURPHY

and

STEWARD C. B. MONTGOMERY

Of the sunk Steamer 'Commodore.'

Part I. Minor Conflicts

THE OPEN BOAT

A Tale intended to be after the Fact. Being the Experience of Four Men from the Sunk Steamer 'Commodore'

I

None of them knew the colour of the sky. Their eyes glanced level, and were fastened upon the waves that swept toward them. These waves were of the hue of slate, save for the tops, which were of foaming white, and all of the men knew the colours of the sea. The horizon narrowed and widened, and dipped and rose, and at all times its edge was jagged with waves that seemed thrust up in points like rocks.

Many a man ought to have a bath-tub larger than the boat which here rode upon the sea. These waves were most wrongfully and barbarously abrupt and tall, and each froth-top was a problem in small boat navigation.

The cook squatted in the bottom and looked with both eyes at the six inches of gunwale which separated him from the ocean. His sleeves were rolled over his fat forearms, and the two flaps of his unbuttoned vest dangled as he bent to bail out the boat. Often he said: "Gawd! That was a narrow clip." As he remarked it he invariably gazed eastward over the broken sea.

The oiler, steering with one of the two oars in the boat, sometimes raised himself suddenly to keep clear of water that swirled in over the stern. It was a thin little oar and it seemed often ready to snap.

The correspondent, pulling at the other oar, watched the waves and wondered why he was there.

The injured captain, lying in the bow, was at this time buried in that profound dejection and indifference which comes, temporarily at least, to even the bravest and most enduring when, willy nilly, the firm fails, the army loses, the ship goes down. The mind of the master of a vessel is rooted deep in the timbers of her, though he commanded for a day or a decade, and this captain had on him the stern impression of a scene in the greys of dawn of seven turned faces, and later a stump of a top-mast with a white ball on it that slashed to and fro at the waves, went low and lower, and down. Thereafter there was something strange in his voice. Although steady, it was deep with mourning, and of a quality beyond oration or tears.

"Keep 'er a little more south, Billie," said he.

"'A little more south,' sir," said the oiler in the stern.

A seat in this boat was not unlike a seat upon a bucking broncho, and, by the same token, a broncho is not much smaller. The craft pranced and reared, and plunged like an animal. As each wave came, and she rose for it, she seemed like a horse making at a fence outrageously high. The manner of her scramble over these walls of water is a mystic thing, and, moreover, at the top of them were ordinarily these problems in white water, the foam racing down from the summit of each wave, requiring a new leap, and a leap from the air. Then, after scornfully bumping a crest, she would slide, and race, and splash down a long incline, and arrive bobbing and nodding in front of the next menace.

A singular disadvantage of the sea lies in the fact that after successfully surmounting one wave you discover that there is another behind it just as important and just as nervously anxious to do something effective in the way of swamping boats. In a ten-foot dingey one can get an idea of the resources of the sea in the line of waves that is not probable to the average experience which is never at sea in a dingey. As each slaty wall of water approached, it shut all else from the view of the men in the boat, and it was not difficult to imagine that this particular wave was the final outburst of the ocean, the last effort of the grim water. There was a terrible grace in the move of the waves, and they came in silence, save for the snarling of the crests.

126

In the wan light, the faces of the men must have been grey. Their eyes must have glinted in strange ways as they gazed steadily astern. Viewed from a balcony, the whole thing would doubtlessly have been weirdly picturesque. But the men in the boat had no time to see it, and if they had had leisure there were other things to occupy their minds. The sun swung steadily up the sky, and they knew it was broad day because the colour of the sea changed from slate to emerald-green, streaked with amber lights, and the foam was like tumbling snow. The process of the breaking day was unknown to them. They were aware only of this effect upon the colour of the waves that rolled toward them.

In disjointed sentences the cook and the correspondent argued as to the difference between a life-saving station and a house of refuge. The cook had said: "There's a house of refuge just north of the Mosquito Inlet Light, and as soon as they see us, they'll come off in their boat and pick us up."

"As soon as who see us?" said the correspondent.

"The crew," said the cook.

"Houses of refuge don't have crews," said the correspondent. "As I understand them, they are only places where clothes and grub are stored for the benefit of shipwrecked people. They don't carry crews."

"Oh, yes, they do," said the cook.

"No, they don't," said the correspondent.

"Well, we're not there yet, anyhow," said the oiler, in the stern.

"Well," said the cook, "perhaps it's not a house of refuge that I'm thinking of as being near Mosquito Inlet Light. Perhaps it's a life-saving station."

"We're not there yet," said the oiler, in the stern.

II

As the boat bounced from the top of each wave, the wind tore through the hair of the hatless men, and as the craft plopped her stern down again the spray slashed past them. The crest of each of these waves was a hill, from the top of which the men surveyed, for a moment, a broad tumultuous expanse, shining and wind-riven. It was probably splendid. It was probably glorious, this play of the free sea, wild with lights of emerald and white and amber.

"Bully good thing it's an on-shore wind," said the cook. "If not, where would we be? Wouldn't have a show."

"That's right," said the correspondent.

The busy oiler nodded his assent.

Then the captain, in the bow, chuckled in a way that expressed humour, contempt, tragedy, all in one. "Do you think we've got much of a show now, boys?" said he.

Whereupon the three were silent, save for a trifle of hemming and hawing. To express any particular optimism at this time they felt to be childish and stupid, but they all doubtless possessed this sense of the situation in their mind. A young man thinks doggedly at such times. On the other hand, the ethics of their condition was decidedly against any open suggestion of hopelessness. So they were silent.

"Oh, well," said the captain, soothing his children, "we'll get ashore all right."

But there was that in his tone which made them think, so the oiler quoth: "Yes! If this wind holds!"

The cook was bailing: "Yes! If we don't catch hell in the surf."

Canton flannel gulls flew near and far. Sometimes they sat down on the sea, near patches of brown sea-weed that rolled over the waves with a movement like carpets on a line in a gale. The birds sat comfortably in groups, and they were envied by some in the dingey, for the wrath of the sea was no more to them than it was to a covey of prairie chickens a thousand miles inland. Often they came very close and stared at the men with black bead-like eyes. At these times they were uncanny and sinister in their unblinking scrutiny, and the men hooted angrily at them, telling them to be gone. One came, and evidently decided to alight on the top of the captain's head. The bird flew parallel to the boat and did not circle, but made short sidelong jumps in the air in chicken-fashion. His black eyes were wistfully fixed upon the captain's head. "Ugly brute," said the oiler to the bird. "You look as if you were made with a jack-knife." The cook and the correspondent swore darkly at the creature. The captain naturally wished to knock it away with the end of the heavy painter; but he did not dare do it, because anything resembling an emphatic gesture would have capsized this freighted boat, and so with his open hand, the captain gently and carefully waved the gull away. After it had been discouraged from the pursuit the captain breathed easier on account of his hair, and others breathed easier because the bird struck their minds at this time as being somehow grewsome and ominous.

In the meantime the oiler and the correspondent rowed. And also they rowed.

They sat together in the same seat, and each rowed an oar. Then the oiler took both oars; then the correspondent took both oars; then the oiler; then the correspondent. They rowed and they rowed. The very ticklish part of the business was when the time came for the reclining one in the stern to take his turn at the oars. By the very last star of truth, it is easier to steal eggs from under a hen than it was to change seats in the dingey. First the man in the stern slid his hand along the thwart and moved with care, as if he were of Sèvres. Then the man in the rowing seat slid his hand along the other thwart. It was all done with the most extraordinary care. As the two sidled past each other, the whole party kept watchful eyes on the coming wave, and the captain cried: "Look out now! Steady there!"

The brown mats of sea-weed that appeared from time to time were like islands, bits of earth. They were travelling, apparently, neither one way nor the other. They were, to all intents, stationary. They informed the men in the boat that it was making progress slowly toward the land.

The captain, rearing cautiously in the bow, after the dingey soared on a great swell, said that he had seen the lighthouse at Mosquito Inlet. Presently the cook remarked that he had seen it. The correspondent was at the oars then, and for some reason he too wished to look at the lighthouse, but his back was toward the far shore and the waves were important, and for some time he could not seize an opportunity to turn his head. But at last there came a wave more gentle than the others, and when at the crest of it he swiftly scoured the western horizon.

"See it?" said the captain.

"No," said the correspondent slowly, "I didn't see anything."

"Look again," said the captain. He pointed. "It's exactly in that direction."

At the top of another wave, the correspondent did as he was bid, and this time his eyes chanced on a small still thing on the edge of the swaying horizon. It was precisely like the point of a pin. It took an anxious eye to find a lighthouse so tiny.

"Think we'll make it, captain?"

"If this wind holds and the boat don't swamp, we can't do much else," said the captain.

The little boat, lifted by each towering sea, and splashed viciously by the crests, made progress that in the absence of sea-weed was not apparent to those in her. She seemed just a wee thing wallowing, miraculously top-up, at the mercy of five oceans. Occasionally, a great spread of water, like white flames, swarmed into her.

"Bail her, cook," said the captain serenely.

"All right, captain," said the cheerful cook.

III

It would be difficult to describe the subtle brotherhood of men that was here established on the seas. No one said that it was so. No one mentioned it. But it dwelt in the boat, and each man felt it warm him. They were a captain, an oiler, a cook, and a correspondent, and they were friends, friends in a more curiously iron-bound degree than may be common. The hurt captain, lying against the water-jar in the bow, spoke always in a low voice and calmly, but he could never command a more ready and swiftly obedient crew than the motley three of the dingey. It was more than a mere recognition of what was best for the common safety. There was surely in it a quality that was personal and heartfelt. And after this devotion to the commander of the boat there was this comradeship that the correspondent, for instance, who had been taught to be cynical of men, knew even at the time was the best experience of his life. But no one said that it was so. No one mentioned it.

"I wish we had a sail," remarked the captain. "We might try my overcoat on the end of an oar and give you two boys a chance to rest." So the cook and the correspondent held the mast and spread wide the overcoat. The oiler steered, and the little boat made good way with her new rig. Sometimes the oiler had to scull sharply to keep a sea from breaking into the boat, but otherwise sailing was a success.

Meanwhile the lighthouse had been growing slowly larger. It had now almost assumed colour, and appeared like a little grey shadow on the sky. The man at the oars could not be prevented from turning his head rather often to try for a glimpse of this little grey shadow.

At last, from the top of each wave the men in the tossing boat could see land. Even as the lighthouse was an upright shadow on the sky, this land seemed but a long black shadow on the sea. It certainly was thinner than paper. "We must be about opposite New Smyrna," said the cook, who had coasted this shore often in schooners. "Captain, by the way, I believe they abandoned that life-saving station there about a year ago."

"Did they?" said the captain.

The wind slowly died away. The cook and the correspondent were not now obliged to slave in order to hold high the oar. But the waves continued their old impetuous swooping at the dingey, and the little craft, no longer under way, struggled woundily over them. The oiler or the correspondent took the oars again.

Shipwrecks are à *propos* of nothing. If men could only train for them and have them occur when the men had reached pink condition, there would be less drowning at sea. Of the four in the dingey none had slept any time worth mentioning for two days and two nights previous to embarking in the dingey, and in the excitement of clambering about the deck of a foundering ship they had also forgotten to eat heartily.

For these reasons, and for others, neither the oiler nor the correspondent was fond of rowing at this time. The correspondent wondered ingenuously how in the name of all that was sane could there be people who thought it amusing to row a boat. It was not an amusement; it was a diabolical punishment, and even a genius of mental aberrations could never conclude that it was anything but a horror to the muscles and a crime against the back. He mentioned to the boat in general how the amusement of rowing struck him, and the weary-faced oiler smiled in full sympathy. Previously to the foundering, by the way, the oiler had worked double-watch in the engine-room of the ship.

"Take her easy, now, boys," said the captain. "Don't spend yourselves. If we have to run a surf you'll need all your strength, because we'll sure have to swim for it. Take your time."

Slowly the land arose from the sea. From a black line it became a line of black and a line of white, trees and sand. Finally, the captain said that he could make out a house on the shore. "That's the house of refuge, sure," said the cook. "They'll see us before long, and come out after us."

The distant lighthouse reared high. "The keeper ought to be able to make us out now, if he's looking through a glass," said the captain. "He'll notify the life-saving people."

"None of those other boats could have got ashore to give word of the wreck," said the oiler, in a low voice. "Else the life-boat would be out hunting us."

Slowly and beautifully the land loomed out of the sea. The wind came again. It had veered from the north-east to the south-east. Finally, a new sound struck the ears of the men in the boat. It was the low thunder of the surf on the shore. "We'll never be able to make the lighthouse now," said the captain. "Swing her head a little more north, Billie," said he.

"'A little more north,' sir," said the oiler.

Whereupon the little boat turned her nose once more down the wind, and all but the oarsman watched the shore grow. Under the influence of this expansion doubt and direful apprehension was leaving the minds of the men. The management of the boat was still most absorbing, but it could not prevent a quiet cheerfulness. In an hour, perhaps, they would be ashore.

Their backbones had become thoroughly used to balancing in the boat, and they now rode this wild colt of a dingey like circus men. The correspondent thought that he had been drenched to the skin, but happening to feel in the top pocket of his coat, he found therein eight cigars. Four of them were soaked with sea-water; four were perfectly scatheless. After a search, somebody produced three dry matches, and thereupon the four waifs rode impudently in their little boat, and with an assurance of an impending rescue shining in their eyes, puffed at the big cigars and judged well and ill of all men. Everybody took a drink of water.

IV

"Cook," remarked the captain, "there don't seem to be any signs of life about your house of refuge."

"No," replied the cook. "Funny they don't see us!"

A broad stretch of lowly coast lay before the eyes of the men. It was of dunes topped with dark vegetation. The roar of the surf was plain, and sometimes they could see the white lip of a wave as it spun up the beach. A tiny house was blocked out black upon the sky. Southward, the slim lighthouse lifted its little grey length.

Tide, wind, and waves were swinging the dingey northward. "Funny they don't see us," said the men.

The surf's roar was here dulled, but its tone was, nevertheless, thunderous and mighty. As the boat swam over the great rollers, the men sat listening to this roar. "We'll swamp sure," said everybody.

It is fair to say here that there was not a life-saving station within twenty miles in either direction, but the men did not know this fact, and in consequence they made dark and opprobrious remarks concerning the eyesight of the nation's life-savers. Four scowling men sat in the dingey and surpassed records in the invention of epithets.

"Funny they don't see us."

The light-heartedness of a former time had completely faded. To their sharpened minds it was easy to conjure pictures of all kinds of incompetency and blindness and, indeed, cowardice. There was the shore of the populous land, and it was bitter and bitter to them that from it came no sign.

"Well," said the captain, ultimately, "I suppose we'll have to make a try for ourselves. If we stay out here too long, we'll none of us have strength left to swim after the boat swamps."

And so the oiler, who was at the oars, turned the boat straight for the shore. There was a sudden tightening of muscles. There was some thinking.

"If we don't all get ashore—" said the captain. "If we don't all get ashore, I suppose you fellows know where to send news of my finish?"

They then briefly exchanged some addresses and admonitions. As for the reflections of the men, there was a great deal of rage in them. Perchance they might be formulated thus: "If I am going to be drowned—if I am going to be drowned—if I am going to be drowned, why, in the name of the seven mad gods who rule the sea, was I allowed to come thus far and contemplate sand and trees? Was I brought here merely to have my nose dragged away as I was about to nibble the sacred cheese of life? It is preposterous. If this old ninny-woman, Fate, cannot do better than this, she should be deprived of the management of men's fortunes. She is an old hen who knows not her intention. If she has decided to drown me, why did she not do it in the beginning and save me all this trouble? The whole affair is absurd.... But no, she cannot mean to drown me. She dare not drown me. She cannot drown me. Not after all this work." Afterward the man might have had an impulse to shake his fist at the clouds: "Just you drown me, now, and then hear what I call you!"

The billows that came at this time were more formidable. They seemed always just about to break and roll over the little boat in a turmoil of foam. There was a preparatory and long growl in the speech of them. No mind unused to the sea would have concluded that the dingey could ascend these sheer heights in time. The shore was still afar. The oiler was a wily surfman. "Boys," he said swiftly, "she won't live three minutes more, and we're too far out to swim. Shall I take her to sea again, captain?"

"Yes! Go ahead!" said the captain.

This oiler, by a series of quick miracles, and fast and steady oarsmanship, turned the boat in the middle of the surf and took her safely to sea again.

There was a considerable silence as the boat bumped over the furrowed sea to deeper water. Then somebody in gloom spoke. "Well, anyhow, they must have seen us from the shore by now."

The gulls went in slanting flight up the wind toward the grey desolate east. A squall, marked by dingy clouds, and clouds brick-red, like smoke from a burning building, appeared from the south-east.

"What do you think of those life-saving people? Ain't they peaches?"

"Funny they haven't seen us."

"Maybe they think we're out here for sport! Maybe they think we're fishin'. Maybe they think we're damned fools."

It was a long afternoon. A changed tide tried to force them southward, but wind and wave said northward. Far ahead, where coast-line, sea, and sky formed their mighty angle, there were little dots which seemed to indicate a city on the shore.

"St. Augustine?"

The captain shook his head. "Too near Mosquito Inlet."

And the oiler rowed, and then the correspondent rowed. Then the oiler rowed. It was a weary business. The human back can become the seat of more aches and pains than are registered in books for the composite anatomy of a regiment. It is a limited area, but it can become the theatre of innumerable muscular conflicts, tangles, wrenches, knots, and other comforts.

"Did you ever like to row, Billie?" asked the correspondent.

"No," said the oiler. "Hang it."

When one exchanged the rowing-seat for a place in the bottom of the boat, he suffered a bodily depression that caused him to be careless of everything save an obligation to wiggle one finger. There was cold sea-water swashing to and fro in the boat, and he lay in it. His head, pillowed on a thwart, was within an inch of the swirl of a wave crest, and sometimes a particularly obstreperous sea came in-board and drenched him once more. But these matters did not annoy him. It is almost certain that if the boat had capsized he would have tumbled comfortably out upon the ocean as if he felt sure that it was a great soft mattress.

"Look! There's a man on the shore!"

"Where?"

"There! See 'im? See 'im?"

"Yes, sure! He's walking along."

"Now he's stopped. Look! He's facing us!"

"He's waving at us!"

"So he is! By thunder!"

"Ah, now we're all right! Now we're all right! There'll be a boat out here for us in half-an-hour."

"He's going on. He's running. He's going up to that house there."

The remote beach seemed lower than the sea, and it required a searching glance to discern the little black figure. The captain saw a floating stick and they rowed to it. A bath-towel was by some weird chance in the boat, and, tying this on the stick, the captain waved it. The oarsman did not dare turn his head, so he was obliged to ask questions.

"What's he doing now?"

"He's standing still again. He's looking, I think.... There he goes again. Towards the house.... Now he's stopped again."

"Is he waving at us?"

"No, not now! he was, though."

"Look! There comes another man!"

"He's running."

"Look at him go, would you."

"Why, he's on a bicycle. Now he's met the other man. They're both waving at us. Look!"

"There comes something up the beach."

"What the devil is that thing?"

"Why, it looks like a boat."

"Why, certainly it's a boat."

"No, it's on wheels."

"Yes, so it is. Well, that must be the life-boat. They drag them along shore on a wagon."

"That's the life-boat, sure."

"No, by ——, it's—it's an omnibus."

"I tell you it's a life-boat."

"It is not! It's an omnibus. I can see it plain. See? One of these big hotel omnibuses."

"By thunder, you're right. It's an omnibus, sure as fate. What do you suppose they are doing with an omnibus? Maybe they are going around collecting the life-crew, hey?"

"That's it, likely. Look! There's a fellow waving a little black flag. He's standing on the steps of the omnibus. There come those other two fellows. Now they're all talking together. Look at the fellow with the flag. Maybe he ain't waving it."

"That ain't a flag, is it? That's his coat. Why certainly, that's his coat."

"So it is. It's his coat. He's taken it off and is waving it around his head. But would you look at him swing it."

"Oh, say, there isn't any life-saving station there. That's just a winter resort hotel omnibus that has brought over some of the boarders to see us drown."

"What's that idiot with the coat mean? What's he signaling, anyhow?"

"It looks as if he were trying to tell us to go north. There must be a life-saving station up there."

"No! He thinks we're fishing. Just giving us a merry hand. See? Ah, there, Willie."

"Well, I wish I could make something out of those signals. What do you suppose he means?"

"He don't mean anything. He's just playing."

"Well, if he'd just signal us to try the surf again, or to go to sea and wait, or go north, or go south, or go to hell—there would be some reason in it. But look at him. He just stands there and keeps his coat revolving like a wheel. The ass!"

"There come more people."

"Now there's quite a mob. Look! Isn't that a boat?"

"Where? Oh, I see where you mean. No, that's no boat."

"That fellow is still waving his coat."

"He must think we like to see him do that. Why don't he quit it? It don't mean anything."

"I don't know. I think he is trying to make us go north. It must be that there's a life-saving station there somewhere."

"Say, he ain't tired yet. Look at 'im wave."

"Wonder how long he can keep that up. He's been revolving his coat ever since he caught sight of us. He's an idiot. Why aren't they getting men to bring a boat out? A fishing boat—one of those big yawls—could come out here all right. Why don't he do something?"

"Oh, it's all right, now."

"They'll have a boat out here for us in less than no time, now that they've seen us."

A faint yellow tone came into the sky over the low land. The shadows on the sea slowly deepened. The wind bore coldness with it, and the men began to shiver.

"Holy smoke!" said one, allowing his voice to express his impious mood, "if we keep on monkeying out here! If we've got to flounder out here all night!"

"Oh, we'll never have to stay here all night! Don't you worry. They've seen us now, and it won't be long before they'll come chasing out after us."

The shore grew dusky. The man waving a coat blended gradually into this gloom, and it swallowed in the same manner the omnibus and the group of people. The spray, when it dashed uproariously over the side, made the voyagers shrink and swear like men who were being branded.

"I'd like to catch the chump who waved the coat. I feel like soaking him one, just for luck."

"Why? What did he do?"

"Oh, nothing, but then he seemed so damned cheerful."

In the meantime the oiler rowed, and then the correspondent rowed, and then the oiler rowed. Grey-faced and bowed forward, they mechanically, turn by turn, plied the leaden oars. The form of the lighthouse had vanished from the southern horizon, but finally a pale star appeared, just lifting from the sea. The streaked saffron in the west passed before the all-merging darkness, and the sea to the east was black. The land had vanished, and was expressed only by the low and drear thunder of the surf.

"If I am going to be drowned—if I am going to be drowned—if I am going to be drowned, why, in the name of the seven mad gods who rule the sea, was I allowed to come thus far and contemplate sand and trees? Was I brought here merely to have my nose dragged away as I was about to nibble the sacred cheese of life?"

The patient captain, drooped over the water-jar, was sometimes obliged to speak to the oarsman.

"Keep her head up! Keep her head up!"

"'Keep her head up,' sir." The voices were weary and low.

This was surely a quiet evening. All save the oarsman lay heavily and listlessly in the boat's bottom. As for him, his eyes were just capable of noting the tall black waves that swept forward in a most sinister silence, save for an occasional subdued growl of a crest.

The cook's head was on a thwart, and he looked without interest at the water under his nose. He was deep in other scenes. Finally he spoke. "Billie," he murmured, dreamfully, "what kind of pie do you like best?"

V

"Pie," said the oiler and the correspondent, agitatedly. "Don't talk about those things, blast you!"

"Well," said the cook, "I was just thinking about ham sandwiches, and——"

140

A night on the sea in an open boat is a long night. As darkness settled finally, the shine of the light, lifting from the sea in the south, changed to full gold. On the northern horizon a new light appeared, a small bluish gleam on the edge of the waters. These two lights were the furniture of the world. Otherwise there was nothing but waves.

Two men huddled in the stern, and distances were so magnificent in the dingey that the rower was enabled to keep his feet partly warmed by thrusting them under his companions. Their legs indeed extended far under the rowing-seat until they touched the feet of the captain forward. Sometimes, despite the efforts of the tired oarsman, a wave came piling into the boat, an icy wave of the night, and the chilling water soaked them anew. They would twist their bodies for a moment and groan, and sleep the dead sleep once more, while the water in the boat gurgled about them as the craft rocked.

The plan of the oiler and the correspondent was for one to row until he lost the ability, and then arouse the other from his sea-water couch in the bottom of the boat.

The oiler plied the oars until his head drooped forward, and the overpowering sleep blinded him. And he rowed yet afterward. Then he touched a man in the bottom of the boat, and called his name. "Will you spell me for a little while?" he said, meekly.

"Sure, Billie," said the correspondent, awakening and dragging himself to a sitting position. They exchanged places carefully, and the oiler, cuddling down in the sea-water at the cook's side, seemed to go to sleep instantly.

The particular violence of the sea had ceased. The waves came without snarling. The obligation of the man at the oars was to keep the boat headed so that the tilt of the rollers would not capsize her, and to preserve her from filling when the crests rushed past. The black waves were silent and hard to be seen in the darkness. Often one was almost upon the boat before the oarsman was aware.

In a low voice the correspondent addressed the captain. He was not sure that the captain was awake, although this iron man seemed to be always awake. "Captain, shall I keep her making for that light north, sir?"

The same steady voice answered him. "Yes. Keep it about two points off the port bow."

The cook had tied a life-belt around himself in order to get even the warmth which this clumsy cork contrivance could donate, and he seemed almost stove-like when a rower, whose teeth invariably chattered wildly as soon as he ceased his labour, dropped down to sleep.

The correspondent, as he rowed, looked down at the two men sleeping under-foot. The cook's arm was around the oiler's shoulders, and, with their fragmentary clothing and haggard faces, they were the babes of the sea, a grotesque rendering of the old babes in the wood.

Later he must have grown stupid at his work, for suddenly there was a growling of water, and a crest came with a roar and a swash into the boat, and it was a wonder that it did not set the cook afloat in his life-belt. The cook continued to sleep, but the oiler sat up, blinking his eyes and shaking with the new cold.

"Oh, I'm awful sorry, Billie," said the correspondent contritely.

"That's all right, old boy," said the oiler, and lay down again and was asleep.

Presently it seemed that even the captain dozed, and the correspondent thought that he was the one man afloat on all the oceans. The wind had a voice as it came over the waves, and it was sadder than the end.

There was a long, loud swishing astern of the boat, and a gleaming trail of phosphorescence, like blue flame, was furrowed on the black waters. It might have been made by a monstrous knife.

Then there came a stillness, while the correspondent breathed with the open mouth and looked at the sea.

Suddenly there was another swish and another long flash of bluish light, and this time it was alongside the boat, and might almost have been reached with an oar. The correspondent saw an enormous fin speed like a shadow through the water, hurling the crystalline spray and leaving the long glowing trail.

The correspondent looked over his shoulder at the captain. His face was hidden, and he seemed to be asleep. He looked at the babes of the sea. They certainly were asleep. So, being bereft of sympathy, he leaned a little way to one side and swore softly into the sea.

But the thing did not then leave the vicinity of the boat. Ahead or astern, on one side or the other, at intervals long or short, fled the long sparkling streak, and there was to be heard the whiroo of the dark fin. The speed and power of the thing was greatly to be admired. It cut the water like a gigantic and keen projectile.

The presence of this biding thing did not affect the man with the same horror that it would if he had been a picnicker. He simply looked at the sea dully and swore in an undertone.

Nevertheless, it is true that he did not wish to be alone. He wished one of his companions to awaken by chance and keep him company with it. But the captain hung motionless over the water-jar, and the oiler and the cook in the bottom of the boat were plunged in slumber.

VI

"If I am going to be drowned—if I am going to be drowned—if I am going to be drowned, why, in the name of the seven mad gods who rule the sea, was I allowed to come thus far and contemplate sand and trees?"

During this dismal night, it may be remarked that a man would conclude that it was really the intention of the seven mad gods to drown him, despite the abominable injustice of it. For it was certainly an abominable injustice to drown a man who had worked so hard, so hard. The man felt it would be a crime most unnatural. Other people had drowned at sea since galleys swarmed with painted sails, but still——

When it occurs to a man that nature does not regard him as important, and that she feels she would not maim the universe by disposing of him, he at first wishes to throw bricks at the temple, and he hates deeply the fact that there are no bricks and no temples. Any visible expression of nature would surely be pelleted with his jeers.

Then, if there be no tangible thing to hoot he feels, perhaps, the desire to confront a personification and indulge in pleas, bowed to one knee, and with hands supplicant, saying: "Yes, but I love myself."

A high cold star on a winter's night is the word he feels that she says to him. Thereafter he knows the pathos of his situation.

The men in the dingey had not discussed these matters, but each had, no doubt, reflected upon them in silence and according to his mind. There was seldom any expression upon their faces save the general one of complete weariness. Speech was devoted to the business of the boat.

To chime the notes of his emotion, a verse mysteriously entered the correspondent's head. He had even forgotten that he had forgotten this verse, but it suddenly was in his mind.

"A soldier of the Legion lay dying in Algiers,

There was lack of woman's nursing, there was dearth of woman's tears;

But a comrade stood beside him, and he took that comrade's hand,

And he said: 'I shall never see my own, my native land.'"

In his childhood, the correspondent had been made acquainted with the fact that a soldier of the Legion lay dying in Algiers, but he had never regarded the fact as important. Myriads of his school-fellows had informed him of the soldier's plight, but the dinning had naturally ended by making him perfectly indifferent. He had never considered it his affair that a soldier of the Legion lay dying in Algiers, nor had it appeared to him as a matter for sorrow. It was less to him than the breaking of a pencil's point.

Now, however, it quaintly came to him as a human, living thing. It was no longer merely a picture of a few throes in the breast of a poet, meanwhile drinking tea and warming his feet at the grate; it was an actuality—stern, mournful, and fine.

The correspondent plainly saw the soldier. He lay on the sand with his feet out straight and still. While his pale left hand was upon his chest in an attempt to thwart the going of his life, the blood came between his fingers. In the far Algerian distance, a city of low square forms was set against a sky that was faint with the last sunset hues. The correspondent, plying the oars and dreaming of the slow and slower movements of the lips of the soldier, was moved by a profound and perfectly impersonal comprehension. He was sorry for the soldier of the Legion who lay dying in Algiers.

The thing which had followed the boat and waited, had evidently grown bored at the delay. There was no longer to be heard the slash of the cut-water, and there was no longer the flame of the long trail. The light in the north still glimmered, but it was apparently no nearer to the boat. Sometimes the boom of the surf rang in the correspondent's ears, and he turned the craft seaward then and rowed harder. Southward, some one had evidently built a watch-fire on the beach. It was too low and too far to be seen, but it made a shimmering, roseate reflection upon the bluff back of it, and this could be discerned from the boat. The wind came stronger, and sometimes a wave suddenly raged out like a mountain-cat, and there was to be seen the sheen and sparkle of a broken crest.

The captain, in the bow, moved on his water-jar and sat erect. "Pretty long night," he observed to the correspondent. He looked at the shore. "Those life-saving people take their time."

"Did you see that shark playing around?"

"Yes, I saw him. He was a big fellow, all right."

"Wish I had known you were awake."

Later the correspondent spoke into the bottom of the boat.

"Billie!" There was a slow and gradual disentanglement. "Billie, will you spell me?"

"Sure," said the oiler.

As soon as the correspondent touched the cold comfortable sea-water in the bottom of the boat, and had huddled close to the cook's life-belt he was deep in sleep, despite the fact that his teeth played all the popular airs. This sleep was so good to him that it was but a moment before he heard a voice call his name in a tone that demonstrated the last stages of exhaustion. "Will you spell me?"

"Sure, Billie."

The light in the north had mysteriously vanished, but the correspondent took his course from the wide-awake captain.

Later in the night they took the boat farther out to sea, and the captain directed the cook to take one oar at the stern and keep the boat facing the seas. He was to call out if he should hear the thunder of the surf. This plan enabled the oiler and the correspondent to get respite together. "We'll give those boys a chance to get into shape again," said the captain. They curled down and, after a few preliminary chatterings and trembles, slept once more the dead sleep. Neither knew they had bequeathed to the cook the company of another shark, or perhaps the same shark.

As the boat caroused on the waves, spray occasionally bumped over the side and gave them a fresh soaking, but this had no power to break their repose. The ominous slash of the wind and the water affected them as it would have affected mummies.

"Boys," said the cook, with the notes of every reluctance in his voice, "she's drifted in pretty close. I guess one of you had better take her to sea again." The correspondent, aroused, heard the crash of the toppled crests.

As he was rowing, the captain gave him some whisky-and-water, and this steadied the chills out of him. "If I ever get ashore and anybody shows me even a photograph of an oar———"

At last there was a short conversation.

"Billie.... Billie, will you spell me?"

"Sure," said the oiler.

VII

When the correspondent again opened his eyes, the sea and the sky were each of the grey hue of the dawning. Later, carmine and gold was painted upon the waters. The morning appeared finally, in its splendour, with a sky of pure blue, and the sunlight flamed on the tips of the waves.

On the distant dunes were set many little black cottages, and a tall white windmill reared above them. No man, nor dog, nor bicycle appeared on the beach. The cottages might have formed a deserted village.

The voyagers scanned the shore. A conference was held in the boat. "Well," said the captain, "if no help is coming we might better try a run through the surf right away. If we stay out here much longer we will be too weak to do anything for ourselves at all." The others silently acquiesced in this reasoning. The boat was headed for the beach. The correspondent wondered if none ever ascended the tall wind-tower, and if then they never looked seaward. This tower was a giant, standing with its back to the plight of the ants. It represented in a degree, to the correspondent, the serenity of nature amid the struggles of the individual—nature in the wind, and nature in the vision of men. She did not seem cruel to him then, nor beneficent, nor treacherous, nor wise. But she was indifferent, flatly indifferent. It is, perhaps, plausible that a man in this situation, impressed with the unconcern of the universe, should see the innumerable flaws of his life, and have them taste wickedly in his mind and wish for another chance. A distinction between right and wrong seems absurdly clear to him, then, in this new ignorance of the grave-edge, and he understands that if he were given another opportunity he would mend his conduct and his words, and be better and brighter during an introduction or at a tea.

"Now, boys," said the captain, "she is going to swamp, sure. All we can do is to work her in as far as possible, and then when she swamps, pile out and scramble for the beach. Keep cool now, and don't jump until she swamps sure."

The oiler took the oars. Over his shoulders he scanned the surf. "Captain," he said, "I think I'd better bring her about, and keep her head-on to the seas and back her in."

"All right, Billie," said the captain. "Back her in." The oiler swung the boat then and, seated in the stern, the cook and the correspondent were obliged to look over their shoulders to contemplate the lonely and indifferent shore.

The monstrous in-shore rollers heaved the boat high until the men were again enabled to see the white sheets of water scudding up the slanted beach. "We won't get in very close," said the captain. Each time a man could wrest his attention from the rollers, he turned his glance toward the shore, and in the expression of the eyes during this contemplation there was a singular quality. The correspondent, observing the others, knew that they were not afraid, but the full meaning of their glances was shrouded.

As for himself, he was too tired to grapple fundamentally with the fact. He tried to coerce his mind into thinking of it, but the mind was dominated at this time by the muscles, and the muscles said they did not care. It merely occurred to him that if he should drown it would be a shame.

There were no hurried words, no pallor, no plain agitation. The men simply looked at the shore. "Now, remember to get well clear of the boat when you jump," said the captain.

Seaward the crest of a roller suddenly fell with a thunderous crash, and the long white comber came roaring down upon the boat.

"Steady now," said the captain. The men were silent. They turned their eyes from the shore to the comber and waited. The boat slid up the incline, leaped at the furious top, bounced over it, and swung down the long back of the wave. Some water had been shipped and the cook bailed it out.

But the next crest crashed also. The tumbling boiling flood of white water caught the boat and whirled it almost perpendicular. Water swarmed in from all sides. The correspondent had his hands on the gunwale at this time, and when the water entered at that place he swiftly withdrew his fingers, as if he objected to wetting them.

148

The little boat, drunken with this weight of water, reeled and snuggled deeper into the sea.

"Bail her out, cook! Bail her out," said the captain.

"All right, captain," said the cook.

"Now, boys, the next one will do for us, sure," said the oiler. "Mind to jump clear of the boat."

The third wave moved forward, huge, furious, implacable. It fairly swallowed the dingey, and almost simultaneously the men tumbled into the sea. A piece of life-belt had lain in the bottom of the boat, and as the correspondent went overboard he held this to his chest with his left hand.

The January water was icy, and he reflected immediately that it was colder than he had expected to find it off the coast of Florida. This appeared to his dazed mind as a fact important enough to be noted at the time. The coldness of the water was sad; it was tragic. This fact was somehow so mixed and confused with his opinion of his own situation that it seemed almost a proper reason for tears. The water was cold.

When he came to the surface he was conscious of little but the noisy water. Afterward he saw his companions in the sea. The oiler was ahead in the race. He was swimming strongly and rapidly. Off to the correspondent's left, the cook's great white and corked back bulged out of the water, and in the rear the captain was hanging with his one good hand to the keel of the overturned dingey.

There is a certain immovable quality to a shore, and the correspondent wondered at it amid the confusion of the sea.

It seemed also very attractive, but the correspondent knew that it was a long journey, and he paddled leisurely. The piece of life-preserver lay under him, and sometimes he whirled down the incline of a wave as if he were on a hand-sled.

But finally he arrived at a place in the sea where travel was beset with difficulty. He did not pause swimming to inquire what manner of current had caught him, but there his progress ceased. The shore was set before him like a bit of scenery on a stage, and he looked at it and understood with his eyes each detail of it.

As the cook passed, much farther to the left, the captain was calling to him, "Turn over on your back, cook! Turn over on your back and use the oar."

"All right, sir." The cook turned on his back, and, paddling with an oar, went ahead as if he were a canoe.

Presently the boat also passed to the left of the correspondent with the captain clinging with one hand to the keel. He would have appeared like a man raising himself to look over a board fence, if it were not for the extraordinary gymnastics of the boat. The correspondent marvelled that the captain could still hold to it.

They passed on, nearer to shore—the oiler, the cook, the captain—and following them went the water-jar, bouncing gaily over the seas.

The correspondent remained in the grip of this strange new enemy—a current. The shore, with its white slope of sand and its green bluff, topped with little silent cottages, was spread like a picture before him. It was very near to him then, but he was impressed as one who in a gallery looks at a scene from Brittany or Holland.

He thought: "I am going to drown? Can it be possible? Can it be possible? Can it be possible?" Perhaps an individual must consider his own death to be the final phenomenon of nature.

But later a wave perhaps whirled him out of this small deadly current, for he found suddenly that he could again make progress toward the shore. Later still, he was aware that the captain, clinging with one hand to the keel of the dingey, had his face turned away from the shore and toward him, and was calling his name. "Come to the boat! Come to the boat!"

In his struggle to reach the captain and the boat, he reflected that when one gets properly wearied, drowning must really be a comfortable arrangement, a cessation of hostilities accompanied by a large degree of relief, and he was glad of it, for the main thing in his mind for some moments had been horror of the temporary agony. He did not wish to be hurt.

Presently he saw a man running along the shore. He was undressing with most remarkable speed. Coat, trousers, shirt, everything flew magically off him.

"Come to the boat," called the captain.

"All right, captain." As the correspondent paddled, he saw the captain let himself down to bottom and leave the boat. Then the correspondent performed his one little marvel of the voyage. A large wave caught him and flung him with ease and supreme speed completely over the boat and far beyond it. It struck him even then as an event in gymnastics, and a true miracle of the sea. An overturned boat in the surf is not a plaything to a swimming man.

The correspondent arrived in water that reached only to his waist, but his condition did not enable him to stand for more than a moment. Each wave knocked him into a heap, and the under-tow pulled at him.

Then he saw the man who had been running and undressing, and undressing and running, come bounding into the water. He dragged ashore the cook, and then waded towards the captain, but the captain waved him away, and sent him to the correspondent. He was naked, naked as a tree in winter, but a halo was about his head, and he shone like a saint. He gave a strong pull, and a long drag, and a bully heave at the correspondent's hand. The correspondent, schooled in the minor formulæ, said: "Thanks, old man." But suddenly the man cried: "What's that?" He pointed a swift finger. The correspondent said: "Go."

In the shallows, face downward, lay the oiler. His forehead touched sand that was periodically, between each wave, clear of the sea.

The correspondent did not know all that transpired afterward. When he achieved safe ground he fell, striking the sand with each particular part of his body. It was as if he had dropped from a roof, but the thud was grateful to him.

It seems that instantly the beach was populated with men with blankets, clothes, and flasks, and women with coffee-pots and all the remedies sacred to their minds. The welcome of the land to the men from the sea was warm and generous, but a still and dripping shape was carried slowly up the beach, and the land's welcome for it could only be the different and sinister hospitality of the grave.

When it came night, the white waves paced to and fro in the moonlight, and the wind brought the sound of the great sea's voice to the men on shore, and they felt that they could then be interpreters.

A MAN AND SOME OTHERS

I

Dark mesquit spread from horizon to horizon. There was no house or horseman from which a mind could evolve a city or a crowd. The world was declared to be a desert and unpeopled. Sometimes, however, on days when no heat-mist arose, a blue shape, dim, of the substance of a spectre's veil, appeared in the south-west, and a pondering sheep-herder might remember that there were mountains.

In the silence of these plains the sudden and childish banging of a tin pan could have made an iron-nerved man leap into the air. The sky was ever flawless; the manoeuvring of clouds was an unknown pageant; but at times a sheep-herder could see, miles away, the long, white streamers of dust rising from the feet of another's flock, and the interest became intense.

Bill was arduously cooking his dinner, bending over the fire, and toiling like a blacksmith. A movement, a flash of strange colour, perhaps, off in the bushes, caused him suddenly to turn his head. Presently he arose, and, shading his eyes with his hand, stood motionless and gazing. He perceived at last a Mexican sheep-herder winding through the brush toward his camp.

"Hello!" shouted Bill.

The Mexican made no answer, but came steadily forward until he was within some twenty yards. There he paused, and, folding his arms, drew himself up in the manner affected by the villain in the play. His serape muffled the lower part of his face, and his great sombrero shaded his brow. Being unexpected and also silent, he had something of the quality of an apparition; moreover, it was clearly his intention to be mysterious and devilish.

The American's pipe, sticking carelessly in the corner of his mouth, was twisted until the wrong side was uppermost, and he held his frying-pan poised in the air. He surveyed with evident surprise this apparition in the mesquit. "Hello, José!" he said; "what's the matter?"

The Mexican spoke with the solemnity of funeral tollings: "Beel, you mus' geet off range. We want you geet off range. We no like. Un'erstan'? We no like."

"What you talking about?" said Bill. "No like what?"

"We no like you here. Un'erstan'? Too mooch. You mus' geet out. We no like. Un'erstan'?"

"Understand? No; I don't know what the blazes you're gittin' at." Bill's eyes wavered in bewilderment, and his jaw fell. "I must git out? I must git off the range? What you givin' us?"

The Mexican unfolded his serape with his small yellow hand. Upon his face was then to be seen a smile that was gently, almost caressingly murderous. "Beel," he said, "geet out!"

Bill's arm dropped until the frying-pan was at his knee. Finally he turned again toward the fire. "Go on, you dog-gone little yaller rat!" he said over his shoulder. "You fellers can't chase me off this range. I got as much right here as anybody."

"Beel," answered the other in a vibrant tone, thrusting his head forward and moving one foot, "you geet out or we keel you."

"Who will?" said Bill.

"I—and the others." The Mexican tapped his breast gracefully.

Bill reflected for a time, and then he said: "You ain't got no manner of license to warn me off'n this range, and I won't move a rod. Understand? I've got rights, and I suppose if I don't see 'em through, no one is likely to give me a good hand and help me lick you fellers, since I'm the only white man in half a day's ride. Now, look; if you fellers try to rush this camp, I'm goin' to plug about fifty per cent. of the gentlemen present, sure. I'm goin' in for trouble, an' I'll git a lot of you. 'Nuther thing: if I was a fine valuable caballero like you, I'd stay in the rear till the shootin' was done, because I'm goin' to make a particular p'int of shootin' you through the chest." He grinned affably, and made a gesture of dismissal.

As for the Mexican, he waved his hands in a consummate expression of indifference. "Oh, all right," he said. Then, in a tone of deep menace and glee, he added: "We will keel you eef you no geet. They have decide'."

"They have, have they?" said Bill. "Well, you tell them to go to the devil!"

II

Bill had been a mine-owner in Wyoming, a great man, an aristocrat, one who possessed unlimited credit in the saloons down the gulch. He had the social weight that could interrupt a lynching or advise a bad man of the particular merits of a remote geographical point. However, the fates exploded the toy balloon with which they had amused Bill, and on the evening of the same day he was a professional gambler with ill-fortune dealing him unspeakable irritation in the shape of three big cards whenever another fellow stood pat. It is well here to inform the world that Bill considered his calamities of life all dwarfs in comparison with the excitement of one particular evening, when three kings came to him with criminal regularity against a man who always filled a straight. Later he became a cow-boy, more weirdly abandoned than if he had never been an aristocrat. By this time all that remained of his former splendour was his pride, or his vanity, which was one thing which need not have remained. He killed the foreman of the ranch over an inconsequent matter as to which of them was a liar, and the midnight train carried him eastward. He became a brakeman on the Union Pacific, and really gained high honours in the hobo war that for many years has devastated the beautiful railroads of our country. A creature of ill-fortune himself, he practised all the ordinary cruelties upon these other creatures of ill-fortune. He was of so fierce a mien that tramps usually surrendered at once whatever coin or tobacco they had in their possession; and if afterward he kicked them from the train, it was only because this was a recognized treachery of the war upon the hoboes. In a famous battle fought in Nebraska in 1879, he would have achieved a lasting distinction if it had not been for a deserter from the United States army. He was at the head of a heroic and sweeping charge, which really broke the power of the hoboes in that country for three months; he had already worsted four tramps with his own coupling-stick, when a stone thrown by the ex-third baseman of F Troop's nine laid him flat on the prairie, and later enforced a stay in the hospital in Omaha. After his recovery he engaged with other railroads, and shuffled cars in countless yards. An order to strike came upon him in Michigan, and afterward the vengeance of the railroad pursued him until he assumed a name. This mask is like the darkness in which the burglar chooses to move. It destroys many of the healthy fears. It is a small thing, but it eats that which we call our conscience. The conductor of No. 419 stood in the caboose within two feet of Bill's nose, and called him a liar. Bill requested him to use a milder term. He had not bored the foreman of Tin Can Ranch with any such request, but had killed him with expedition. The conductor seemed to insist, and so Bill let the matter drop.

He became the bouncer of a saloon on the Bowery in New York. Here most of his fights were as successful as had been his brushes with the hoboes in the West. He gained the complete admiration of the four clean bar-tenders who stood behind the great and glittering bar. He was an honoured man. He nearly killed Bad Hennessy, who, as a matter of fact, had more reputation than ability, and his fame moved up the Bowery and down the Bowery.

But let a man adopt fighting as his business, and the thought grows constantly within him that it is his business to fight. These phrases became mixed in Bill's mind precisely as they are here mixed; and let a man get this idea in his mind, and defeat begins to move toward him over the unknown ways of circumstances. One summer night three sailors from the U.S.S. *Seattle* sat in the saloon drinking and attending to other people's affairs in an amiable fashion. Bill was a proud man since he had thrashed so many citizens, and it suddenly occurred to him that the loud talk of the sailors was very offensive. So he swaggered upon their attention, and warned them that the saloon was the flowery abode of peace and gentle silence. They glanced at him in surprise, and without a moment's pause consigned him to a worse place than any stoker of them knew. Whereupon he flung one of them through the side door before the others could prevent it. On the sidewalk there was a short struggle, with many hoarse epithets in the air, and then Bill slid into the saloon again. A frown of false rage was upon his brow, and he strutted like a savage king. He took a long yellow night-stick from behind the lunch-counter, and started importantly toward the main doors to see that the incensed seamen did not again enter.

The ways of sailormen are without speech, and, together in the street, the three sailors exchanged no word, but they moved at once. Landsmen would have required two years of discussion to gain such unanimity. In silence, and immediately, they seized a long piece of scantling that lay handily. With one forward to guide the battering-ram, and with two behind him to furnish the power, they made a beautiful curve, and came down like the Assyrians on the front door of that saloon.

Mystic and still mystic are the laws of fate. Bill, with his kingly frown and his long night-stick, appeared at precisely that moment in the doorway. He stood like a statue of victory; his pride was at its zenith; and in the same second this atrocious piece of scantling punched him in the bulwarks of his stomach, and he vanished like a mist. Opinions differed as to where the end of the scantling landed him, but it was ultimately clear that it landed him in south-western Texas, where he became a sheep-herder.

The sailors charged three times upon the plate-glass front of the saloon, and when they had finished, it looked as if it had been the victim of a rural fire company's success in saving it from the flames. As the proprietor of the place surveyed the ruins, he remarked that Bill was a very zealous guardian of property. As the ambulance surgeon surveyed Bill, he remarked that the wound was really an excavation.

III

As his Mexican friend tripped blithely away, Bill turned with a thoughtful face to his frying-pan and his fire. After dinner he drew his revolver from its scarred old holster, and examined every part of it. It was the revolver that had dealt death to the foreman, and it had also been in free fights in which it had dealt death to several or none. Bill loved it because its allegiance was more than that of man, horse, or dog. It questioned neither social nor moral position; it obeyed alike the saint and the assassin. It was the claw of the eagle, the tooth of the lion, the poison of the snake; and when he swept it from its holster, this minion smote where he listed, even to the battering of a far penny. Wherefore it was his dearest possession, and was not to be exchanged in south-western Texas for a handful of rubies, nor even the shame and homage of the conductor of No. 419.

During the afternoon he moved through his monotony of work and leisure with the same air of deep meditation. The smoke of his supper-time fire was curling across the shadowy sea of mesquit when the instinct of the plainsman warned him that the stillness, the desolation, was again invaded. He saw a motionless horseman in black outline against the pallid sky. The silhouette displayed serape and sombrero, and even the Mexican spurs as large as pies. When this black figure began to move toward the camp, Bill's hand dropped to his revolver.

The horseman approached until Bill was enabled to see pronounced American features, and a skin too red to grow on a Mexican face. Bill released his grip on his revolver.

"Hello!" called the horseman.

"Hello!" answered Bill.

The horseman cantered forward. "Good evening," he said, as he again drew rein.

"Good evenin'," answered Bill, without committing himself by too much courtesy.

For a moment the two men scanned each other in a way that is not ill-mannered on the plains, where one is in danger of meeting horse-thieves or tourists.

Bill saw a type which did not belong in the mesquit. The young fellow had invested in some Mexican trappings of an expensive kind. Bill's eyes searched the outfit for some sign of craft, but there was none. Even with his local regalia, it was clear that the young man was of a far, black Northern city. He had discarded the enormous stirrups of his Mexican saddle; he used the small English stirrup, and his feet were thrust forward until the steel tightly gripped his ankles. As Bill's eyes travelled over the stranger, they lighted suddenly upon the stirrups and the thrust feet, and immediately he smiled in a friendly way. No dark purpose could dwell in the innocent heart of a man who rode thus on the plains.

As for the stranger, he saw a tattered individual with a tangle of hair and beard, and with a complexion turned brick-colour from the sun and whisky. He saw a pair of eyes that at first looked at him as the wolf looks at the wolf, and then became childlike, almost timid, in their glance. Here was evidently a man who had often stormed the iron walls of the city of success, and who now sometimes valued himself as the rabbit values his prowess.

The stranger smiled genially, and sprang from his horse. "Well, sir, I suppose you will let me camp here with you to-night?"

"Eh?" said Bill.

"I suppose you will let me camp here with you to-night?"

Bill for a time seemed too astonished for words. "Well,"—he answered, scowling in inhospitable annoyance—"well, I don't believe this here is a good place to camp to-night, mister."

The stranger turned quickly from his saddle-girth.

"What?" he said in surprise. "You don't want me here? You don't want me to camp here?"

Bill's feet scuffled awkwardly, and he looked steadily at a cactus plant. "Well, you see, mister," he said, "I'd like your company well enough, but— you see, some of these here greasers are goin' to chase me off the range to-night; and while I might like a man's company all right, I couldn't let him in for no such game when he ain't got nothin' to do with the trouble."

"Going to chase you off the range?" cried the stranger.

"Well, they said they were goin' to do it," said Bill.

"And—great heavens! will they kill you, do you think?"

"Don't know. Can't tell till afterwards. You see, they take some feller that's alone like me, and then they rush his camp when he ain't quite ready for 'em, and generally plug 'im with a sawed-off shot-gun load before he has a chance to git at 'em. They lay around and wait for their chance, and it comes soon enough. Of course a feller alone like me has got to let up watching some time. Maybe they ketch 'im asleep. Maybe the feller gits tired waiting, and goes out in broad day, and kills two or three just to make the whole crowd pile on him and settle the thing. I heard of a case like that once. It's awful hard on a man's mind—to git a gang after him."

"And so they're going to rush your camp to-night?" cried the stranger. "How do you know? Who told you?"

"Feller come and told me."

"And what are you going to do? Fight?"

"Don't see nothin' else to do," answered Bill gloomily, still staring at the cactus plant.

There was a silence. Finally the stranger burst out in an amazed cry. "Well, I never heard of such a thing in my life! How many of them are there?"

"Eight," answered Bill. "And now look-a-here; you ain't got no manner of business foolin' around here just now, and you might better lope off before dark. I don't ask no help in this here row. I know your happening along here just now don't give me no call on you, and you better hit the trail."

"Well, why in the name of wonder don't you go get the sheriff?" cried the stranger.

"Oh, h——!" said Bill.

IV

Long, smoldering clouds spread in the western sky, and to the east silver mists lay on the purple gloom of the wilderness.

Finally, when the great moon climbed the heavens and cast its ghastly radiance upon the bushes, it made a new and more brilliant crimson of the campfire, where the flames capered merrily through its mesquit branches, filling the silence with the fire chorus, an ancient melody which surely bears a message of the inconsequence of individual tragedy—a message that is in the boom of the sea, the sliver of the wind through the grass-blades, the silken clash of hemlock boughs.

No figures moved in the rosy space of the camp, and the search of the moonbeams failed to disclose a living thing in the bushes. There was no owl-faced clock to chant the weariness of the long silence that brooded upon the plain.

The dew gave the darkness under the mesquit a velvet quality that made air seem nearer to water, and no eye could have seen through it the black things that moved like monster lizards toward the camp. The branches, the leaves, that are fain to cry out when death approaches in the wilds, were frustrated by these uncanny bodies gliding with the finesse of the escaping serpent. They crept forward to the last point where assuredly no frantic attempt of the fire could discover them, and there they paused to locate the prey. A romance relates the tale of the black cell hidden deep in the earth, where, upon entering, one sees only the little eyes of snakes fixing him in menaces. If a man could have approached a certain spot in the bushes, he would not have found it romantically necessary to have his hair rise. There would have been a sufficient expression of horror in the feeling of the death-hand at the nape of his neck and in his rubber knee-joints.

Two of these bodies finally moved toward each other until for each there grew out of the darkness a face placidly smiling with tender dreams of assassination. "The fool is asleep by the fire, God be praised!" The lips of the other widened in a grin of affectionate appreciation of the fool and his plight.

There was some signaling in the gloom, and then began a series of subtle rustlings, interjected often with pauses, during which no sound arose but the sound of faint breathing.

A bush stood like a rock in the stream of firelight, sending its long shadow backward. With painful caution the little company travelled along this shadow, and finally arrived at the rear of the bush. Through its branches they surveyed for a moment of comfortable satisfaction a form in a grey blanket extended on the ground near the fire. The smile of joyful anticipation fled quickly, to give place to a quiet air of business. Two men lifted shotguns with much of the barrels gone, and sighting these weapons through the branches, pulled trigger together.

The noise of the explosions roared over the lonely mesquit as if these guns wished to inform the entire world; and as the grey smoke fled, the dodging company back of the bush saw the blanketed form twitching; whereupon they burst out in chorus in a laugh, and arose as merry as a lot of banqueters. They gleefully gestured congratulations, and strode bravely into the light of the fire.

Then suddenly a new laugh rang from some unknown spot in the darkness. It was a fearsome laugh of ridicule, hatred, ferocity. It might have been demoniac. It smote them motionless in their gleeful prowl, as the stern voice from the sky smites the legendary malefactor. They might have been a weird group in wax, the light of the dying fire on their yellow faces, and shining athwart their eyes turned toward the darkness whence might come the unknown and the terrible.

The thing in the grey blanket no longer twitched; but if the knives in their hands had been thrust toward it, each knife was now drawn back, and its owner's elbow was thrown upward, as if he expected death from the clouds.

This laugh had so chained their reason that for a moment they had no wit to flee. They were prisoners to their terror. Then suddenly the belated decision arrived, and with bubbling cries they turned to run; but at that instant there was a long flash of red in the darkness, and with the report one of the men shouted a bitter shout, spun once, and tumbled headlong. The thick bushes failed to impede the route of the others.

162

The silence returned to the wilderness. The tired flames faintly illumined the blanketed thing and the flung corpse of the marauder, and sang the fire chorus, the ancient melody which bears the message of the inconsequence of human tragedy.

V

"Now you are worse off than ever," said the young man, dry-voiced and awed.

"No, I ain't," said Bill rebelliously. "I'm one ahead."

After reflection, the stranger remarked, "Well, there's seven more."

They were cautiously and slowly approaching the camp. The sun was flaring its first warming rays over the grey wilderness. Upreared twigs, prominent branches, shone with golden light, while the shadows under the mesquit were heavily blue.

Suddenly the stranger uttered a frightened cry. He had arrived at a point whence he had, through openings in the thicket, a clear view of a dead face.

"Gosh!" said Bill, who at the next instant had seen the thing; "I thought at first it was that there José. That would have been queer, after what I told 'im yesterday."

They continued their way, the stranger wincing in his walk, and Bill exhibiting considerable curiosity.

The yellow beams of the new sun were touching the grim hues of the dead Mexican's face, and creating there an inhuman effect, which made his countenance more like a mask of dulled brass. One hand, grown curiously thinner, had been flung out regardlessly to a cactus bush.

Bill walked forward and stood looking respectfully at the body. "I know that feller; his name is Miguel. He——"

The stranger's nerves might have been in that condition when there is no backbone to the body, only a long groove. "Good heavens!" he exclaimed, much agitated; "don't speak that way!"

"What way?" said Bill. "I only said his name was Miguel."

After a pause the stranger said:

"Oh, I know; but——" He waved his hand. "Lower your voice, or something. I don't know. This part of the business rattles me, don't you see?"

"Oh, all right," replied Bill, bowing to the other's mysterious mood. But in a moment he burst out violently and loud in the most extraordinary profanity, the oaths winging from him as the sparks go from the funnel.

He had been examining the contents of the bundled grey blanket, and he had brought forth, among other things, his frying-pan. It was now only a rim with a handle; the Mexican volley had centered upon it. A Mexican shot-gun of the abbreviated description is ordinarily loaded with flat-irons, stove-lids, lead pipe, old horseshoes, sections of chain, window weights, railroad sleepers and spikes, dumb-bells, and any other junk which may be at hand. When one of these loads encounters a man vitally, it is likely to make an impression upon him, and a cooking-utensil may be supposed to subside before such an assault of curiosities.

Bill held high his desecrated frying-pan, turning it this way and that way. He swore until he happened to note the absence of the stranger. A moment later he saw him leading his horse from the bushes. In silence and sullenly the young man went about saddling the animal. Bill said, "Well, goin' to pull out?"

The stranger's hands fumbled uncertainly at the throat-latch. Once he exclaimed irritably, blaming the buckle for the trembling of his fingers. Once he turned to look at the dead face with the light of the morning sun upon it. At last he cried, "Oh, I know the whole thing was all square enough—couldn't be squarer—but—somehow or other, that man there takes the heart out of me." He turned his troubled face for another look. "He seems to be all the time calling me a—he makes me feel like a murderer."

"But," said Bill, puzzling, "you didn't shoot him, mister; I shot him."

"I know; but I feel that way, somehow. I can't get rid of it."

Bill considered for a time; then he said diffidently, "Mister, you're a eddycated man, ain't you?"

"What?"

"You're what they call a—a eddycated man, ain't you?"

The young man, perplexed, evidently had a question upon his lips, when there was a roar of guns, bright flashes, and in the air such hooting and whistling as would come from a swift flock of steam-boilers. The stranger's horse gave a mighty, convulsive spring, snorting wildly in its sudden anguish, fell upon its knees, scrambled afoot again, and was away in the uncanny death run known to men who have seen the finish of brave horses.

"This comes from discussin' things," cried Bill angrily.

He had thrown himself flat on the ground facing the thicket whence had come the firing. He could see the smoke winding over the bush-tops. He lifted his revolver, and the weapon came slowly up from the ground and poised like the glittering crest of a snake. Somewhere on his face there was a kind of smile, cynical, wicked, deadly, of a ferocity which at the same time had brought a deep flush to his face, and had caused two upright lines to glow in his eyes.

"Hello, José!" he called, amiable for satire's sake. "Got your old blunderbusses loaded up again yet?"

The stillness had returned to the plain. The sun's brilliant rays swept over the sea of mesquit, painting the far mists of the west with faint rosy light, and high in the air some great bird fled toward the south.

"You come out here," called Bill, again addressing the landscape, "and I'll give you some shootin' lessons. That ain't the way to shoot." Receiving no reply, he began to invent epithets and yell them at the thicket. He was something of a master of insult, and, moreover, he dived into his memory to bring forth imprecations tarnished with age, unused since fluent Bowery days. The occupation amused him, and sometimes he laughed so that it was uncomfortable for his chest to be against the ground.

Finally the stranger, prostrate near him, said wearily, "Oh, they've gone."

"Don't you believe it," replied Bill, sobering swiftly. "They're there yet—every man of 'em."

"How do you know?"

"Because I do. They won't shake us so soon. Don't put your head up, or they'll get you, sure."

Bill's eyes, meanwhile, had not wavered from their scrutiny of the thicket in front. "They're there all right; don't you forget it. Now you listen." So he called out: "José! Ojo, José! Speak up, *hombre*! I want have talk. Speak up, you yaller cuss, you!"

Whereupon a mocking voice from off in the bushes said, "Señor?"

"There," said Bill to his ally; "didn't I tell you? The whole batch." Again he lifted his voice. "José—look—ain't you gittin' kinder tired? You better go home, you fellers, and git some rest."

The answer was a sudden furious chatter of Spanish, eloquent with hatred, calling down upon Bill all the calamities which life holds. It was as if some one had suddenly enraged a cageful of wild cats. The spirits of all the revenges which they had imagined were loosened at this time, and filled the air.

"They're in a holler," said Bill, chuckling, "or there'd be shootin'."

Presently he began to grow angry. His hidden enemies called him nine kinds of coward, a man who could fight only in the dark, a baby who would run from the shadows of such noble Mexican gentlemen, a dog that sneaked. They described the affair of the previous night, and informed him of the base advantage he had taken of their friend. In fact, they in all sincerity endowed him with every quality which he no less earnestly believed them to possess. One could have seen the phrases bite him as he lay there on the ground fingering his revolver.

VI

It is sometimes taught that men do the furious and desperate thing from an emotion that is as even and placid as the thoughts of a village clergyman on Sunday afternoon. Usually, however, it is to be believed that a panther is at the time born in the heart, and that the subject does not resemble a man picking mulberries.

"B' G——!" said Bill, speaking as from a throat filled with dust, "I'll go after 'em in a minute."

"Don't you budge an inch!" cried the stranger, sternly. "Don't you budge!"

"Well," said Bill, glaring at the bushes—"well—"

"Put your head down!" suddenly screamed the stranger, in white alarm. As the guns roared, Bill uttered a loud grunt, and for a moment leaned panting on his elbow, while his arm shook like a twig. Then he upreared like a great and bloody spirit of vengeance, his face lighted with the blaze of his last passion. The Mexicans came swiftly and in silence.

The lightning action of the next few moments was of the fabric of dreams to the stranger. The muscular struggle may not be real to the drowning man. His mind may be fixed on the far, straight shadows back of the stars, and the terror of them. And so the fight, and his part in it, had to the stranger only the quality of a picture half drawn. The rush of feet, the spatter of shots, the cries, the swollen faces seen like masks on the smoke, resembled a happening of the night.

And yet afterward certain lines, forms, lived out so strongly from the incoherence that they were always in his memory.

He killed a man, and the thought went swiftly by him, like the feather on the gale, that it was easy to kill a man.

Moreover, he suddenly felt for Bill, this grimy sheep-herder, some deep form of idolatry. Bill was dying, and the dignity of last defeat, the superiority of him who stands in his grave, was in the pose of the lost sheep-herder.

The stranger sat on the ground idly mopping the sweat and powder-stain from his brow. He wore the gentle idiot smile of an aged beggar as he watched three Mexicans limping and staggering in the distance. He noted at this time that one who still possessed a serape had from it none of the grandeur of the cloaked Spaniard, but that against the sky the silhouette resembled a cornucopia of childhood's Christmas.

They turned to look at him, and he lifted his weary arm to menace them with his revolver. They stood for a moment banded together, and hooted curses at him.

Finally he arose, and, walking some paces, stooped to loosen Bill's grey hands from a throat. Swaying as if slightly drunk, he stood looking down into the still face.

Struck suddenly with a thought, he went about with dulled eyes on the ground, until he plucked his gaudy blanket from where it lay dirty from trampling feet. He dusted it carefully, and then returned and laid it over Bill's form. There he again stood motionless, his mouth just agape and the same stupid glance in his eyes, when all at once he made a gesture of fright and looked wildly about him.

He had almost reached the thicket when he stopped, smitten with alarm. A body contorted, with one arm stiff in the air, lay in his path. Slowly and warily he moved around it, and in a moment the bushes, nodding and whispering, their leaf-faces turned toward the scene behind him, swung and swung again into stillness and the peace of the wilderness.

THE BRIDE COMES TO YELLOW SKY

I

The great Pullman was whirling onward with such dignity of motion that a glance from the window seemed simply to prove that the plains of Texas were pouring eastward. Vast flats of green grass, dull-hued spaces of mesquit and cactus, little groups of frame houses, woods of light and tender trees, all were sweeping into the east, sweeping over the horizon, a precipice.

A newly-married pair had boarded this train at San Antonio. The man's face was reddened from many days in the wind and sun, and a direct result of his new black clothes was that his brick-coloured hands were constantly performing in a most conscious fashion. From time to time he looked down respectfully at his attire. He sat with a hand on each knee, like a man waiting in a barber's shop. The glances he devoted to other passengers were furtive and shy.

The bride was not pretty, nor was she very young. She wore a dress of blue cashmere, with small reservations of velvet here and there, and with steel buttons abounding. She continually twisted her head to regard her puff-sleeves, very stiff, straight, and high. They embarrassed her. It was quite apparent that she had cooked, and that she expected to cook, dutifully. The blushes caused by the careless scrutiny of some passengers as she had entered the car were strange to see upon this plain, under-class countenance, which was drawn in placid, almost emotionless lines.

They were evidently very happy. "Ever been in a parlour-car before?" he asked, smiling with delight.

"No," she answered; "I never was. It's fine, ain't it?"

"Great. And then, after a while, we'll go forward to the diner, and get a big lay-out. Finest meal in the world. Charge, a dollar."

"Oh, do they?" cried the bride. "Charge a dollar? Why, that's too much—for us—ain't it, Jack?"

"Not this trip, anyhow," he answered bravely. "We're going to go the whole thing."

Later, he explained to her about the train. "You see, it's a thousand miles from one end of Texas to the other, and this train runs right across it, and never stops but four times."

He had the pride of an owner. He pointed out to her the dazzling fittings of the coach, and, in truth, her eyes opened wider as she contemplated the sea-green figured velvet, the shining brass, silver, and glass, the wood that gleamed as darkly brilliant as the surface of a pool of oil. At one end a bronze figure sturdily held a support for a separated chamber, and at convenient places on the ceiling were frescoes in olive and silver.

To the minds of the pair, their surroundings reflected the glory of their marriage that morning in San Antonio. This was the environment of their new estate, and the man's face, in particular, beamed with an elation that made him appear ridiculous to the negro porter. This individual at times surveyed them from afar with an amused and superior grin. On other occasions he bullied them with skill in ways that did not make it exactly plain to them that they were being bullied. He subtly used all the manners of the most unconquerable kind of snobbery. He oppressed them, but of this oppression they had small knowledge, and they speedily forgot that unfrequently a number of travellers covered them with stares of derisive enjoyment. Historically there was supposed to be something infinitely humorous in their situation.

"We are due in Yellow Sky at 3.42," he said, looking tenderly into her eyes.

"Oh, are we?" she said, as if she had not been aware of it.

To evince surprise at her husband's statement was part of her wifely amiability. She took from a pocket a little silver watch, and as she held it before her, and stared at it with a frown of attention, the new husband's face shone.

"I bought it in San Anton' from a friend of mine," he told her gleefully.

"It's seventeen minutes past twelve," she said, looking up at him with a kind of shy and clumsy coquetry.

A passenger, noting this play, grew excessively sardonic, and winked at himself in one of the numerous mirrors.

At last they went to the dining-car. Two rows of negro waiters in dazzling white suits surveyed their entrance with the interest, and also the equanimity, of men who had been forewarned. The pair fell to the lot of a waiter who happened to feel pleasure in steering them through their meal. He viewed them with the manner of a fatherly pilot, his countenance radiant with benevolence. The patronage entwined with the ordinary deference was not palpable to them. And yet as they returned to their coach they showed in their faces a sense of escape.

To the left, miles down a long purple slope, was a little ribbon of mist, where moved the keening Rio Grande. The train was approaching it at an angle, and the apex was Yellow Sky. Presently it was apparent that as the distance from Yellow Sky grew shorter, the husband became commensurately restless. His brick-red hands were more insistent in their prominence. Occasionally he was even rather absent-minded and far away when the bride leaned forward and addressed him.

As a matter of truth, Jack Potter was beginning to find the shadow of a deed weigh upon him like a leaden slab. He, the town-marshal of Yellow Sky, a man known, liked, and feared in his corner, a prominent person, had gone to San Antonio to meet a girl he believed he loved, and there, after the usual prayers, had actually induced her to marry him without consulting Yellow Sky for any part of the transaction. He was now bringing his bride before an innocent and unsuspecting community.

Of course, people in Yellow Sky married as it pleased them in accordance with a general custom, but such was Potter's thought of his duty to his friends, or of their idea of his duty, or of an unspoken form which does not control men in these matters, that he felt he was heinous. He had committed an extraordinary crime. Face to face with this girl in San Antonio, and spurred by his sharp impulse, he had gone headlong over all the social hedges. At San Antonio he was like a man hidden in the dark. A knife to sever any friendly duty, any form, was easy to his hand in that remote city. But the hour of Yellow Sky, the hour of daylight, was approaching.

He knew full well that his marriage was an important thing to his town. It could only be exceeded by the burning of the new hotel. His friends would not forgive him. Frequently he had reflected upon the advisability of telling them by telegraph, but a new cowardice had been upon him. He feared to do it. And now the train was hurrying him toward a scene of amazement, glee, reproach. He glanced out of the window at the line of haze swinging slowly in toward the train.

Yellow Sky had a kind of brass band which played painfully to the delight of the populace. He laughed without heart as he thought of it. If the citizens could dream of his prospective arrival with his bride, they would parade the band at the station, and escort them, amid cheers and laughing congratulations, to his adobe home.

He resolved that he would use all the devices of speed and plainscraft in making the journey from the station to his house. Once within that safe citadel, he could issue some sort of a vocal bulletin, and then not go among the citizens until they had time to wear off a little of their enthusiasm.

The bride looked anxiously at him. "What's worrying you, Jack?"

He laughed again. "I'm not worrying, girl. I'm only thinking of Yellow Sky."

She flushed in comprehension.

A sense of mutual guilt invaded their minds, and developed a finer tenderness. They looked at each other with eyes softly aglow. But Potter often laughed the same nervous laugh. The flush upon the bride's face seemed quite permanent.

The traitor to the feelings of Yellow Sky narrowly watched the speeding landscape.

"We're nearly there," he said.

Presently the porter came and announced the proximity of Potter's home. He held a brush in his hand, and, with all his airy superiority gone, he brushed Potter's new clothes, as the latter slowly turned this way and that way. Potter fumbled out a coin, and gave it to the porter as he had seen others do. It was a heavy and muscle-bound business, as that of a man shoeing his first horse.

The porter took their bag, and, as the train began to slow, they moved forward to the hooded platform of the car. Presently the two engines and their long string of coaches rushed into the station of Yellow Sky.

"They have to take water here," said Potter, from a constricted throat, and in mournful cadence as one announcing death. Before the train stopped his eye had swept the length of the platform, and he was glad and astonished to see there was no one upon it but the station-agent, who, with a slightly hurried and anxious air, was walking toward the water-tanks. When the train had halted, the porter alighted first and placed in position a little temporary step.

"Come on, girl," said Potter, hoarsely.

As he helped her down, they each laughed on a false note. He took the bag from the negro, and bade his wife cling to his arm. As they slunk rapidly away, his hang-dog glance perceived that they were unloading the two trunks, and also that the station-agent, far ahead, near the baggage-car, had turned, and was running toward him, making gestures. He laughed, and groaned as he laughed, when he noted the first effect of his marital bliss upon Yellow Sky. He gripped his wife's arm firmly to his side, and they fled. Behind them the porter stood chuckling fatuously.

II

The California Express on the Southron Railway was due at Yellow Sky in twenty-one minutes. There were six men at the bar of the Weary Gentleman saloon. One was a drummer, who talked a great deal and rapidly; three were

Texans, who did not care to talk at that time; and two were Mexican sheep-herders, who did not talk as a general practice in the Weary Gentleman saloon. The bar-keeper's dog lay on the board-walk that crossed in front of the door. His head was on his paws, and he glanced drowsily here and there with the constant vigilance of a dog that is kicked on occasion. Across the sandy street were some vivid green grass plots, so wonderful in appearance amid the sands that burned near them in a blazing sun, that they caused a doubt in the mind. They exactly resembled the grass-mats used to represent lawns on the stage. At the cooler end of the railway-station a man without a coat sat in a tilted chair and smoked his pipe. The fresh-cut bank of the Rio Grande circled near the town, and there could be seen beyond it a great plum-coloured plain of mesquit.

Save for the busy drummer and his companions in the saloon, Yellow Sky was dozing. The new-comer leaned gracefully upon the bar, and recited many tales with the confidence of a bard who has come upon a new field.

"And at the moment that the old man fell down-stairs, with the bureau in his arms, the old woman was coming up with two scuttles of coal, and, of course——"

The drummer's tale was interrupted by a young man who suddenly appeared in the open door. He cried—

"Scratchy Wilson's drunk, and has turned loose with both hands."

The two Mexicans at once set down their glasses, and faded out of the rear entrance of the saloon.

The drummer, innocent and jocular, answered—

"All right, old man. S'pose he has. Come and have a drink, anyhow."

But the information had made such an obvious cleft in every skull in the room, that the drummer was obliged to see its importance. All had become instantly morose.

"Say," said he, mystified, "what is this?"

His three companions made the introductory gesture of eloquent speech, but the young man at the door forestalled them.

"It means, my friend," he answered, as he came into the saloon, "that for the next two hours this town won't be a health resort."

The bar-keeper went to the door, and locked and barred it. Reaching out of the window, he pulled in heavy wooden shutters and barred them. Immediately a solemn, chapel-like gloom was upon the place. The drummer was looking from one to another.

"But say," he cried, "what is this, anyhow? You don't mean there is going to be a gun-fight?"

"Don't know whether there'll be a fight or not," answered one man grimly. "But there'll be some shootin'—some good shootin'."

The young man who had warned them waved his hand. "Oh, there'll be a fight, fast enough, if any one wants it. Anybody can get a fight out there in the street. There's a fight just waiting."

The drummer seemed to be swayed between the interest of a foreigner, and a perception of personal danger.

"What did you say his name was?" he asked.

"Scratchy Wilson," they answered in chorus.

"And will he kill anybody? What are you going to do? Does this happen often? Does he rampage round like this once a week or so? Can he break in that door?"

"No, he can't break down that door," replied the bar-keeper. "He's tried it three times. But when he comes you'd better lay down on the floor, stranger. He's dead sure to shoot at it, and a bullet may come through."

Thereafter the drummer kept a strict eye on the door. The time had not yet been called for him to hug the floor, but as a minor precaution he sidled near to the wall.

"Will he kill anybody?" he said again.

The men laughed low and scornfully at the question.

"He's out to shoot, and he's out for trouble. Don't see any good in experimentin' with him."

"But what do you do in a case like this? What do you do?"

A man responded—"Why, he and Jack Potter——"

But, in chorus, the other men interrupted—"Jack Potter's in San Anton'."

"Well, who is he? What's he got to do with it?"

"Oh, he's the town-marshal. He goes out and fights Scratchy when he gets on one of these tears."

"Whow!" said the drummer, mopping his brow. "Nice job he's got."

The voices had toned away to mere whisperings. The drummer wished to ask further questions, which were born of an increasing anxiety and bewilderment, but when he attempted them, the men merely looked at him in irritation, and motioned him to remain silent. A tense waiting hush was upon them. In the deep shadows of the room their eyes shone as they listened for sounds from the street. One man made three gestures at the bar-keeper, and the latter, moving like a ghost, handed him a glass and a bottle. The man poured a full glass of whisky, and set down the bottle noiselessly. He gulped the whisky in a swallow, and turned again toward the door in immovable silence. The drummer saw that the bar-keeper, without a sound, had taken a Winchester from beneath the bar. Later, he saw this individual beckoning to him, so he tip-toed across the room.

"You better come with me back of the bar."

"No, thanks," said the drummer, perspiring. "I'd rather be where I can make a break for the back-door."

Whereupon the man of bottles made a kindly but peremptory gesture.

The drummer obeyed it, and finding himself seated on a box, with his head below the level of the bar, balm was laid upon his soul at sight of various zinc and copper fittings that bore a resemblance to plate armour. The bar-keeper took a seat comfortably upon an adjacent box.

"You see," he whispered, "this here Scratchy Wilson is a wonder with a gun—a perfect wonder—and when he goes on the war-trail, we hunt our holes—naturally. He's about the last one of the old gang that used to hang out along the river here. He's a terror when he's drunk. When he's sober he's all right—kind of simple—wouldn't hurt a fly—nicest fellow in town. But when he's drunk—whoo!"

There were periods of stillness.

"I wish Jack Potter was back from San Anton'," said the bar-keeper. "He shot Wilson up once—in the leg—and he would sail in and pull out the kinks in this thing."

Presently they heard from a distance the sound of a shot, followed by three wild yells. It instantly removed a bond from the men in the darkened saloon. There was a shuffling of feet. They looked at each other.

"Here he comes," they said.

III

A man in a maroon-coloured flannel shirt, which had been purchased for purposes of decoration, and made, principally, by some Jewish women on the east side of New York, rounded a corner and walked into the middle of the main street of Yellow Sky. In either hand the man held a long, heavy blue-black revolver. Often he yelled, and these cries rang through a semblance of a deserted village, shrilly flying over the roofs in a volume that seemed to have no relation to the ordinary vocal strength of a man. It was as if the surrounding stillness formed the arch of a tomb over him. These cries of ferocious challenge rang against walls of silence. And his boots had red tops with gilded imprints, of the kind beloved in winter by little sledging boys on the hillsides of New England.

The man's face flamed in a rage begot of whisky. His eyes, rolling and yet keen for ambush, hunted the still door-ways and windows. He walked with the creeping movement of the midnight cat. As it occurred to him, he roared menacing information. The long revolvers in his hands were as easy as straws; they were moved with an electric swiftness. The little fingers of each hand played sometimes in a musician's way. Plain from the low collar of the shirt, the cords of his neck straightened and sank as passion moved him. The only sounds were his terrible invitations. The calm adobes preserved their demeanour at the passing of this small thing in the middle of the street.

There was no offer of fight—no offer of fight. The man called to the sky. There were no attractions. He bellowed and fumed and swayed his revolver here and everywhere.

The dog of the bar-keeper of the Weary Gentleman saloon had not appreciated the advance of events. He yet lay dozing in front of his master's door. At sight of the dog, the man paused and raised his revolver humorously. At sight of the man, the dog sprang up and walked diagonally away, with a sullen head and growling. The man yelled, and the dog broke into a gallop. As it was about to enter an alley, there was a loud noise, a whistling, and something spat the ground directly before it. The dog screamed, and, wheeling in terror, galloped headlong in a new direction. Again there was a noise, a whistling, and sand was kicked viciously before it. Fear-stricken, the dog turned and flurried like an animal in a pen. The man stood laughing, his weapons at his hips.

Ultimately the man was attracted by the closed door of the Weary Gentleman saloon. He went to it, and, hammering with a revolver, demanded drink.

The door remaining imperturbable, he picked a bit of paper from the walk, and nailed it to the framework with a knife. He then turned his back contemptuously upon this popular resort, and, walking to the opposite side of the street and spinning there on his heel quickly and lithely, fired at the bit of paper. He missed it by a half-inch. He swore at himself, and went away. Later, he comfortably fusiladed the windows of his most intimate friend. The man was playing with this town. It was a toy for him.

178

But still there was no offer of fight. The name of Jack Potter, his ancient antagonist, entered his mind, and he concluded that it would be a glad thing if he should go to Potter's house, and, by bombardment, induce him to come out and fight. He moved in the direction of his desire, chanting Apache scalp music.

When he arrived at it, Potter's house presented the same still, calm front as had the other adobes. Taking up a strategic position, the man howled a challenge. But this house regarded him as might a great stone god. It gave no sign. After a decent wait, the man howled further challenges, mingling with them wonderful epithets.

Presently there came the spectacle of a man churning himself into deepest rage over the immobility of a house. He fumed at it as the winter wind attacks a prairie cabin in the north. To the distance there should have gone the sound of a tumult like the fighting of two hundred Mexicans. As necessity bade him, he paused for breath or to reload his revolvers.

IV

Potter and his bride walked sheepishly and with speed. Sometimes they laughed together shamefacedly and low.

"Next corner, dear," he said finally.

They put forth the efforts of a pair walking bowed against a strong wind. Potter was about to raise a finger to point the first appearance of the new home, when, as they circled the corner, they came face to face with a man in a maroon-coloured shirt, who was feverishly pushing cartridges into a large revolver. Upon the instant the man dropped this revolver to the ground, and, like lightning, whipped another from its holster. The second weapon was aimed at the bridegroom's chest.

There was a silence. Potter's mouth seemed to be merely a grave for his tongue. He exhibited an instinct to at once loosen his arm from the woman's grip, and he dropped the bag to the sand. As for the bride, her face had gone as yellow as old cloth. She was a slave to hideous rites, gazing at the apparitional snake.

The two men faced each other at a distance of three paces. He of the revolver smiled with a new and quiet ferocity. "Tried to sneak up on me!" he said. "Tried to sneak up on me!" His eyes grew more baleful. As Potter made a slight movement, the man thrust his revolver venomously forward. "No; don't you do it, Jack Potter. Don't you move a finger towards a gun just yet. Don't you move an eyelash. The time has come for me to settle with you, and I'm going to do it my own way, and loaf along with no interferin'. So if you don't want a gun bent on you, just mind what I tell you."

Potter looked at his enemy. "I ain't got a gun on me, Scratchy," he said. "Honest, I ain't." He was stiffening and steadying, but yet somewhere at the back of his mind a vision of the Pullman floated—the sea-green figured velvet, the shining brass, silver, and glass, the wood that gleamed as darkly brilliant as the surface of a pool of oil—all the glory of their marriage, the environment of the new estate.

"You know I fight when it comes to fighting, Scratchy Wilson, but I ain't got a gun on me. You'll have to do all the shootin' yourself."

His enemy's face went livid. He stepped forward, and lashed his weapon to and fro before Potter's chest.

"Don't you tell me you ain't got no gun on you, you whelp. Don't tell me no lie like that. There ain't a man in Texas ever seen you without no gun. Don't take me for no kid."

His eyes blazed with light and his throat worked like a pump.

"I ain't takin' you for no kid," answered Potter. His heels had not moved an inch backward. "I'm takin' you for a —— fool. I tell you I ain't got a gun, and I ain't. If you're goin' to shoot me up, you'd better begin now. You'll never get a chance like this again."

So much enforced reasoning had told on Wilson's rage. He was calmer.

"If you ain't got a gun, why ain't you got a gun?" he sneered. "Been to Sunday school?"

"I ain't got a gun because I've just come from San Anton' with my wife.

I'm married," said Potter. "And if I'd thought there was going to be any galoots like you prowling around when I brought my wife home, I'd had a gun, and don't you forget it."

"Married!" said Scratchy, not at all comprehending.

"Yes, married! I'm married," said Potter, distinctly.

"Married!" said Scratchy; seeming for the first time he saw the drooping drowning woman at the other man's side. "No!" he said. He was like a creature allowed a glimpse of another world. He moved a pace backward, and his arm with the revolver dropped to his side. "Is this—is this the lady?" he asked.

"Yes, this is the lady," answered Potter.

There was another period of silence.

"Well," said Wilson at last, slowly, "I s'pose it's all off now?"

"It's all off if you say so, Scratchy. You know I didn't make the trouble."

Potter lifted his valise.

"Well, I 'low it's off, Jack," said Wilson. He was looking at the ground. "Married!" He was not a student of chivalry; it was merely that in the presence of this foreign condition he was a simple child of the earlier plains. He picked up his starboard revolver, and placing both weapons in their holsters, he went away. His feet made funnel-shaped tracks in the heavy sand.

THE WISE MEN

They were youths of subtle mind. They were very wicked according to report, and yet they managed to have it reflect great credit upon them. They often had the well-informed and the great talkers of the American colony engaged in reciting their misdeeds, and facts relating to their sins were usually told with a flourish of awe and fine admiration.

One was from San Francisco and one was from New York, but they resembled each other in appearance. This is an idiosyncrasy of geography.

They were never apart in the City of Mexico, at any rate, excepting perhaps when one had retired to his hotel for a respite, and then the other was usually camped down at the office sending up servants with clamorous messages. "Oh, get up and come on down."

They were two lads—they were called the kids—and far from their mothers. Occasionally some wise man pitied them, but he usually was alone in his wisdom. The other folk frankly were transfixed at the splendour of the audacity and endurance of these kids.

"When do those boys ever sleep?" murmured a man as he viewed them entering a café about eight o'clock one morning. Their smooth infantile faces looked bright and fresh enough, at any rate. "Jim told me he saw them still at it about 4.30 this morning."

"Sleep!" ejaculated a companion in a glowing voice. "They never sleep! They go to bed once in every two weeks." His boast of it seemed almost a personal pride.

"They'll end with a crash, though, if they keep it up at this pace," said a gloomy voice from behind a newspaper.

The Café Colorado has a front of white and gold, in which is set larger plate-glass windows than are commonly to be found in Mexico. Two little wings of willow flip-flapping incessantly serve as doors. Under them small stray dogs go furtively into the café, and are shied into the street again by the waiters. On the side-walk there is always a decorative effect of loungers, ranging from the newly-arrived and superior tourist to the old veteran of the silver mines bronzed by violent suns. They contemplate with various shades of interest the show of the street—the red, purple, dusty white, glaring forth against the walls in the furious sunshine.

One afternoon the kids strolled into the Café Colorado. A half-dozen of the men who sat smoking and reading with a sort of Parisian effect at the little tables which lined two sides of the room, looked up and bowed smiling, and although this coming of the kids was anything but an unusual event, at least a dozen men wheeled in their chairs to stare after them. Three waiters polished tables, and moved chairs noisily, and appeared to be eager. Distinctly these kids were of importance.

Behind the distant bar, the tall form of old Pop himself awaited them smiling with broad geniality. "Well, my boys, how are you?" he cried in a voice of profound solicitude. He allowed five or six of his customers to languish in the care of Mexican bartenders, while he himself gave his eloquent attention to the kids, lending all the dignity of a great event to their arrival. "How are the boys to-day, eh?"

"You're a smooth old guy," said one, eying him. "Are you giving us this welcome so we won't notice it when you push your worst whisky at us?"

Pop turned in appeal from one kid to the other kid. "There, now, hear that, will you?" He assumed an oratorical pose. "Why, my boys, you always get the best that this house has got."

"Yes, we do!" The kids laughed. "Well, bring it out, anyhow, and if it's the same you sold us last night, we'll grab your cash register and run."

Pop whirled a bottle along the bar and then gazed at it with a rapt expression. "Fine as silk," he murmured. "Now just taste that, and if it isn't the best whisky you ever put in your face, why I'm a liar, that's all."

The kids surveyed him with scorn, and poured their allowances. Then they stood for a time insulting Pop about his whisky. "Usually it tastes exactly like new parlour furniture," said the San Francisco kid. "Well, here goes, and you want to look out for your cash register."

"Your health, gentlemen," said Pop with a grand air, and as he wiped his bristling grey moustaches he wagged his head with reference to the cash register question. "I could catch you before you got very far."

"Why, are you a runner?" said one derisively.

"You just bank on me, my boy," said Pop, with deep emphasis. "I'm a flier."

The kids sat down their glasses suddenly and looked at him. "You must be," they said. Pop was tall and graceful and magnificent in manner, but he did not display those qualities of form which mean speed in the animal. His hair was grey; his face was round and fat from much living. The buttons of his glittering white waistcoat formed a fine curve, so that if the concave surface of a piece of barrel-hoop had been laid against Pop it would have touched every button. "You must be," observed the kids again.

"Well, you can laugh all you like, but—no jolly now, boys, I tell you I'm a winner. Why, I bet you I can skin anything in this town on a square go. When I kept my place in Eagle Pass there wasn't anybody who could touch me. One of these sure things came down from San Anton'. Oh, he was a runner he was. One of these people with wings. Well, I skinned 'im. What? Certainly I did. Never touched me."

The kids had been regarding him in grave silence, but at this moment they grinned, and said quite in chorus, "Oh, you old liar!"

Pop's voice took on a whining tone of earnestness. "Boys, I'm telling it to you straight. I'm a flier."

One of the kids had had a dreamy cloud in his eye and he cried out suddenly—"Say, what a joke to play this on Freddie."

The other jumped ecstatically. "Oh, wouldn't it though. Say he wouldn't do a thing but howl! He'd go crazy."

184

They looked at Pop as if they longed to be certain that he was, after all, a runner. "Now, Pop, on the level," said one of them wistfully, "can you run?"

"Boys," swore Pop, "I'm a peach! On the dead level, I'm a peach."

"By golly, I believe the old Indian can run," said one to the other, as if they were alone in confidence.

"That's what I can," cried Pop.

The kids said—"Well, so long, old man." They went to a table and sat down. They ordered a salad. They were always ordering salads. This was because one kid had a wild passion for salads, and the other didn't care. So at any hour of the day they might be seen ordering a salad. When this one came they went into a sort of executive session. It was a very long consultation. Men noted it. Occasionally the kids laughed in supreme enjoyment of something unknown. The low rumble of wheels came from the street. Often could be heard the parrot-like cries of distant vendors. The sunlight streamed through the green curtains, and made little amber-coloured flitterings on the marble floor. High up among the severe decorations of the ceiling—reminiscent of the days when the great building was a palace—a small white butterfly was wending through the cool air spaces. The long billiard hall led back to a vague gloom. The balls were always clicking, and one could see countless crooked elbows. Beggars slunk through the wicker doors, and were ejected by the nearest waiter. At last the kids called Pop to them.

"Sit down, Pop. Have a drink." They scanned him carefully. "Say now, Pop, on your solemn oath, can you run?"

"Boys," said Pop piously, and raising his hand, "I can run like a rabbit."

"On your oath?"

"On my oath."

"Can you beat Freddie?"

Pop appeared to look at the matter from all sides. "Well, boys, I'll tell you. No man is ever cock-sure of anything in this world, and I don't want to say that I can best any man, but I've seen Freddie run, and I'm ready to swear I can beat him. In a hundred yards I'd just about skin 'im neat—you understand, just about neat. Freddie is a good average runner, but I—you understand—I'm just—a little—bit—better." The kids had been listening with the utmost attention. Pop spoke the latter part slowly and meanfully. They thought he intended them to see his great confidence.

One said—"Pop, if you throw us in this thing, we'll come here and drink for two weeks without paying. We'll back you and work a josh on Freddie! But O!—if you throw us!"

To this menace Pop cried—"Boys, I'll make the run of my life! On my oath!"

The salad having vanished, the kids arose. "All right, now," they warned him. "If you play us for duffers, we'll get square. Don't you forget it."

"Boys, I'll give you a race for your money. Book on that. I may lose—understand, I may lose—no man can help meeting a better man. But I think I can skin him, and I'll give you a run for your money, you bet."

"All right, then. But, look here," they told him, "you keep your face closed. Nobody gets in on this but us. Understand?"

"Not a soul," Pop declared. They left him, gesturing a last warning from the wicker doors.

In the street they saw Benson, his cane gripped in the middle, strolling through the white-clothed jabbering natives on the shady side. They semaphored to him eagerly. He came across cautiously, like a man who ventures into dangerous company.

"We're going to get up a race. Pop and Fred. Pop swears he can skin 'im. This is a tip. Keep it dark. Say, won't Freddie be hot?"

Benson looked as if he had been compelled to endure these exhibitions of insanity for a century. "Oh, you fellows are off. Pop can't beat Freddie. He's an old bat. Why, it's impossible. Pop can't beat Freddie."

"Can't he? Want to bet he can't?" said the kids. "There now, let's see—you're talking so large."

"Well, you——"

"Oh, bet. Bet or else close your trap. That's the way."

"How do you know you can pull off the race? Seen Freddie?"

"No, but——"

"Well, see him then. Can't bet with no race arranged. I'll bet with you all right—all right. I'll give you fellows a tip though—you're a pair of asses. Pop can't run any faster than a brick school-house."

The kids scowled at him and defiantly said—"Can't he?" They left him and went to the Casa Verde. Freddie, beautiful in his white jacket, was holding one of his innumerable conversations across the bar. He smiled when he saw them. "Where you boys been?" he demanded, in a paternal tone. Almost all the proprietors of American cafés in the city used to adopt a paternal tone when they spoke to the kids.

"Oh, been 'round,'" they replied.

"Have a drink?" said the proprietor of the Casa Verde, forgetting his other social obligations. During the course of this ceremony one of the kids remarked—

"Freddie, Pop says he can beat you running."

"Does he?" observed Freddie without excitement. He was used to various snares of the kids.

"That's what. He says he can leave you at the wire and not see you again."

"Well, he lies," replied Freddie placidly.

"And I'll bet you a bottle of wine that he can do it, too."

"Rats!" said Freddie.

"Oh, that's all right," pursued a kid. "You can throw bluffs all you like, but he can lose you in a hundred yards' dash, you bet."

Freddie drank his whisky, and then settled his elbows on the bar.

"Say, now, what do you boys keep coming in here with some pipe-story all the time for? You can't josh me. Do you think you can scare me about Pop? Why, I know I can beat him. He can't run with me. Certainly not. Why, you fellows are just jollying me."

"Are we though!" said the kids. "You daren't bet the bottle of wine."

"Oh, of course I can bet you a bottle of wine," said Freddie disdainfully. "Nobody cares about a bottle of wine, but——"

"Well, make it five then," advised one of the kids.

Freddie hunched his shoulders. "Why, certainly I will. Make it ten if you like, but——"

"We do," they said.

"Ten, is it? All right; that goes." A look of weariness came over Freddie's face. "But you boys are foolish. I tell you Pop is an old man. How can you expect him to run? Of course, I'm no great runner, but then I'm young and healthy and—and a pretty smooth runner too. Pop is old and fat, and then he doesn't do a thing but tank all day. It's a cinch."

The kids looked at him and laughed rapturously. They waved their fingers at him. "Ah, there!" they cried. They meant that they had made a victim of him.

But Freddie continued to expostulate. "I tell you he couldn't win—an old man like him. You're crazy. Of course, I know you don't care about ten bottles of wine, but, then—to make such bets as that. You're twisted."

"Are we, though?" cried the kids in mockery. They had precipitated Freddie into a long and thoughtful treatise on every possible chance of the thing as he saw it. They disputed with him from time to time, and jeered at him. He laboured on through his argument. Their childish faces were bright with glee.

In the midst of it Wilburson entered. Wilburson worked; not too much, though. He had hold of the Mexican end of a great importing house of New York, and as he was a junior partner, he worked. But not too much, though. "What's the howl?" he said.

The kids giggled. "We've got Freddie rattled."

"Why," said Freddie, turning to him, "these two Indians are trying to tell me that Pop can beat me running."

"Like the devil," said Wilburson, incredulously.

"Well, can't he?" demanded a kid.

"Why, certainly not," said Wilburson, dismissing every possibility of it with a gesture. "That old bat? Certainly not. I'll bet fifty dollars that Freddie——"

"Take you," said a kid.

"What?" said Wilburson, "that Freddie won't beat Pop?"

The kid that had spoken now nodded his head.

"That Freddie won't beat Pop?" repeated Wilburson.

"Yes. It's a go?"

"Why, certainly," retorted Wilburson. "Fifty? All right."

"Bet you five bottles on the side," ventured the other kid.

"Why, certainly," exploded Wilburson wrathfully. "You fellows must take me for something easy. I'll take all those kinds of bets I can get. Cer—tain—ly."

They settled the details. The course was to be paced off on the asphalt of one of the adjacent side-streets, and then, at about eleven o'clock in the evening, the match would be run. Usually in Mexico the streets of a city grow lonely and dark but a little after nine o'clock. There are occasional lurking figures, perhaps, but no crowds, lights and noise. The course would doubtless be undisturbed. As for the policeman in the vicinity, they—well, they were conditionally amiable.

The kids went to see Pop; they told him of the arrangement, and then in deep tones they said, "Oh, Pop, if you throw us!"

Pop appeared to be a trifle shaken by the weight of responsibility thrust upon him, but he spoke out bravely. "Boys, I'll pinch that race. Now you watch me. I'll pinch it."

The kids went then on some business of their own, for they were not seen again till evening. When they returned to the neighbourhood of the Café Colorado the usual stream of carriages was whirling along the calle. The wheels hummed on the asphalt, and the coachmen towered in their great sombreros. On the sidewalk a gazing crowd sauntered, the better class self-satisfied and proud, in their Derby hats and cut-away coats, the lower classes muffling their dark faces in their blankets, slipping along in leather sandals. An electric light sputtered and fumed over the throng. The afternoon shower had left the pave wet and glittering. The air was still laden with the odour of rain on flowers, grass, leaves.

In the Café Colorado a cosmopolitan crowd ate, drank, played billiards, gossiped, or read in the glaring yellow light. When the kids entered a large circle of men that had been gesticulating near the bar greeted them with a roar.

"Here they are now!"

"Oh, you pair of peaches!"

"Say, got any more money to bet with?" Colonel Hammigan, grinning, pushed his way to them. "Say, boys, we'll all have a drink on you now because you won't have any money after eleven o'clock. You'll be going down the back stairs in your stocking feet."

Although the kids remained unnaturally serene and quiet, argument in the Café Colorado became tumultuous. Here and there a man who did not intend to bet ventured meekly that perchance Pop might win, and the others swarmed upon him in a whirlwind of angry denial and ridicule.

Pop, enthroned behind the bar, looked over at this storm with a shadow of anxiety upon his face. This widespread flouting affected him, but the kids looked blissfully satisfied with the tumult they had stirred.

Blanco, honest man, ever worrying for his friends, came to them. "Say, you fellows, you aren't betting too much? This thing looks kind of shaky, don't it?"

The faces of the kids grew sober, and after consideration one said—"No, I guess we've got a good thing, Blanco. Pop is going to surprise them, I think."

"Well, don't———"

"All right, old boy. We'll watch out."

From time to time the kids had much business with certain orange, red, blue, purple, and green bills. They were making little memoranda on the back of visiting cards. Pop watched them closely, the shadow still upon his face. Once he called to them, and when they came he leaned over the bar and said intensely—"Say, boys, remember, now—I might lose this race. Nobody can ever say for sure, and if I do, why———"

"Oh, that's all right, Pop," said the kids, reassuringly. "Don't mind it. Do your derndest, and let it go at that."

When they had left him, however, they went to a corner to consult. "Say, this is getting interesting. Are you in deep?" asked one anxiously of his friend.

"Yes, pretty deep," said the other stolidly. "Are you?"

"Deep as the devil," replied the other in the same tone.

They looked at each other stonily and went back to the crowd. Benson had just entered the café. He approached them with a gloating smile of victory. "Well, where's all that money you were going to bet?"

"Right here," said the kids, thrusting into their waistcoat pockets.

At eleven o'clock a curious thing was learned. When Pop and Freddie, the kids and all, came to the little side street, it was thick with people. It seemed that the news of this race had spread like the wind among the Americans, and they had come to witness the event. In the darkness the crowd moved, mumbling in argument.

The principals—the kids and those with them—surveyed this scene with some dismay. "Say—here's a go." Even then a policeman might be seen approaching, the light from his little lantern flickering on his white cap, gloves, brass buttons, and on the butt of the old-fashioned Colt's revolver which hung at his belt. He addressed Freddie in swift Mexican. Freddie listened, nodding from time to time. Finally Freddie turned to the others to translate. "He says he'll get into trouble if he allows this race when all this crowd is here."

There was a murmur of discontent. The policeman looked at them with an expression of anxiety on his broad, brown face.

"Oh, come on. We'll go hold it on some other fellow's beat," said one of the kids. The group moved slowly away debating. Suddenly the other kid cried, "I know! The Paseo!"

"By jiminy," said Freddie, "just the thing. We'll get a cab and go out to the Paseo. S-s-h! Keep it quiet; we don't want all this mob."

Later they tumbled into a cab—Pop, Freddie, the kids, old Colonel Hammigan and Benson. They whispered to the men who had wagered, "The Paseo." The cab whirled away up the black street. There were occasional grunts and groans, cries of "Oh, get off me feet," and of "Quit! you're killing me." Six people do not have fun in one cab. The principals spoke to each other with the respect and friendliness which comes to good men at such times. Once a kid put his head out of the window and looked backward. He pulled it in again and cried, "Great Scott! Look at that, would you!"

The others struggled to do as they were bid, and afterwards shouted, "Holy smoke! Well, I'll be blowed! Thunder and turf!"

Galloping after them came innumerable cabs, their lights twinkling, streaming in a great procession through the night.

"The street is full of them," ejaculated the old colonel.

The Paseo de la Reforma is the famous drive of the city of Mexico, leading to the Castle of Chapultepec, which last ought to be well known in the United States.

It is a fine broad avenue of macadam with a much greater quality of dignity than anything of the kind we possess in our own land. It seems of the old world, where to the beauty of the thing itself is added the solemnity of tradition and history, the knowledge that feet in buskins trod the same stones, that cavalcades of steel thundered there before the coming of carriages.

When the Americans tumbled out of their cabs the giant bronzes of Aztec and Spaniard loomed dimly above them like towers. The four roads of poplar trees rustled weirdly off there in the darkness. Pop took out his watch and struck a match. "Well, hurry up this thing. It's almost midnight."

The other cabs came swarming, the drivers lashing their horses, for these Americans, who did all manner of strange things, nevertheless always paid well for it. There was a mighty hubbub then in the darkness. Five or six men began to pace the distance and quarrel. Others knotted their handkerchiefs together to make a tape. Men were swearing over bets, fussing and fuming about the odds. Benson came to the kids swaggering. "You're a pair of asses." The cabs waited in a solid block down the avenue. Above the crowd the tall statues hid their visages in the night.

At last a voice floated through the darkness. "Are you ready there?" Everybody yelled excitedly. The men at the tape pulled it out straight. "Hold it higher, Jim, you fool," and silence fell then upon the throng. Men bended down trying to pierce the deep gloom with their eyes. From out at the starting point came muffled voices. The crowd swayed and jostled.

The racers did not come. The crowd began to fret, its nerves burning. "Oh, hurry up," shrilled some one.

The voice called again—"Ready there?" Everybody replied—"Yes, all ready. Hurry up!"

There was a more muffled discussion at the starting point. In the crowd a man began to make a proposition. "I'll bet twenty——" but the crowd interrupted with a howl. "Here they come!" The thickly-packed body of men swung as if the ground had moved. The men at the tape shouldered madly at their fellows, bawling, "Keep back! Keep back!"

From the distance came the noise of feet pattering furiously. Vague forms flashed into view for an instant. A hoarse roar broke from the crowd. Men bended and swayed and fought. The kids back near the tape exchanged another stolid look. A white form shone forth. It grew like a spectre. Always could be heard the wild patter. A scream broke from the crowd. "By Gawd, it's Pop! Pop! Pop's ahead!"

The old man spun towards the tape like a madman, his chin thrown back, his grey hair flying. His legs moved like oiled machinery. And as he shot forward a howl as from forty cages of wild animals went toward the imperturbable chieftains in bronze. The crowd flung themselves forward. "Oh, you old Indian! You savage! Did anybody ever see such running?"

"Ain't he a peach! Well!"

"Where's the kids? H-e-y, kids!"

"Look at him, would you? Did you ever think?" These cries flew in the air blended in a vast shout of astonishment and laughter.

For an instant the whole tragedy was in view. Freddie, desperate, his teeth shining, his face contorted, whirling along in deadly effort, was twenty feet behind the tall form of old Pop, who, dressed only in his—only in his underclothes—gained with each stride. One grand insane moment, and then Pop had hurled himself against the tape—victor!

Freddie, fallen into the arms of some men, struggled with his breath, and at last managed to stammer—

"Say, can't—can't—that old—old—man run!"

Pop, puffing and heaving, could only gasp—"Where's my shoes? Who's got my shoes?"

Later Freddie scrambled panting through the crowd, and held out his hand. "Good man, Pop!" And then he looked up and down the tall, stout form. "Hell! who would think you could run like that?"

The kids were surrounded by a crowd, laughing tempestuously.

"How did you know he could run?"

"Why didn't you give me a line on him?"

"Say—great snakes!—you fellows had a nerve to bet on Pop."

"Why, I was cock-sure he couldn't win."

"Oh, you fellows must have seen him run before."

"Who would ever think it?"

Benson came by, filling the midnight air with curses. They turned to jibe him.

"What's the matter, Benson?"

"Somebody pinched my handkerchief. I tied it up in that string. Damn it."

The kids laughed blithely. "Why, hello! Benson," they said.

There was a great rush for cabs. Shouting, laughing, wondering, the crowd hustled into their conveyances, and the drivers flogged their horses toward the city again.

"Won't Freddie be crazy! Say, he'll be guyed about this for years."

"But who would ever think that old tank could run so?"

One cab had to wait while Pop and Freddie resumed various parts of their clothing.

As they drove home, Freddie said—"Well, Pop, you beat me."

Pop said—"That's all right, old man."

The kids, grinning, said—"How much did you lose, Benson?"

Benson said defiantly—"Oh, not so much. How much did you win?"

"Oh, not so much."

Old Colonel Hammigan, squeezed down in a corner, had apparently been reviewing the event in his mind, for he suddenly remarked, "Well, I'm damned!"

They were late in reaching the Café Colorado, but when they did, the bottles were on the bar as thick as pickets on a fence.

THE FIVE WHITE MICE

Freddie was mixing a cock-tail. His hand with the long spoon was whirling swiftly, and the ice in the glass hummed and rattled like a cheap watch. Over by the window, a gambler, a millionaire, a railway conductor, and the agent of a vast American syndicate were playing seven-up. Freddie surveyed them with the ironical glance of a man who is mixing a cock-tail.

From time to time a swarthy Mexican waiter came with his tray from the rooms at the rear, and called his orders across the bar. The sounds of the indolent stir of the city, awakening from its siesta, floated over the screens which barred the sun and the inquisitive eye. From the far-away kitchen could be heard the roar of the old French *chef*, driving, herding, and abusing his Mexican helpers.

A string of men came suddenly in from the street. They stormed up to the bar. There were impatient shouts. "Come now, Freddie, don't stand there like a portrait of yourself. Wiggle!" Drinks of many kinds and colours, amber, green, mahogany, strong and mild, began to swarm upon the bar with all the attendants of lemon, sugar, mint and ice. Freddie, with Mexican support, worked like a sailor in the provision of them, sometimes talking with that scorn for drink and admiration for those who drink which is the attribute of a good bar-keeper.

At last a man was afflicted with a stroke of dice-shaking. A herculean discussion was waging, and he was deeply engaged in it, but at the same time he lazily flirted the dice. Occasionally he made great combinations. "Look at that, would you?" he cried proudly. The others paid little heed. Then violently the craving took them. It went along the line like an epidemic, and involved them all. In a moment they had arranged a carnival of dice-shaking with money penalties and liquid prizes. They clamorously made it a point of honour with Freddie that he should play and take his chance of sometimes providing this large group with free refreshment. With bended heads like football players, they surged over the tinkling dice, jostling, cheering, and bitterly arguing. One of the quiet company playing seven-up at the corner table said profanely that the row reminded him of a bowling contest at a picnic.

After the regular shower, many carriages rolled over the smooth calle, and sent a musical thunder through the Casa Verde. The shop-windows became aglow with light, and the walks were crowded with youths, callow and ogling, dressed vainly according to superstitious fashions. The policemen had muffled themselves in their gnome-like cloaks, and placed their lanterns as obstacles for the carriages in the middle of the street. The city of Mexico gave forth the deep organ-mellow tones of its evening resurrection.

But still the group at the bar of the Casa Verde were shaking dice. They had passed beyond shaking for drinks for the crowd, for Mexican dollars, for dinners, for the wine at dinner. They had even gone to the trouble of separating the cigars and cigarettes from the dinner's bill, and causing a distinct man to be responsible for them. Finally they were aghast. Nothing remained in sight of their minds which even remotely suggested further gambling. There was a pause for deep consideration.

"Well——"

"Well——"

A man called out in the exuberance of creation. "I know! Let's shake for a box to-night at the circus! A box at the circus!" The group was profoundly edified. "That's it! That's it! Come on now! Box at the circus!" A dominating voice cried—"Three dashes—high man out!" An American, tall, and with a face of copper red from the rays that flash among the Sierra Madres and burn on the cactus deserts, took the little leathern cup and spun the dice out upon the polished wood. A fascinated assemblage hung upon the bar-rail. Three kings turned their pink faces upward. The tall man flourished the cup, burlesquing, and flung the two other dice. From them he ultimately extracted one more pink king. "There," he said. "Now, let's see! Four kings!" He began to swagger in a sort of provisional way.

The next man took the cup, and blew softly in the top of it. Poising it in his hand, he then surveyed the company with a stony eye and paused. They knew perfectly well that he was applying the magic of deliberation and ostentatious indifference, but they could not wait in tranquillity during the performance of all these rites. They began to call out impatiently. "Come now—hurry up." At last the man, with a gesture that was singularly impressive, threw the dice. The others set up a howl of joy. "Not a pair!" There was another solemn pause. The men moved restlessly. "Come, now, go ahead!" In the end, the man, induced and abused, achieved something that was nothing in the presence of four kings. The tall man climbed on the foot-rail and leaned hazardously forward. "Four kings! My four kings are good to go out," he bellowed into the middle of the mob, and although in a moment he did pass into the radiant region of exemption, he continued to bawl advice and scorn.

The mirrors and oiled woods of the Casa Verde were now dancing with blue flashes from a great buzzing electric lamp. A host of quiet members of the Anglo-Saxon colony had come in for their pre-dinner cock-tails. An amiable person was exhibiting to some tourists this popular American saloon. It was a very sober and respectable time of day. Freddie reproved courageously the dice-shaking brawlers, and, in return, he received the choicest advice in a tumult of seven combined vocabularies. He laughed; he had been compelled to retire from the game, but he was keeping an interested, if furtive, eye upon it.

Down at the end of the line there was a youth at whom everybody railed for his flaming ill-luck. At each disaster, Freddie swore from behind the bar in a sort of affectionate contempt. "Why, this kid has had no luck for two days. Did you ever see such throwin'?"

The contest narrowed eventually to the New York kid and an individual who swung about placidly on legs that moved in nefarious circles. He had a grin that resembled a bit of carving. He was obliged to lean down and blink rapidly to ascertain the facts of his venture, but fate presented him with five queens. His smile did not change, but he puffed gently like a man who has been running.

The others, having emerged unscathed from this part of the conflict, waxed hilarious with the kid. They smote him on either shoulders. "We've got you stuck for it, kid! You can't beat that game! Five queens!"

Up to this time the kid had displayed only the temper of the gambler, but the cheerful hoots of the players, supplemented now by a ring of guying non-combatants, caused him to feel profoundly that it would be fine to beat the five queens. He addressed a gambler's slogan to the interior of the cup.

"Oh, five white mice of chance,

Shirts of wool and corduroy pants,

Gold and wine, women and sin,

All for you if you let me come in—

Into the house of chance."

Flashing the dice sardonically out upon the bar, he displayed three aces. From two dice in the next throw he achieved one more ace. For his last throw, he rattled the single dice for a long time. He already had four aces; if he accomplished another one, the five queens were vanquished and the box at the circus came from the drunken man's pocket. All the kid's movements were slow and elaborate. For the last throw he planted the cup bottom-down on the bar with the one dice hidden under it. Then he turned and faced the crowd with the air of a conjuror or a cheat.

"Oh, maybe it's an ace," he said in boastful calm. "Maybe it's an ace."

Instantly he was presiding over a little drama in which every man was absorbed. The kid leaned with his back against the bar-rail and with his elbows upon it.

"Maybe it's an ace," he repeated.

A jeering voice in the background said—"Yes, maybe it is, kid!"

The kid's eyes searched for a moment among the men. "I'll bet fifty dollars it is an ace," he said.

Another voice asked—"American money?"

"Yes," answered the kid.

"Oh!" There was a genial laugh at this discomfiture. However, no one came forward at the kid's challenge, and presently he turned to the cup. "Now, I'll show you." With the manner of a mayor unveiling a statue, he lifted the cup. There was revealed naught but a ten-spot. In the roar which arose could be heard each man ridiculing the cowardice of his neighbour, and above all the din rang the voice of Freddie be-rating every one. "Why, there isn't one liver to every five men in the outfit. That was the greatest cold bluff I ever saw worked. He wouldn't know how to cheat with dice if he wanted to. Don't know the first thing about it. I could hardly keep from laughin' when I seen him drillin' you around. Why, I tell you, I had that fifty dollars right in my pocket if I wanted to be a chump. You're an easy lot——"

Nevertheless the group who had won in the theatre-box game did not relinquish their triumph. They burst like a storm about the head of the kid, swinging at him with their fists. "'Five white mice'!" they quoted, choking. "'Five white mice'!"

"Oh, they are not so bad," said the kid.

Afterward it often occurred that a man would jeer a finger at the kid and derisively say—"'Five white mice.'"

On the route from the dinner to the circus, others of the party often asked the kid if he had really intended to make his appeal to mice. They suggested other animals—rabbits, dogs, hedgehogs, snakes, opossums. To this banter the kid replied with a serious expression of his belief in the fidelity and wisdom of the five white mice. He presented a most eloquent case, decorated with fine language and insults, in which he proved that if one was going to believe in anything at all, one might as well choose the five white mice. His companions, however, at once and unanimously pointed out to him that his recent exploit did not place him in the light of a convincing advocate.

The kid discerned two figures in the street. They were making imperious signs at him. He waited for them to approach, for he recognized one as the other kid—the Frisco kid: there were two kids. With the Frisco kid was Benson. They arrived almost breathless. "Where you been?" cried the Frisco kid. It was an arrangement that upon a meeting the one that could first ask this question was entitled to use a tone of limitless injury. "What you been doing? Where you going? Come on with us. Benson and I have got a little scheme."

The New York kid pulled his arm from the grapple of the other. "I can't. I've got to take these sutlers to the circus. They stuck me for it shaking dice at Freddie's. I can't, I tell you."

The two did not at first attend to his remarks. "Come on! We've got a little scheme."

"I can't. They stuck me. I've got to take'm to the circus."

At this time it did not suit the men with the scheme to recognize these objections as important. "Oh, take'm some other time. Well, can't you take'm some other time? Let 'em go. Damn the circus. Get cold feet. What did you get stuck for? Get cold feet."

But despite their fighting, the New York kid broke away from them. "I can't, I tell you. They stuck me." As he left them, they yelled with rage. "Well, meet us, now, do you hear? In the Casa Verde as soon as the circus quits! Hear?" They threw maledictions after him.

In the city of Mexico, a man goes to the circus without descending in any way to infant amusements, because the Circo Teatro Orrin is one of the best in the world, and too easily surpasses anything of the kind in the United States, where it is merely a matter of a number of rings, if possible, and a great professional agreement to lie to the public. Moreover, the American clown, who in the Mexican arena prances and gabbles, is the clown to whom writers refer as the delight of their childhood, and lament that he is dead. At this circus the kid was not debased by the sight of mournful prisoner elephants and caged animals forlorn and sickly. He sat in his box until late, and laughed and swore when past laughing at the comic foolish-wise clown.

When he returned to the Casa Verde there was no display of the Frisco kid and Benson. Freddie was leaning on the bar listening to four men terribly discuss a question that was not plain. There was a card-game in the corner, of course. Sounds of revelry pealed from the rear rooms.

When the kid asked Freddie if he had seen his friend and Benson, Freddie looked bored. "Oh, yes, they were in here just a minute ago, but I don't know where they went. They've got their skates on. Where've they been? Came in here rolling across the floor like two little gilt gods. They wobbled around for a time, and then Frisco wanted me to send six bottles of wine around to Benson's rooms, but I didn't have anybody to send this time of night, and so they got mad and went out. Where did they get their loads?"

In the first deep gloom of the street the kid paused a moment debating. But presently he heard quavering voices. "Oh, kid! kid! Com'ere!" Peering, he recognized two vague figures against the opposite wall. He crossed the street, and they said—"Hello-kid."

"Say, where did you get it?" he demanded sternly. "You Indians better go home. What did you want to get scragged for?" His face was luminous with virtue.

As they swung to and fro, they made angry denials. "We ain' load'! We ain' load'. Big chump. Comonangetadrink."

The sober youth turned then to his friend. "Hadn't you better go home, kid? Come on, it's late. You'd better break away."

The Frisco kid wagged his head decisively. "Got take Benson home first. He'll be wallowing around in a minute. Don't mind me. I'm all right."

"Cerly, he's all right," said Benson, arousing from deep thought. "He's all right. But better take'm home, though. That's ri—right. He's load'. But he's all right. No need go home any more'n you. But better take'm home. He's load'." He looked at his companion with compassion. "Kid, you're load'."

The sober kid spoke abruptly to his friend from San Francisco. "Kid, pull yourself together, now. Don't fool. We've got to brace this ass of a Benson all the way home. Get hold of his other arm."

The Frisco kid immediately obeyed his comrade without a word or a glower. He seized Benson and came to attention like a soldier. Later, indeed, he meekly ventured—"Can't we take cab?" But when the New York kid snapped out that there were no convenient cabs he subsided to an impassive silence. He seemed to be reflecting upon his state, without astonishment, dismay, or any particular emotion. He submitted himself woodenly to the direction of his friend.

Benson had protested when they had grasped his arms. "Washa doing?" he said in a new and guttural voice. "Washa doing? I ain' load'. Comonangetadrink. I——"

"Oh, come along, you idiot," said the New York kid. The Frisco kid merely presented the mien of a stoic to the appeal of Benson, and in silence dragged away at one of his arms. Benson's feet came from that particular spot on the pavement with the reluctance of roots and also with the ultimate suddenness of roots. The three of them lurched out into the street in the abandon of tumbling chimneys. Benson was meanwhile noisily challenging the others to produce any reasons for his being taken home. His toes clashed into the kerb when they reached the other side of the calle, and for a moment the kids hauled him along with the points of his shoes scraping musically on the pavement. He balked formidably as they were about to pass the Casa Verde. "No! No! Leshavanothdrink! Anothdrink! Onemore!"

But the Frisco kid obeyed the voice of his partner in a manner that was blind but absolute, and they scummed Benson on past the door. Locked together the three swung into a dark street. The sober kid's flank was continually careering ahead of the other wing. He harshly admonished the Frisco child, and the latter promptly improved in the same manner of unthinking complete obedience. Benson began to recite the tale of a love affair, a tale that didn't even have a middle. Occasionally the New York kid swore. They toppled on their way like three comedians playing at it on the stage.

At midnight a little Mexican street burrowing among the walls of the city is as dark as a whale's throat at deep sea. Upon this occasion heavy clouds hung over the capital and the sky was a pall. The projecting balconies could make no shadows.

"Shay," said Benson, breaking away from his escort suddenly, "what want gome for? I ain't load'. You got reg'lar spool-fact'ry in your head—you N' York kid there. Thish oth' kid, he's mos' proper shober, mos' proper shober. He's drunk, but—but he's shober."

"Ah, shup up, Benson," said the New York kid. "Come along now. We can't stay here all night." Benson refused to be corralled, but spread his legs and twirled like a dervish, meanwhile under the evident impression that he was conducting himself most handsomely. It was not long before he gained the opinion that he was laughing at the others. "Eight purple dogsh—dogs! Eight purple dogs. Thas what kid'll see in the morn'. Look ou' for 'em. They—"

As Benson, describing the canine phenomena, swung wildly across the sidewalk, it chanced that three other pedestrians were passing in shadowy rank. Benson's shoulder jostled one of them.

A Mexican wheeled upon the instant. His hand flashed to his hip. There was a moment of silence, during which Benson's voice was not heard raised in apology. Then an indescribable comment, one burning word, came from between the Mexican's teeth.

Benson, rolling about in a semi-detached manner, stared vacantly at the Mexican, who thrust his lean face forward while his fingers played nervously at his hip. The New York kid could not follow Spanish well, but he understood when the Mexican breathed softly: "Does the señor want to fight?"

Benson simply gazed in gentle surprise. The woman next to him at dinner had said something inventive. His tailor had presented his bill. Something had occurred which was mildly out of the ordinary, and his surcharged brain refused to cope with it. He displayed only the agitation of a smoker temporarily without a light.

The New York kid had almost instantly grasped Benson's arm, and was about to jerk him away, when the other kid, who up to this time had been an automaton, suddenly projected himself forward, thrust the rubber Benson aside, and said—"Yes."

There was no sound nor light in the world. The wall at the left happened to be of the common prison-like construction—no door, no window, no opening at all. Humanity was enclosed and asleep. Into the mouth of the sober kid came a wretched bitter taste as if it had filled with blood. He was transfixed as if he was already seeing the lightning ripples on the knife-blade.

But the Mexican's hand did not move at that time. His face went still further forward and he whispered—"So?" The sober kid saw this face as if he and it were alone in space—a yellow mask smiling in eager cruelty, in satisfaction, and above all it was lit with sinister decision. As for the features, they were reminiscent of an unplaced, a forgotten type, which really resembled with precision those of a man who had shaved him three times in Boston in 1888. But the expression burned his mind as sealing-wax burns the palm, and fascinated, stupefied, he actually watched the progress of the man's thought toward the point where a knife would be wrenched from its sheath. The emotion, a sort of mechanical fury, a breeze made by electric fans, a rage made by vanity, smote the dark countenance in wave after wave.

Then the New York kid took a sudden step forward. His hand was at his hip. He was gripping there a revolver of robust size. He recalled that upon its black handle was stamped a hunting scene in which a sportsman in fine leggings and a peaked cap was taking aim at a stag less than one-eighth of an inch away.

His pace forward caused instant movement of the Mexicans. One immediately took two steps to face him squarely. There was a general adjustment, pair and pair. This opponent of the New York kid was a tall man and quite stout. His sombrero was drawn low over his eyes. His serape was flung on his left shoulder. His back was bended in the supposed manner of a Spanish grandee. This concave gentleman cut a fine and terrible figure. The lad, moved by the spirits of his modest and perpendicular ancestors, had time to feel his blood roar at sight of the pose.

He was aware that the third Mexican was over on the left fronting Benson, and he was aware that Benson was leaning against the wall sleepily and peacefully eying the convention. So it happened that these six men stood, side fronting side, five of them with their right hands at their hips and with their bodies lifted nervously, while the central pair exchanged a crescendo of provocations. The meaning of their words rose and rose. They were travelling in a straight line toward collision.

The New York kid contemplated his Spanish grandee. He drew his revolver upward until the hammer was surely free of the holster. He waited immovable and watchful while the garrulous Frisco kid expended two and a half lexicons on the middle Mexican.

The eastern lad suddenly decided that he was going to be killed. His mind leaped forward and studied the aftermath. The story would be a marvel of brevity when first it reached the far New York home, written in a careful hand on a bit of cheap paper, topped and footed and backed by the printed fortifications of the cable company. But they are often as stones flung into mirrors, these bits of paper upon which are laconically written all the most terrible chronicles of the times. He witnessed the uprising of his mother and sister, and the invincible calm of his hard-mouthed old father, who would probably shut himself in his library and smoke alone. Then his father would come, and they would bring him here and say—"This is the place." Then, very likely, each would remove his hat. They would stand quietly with their hats in their hands for a decent minute. He pitied his old financing father, unyielding and millioned, a man who commonly spoke twenty-two words a year to his beloved son. The kid understood it at this time. If his fate was not impregnable, he might have turned out to be a man and have been liked by his father.

The other kid would mourn his death. He would be preternaturally correct for some weeks, and recite the tale without swearing. But it would not bore him. For the sake of his dead comrade he would be glad to be preternaturally correct, and to recite the tale without swearing.

These views were perfectly stereopticon, flashing in and away from his thought with an inconceivable rapidity until after all they were simply one quick dismal impression. And now here is the unreal real: into this kid's nostrils, at the expectant moment of slaughter, had come the scent of new-mown hay, a fragrance from a field of prostrate grass, a fragrance which contained the sunshine, the bees, the peace of meadows, and the wonder of a distant crooning stream. It had no right to be supreme, but it was supreme, and he breathed it as he waited for pain and a sight of the unknown.

But in the same instant, it may be, his thought flew to the Frisco kid, and it came upon him like a flicker of lightning that the Frisco kid was not going to be there to perform, for instance, the extraordinary office of respectable mourner. The other kid's head was muddled, his hand was unsteady, his agility was gone. This other kid was facing the determined and most ferocious gentleman of the enemy. The New York kid became convinced that his friend was lost. There was going to be a screaming murder. He was so certain of it that he wanted to shield his eyes from sight of the leaping arm and the knife. It was sickening, utterly sickening. The New York kid might have been taking his first sea-voyage. A combination of honourable manhood and inability prevented him from running away.

He suddenly knew that it was possible to draw his own revolver, and by a swift manoeuvre face down all three Mexicans. If he was quick enough he would probably be victor. If any hitch occurred in the draw he would undoubtedly be dead with his friends. It was a new game; he had never been obliged to face a situation of this kind in the Beacon Club in New York. In this test, the lungs of the kid still continued to perform their duty.

"Oh, five white mice of chance,

Shirts of wool and corduroy pants,

Gold and wine, women and sin,

All for you if you let me come in—

Into the house of chance."

He thought of the weight and size of his revolver, and dismay pierced him. He feared that in his hands it would be as unwieldy as a sewing-machine for this quick work. He imagined, too, that some singular providence might cause him to lose his grip as he raised his weapon. Or it might get fatally entangled in the tails of his coat. Some of the eels of despair lay wet and cold against his back.

But at the supreme moment the revolver came forth as if it were greased and it arose like a feather. This somnolent machine, after months of repose, was finally looking at the breasts of men.

Perhaps in this one series of movements, the kid had unconsciously used nervous force sufficient to raise a bale of hay. Before he comprehended it he was standing behind his revolver glaring over the barrel at the Mexicans, menacing first one and then another. His finger was tremoring on the trigger. The revolver gleamed in the darkness with a fine silver light.

The fulsome grandee sprang backward with a low cry. The man who had been facing the Frisco kid took a quick step away. The beautiful array of Mexicans was suddenly disorganized.

The cry and the backward steps revealed something of great importance to the New York kid. He had never dreamed that he did not have a complete monopoly of all possible trepidations. The cry of the grandee was that of a man who suddenly sees a poisonous snake. Thus the kid was able to understand swiftly that they were all human beings. They were unanimous in not wishing for too bloody combat. There was a sudden expression of the equality. He had vaguely believed that they were not going to evince much consideration for his dramatic development as an active factor. They even might be exasperated into an onslaught by it. Instead, they had respected his movement with a respect as great even as an ejaculation of fear and backward steps. Upon the instant he pounced forward and began to swear, unreeling great English oaths as thick as ropes, and lashing the faces of the Mexicans with them. He was bursting with rage, because these men had not previously confided to him that they were vulnerable. The whole thing had been an absurd imposition. He had been seduced into respectful alarm by the concave attitude of the grandee. And after all there had been an equality of emotion, an equality: he was furious. He wanted to take the serape of the grandee and swaddle him in it.

The Mexicans slunk back, their eyes burning wistfully. The kid took aim first at one and then at another. After they had achieved a certain distance they paused and drew up in a rank. They then resumed some of their old splendour of manner. A voice hailed him in a tone of cynical bravado as if it had come from between lips of smiling mockery. "Well, señor, it is finished?"

The kid scowled into the darkness, his revolver drooping at his side. After a moment he answered—"I am willing." He found it strange that he should be able to speak after this silence of years.

"Good-night, señor."

"Good-night."

When he turned to look at the Frisco kid he found him in his original position, his hand upon his hip. He was blinking in perplexity at the point from whence the Mexicans had vanished.

"Well," said the sober kid crossly, "are you ready to go home now?"

The Frisco kid said—"Where they gone?" His voice was undisturbed but inquisitive.

Benson suddenly propelled himself from his dreamful position against the wall. "Frishco kid's all right. He's drunk's fool and he's all right. But you New York kid, you're shober." He passed into a state of profound investigation. "Kid shober 'cause didn't go with us. Didn't go with us 'cause went to damn circus. Went to damn circus 'cause lose shakin' dice. Lose shakin' dice 'cause— what make lose shakin' dice, kid?"

The New York kid eyed the senile youth. "I don't know. The five white mice, maybe."

Benson puzzled so over this reply that he had to be held erect by his friends. Finally the Frisco kid said—"Let's go home."

Nothing had happened.

FLANAGAN AND HIS SHORT FILIBUSTERING ADVENTURE

I

"I have got twenty men at me back who will fight to the death," said the warrior to the old filibuster.

"And they can be blowed for all me," replied the old filibuster. "Common as sparrows. Cheap as cigarettes. Show me twenty men with steel clamps on their mouths, with holes in their heads where memory ought to be, and I want 'em. But twenty brave men merely? I'd rather have twenty brave onions."

Thereupon the warrior removed sadly, feeling that no salaams were paid to valour in these days of mechanical excellence.

Valour, in truth, is no bad thing to have when filibustering; but many medals are to be won by the man who knows not the meaning of "pow-wow," before or afterwards. Twenty brave men with tongues hung lightly may make trouble rise from the ground like smoke from grass, because of their subsequent fiery pride; whereas twenty cow-eyed villains who accept unrighteous and far-compelling kicks as they do the rain from heaven may halo the ultimate history of an expedition with gold, and plentifully bedeck their names, winning forty years of gratitude from patriots, simply by remaining silent. As for the cause, it may be only that they have no friends or other credulous furniture.

If it were not for the curse of the swinging tongue, it is surely to be said that the filibustering industry, flourishing now in the United States, would be pie. Under correct conditions, it is merely a matter of dealing with some little detectives whose skill at search is rated by those who pay them at a value of twelve or twenty dollars each week. It is nearly axiomatic that normally a twelve dollar per week detective cannot defeat a one hundred thousand dollar filibustering excursion. Against the criminal, the detective represents the commonwealth, but in this other case he represents his desire to show cause why his salary should be paid. He represents himself merely, and he counts no more than a grocer's clerk.

But the pride of the successful filibuster often smites him and his cause like an axe, and men who have not confided in their mothers go prone with him. It can make the dome of the Capitol tremble and incite the Senators to over-turning benches. It can increase the salaries of detectives who could not detect the location of a pain in the chest. It is a wonderful thing, this pride.

Filibustering was once such a simple game. It was managed blandly by gentle captains and smooth and undisturbed gentlemen, who at other times dealt in law, soap, medicine, and bananas. It was a great pity that the little cote of doves in Washington were obliged to rustle officially, and naval men were kept from their berths at night, and sundry Custom House people got wiggings, all because the returned adventurer pow-wowed in his pride. A yellow and red banner would have been long since smothered in a shame of defeat if a contract to filibuster had been let to some admirable organization like one of our trusts.

And yet the game is not obsolete. It is still played by the wise and the silent men whose names are not display-typed and blathered from one end of the country to the other.

There is in mind now a man who knew one side of a fence from the other side when he looked sharply. They were hunting for captains then to command the first vessels of what has since become a famous little fleet. One was recommended to this man, and he said, "Send him down to my office and I'll look him over." He was an attorney, and he liked to lean back in his chair, twirl a paper-knife, and let the other fellow talk.

The sea-faring man came and stood and appeared confounded. The attorney asked the terrible first question of the filibuster to the applicant. He said, "Why do you want to go?"

The captain reflected, changed his attitude three times, and decided ultimately that he didn't know. He seemed greatly ashamed. The attorney, looking at him, saw that he had eyes that resembled a lambkin's eyes.

"Glory?" said the attorney at last.

"No-o," said the captain.

"Pay?"

"No-o. Not that so much."

"Think they'll give you a land grant when they win out?"

"No; never thought."

"No glory; no immense pay; no land grant. What are you going for, then?"

"Well, I don't know," said the captain, with his glance on the floor and shifting his position again. "I don't know. I guess it's just for fun mostly." The attorney asked him out to have a drink.

When he stood on the bridge of his out-going steamer, the attorney saw him again. His shore meekness and uncertainty were gone. He was clear-eyed and strong, aroused like a mastiff at night. He took his cigar out of his mouth and yelled some sudden language at the deck.

This steamer had about her a quality of unholy mediæval disrepair, which is usually accounted the principal prerogative of the United States Revenue Marine. There is many a seaworthy ice-house if she were a good ship. She swashed through the seas as genially as an old wooden clock, burying her head under waves that came only like children at play, and, on board, it cost a ducking to go from anywhere to anywhere.

The captain had commanded vessels that shore-people thought were liners; but when a man gets the ant of desire-to-see-what-it's-like stirring in his heart, he will wallow out to sea in a pail. The thing surpasses a man's love for his sweetheart. The great tank-steamer *Thunder-Voice* had long been Flanagan's sweetheart, but he was far happier off Hatteras watching this wretched little portmanteau boom down the slant of a wave.

The crew scraped acquaintance one with another gradually. Each man came ultimately to ask his neighbour what particular turn of ill-fortune or inherited deviltry caused him to try this voyage. When one frank, bold man saw another frank, bold man aboard, he smiled, and they became friends. There was not a mind on board the ship that was not fastened to the dangers of the coast of Cuba, and taking wonder at this prospect and delight in it. Still, in jovial moments they termed each other accursed idiots.

At first there was some trouble in the engine-room, where there were many steel animals, for the most part painted red and in other places very shiny—bewildering, complex, incomprehensible to any one who don't care, usually thumping, thumping, thumping with the monotony of a snore.

It seems that this engine was as whimsical as a gas-meter. The chief engineer was a fine old fellow with a grey moustache, but the engine told him that it didn't intend to budge until it felt better. He came to the bridge and said, "The blamed old thing has laid down on us, sir."

"Who was on duty?" roared the captain.

"The second, sir."

"Why didn't he call you?"

"Don't know, sir." Later the stokers had occasion to thank the stars that they were not second engineers.

The *Foundling* was soundly thrashed by the waves for loitering while the captain and the engineers fought the obstinate machinery. During this wait on the sea, the first gloom came to the faces of the company. The ocean is wide, and a ship is a small place for the feet, and an ill ship is worriment. Even when she was again under way, the gloom was still upon the crew. From time to time men went to the engine-room doors, and looking down, wanted to ask questions of the chief engineer, who slowly prowled to and fro, and watched with careful eye his red-painted mysteries. No man wished to have a companion know that he was anxious, and so questions were caught at the lips. Perhaps none commented save the first mate, who remarked to the captain, "Wonder what the bally old thing will do, sir, when we're chased by a Spanish cruiser?"

214

The captain merely grinned. Later he looked over the side and said to himself with scorn, "Sixteen knots! sixteen knots! Sixteen hinges on the inner gates of Hades! Sixteen knots! Seven is her gait, and nine if you crack her up to it."

There may never be a captain whose crew can't sniff his misgivings. They scent it as a herd scents the menace far through the trees and over the ridges. A captain that does not know that he is on a foundering ship sometimes can take his men to tea and buttered toast twelve minutes before the disaster, but let him fret for a moment in the loneliness of his cabin, and in no time it affects the liver of a distant and sensitive seaman. Even as Flanagan reflected on the *Foundling*, viewing her as a filibuster, word arrived that a winter of discontent had come to the stoke-room.

The captain knew that it requires sky to give a man courage. He sent for a stoker and talked to him on the bridge. The man, standing under the sky, instantly and shamefacedly denied all knowledge of the business; nevertheless, a jaw had presently to be broken by a fist because the *Foundling* could only steam nine knots, and because the stoke-room has no sky, no wind, no bright horizon.

When the *Foundling* was somewhere off Savannah a blow came from the north-east, and the steamer, headed south-east, rolled like a boiling potato. The first mate was a fine officer, and so a wave crashed him into the deck-house and broke his arm. The cook was a good cook, and so the heave of the ship flung him heels over head with a pot of boiling water, and caused him to lose interest in everything save his legs. "By the piper," said Flanagan to himself, "this filibustering is no trick with cards."

Later there was more trouble in the stoke-room. All the stokers participated save the one with a broken jaw, who had become discouraged. The captain had an excellent chest development. When he went aft, roaring, it was plain that a man could beat carpets with a voice like that one.

II

One night the *Foundling* was off the southern coast of Florida, and running at half-speed towards the shore. The captain was on the bridge. "Four flashes at intervals of one minute," he said to himself, gazing steadfastly towards the beach. Suddenly a yellow eye opened in the black face of the night, and looked at the *Foundling* and closed again. The captain studied his watch and the shore. Three times more the eye opened and looked at the *Foundling* and closed again. The captain called to the vague figures on the deck below him. "Answer it." The flash of a light from the bow of the steamer displayed for a moment in golden colour the crests of the inriding waves.

The *Foundling* lay to and waited. The long swells rolled her gracefully, and her two stub masts reaching into the darkness swung with the solemnity of batons timing a dirge. When the ship had left Boston she had been as encrusted with ice as a Dakota stage-driver's beard, but now the gentle wind of Florida softly swayed the lock on the forehead of the coatless Flanagan, and he lit a new cigar without troubling to make a shield of his hands.

Finally a dark boat came plashing over the waves. As it came very near, the captain leaned forward and perceived that the men in her rowed like seamstresses, and at the same time a voice hailed him in bad English. "It's a dead sure connection," said he to himself.

At sea, to load two hundred thousand rounds of rifle ammunition, seven hundred and fifty rifles, two rapid-fire field guns with a hundred shells, forty bundles of machetes, and a hundred pounds of dynamite, from yawls, and by men who are not born stevedores, and in a heavy ground swell, and with the searchlight of a United States cruiser sometimes flashing like lightning in the sky to the southward, is no business for a Sunday-school class. When at last the *Foundling* was steaming for the open over the grey sea at dawn, there was not a man of the forty come aboard from the Florida shore, nor of the fifteen sailed from Boston, who was not glad, standing with his hair matted to his forehead with sweat, smiling at the broad wake of the *Foundling* and the dim streak on the horizon which was Florida.

But there is a point of the compass in these waters men call the north-east. When the strong winds come from that direction they kick up a turmoil that is not good for a *Foundling* stuffed with coals and war-stores. In the gale which came, this ship was no more than a drunken soldier.

The Cuban leader, standing on the bridge with the captain, was presently informed that of his men, thirty-nine out of a possible thirty-nine were sea-sick. And in truth they were sea-sick. There are degrees in this complaint, but that matter was waived between them. They were all sick to the limits. They strewed the deck in every posture of human anguish, and when the *Foundling* ducked and water came sluicing down from the bows, they let it sluice. They were satisfied if they could keep their heads clear of the wash; and if they could not keep their heads clear of the wash, they didn't care. Presently the *Foundling* swung her course to the south-east, and the waves pounded her broadside. The patriots were all ordered below decks, and there they howled and measured their misery one against another. All day the *Foundling* plopped and floundered over a blazing bright meadow of an ocean whereon the white foam was like flowers.

The captain on the bridge mused and studied the bare horizon. "Hell!" said he to himself, and the word was more in amazement than in indignation or sorrow. "Thirty-nine sea-sick passengers, the mate with a broken arm, a stoker with a broken jaw, the cook with a pair of scalded legs, and an engine likely to be taken with all these diseases, if not more! If I get back to a home port with a spoke of the wheel gripped in my hands, it'll be fair luck!"

There is a kind of corn-whisky bred in Florida which the natives declare is potent in the proportion of seven fights to a drink. Some of the Cuban volunteers had had the forethought to bring a small quantity of this whisky aboard with them, and being now in the fire-room and sea-sick, feeling that they would not care to drink liquor for two or three years to come, they gracefully tendered their portions to the stokers. The stokers accepted these gifts without avidity, but with a certain earnestness of manner.

As they were stokers, and toiling, the whirl of emotion was delayed, but it arrived ultimately, and with emphasis. One stoker called another stoker a weird name, and the latter, righteously inflamed at it, smote his mate with an iron shovel, and the man fell headlong over a heap of coal, which crashed gently while piece after piece rattled down upon the deck.

A third stoker was providently enraged at the scene, and assailed the second stoker. They fought for some moments, while the sea-sick Cubans sprawled on the deck watched with languid rolling glances the ferocity of this scuffle. One was so indifferent to the strategic importance of the space he occupied that he was kicked on the shins.

When the second engineer came to separating the combatants, he was sincere in his efforts, and he came near to disabling them for life.

The captain said, "I'll go down there and——" But the leader of the Cubans restrained him. "No, no," he cried, "you must not. We must treat them like children, very gently, all the time, you see, or else when we get back to a United States port they will—what you call? Spring? Yes, spring the whole business. We must—jolly them, you see?"

"You mean," said the captain thoughtfully, "they are likely to get mad, and give the expedition dead away when we reach port again unless we blarney them now?"

"Yes, yes," cried the Cuban leader, "unless we are so very gentle with them they will make many troubles afterwards for us in the newspapers and then in court."

"Well, but I won't have my crew——" began the captain.

"But you must," interrupted the Cuban, "you must. It is the only thing. You are like the captain of a pirate ship. You see? Only you can't throw them overboard like him. You see?"

"Hum," said the captain, "this here filibustering business has got a lot to it when you come to look it over."

He called the fighting stokers to the bridge, and the three came, meek and considerably battered. He was lecturing them soundly but sensibly, when he suddenly tripped a sentence and cried—"Here! Where's that other fellow? How does it come he wasn't in the fight?"

The row of stokers cried at once eagerly, "He's hurt, sir. He's got a broken jaw, sir."

"So he has; so he has," murmured the captain, much embarrassed.

And because of all these affairs, the *Foundling* steamed toward Cuba with its crew in a sling, if one may be allowed to speak in that way.

III

At night the *Foundling* approached the coast like a thief. Her lights were muffled, so that from the deck the sea shone with its own radiance, like the faint shimmer of some kinds of silk. The men on deck spoke in whispers, and even down in the fire-room the hidden stokers working before the blood-red furnace doors used no words and walked on tip-toe. The stars were out in the blue-velvet sky, and their light with the soft shine of the sea caused the coast to appear black as the side of a coffin. The surf boomed in low thunder on the distant beach.

The *Foundling*'s engines ceased their thumping for a time. She glided quietly forward until a bell chimed faintly in the engine-room. Then she paused with a flourish of phosphorescent waters.

"Give the signal," said the captain. Three times a flash of light went from the bow. There was a moment of waiting. Then an eye like the one on the coast of Florida opened and closed, opened and closed, opened and closed. The Cubans, grouped in a great shadow on deck, burst into a low chatter of delight. A hiss from their leader silenced them.

"Well?" said the captain.

"All right," said the leader.

At the giving of the word it was not apparent that any one on board of the *Foundling* had ever been sea-sick. The boats were lowered swiftly— too swiftly. Boxes of cartridges were dragged from the hold and passed over the side with a rapidity that made men in the boats exclaim against it. They were being bombarded. When a boat headed for shore its rowers pulled like madmen. The captain paced slowly to and fro on the bridge. In the engine-room the engineers stood at their station, and in the stoke-hold the firemen fidgeted silently around the furnace doors.

On the bridge Flanagan reflected. "Oh, I don't know!" he observed. "This filibustering business isn't so bad. Pretty soon it'll be off to sea again with nothing to do but some big lying when I get into port."

In one of the boats returning from shore came twelve Cuban officers, the greater number of them convalescing from wounds, while two or three of them had been ordered to America on commissions from the insurgents. The captain welcomed them, and assured them of a speedy and safe voyage.

Presently he went again to the bridge and scanned the horizon. The sea was lonely like the spaces amid the suns. The captain grinned and softly smote his chest. "It's dead easy," he said.

It was near the end of the cargo, and the men were breathing like spent horses, although their elation grew with each moment, when suddenly a voice spoke from the sky. It was not a loud voice, but the quality of it brought every man on deck to full stop and motionless, as if they had all been changed to wax. "Captain," said the man at the masthead, "there's a light to the west'ard, sir. Think it's a steamer, sir."

There was a still moment until the captain called, "Well, keep your eye on it now." Speaking to the deck, he said, "Go ahead with your unloading."

The second engineer went to the galley to borrow a tin cup. "Hear the news, second?" asked the cook. "Steamer coming up from the west'ard."

"Gee!" said the second engineer. In the engine-room he said to the chief, "Steamer coming up from the west'ard, sir." The chief engineer began to test various little machines with which his domain was decorated. Finally he addressed the stoke-room. "Boys, I want you to look sharp now. There's a steamer coming up to the west'ard."

"All right, sir," said the stoke-room.

From time to time the captain hailed the masthead. "How is she now?"

"Seems to be coming down on us pretty fast, sir."

The Cuban leader came anxiously to the captain. "Do you think we can save all the cargo? It is rather delicate business. No?"

"Go ahead," said Flanagan. "Fire away! I'll wait."

There continued the hurried shuffling of feet on deck, and the low cries of the men unloading the cargo. In the engine-room the chief and his assistant were staring at the gong. In the stoke-room the firemen breathed through their teeth. A shovel slipped from where it leaned against the side and banged on the floor. The stokers started and looked around quickly.

Climbing to the rail and holding on to a stay, the captain gazed westward. A light had raised out of the deep. After watching this light for a time he called to the Cuban leader. "Well, as soon as you're ready now, we might as well be skipping out."

Finally, the Cuban leader told him, "Well, this is the last load. As soon as the boats come back you can be off."

"Shan't wait for all the boats," said the captain. "That fellow is too close." As the second boat came aboard, the *Foundling* turned, and like a black shadow stole seaward to cross the bows of the oncoming steamer. "Waited about ten minutes too long," said the captain to himself.

Suddenly the light in the west vanished. "Hum!" said Flanagan, "he's up to some meanness." Every one outside of the engine-rooms was set on watch. The *Foundling*, going at full speed into the north-east, slashed a wonderful trail of blue silver on the dark bosom of the sea.

A man on deck cried out hurriedly, "There she is, sir." Many eyes searched the western gloom, and one after another the glances of the men found a tiny shadow on the deep with a line of white beneath it. "He couldn't be heading better if he had a line to us," said Flanagan.

There was a thin flash of red in the darkness. It was long and keen like a crimson rapier. A short, sharp report sounded, and then a shot whined swiftly in the air and blipped into the sea. The captain had been about to take a bite of plug tobacco at the beginning of this incident, and his arm was raised. He remained like a frozen figure while the shot whined, and then, as it blipped into the sea, his hand went to his mouth and he bit the plug. He looked wide-eyed at the shadow with its line of white.

The senior Cuban officer came hurriedly to the bridge. "It is no good to surrender," he cried. "They would only shoot or hang all of us."

There was another thin red flash and a report. A loud whirring noise passed over the ship.

"I'm not going to surrender," said the captain, hanging with both hands to the rail. He appeared like a man whose traditions of peace are clinched in his heart. He was as astonished as if his hat had turned into a dog. Presently he wheeled quickly and said—"What kind of a gun is that?"

"It is a one-pounder," cried the Cuban officer. "The boat is one of those little gunboats made from a yacht. You see?"

"Well, if it's only a yawl, he'll sink us in five more minutes," said Flanagan. For a moment he looked helplessly off at the horizon. His under-jaw hung low. But a moment later, something touched him, like a stiletto point of inspiration. He leaped to the pilothouse and roared at the man at the wheel. The *Foundling* sheered suddenly to starboard, made a clumsy turn, and Flanagan was bellowing through the tube to the engine-room before everybody discovered that the old basket was heading straight for the Spanish gun-boat. The ship lunged forward like a draught-horse on the gallop.

This strange manoeuvre by the *Foundling* first dealt consternation on board of the *Foundling*. Men instinctively crouched on the instant, and then swore their supreme oath, which was unheard by their own ears.

Later the manoeuvre of the *Foundling* dealt consternation on board of the gunboat. She had been going victoriously forward dim-eyed from the fury of her pursuit. Then this tall threatening shape had suddenly loomed over her like a giant apparition.

The people on board the *Foundling* heard panic shouts, hoarse orders. The little gunboat was paralyzed with astonishment.

Suddenly Flanagan yelled with rage and sprang for the wheel. The helmsman had turned his eyes away. As the captain whirled the wheel far to starboard he heard a crunch as the *Foundling*, lifted on a wave, smashed her shoulder against the gunboat, and he saw shooting past a little launch sort of a thing with men on her that ran this way and that way. The Cuban officers, joined by the cook and a seaman, emptied their revolvers into the surprised terror of the seas.

There was naturally no pursuit. Under comfortable speed the *Foundling* stood to the northwards.

The captain went to his berth chuckling. "There, by God!" he said. "There now!"

IV

When Flanagan came again on deck, the first mate, his arm in a sling, walked the bridge. Flanagan was smiling a wide smile. The bridge of the *Foundling* was dipping afar and then afar. With each lunge of the little steamer the water seethed and boomed alongside, and the spray dashed high and swiftly.

"Well," said Flanagan, inflating himself, "we've had a great deal of a time, and we've come through it all right, and thank Heaven it is all over."

The sky in the north-east was of a dull brick-red in tone, shaded here and there by black masses that billowed out in some fashion from the flat heavens.

"Look there," said the mate.

"Hum!" said the captain. "Looks like a blow, don't it?"

Later the surface of the water rippled and flickered in the preliminary wind. The sea had become the colour of lead. The swashing sound of the waves on the sides of the *Foundling* was now provided with some manner of ominous significance. The men's shouts were hoarse.

A squall struck the *Foundling* on her starboard quarter, and she leaned under the force of it as if she were never to return to the even keel. "I'll be glad when we get in," said the mate. "I'm going to quit then. I've got enough."

"Hell!" said the beaming Flanagan.

The steamer crawled on into the north-west. The white water, sweeping out from her, deadened the chug-chug-chug of the tired old engines.

Once, when the boat careened, she laid her shoulder flat on the sea and rested in that manner. The mate, looking down the bridge, which slanted more than a coal-shute, whistled softly to himself. Slowly, heavily, the *Foundling* arose to meet another sea.

At night waves thundered mightily on the bows of the steamer, and water lit with the beautiful phosphorescent glamour went boiling and howling along deck.

By good fortune the chief engineer crawled safely, but utterly drenched, to the galley for coffee. "Well, how goes it, chief?" said the cook, standing with his fat arms folded in order to prove that he could balance himself under any conditions.

The engineer shook his head dejectedly. "This old biscuit-box will never see port again. Why, she'll fall to pieces."

Finally at night the captain said, "Launch the boats." The Cubans hovered about him. "Is the ship going to sink?" The captain addressed them politely. "Gentlemen, we are in trouble, but all I ask of you is that you just do what I tell you, and no harm will come to anybody."

The mate directed the lowering of the first boat, and the men performed this task with all decency, like people at the side of a grave.

A young oiler came to the captain. "The chief sends word, sir, that the water is almost up to the fires."

"Keep at it as long as you can."

"Keep at it as long as we can, sir?"

Flanagan took the senior Cuban officer to the rail, and, as the steamer sheered high on a great sea, showed him a yellow dot on the horizon. It was smaller than a needle when its point is towards you.

"There," said the captain. The wind-driven spray was lashing his face. "That's Jupiter Light on the Florida coast. Put your men in the boat we've just launched, and the mate will take you to that light."

Afterwards Flanagan turned to the chief engineer. "We can never beach," said the old man. "The stokers have got to quit in a minute." Tears were in his eyes.

The *Foundling* was a wounded thing. She lay on the water with gasping engines, and each wave resembled her death-blow.

Now the way of a good ship on the sea is finer than sword-play. But this is when she is alive. If a time comes that the ship dies, then her way is the way of a floating old glove, and she has that much vim, spirit, buoyancy. At this time many men on the *Foundling* suddenly came to know that they were clinging to a corpse.

The captain went to the stoke-room, and what he saw as he swung down the companion suddenly turned him hesitant and dumb. Water was swirling to and fro with the roll of the ship, fuming greasily around half-strangled machinery that still attempted to perform its duty. Steam arose from the water, and through its clouds shone the red glare of the dying fires. As for the stokers, death might have been with silence in this room. One lay in his berth, his hands under his head, staring moodily at the wall. One sat near the foot of the companion, his face hidden in his arms. One leaned against the side and gazed at the snarling water as it rose, and its mad eddies among the machinery. In the unholy red light and grey mist of this stifling dim Inferno they were strange figures with their silence and their immobility. The wretched *Foundling* groaned deeply as she lifted, and groaned deeply as she sank into the trough, while hurried waves then thundered over her with the noise of landslides. The terrified machinery was making gestures.

But Flanagan took control of himself suddenly. Then he stirred the fire-room. The stillness had been so unearthly that he was not altogether inapprehensive of strange and grim deeds when he charged into them; but precisely as they had submitted to the sea so they submitted to Flanagan. For a moment they rolled their eyes like hurt cows, but they obeyed the Voice. The situation simply required a Voice.

225

When the captain returned to the deck the hue of this fire-room was in his mind, and then he understood doom and its weight and complexion.

When finally the *Foundling* sank she shifted and settled as calmly as an animal curls down in the bush grass. Away over the waves two bobbing boats paused to witness this quiet death. It was a slow manoeuvre, altogether without the pageantry of uproar, but it flashed pallor into the faces of all men who saw it, and they groaned when they said, "There she goes!" Suddenly the captain whirled and knocked his hand on the gunwale. He sobbed for a time, and then he sobbed and swore also.

There was a dance at the Imperial Inn. During the evening some irresponsible young men came from the beach bringing the statement that several boatloads of people had been perceived off shore. It was a charming dance, and none cared to take time to believe this tale. The fountain in the court-yard splashed softly, and couple after couple paraded through the aisles of palms, where lamps with red shades threw a rose light upon the gleaming leaves. The band played its waltzes slumberously, and its music came faintly to the people among the palms.

Sometimes a woman said—"Oh, it is not really true, is it, that there was a wreck out at sea?"

A man usually said—"No, of course not."

At last, however, a youth came violently from the beach. He was triumphant in manner. "They're out there," he cried. "A whole boat-load!" He received eager attention, and he told all that he supposed. His news destroyed the dance. After a time the band was playing beautifully to space. The guests had hurried to the beach. One little girl cried, "Oh, mamma, may I go too?" Being refused permission she pouted.

As they came from the shelter of the great hotel, the wind was blowing swiftly from the sea, and at intervals a breaker shone livid. The women shuddered, and their bending companions seized the opportunity to draw the cloaks closer.

"Oh, dear!" said a girl; "supposin' they were out there drowning while we were dancing!"

"Oh, nonsense!" said her younger brother; "that don't happen."

"Well, it might, you know, Roger. How can you tell?"

A man who was not her brother gazed at her then with profound admiration. Later, she complained of the damp sand, and, drawing back her skirts, looked ruefully at her little feet.

A mother's son was venturing too near to the water in his interest and excitement. Occasionally she cautioned and reproached him from the background.

Save for the white glare of the breakers, the sea was a great wind-crossed void. From the throng of charming women floated the perfume of many flowers. Later there floated to them a body with a calm face of an Irish type. The expedition of the *Foundling* will never be historic.

HORSES

Richardson pulled up his horse, and looked back over the trail where the crimson serape of his servant flamed amid the dusk of the mesquit. The hills in the west were carved into peaks, and were painted the most profound blue. Above them the sky was of that marvellous tone of green—like still, sun-shot water—which people denounce in pictures.

José was muffled deep in his blanket, and his great toppling sombrero was drawn low over his brow. He shadowed his master along the dimming trail in the fashion of an assassin. A cold wind of the impending night swept over the wilderness of mesquit.

"Man," said Richardson in lame Mexican as the servant drew near, "I want eat! I want sleep! Understand—no? Quickly! Understand?"

"Si, señor," said José, nodding. He stretched one arm out of his blanket and pointed a yellow finger into the gloom. "Over there, small village. Si, señor."

They rode forward again. Once the American's horse shied and breathed quiveringly at something which he saw or imagined in the darkness, and the rider drew a steady, patient rein, and leaned over to speak tenderly as if he were addressing a frightened woman. The sky had faded to white over the mountains, and the plain was a vast, pointless ocean of black.

Suddenly some low houses appeared squatting amid the bushes. The horsemen rode into a hollow until the houses rose against the sombre sundown sky, and then up a small hillock, causing these habitations to sink like boats in the sea of shadow.

A beam of red firelight fell across the trail. Richardson sat sleepily on his horse while his servant quarrelled with somebody—a mere voice in the gloom—over the price of bed and board. The houses about him were for the most part like tombs in their whiteness and silence, but there were scudding black figures that seemed interested in his arrival.

José came at last to the horses' heads, and the American slid stiffly from his seat. He muttered a greeting, as with his spurred feet he clicked into the adobe house that confronted him. The brown stolid face of a woman shone in the light of the fire. He seated himself on the earthen floor and blinked drowsily at the blaze. He was aware that the woman was clinking earthenware, and hieing here and everywhere in the manoeuvres of the housewife. From a dark corner there came the sound of two or three snores twining together.

The woman handed him a bowl of tortillas. She was a submissive creature, timid and large-eyed. She gazed at his enormous silver spurs, his large and impressive revolver, with the interest and admiration of the highly-privileged cat of the adage. When he ate, she seemed transfixed off there in the gloom, her white teeth shining.

José entered, staggering under two Mexican saddles, large enough for building-sites. Richardson decided to smoke a cigarette, and then changed his mind. It would be much finer to go to sleep. His blanket hung over his left shoulder, furled into a long pipe of cloth, according to the Mexican fashion. By doffing his sombrero, unfastening his spurs and his revolver belt, he made himself ready for the slow, blissful twist into the blanket. Like a cautious man he lay close to the wall, and all his property was very near his hand.

The mesquit brush burned long. José threw two gigantic wings of shadow as he flapped his blanket about him—first across his chest under his arms, and then around his neck and across his chest again—this time over his arms, with the end tossed on his right shoulder. A Mexican thus snugly enveloped can nevertheless free his fighting arm in a beautifully brisk way, merely shrugging his shoulder as he grabs for the weapon at his belt. (They always wear their serapes in this manner.)

The firelight smothered the rays which, streaming from a moon as large as a drum-head, were struggling at the open door. Richardson heard from the plain the fine, rhythmical trample of the hoofs of hurried horses. He went to sleep wondering who rode so fast and so late. And in the deep silence the pale rays of the moon must have prevailed against the red spears of the fire until the room was slowly flooded to its middle with a rectangle of silver light.

Richardson was awakened by the sound of a guitar. It was badly played—in this land of Mexico, from which the romance of the instrument ascends to us like a perfume. The guitar was groaning and whining like a badgered soul. A noise of scuffling feet accompanied the music. Sometimes laughter arose, and often the voices of men saying bitter things to each other, but always the guitar cried on, the treble sounding as if some one were beating iron, and the bass humming like bees. "Damn it—they're having a dance," he muttered, fretfully. He heard two men quarrelling in short, sharp words, like pistol shots; they were calling each other worse names than common people know in other countries. He wondered why the noise was so loud. Raising his head from his saddle pillow, he saw, with the help of the valiant moonbeams, a blanket hanging flat against the wall at the further end of the room. Being of opinion that it concealed a door, and remembering that Mexican drink made men very drunk, he pulled his revolver closer to him and prepared for sudden disaster.

Richardson was dreaming of his far and beloved north.

"Well, I would kill him, then!"

"No, you must not!"

"Yes, I will kill him! Listen! I will ask this American beast for his beautiful pistol and spurs and money and saddle, and if he will not give them—you will see!"

"But these Americans—they are a strange people. Look out, señor."

Then twenty voices took part in the discussion. They rose in quavering shrillness, as from men badly drunk. Richardson felt the skin draw tight around his mouth, and his knee-joints turned to bread. He slowly came to a sitting posture, glaring at the motionless blanket at the far end of the room. This stiff and mechanical movement, accomplished entirely by the muscles of the waist, must have looked like the rising of a corpse in the wan moonlight, which gave everything a hue of the grave.

My friend, take my advice and never be executed by a hangman who doesn't talk the English language. It, or anything that resembles it, is the most difficult of deaths. The tumultuous emotions of Richardson's terror destroyed that slow and careful process of thought by means of which he understood Mexican. Then he used his instinctive comprehension of the first and universal language, which is tone. Still, it is disheartening not to be able to understand the detail of threats against the blood of your body.

Suddenly, the clamour of voices ceased. There was a silence—a silence of decision. The blanket was flung aside, and the red light of a torch flared into the room. It was held high by a fat, round-faced Mexican, whose little snake-like moustache was as black as his eyes, and whose eyes were black as jet. He was insane with the wild rage of a man whose liquor is dully burning at his brain. Five or six of his fellows crowded after him. The guitar, which had been thrummed doggedly during the time of the high words, now suddenly stopped. They contemplated each other. Richardson sat very straight and still, his right hand lost in his blanket. The Mexicans jostled in the light of the torch, their eyes blinking and glittering.

The fat one posed in the manner of a grandee. Presently his hand dropped to his belt, and from his lips there spun an epithet—a hideous word which often foreshadows knife-blows, a word peculiarly of Mexico, where people have to dig deep to find an insult that has not lost its savour. The American did not move. He was staring at the fat Mexican with a strange fixedness of gaze, not fearful, not dauntless, not anything that could be interpreted. He simply stared.

The fat Mexican must have been disconcerted, for he continued to pose as a grandee, with more and more sublimity, until it would have been easy for him to have fallen over backward. His companions were swaying very drunkenly. They still blinked their little beady eyes at Richardson. Ah, well, sirs, here was a mystery! At the approach of their menacing company, why did not this American cry out and turn pale, or run, or pray them mercy? The animal merely sat still, and stared, and waited for them to begin. Well, evidently he was a great fighter! Or perhaps he was an idiot? Indeed, this was an embarrassing situation, for who was going forward to discover whether he was a great fighter or an idiot?

To Richardson, whose nerves were tingling and twitching like live wires, and whose heart jolted inside him, this pause was a long horror; and for these men, who could so frighten him, there began to swell in him a fierce hatred—a hatred that made him long to be capable of fighting all of them, a hatred that made him capable of fighting all of them. A 44-calibre revolver can make a hole large enough for little boys to shoot marbles through; and there was a certain fat Mexican with a moustache like a snake who came extremely near to have eaten his last tomale merely because he frightened a man too much.

José had slept the first part of the night in his fashion, his body hunched into a heap, his legs crooked, his head touching his knees. Shadows had obscured him from the sight of the invaders. At this point he arose, and began to prowl quakingly over toward Richardson, as if he meant to hide behind him.

Of a sudden the fat Mexican gave a howl of glee. José had come within the torch's circle of light. With roars of ferocity the whole group of Mexicans pounced on the American's servant. He shrank shuddering away from them, beseeching by every device of word and gesture. They pushed him this way and that. They beat him with their fists. They stung him with their curses. As he grovelled on his knees, the fat Mexican took him by the throat and said—"I am going to kill you!" And continually they turned their eyes to see if they were to succeed in causing the initial demonstration by the American. But he looked on impassively. Under the blanket his fingers were clenched, as iron, upon the handle of his revolver.

Here suddenly two brilliant clashing chords from the guitar were heard, and a woman's voice, full of laughter and confidence, cried from without—"Hello! hello! Where are you?" The lurching company of Mexicans instantly paused and looked at the ground. One said, as he stood with his legs wide apart in order to balance himself—"It is the girls. They have come!" He screamed in answer to the question of the woman—"Here!" And without waiting he started on a pilgrimage toward the blanket-covered door. One could now hear a number of female voices giggling and chattering.

Two other Mexicans said—"Yes, it is the girls! Yes!" They also started quietly away. Even the fat Mexican's ferocity seemed to be affected. He looked uncertainly at the still immovable American. Two of his friends grasped him gaily—"Come, the girls are here! Come!" He cast another glower at Richardson. "But this———," he began. Laughing, his comrades hustled him toward the door. On its threshold, and holding back the blanket, with one hand, he turned his yellow face with a last challenging glare toward the American. José, bewailing his state in little sobs of utter despair and woe, crept to Richardson and huddled near his knee. Then the cries of the Mexicans meeting the girls were heard, and the guitar burst out in joyous humming.

The moon clouded, and but a faint square of light fell through the open main door of the house. The coals of the fire were silent, save for occasional sputters. Richardson did not change his position. He remained staring at the blanket which hid the strategic door in the far end. At his knees José was arguing, in a low, aggrieved tone, with the saints. Without, the Mexicans laughed and danced, and—it would appear from the sound—drank more.

In the stillness and the night Richardson sat wondering if some serpent-like Mexican were sliding towards him in the darkness, and if the first thing he knew of it would be the deadly sting of a knife. "Sssh," he whispered, to José. He drew his revolver from under the blanket, and held it on his leg. The blanket over the door fascinated him. It was a vague form, black and unmoving. Through the opening it shielded were to come, probably, threats, death. Sometimes he thought he saw it move. As grim white sheets, the black and silver of coffins, all the panoply of death, affect us, because of that which they hide, so this blanket, dangling before a hole in an adobe wall, was to Richardson a horrible emblem, and a horrible thing in itself. In his present mood he could not have been brought to touch it with his finger.

The celebrating Mexicans occasionally howled in song. The guitarist played with speed and enthusiasm. Richardson longed to run. But in this vibrating and threatening gloom his terror convinced him that a move on his part would be a signal for the pounce of death. José, crouching abjectly, mumbled now and again. Slowly, and ponderous as stars, the minutes went.

Suddenly Richardson thrilled and started. His breath for a moment left him. In sleep his nerveless fingers had allowed his revolver to fall and clang upon the hard floor. He grabbed it up hastily, and his glance swept apprehensively over the room. A chill blue light of dawn was in the place. Every outline was slowly growing; detail was following detail. The dread blanket did not move. The riotous company had gone or fallen silent. He felt the effect of this cold dawn in his blood. The candour of breaking day brought his nerve. He touched José. "Come," he said. His servant lifted his lined yellow face, and comprehended. Richardson buckled on his spurs and strode up; José obediently lifted the two great saddles. Richardson held two bridles and a blanket on his left arm; in his right hand he had his revolver. They sneaked toward the door.

The man who said that spurs jingled was insane. Spurs have a mellow clash—clash—clash. Walking in spurs—notably Mexican spurs—you remind yourself vaguely of a telegraphic linesman. Richardson was inexpressibly shocked when he came to walk. He sounded to himself like a pair of cymbals. He would have known of this if he had reflected; but then, he was escaping, not reflecting. He made a gesture of despair, and from under the two saddles José tried to make one of hopeless horror. Richardson stooped, and with shaking fingers unfastened the spurs. Taking them in his left hand, he picked up his revolver, and they slunk on toward the door. On the threshold he looked back. In a corner he saw, watching him with large eyes, the Indian man and woman who had been his hosts. Throughout the night they had made no sign, and now they neither spoke nor moved. Yet Richardson thought he detected meek satisfaction at his departure.

The street was still and deserted. In the eastern sky there was a lemon-coloured patch. José had picketed the horses at the side of the house. As the two men came round the corner Richardson's beast set up a whinny of welcome. The little horse had heard them coming. He stood facing them, his ears cocked forward, his eyes bright with welcome.

Richardson made a frantic gesture, but the horse, in his happiness at the appearance of his friends, whinnied with enthusiasm. The American felt that he could have strangled his well-beloved steed. Upon the threshold of safety, he was being betrayed by his horse, his friend! He felt the same hate that he would have felt for a dragon. And yet, as he glanced wildly about him, he could see nothing stirring in the street, nothing at the doors of the tomb-like houses.

José had his own saddle-girth and both bridles buckled in a moment. He curled the picket-ropes with a few sweeps of his arm. The American's fingers, however, were shaking so that he could hardly buckle the girth. His hands were in invisible mittens. He was wondering, calculating, hoping about his horse. He knew the little animal's willingness and courage under all circumstances up to this time; but then—here it was different. Who could tell if some wretched instance of equine perversity was not about to develop? Maybe the little fellow would not feel like smoking over the plain at express speed this morning, and so he would rebel, and kick, and be wicked. Maybe he would be without feeling of interest, and run listlessly. All riders who have had to hurry in the saddle know what it is to be on a horse who does not understand the dramatic situation. Riding a lame sheep is bliss to it. Richardson, fumbling furiously at the girth, thought of these things.

Presently he had it fastened. He swung into the saddle, and as he did so his horse made a mad jump forward. The spurs of José scratched and tore the flanks of his great black beast, and side by side the two horses raced down the village street. The American heard his horse breathe a quivering sigh of excitement. Those four feet skimmed. They were as light as fairy puff balls. The houses glided past in a moment, and the great, clear, silent plain appeared like a pale blue sea of mist and wet bushes. Above the mountains the colours of the sunlight were like the first tones, the opening chords of the mighty hymn of the morning.

The American looked down at his horse. He felt in his heart the first thrill of confidence. The little animal, unurged and quite tranquil, moving his ears this way and that way with an air of interest in the scenery, was nevertheless bounding into the eye of the breaking day with the speed of a frightened antelope. Richardson, looking down, saw the long, fine reach of forelimb as steady as steel machinery. As the ground reeled past, the long, dried grasses hissed, and cactus plants were dull blurs. A wind whirled the horse's mane over his rider's bridle hand.

José's profile was lined against the pale sky. It was as that of a man who swims alone in an ocean. His eyes glinted like metal, fastened on some unknown point ahead of him, some fabulous place of safety. Occasionally his mouth puckered in a little unheard cry; and his legs, bended back, worked spasmodically as his spurred heels sliced his charger's sides.

Richardson consulted the gloom in the west for signs of a hard-riding, yelling cavalcade. He knew that, whereas his friends the enemy had not attacked him when he had sat still and with apparent calmness confronted them, they would take furiously after him now that he had run from them—now that he had confessed himself the weaker. Their valour would grow like weeds in the spring, and upon discovering his escape they would ride forth dauntless warriors. Sometimes he was sure he saw them. Sometimes he was sure he heard them. Continually looking backward over his shoulder, he studied the purple expanses where the night was marching away. José rolled and shuddered in his saddle, persistently disturbing the stride of the black horse, fretting and worrying him until the white foam flew, and the great shoulders shone like satin from the sweat.

At last, Richardson drew his horse carefully down to a walk. José wished to rush insanely on, but the American spoke to him sternly. As the two paced forward side by side, Richardson's little horse thrust over his soft nose and inquired into the black's condition.

Riding with José was like riding with a corpse. His face resembled a cast in lead. Sometimes he swung forward and almost pitched from his seat. Richardson was too frightened himself to do anything but hate this man for his fear. Finally, he issued a mandate which nearly caused José's eyes to slide out of his head and fall to the ground, like two coins:—"Ride behind me—about fifty paces."

"Señor——" stuttered the servant. "Go," cried the American furiously. He glared at the other and laid his hand on his revolver. José looked at his master wildly. He made a piteous gesture. Then slowly he fell back, watching the hard face of the American for a sign of mercy. But Richardson had resolved in his rage that at any rate he was going to use the eyes and ears of extreme fear to detect the approach of danger; so he established his panic-stricken servant as a sort of outpost.

As they proceeded, he was obliged to watch sharply to see that the servant did not slink forward and join him. When José made beseeching circles in the air with his arm, he replied by menacingly gripping his revolver. José had a revolver too; nevertheless it was very clear in his mind that the revolver was distinctly an American weapon. He had been educated in the Rio Grande country.

Richardson lost the trail once. He was recalled to it by the loud sobs of his servant.

Then at last José came clattering forward, gesticulating and wailing. The little horse sprang to the shoulder of the black. They were off.

Richardson, again looking backward, could see a slanting flare of dust on the whitening plain. He thought that he could detect small moving figures in it.

José's moans and cries amounted to a university course in theology. They broke continually from his quivering lips. His spurs were as motors. They forced the black horse over the plain in great headlong leaps. But under Richardson there was a little insignificant rat-coloured beast who was running apparently with almost as much effort as it takes a bronze statue to stand still. The ground seemed merely something to be touched from time to time with hoofs that were as light as blown leaves. Occasionally Richardson lay back and pulled stoutly at the bridle to keep from abandoning his servant. José harried at his horse's mouth, flopped about in the saddle, and made his two heels beat like flails. The black ran like a horse in despair.

Crimson serapes in the distance resemble drops of blood on the great cloth of plain. Richardson began to dream of all possible chances. Although quite a humane man, he did not once think of his servant. José being a Mexican, it was natural that he should be killed in Mexico; but for himself, a New Yorker——! He remembered all the tales of such races for life, and he thought them badly written.

The great black horse was growing indifferent. The jabs of José's spurs no longer caused him to bound forward in wild leaps of pain. José had at last succeeded in teaching him that spurring was to be expected, speed or no speed, and now he took the pain of it dully and stolidly, as an animal who finds that doing his best gains him no respite. José was turned into a raving maniac. He bellowed and screamed, working his arms and his heels like one in a fit. He resembled a man on a sinking ship, who appeals to the ship. Richardson, too, cried madly to the black horse. The spirit of the horse responded to these calls, and quivering and breathing heavily he made a great effort, a sort of a final rush, not for himself apparently, but because he understood that his life's sacrifice, perhaps, had been invoked by these two men who cried to him in the universal tongue. Richardson had no sense of appreciation at this time—he was too frightened; but often now he remembers a certain black horse.

From the rear could be heard a yelling, and once a shot was fired—in the air, evidently. Richardson moaned as he looked back. He kept his hand on his revolver. He tried to imagine the brief tumult of his capture—the flurry of dust from the hoofs of horses pulled suddenly to their haunches, the shrill, biting curses of the men, the ring of the shots, his own last contortion. He wondered, too, if he could not somehow manage to pelt that fat Mexican, just to cure his abominable egotism.

It was José, the terror-stricken, who at last discovered safety. Suddenly he gave a howl of delight and astonished his horse into a new burst of speed. They were on a little ridge at the time, and the American at the top of it saw his servant gallop down the slope and into the arms, so to speak, of a small column of horsemen in grey and silver clothes. In the dim light of the early morning they were as vague as shadows, but Richardson knew them at once for a detachment of Rurales, that crack cavalry corps of the Mexican army which polices the plain so zealously, being of themselves the law and the arm of it—a fierce and swift-moving body that knows little of prevention but much of vengeance. They drew up suddenly, and the rows of great silver-trimmed sombreros bobbed in surprise.

Richardson saw José throw himself from his horse and begin to jabber at the leader. When he arrived he found that his servant had already outlined the entire situation, and was then engaged in describing him, Richardson, as an American señor of vast wealth, who was the friend of almost every governmental potentate within two hundred miles. This seemed profoundly to impress the officer. He bowed gravely to Richardson and smiled significantly at his men, who unslung their carbines.

The little ridge hid the pursuers from view, but the rapid thud of their horses' feet could be heard. Occasionally they yelled and called to each other. Then at last they swept over the brow of the hill, a wild mob of almost fifty drunken horsemen. When they discerned the pale-uniformed Rurales, they were sailing down the slope at top speed.

If toboggans half-way down a hill should suddenly make up their minds to turn round and go back, there would be an effect something like that produced by the drunken horsemen. Richardson saw the Rurales serenely swing their carbines forward, and, peculiar-minded person that he was, felt his heart leap into his throat at the prospective volley. But the officer rode forward alone.

It appeared that the man who owned the best horse in this astonished company was the fat Mexican with the snaky moustache, and, in consequence, this gentleman was quite a distance in the van. He tried to pull up, wheel his horse, and scuttle back over the hill as some of his companions had done, but the officer called to him in a voice harsh with rage. "——!" howled the officer. "This señor is my friend, the friend of my friends. Do you dare pursue him, ——?——!——!——!——!" These dashes represent terrible names, all different, used by the officer.

The fat Mexican simply grovelled on his horse's neck. His face was green: it could be seen that he expected death. The officer stormed with magnificent intensity: "——!——!——!" Finally he sprang from his saddle, and, running to the fat Mexican's side, yelled—"Go!" and kicked the horse in the belly with all his might. The animal gave a mighty leap into the air, and the fat Mexican, with one wretched glance at the contemplative Rurales, aimed his steed for the top of the ridge. Richardson gulped again in expectation of a volley, for— it is said—this is a favourite method for disposing of objectionable people.

The fat, green Mexican also thought that he was to be killed on the run, from the miserable look he cast at the troops. Nevertheless, he was allowed to vanish in a cloud of yellow dust at the ridge-top.

José was exultant, defiant, and, oh! bristling with courage. The black horse was drooping sadly, his nose to the ground. Richardson's little animal, with his ears bent forward, was staring at the horses of the Rurales as if in an intense study. Richardson longed for speech, but he could only bend forward and pat the shining, silken shoulders. The little horse turned his head and looked back gravely.

DEATH AND THE CHILD

I

The peasants who were streaming down the mountain trail had in their sharp terror evidently lost their ability to count. The cattle and the huge round bundles seemed to suffice to the minds of the crowd if there were now two in each case where there had been three. This brown stream poured on with a constant wastage of goods and beasts. A goat fell behind to scout the dried grass and its owner, howling, flogging his donkeys, passed far ahead. A colt, suddenly frightened, made a stumbling charge up the hill-side. The expenditure was always profligate and always unnamed, unnoted. It was as if fear was a river, and this horde had simply been caught in the torrent, man tumbling over beast, beast over man, as helpless in it as the logs that fall and shoulder grindingly through the gorges of a lumber country. It was a freshet that might sear the face of the tall quiet mountain; it might draw a livid line across the land, this downpour of fear with a thousand homes adrift in the current—men, women, babes, animals. From it there arose a constant babble of tongues, shrill, broken, and sometimes choking as from men drowning. Many made gestures, painting their agonies on the air with fingers that twirled swiftly.

The blue bay with its pointed ships and the white town lay below them, distant, flat, serene. There was upon this vista a peace that a bird knows when high in the air it surveys the world, a great calm thing rolling noiselessly toward the end of the mystery. Here on the height one felt the existence of the universe scornfully defining the pain in ten thousand minds. The sky was an arch of stolid sapphire. Even to the mountains raising their mighty shapes from the valley, this headlong rush of the fugitives was too minute. The sea, the sky, and the hills combined in their grandeur to term this misery inconsequent. Then too it sometimes happened that a face seen as it passed on the flood reflected curiously the spirit of them all and still more. One saw then a woman of the opinion of the vaults above the clouds. When a child cried it cried always because of some adjacent misfortune, some discomfort of a pack-saddle or rudeness of an encircling arm. In the dismal melody of this flight there were often sounding chords of apathy. Into these preoccupied countenances, one felt that needles could be thrust without purchasing a scream. The trail wound here and there as the sheep had willed in the making of it.

Although this throng seemed to prove that the whole of humanity was fleeing in one direction—with every tie severed that binds us to the soil—a young man was walking rapidly up the mountain, hastening to a side of the path from time to time to avoid some particularly wide rush of people and cattle. He looked at everything in agitation and pity. Frequently he called admonitions to maniacal fugitives, and at other moments he exchanged strange stares with the imperturbable ones. They seemed to him to wear merely the expressions of so many boulders rolling down the hill. He exhibited wonder and awe with his pitying glances.

Turning once toward the rear, he saw a man in the uniform of a lieutenant of infantry marching the same way. He waited then, subconsciously elate at a prospect of being able to make into words the emotion which heretofore had only been expressed in the flash of eyes and sensitive movements of his flexible mouth. He spoke to the officer in rapid French, waving his arms wildly, and often pointing with a dramatic finger. "Ah, this is too cruel, too cruel, too cruel. Is it not? I did not think it would be as bad as this. I did not think—God's mercy—I did not think at all. And yet I am a Greek. Or at least my father was a Greek. I did not come here to fight. I am really a correspondent, you see? I was to write for an Italian paper. I have been educated in Italy. I have spent nearly all my life in Italy. At the schools and universities! I knew nothing of war! I was a student—a student. I came here merely because my father was a Greek, and for his sake I thought of Greece—I loved Greece. But I did not dream——"

He paused, breathing heavily. His eyes glistened from that soft overflow which comes on occasion to the glance of a young woman. Eager, passionate, profoundly moved, his first words, while facing the procession of fugitives, had been an active definition of his own dimension, his personal relation to men, geography, life. Throughout he had preserved the fiery dignity of a tragedian.

The officer's manner at once deferred to this outburst. "Yes," he said, polite but mournful, "these poor people! These poor people! I do not know what is to become of these poor people."

The young man declaimed again. "I had no dream—I had no dream that it would be like this! This is too cruel! Too cruel! Now I want to be a soldier. Now I want to fight. Now I want to do battle for the land of my father." He made a sweeping gesture into the north-west.

The officer was also a young man, but he was very bronzed and steady. Above his high military collar of crimson cloth with one silver star upon it, appeared a profile stern, quiet, and confident, respecting fate, fearing only opinion. His clothes were covered with dust; the only bright spot was the flame of the crimson collar. At the violent cries of his companion he smiled as if to himself, meanwhile keeping his eyes fixed in a glance ahead.

From a land toward which their faces were bent came a continuous boom of artillery fire. It was sounding in regular measures like the beating of a colossal clock, a clock that was counting the seconds in the lives of the stars, and men had time to die between the ticks. Solemn, oracular, inexorable, the great seconds tolled over the hills as if God fronted this dial rimmed by the horizon. The soldier and the correspondent found themselves silent. The latter in particular was sunk in a great mournfulness, as if he had resolved willy-nilly to swing to the bottom of the abyss where dwell secrets of his kind, and had learned beforehand that all to be met there was cruelty and hopelessness. A strap of his bright new leather leggings came unfastened, and he bowed over it slowly, impressively, as one bending over the grave of a child.

Then suddenly, the reverberations mingled until one could not separate an explosion from another, and into the hubbub came the drawling sound of a leisurely musketry fire. Instantly, for some reason of cadence, the noise was irritating, silly, infantile. This uproar was childish. It forced the nerves to object, to protest against this racket which was as idle as the din of a lad with a drum.

243

The lieutenant lifted his finger and pointed. He spoke in vexed tones, as if he held the other man personally responsible for the noise. "Well, there!" he said. "If you wish for war you now have an opportunity magnificent."

The correspondent raised himself upon his toes. He tapped his chest with gloomy pride. "Yes! There is war! There is the war I wish to enter. I fling myself in. I am a Greek, a Greek, you understand. I wish to fight for my country. You know the way. Lead me. I offer myself." Struck by a sudden thought he brought a case from his pocket, and extracting a card handed it to the officer with a bow. "My name is Peza," he said simply.

A strange smile passed over the soldier's face. There was pity and pride— the vanity of experience—and contempt in it. "Very well," he said, returning the bow. "If my company is in the middle of the fight I shall be glad for the honour of your companionship. If my company is not in the middle of the fight—I will make other arrangements for you."

Peza bowed once more, very stiffly, and correctly spoke his thanks. On the edge of what he took to be a great venture toward death, he discovered that he was annoyed at something in the lieutenant's tone. Things immediately assumed new and extraordinary proportions. The battle, the great carnival of woe, was sunk at once to an equation with a vexation by a stranger. He wanted to ask the lieutenant what was his meaning. He bowed again majestically; the lieutenant bowed. They flung a shadow of manners, of capering tinsel ceremony across a land that groaned, and it satisfied something within themselves completely.

In the meantime, the river of fleeing villagers had changed to simply a last dropping of belated creatures, who fled past stammering and flinging their hands high. The two men had come to the top of the great hill. Before them was a green plain as level as an inland sea. It swept northward, and merged finally into a length of silvery mist. Upon the near part of this plain, and upon two grey treeless mountains at the side of it, were little black lines from which floated slanting sheets of smoke. It was not a battle to the nerves. One could survey it with equanimity, as if it were a tea-table; but upon Peza's mind it struck a loud clanging blow. It was war. Edified, aghast, triumphant, he paused suddenly, his lips apart. He remembered the pageants of carnage that had marched through the dreams of his childhood. Love he knew that he had confronted, alone, isolated, wondering, an individual, an atom taking the hand of a titanic principle. But, like the faintest breeze on his forehead, he felt here the vibration from the hearts of forty thousand men.

The lieutenant's nostrils were moving. "I must go at once," he said. "I must go at once."

"I will go with you wherever you go," shouted Peza loudly.

A primitive track wound down the side of the mountain, and in their rush they bounded from here to there, choosing risks which in the ordinary caution of man would surely have seemed of remarkable danger. The ardour of the correspondent surpassed the full energy of the soldier. Several times he turned and shouted, "Come on! Come on!"

At the foot of the path they came to a wide road, which extended toward the battle in a yellow and straight line. Some men were trudging wearily to the rear. They were without rifles; their clumsy uniforms were dirty and all awry. They turned eyes dully aglow with fever upon the pair striding toward the battle. Others were bandaged with the triangular kerchief upon which one could still see through bloodstains the little explanatory pictures illustrating the ways to bind various wounds. "Fig. 1."—"Fig. 2."—"Fig. 7." Mingled with the pacing soldiers were peasants, indifferent, capable of smiling, gibbering about the battle, which was to them an ulterior drama. A man was leading a string of three donkeys to the rear, and at intervals he was accosted by wounded or fevered soldiers, from whom he defended his animals with ape-like cries and mad gesticulation. After much chattering they usually subsided gloomily, and allowed him to go with his sleek little beasts unburdened. Finally he encountered a soldier who walked slowly with the assistance of a staff. His head was bound with a wide bandage, grimey from blood and mud. He made application to the peasant, and immediately they were involved in a hideous Levantine discussion. The peasant whined and clamoured, sometimes spitting like a kitten. The wounded soldier jawed on thunderously, his great hands stretched in claw-like graspings over the peasant's head. Once he raised his staff and made threat with it. Then suddenly the row was at an end. The other sick men saw their comrade mount the leading donkey and at once begin to drum with his heels. None attempted to gain the backs of the remaining animals. They gazed after them dully. Finally they saw the caravan outlined for a moment against the sky. The soldier was still waving his arms passionately, having it out with the peasant.

Peza was alive with despair for these men who looked at him with such doleful, quiet eyes. "Ah, my God!" he cried to the lieutenant, "these poor souls! These poor souls!"

The officer faced about angrily. "If you are coming with me there is no time for this." Peza obeyed instantly and with a sudden meekness. In the moment some portion of egotism left him, and he modestly wondered if the universe took cognizance of him to an important degree. This theatre for slaughter, built by the inscrutable needs of the earth, was an enormous affair, and he reflected that the accidental destruction of an individual, Peza by name, would perhaps be nothing at all.

With the lieutenant he was soon walking along behind a series of little crescent-shape trenches, in which were soldiers, tranquilly interested, gossiping with the hum of a tea-party. Although these men were not at this time under fire, he concluded that they were fabulously brave. Else they would not be so comfortable, so at home in their sticky brown trenches. They were certain to be heavily attacked before the day was old. The universities had not taught him to understand this attitude.

At the passing of the young man in very nice tweed, with his new leggings, his new white helmet, his new field-glass case, his new revolver holster, the soiled soldiers turned with the same curiosity which a being in strange garb meets at the corners of streets. He might as well have been promenading a populous avenue. The soldiers volubly discussed his identity.

To Peza there was something awful in the absolute familiarity of each tone, expression, gesture. These men, menaced with battle, displayed the curiosity of the café. Then, on the verge of his great encounter toward death, he found himself extremely embarrassed, composing his face with difficulty, wondering what to do with his hands, like a gawk at a levée.

He felt ridiculous, and also he felt awed, aghast, at these men who could turn their faces from the ominous front and debate his clothes, his business. There was an element which was new born into his theory of war. He was not averse to the brisk pace at which the lieutenant moved along the line.

The roar of fighting was always in Peza's ears. It came from some short hills ahead and to the left. The road curved suddenly and entered a wood. The trees stretched their luxuriant and graceful branches over grassy slopes. A breeze made all this verdure gently rustle and speak in long silken sighs. Absorbed in listening to the hurricane racket from the front, he still remembered that these trees were growing, the grass-blades were extending according to their process. He inhaled a deep breath of moisture and fragrance from the grove, a wet odour which expressed all the opulent fecundity of unmoved nature, marching on with her million plans for multiple life, multiple death.

Further on, they came to a place where the Turkish shells were landing. There was a long hurtling sound in the air, and then one had sight of a shell. To Peza it was of the conical missiles which friendly officers had displayed to him on board warships. Curiously enough, too, this first shell smacked of the foundry, of men with smudged faces, of the blare of furnace fires. It brought machinery immediately into his mind. He thought that if he was killed there at that time it would be as romantic, to the old standards, as death by a bit of falling iron in a factory.

II

A child was playing on a mountain and disregarding a battle that was waging on the plain. Behind him was the little cobbled hut of his fled parents. It was now occupied by a pearl-coloured cow that stared out from the darkness thoughtful and tender-eyed. The child ran to and fro, fumbling with sticks and making great machinations with pebbles. By a striking exercise of artistic license the sticks were ponies, cows, and dogs, and the pebbles were sheep. He was managing large agricultural and herding affairs. He was too intent on them to pay much heed to the fight four miles away, which at that distance resembled in sound the beating of surf upon rocks. However, there were occasions when some louder outbreak of that thunder stirred him from his serious occupation, and he turned then a questioning eye upon the battle, a small stick poised in his hand, interrupted in the act of sending his dog after his sheep. His tranquillity in regard to the death on the plain was as invincible as that of the mountain on which he stood.

It was evident that fear had swept the parents away from their home in a manner that could make them forget this child, the first-born. Nevertheless, the hut was clean bare. The cow had committed no impropriety in billeting herself at the domicile of her masters. This smoke-coloured and odorous interior contained nothing as large as a humming-bird. Terror had operated on these runaway people in its sinister fashion, elevating details to enormous heights, causing a man to remember a button while he forgot a coat, overpowering every one with recollections of a broken coffee-cup, deluging them with fears for the safety of an old pipe, and causing them to forget their first-born. Meanwhile the child played soberly with his trinkets.

He was solitary; engrossed in his own pursuits, it was seldom that he lifted his head to inquire of the world why it made so much noise. The stick in his hand was much larger to him than was an army corps of the distance. It was too childish for the mind of the child. He was dealing with sticks.

The battle lines writhed at times in the agony of a sea-creature on the sands. These tentacles flung and waved in a supreme excitement of pain, and the struggles of the great outlined body brought it nearer and nearer to the child. Once he looked at the plain and saw some men running wildly across a field. He had seen people chasing obdurate beasts in such fashion, and it struck him immediately that it was a manly thing which he would incorporate in his game. Consequently he raced furiously at his stone sheep, flourishing a cudgel, crying the shepherd calls. He paused frequently to get a cue of manner from the soldiers fighting on the plain. He reproduced, to a degree, any movements which he accounted rational to his theory of sheep-herding, the business of men, the traditional and exalted living of his father.

III

It was as if Peza was a corpse walking on the bottom of the sea, and finding there fields of grain, groves, weeds, the faces of men, voices. War, a strange employment of the race, presented to him a scene crowded with familiar objects which wore the livery of their commonness, placidly, undauntedly. He was smitten with keen astonishment; a spread of green grass lit with the flames of poppies was too old for the company of this new ogre. If he had been devoting the full lens of his mind to this phase, he would have known he was amazed that the trees, the flowers, the grass, all tender and peaceful nature had not taken to heels at once upon the outbreak of battle. He venerated the immovable poppies.

The road seemed to lead into the apex of an angle formed by the two defensive lines of the Greeks. There was a straggle of wounded men and of gunless and jaded men. These latter did not seem to be frightened. They remained very cool, walking with unhurried steps and busy in gossip. Peza tried to define them. Perhaps during the fight they had reached the limit of their mental storage, their capacity for excitement, for tragedy, and had then simply come away. Peza remembered his visit to a certain place of pictures, where he had found himself amid heavenly skies and diabolic midnights—the sunshine beating red upon desert sands, nude bodies flung to the shore in the green moon-glow, ghastly and starving men clawing at a wall in darkness, a girl at her bath with screened rays falling upon her pearly shoulders, a dance, a funeral, a review, an execution, all the strength of argus-eyed art: and he had whirled and whirled amid this universe with cries of woe and joy, sin and beauty piercing his ears until he had been obliged to simply come away. He remembered that as he had emerged he had lit a cigarette with unction and advanced promptly to a café. A great hollow quiet seemed to be upon the earth.

This was a different case, but in his thoughts he conceded the same causes to many of these gunless wanderers. They too may have dreamed at lightning speed until the capacity for it was overwhelmed. As he watched them, he again saw himself walking toward the café, puffing upon his cigarette. As if to reinforce his theory, a soldier stopped him with an eager but polite inquiry for a match. He watched the man light his little roll of tobacco and paper and begin to smoke ravenously.

Peza no longer was torn with sorrow at the sight of wounded men. Evidently he found that pity had a numerical limit, and when this was passed the emotion became another thing. Now, as he viewed them, he merely felt himself very lucky, and beseeched the continuance of his superior fortune. At the passing of these slouched and stained figures he now heard a reiteration of warning. A part of himself was appealing through the medium of these grim shapes. It was plucking at his sleeve and pointing, telling him to beware; and so it had come to pass that he cared for the implacable misery of these soldiers only as he would have cared for the harms of broken dolls. His whole vision was focussed upon his own chance.

The lieutenant suddenly halted. "Look," he said. "I find that my duty is in another direction. I must go another way. But if you wish to fight you have only to go forward, and any officer of the fighting line will give you opportunity." He raised his cap ceremoniously; Peza raised his new white helmet. The stranger to battles uttered thanks to his chaperon, the one who had presented him. They bowed punctiliously, staring at each other with civil eyes.

The lieutenant moved quietly away through a field. In an instant it flashed upon Peza's mind that this desertion was perfidious. He had been subjected to a criminal discourtesy. The officer had fetched him into the middle of the thing, and then left him to wander helplessly toward death. At one time he was upon the point of shouting at the officer.

In the vale there was an effect as if one was then beneath the battle. It was going on above somewhere. Alone, unguided, Peza felt like a man groping in a cellar. He reflected too that one should always see the beginning of a fight. It was too difficult to thus approach it when the affair was in full swing. The trees hid all movements of troops from him, and he thought he might be walking out to the very spot which chance had provided for the reception of a fool. He asked eager questions of passing soldiers. Some paid no heed to him; others shook their heads mournfully. They knew nothing save war was hard work. If they talked at all it was in testimony of having fought well, savagely. They did not know if the army was going to advance, hold its ground, or retreat; they were weary.

A long pointed shell flashed through the air and struck near the base of a tree, with a fierce upheaval, compounded of earth and flames. Looking back, Peza could see the shattered tree quivering from head to foot. Its whole being underwent a convulsive tremor which was an exhibition of pain, and, furthermore, deep amazement. As he advanced through the vale, the shells continued to hiss and hurtle in long low flights, and the bullets purred in the air. The missiles were flying into the breast of an astounded nature. The landscape, bewildered, agonized, was suffering a rain of infamous shots, and Peza imagined a million eyes gazing at him with the gaze of startled antelopes.

There was a resolute crashing of musketry from the tall hill on the left, and from directly in front there was a mingled din of artillery and musketry firing. Peza felt that his pride was playing a great trick in forcing him forward in this manner under conditions of strangeness, isolation, and ignorance. But he recalled the manner of the lieutenant, the smile on the hill-top among the flying peasants. Peza blushed and pulled the peak of his helmet down on his forehead. He strode onward firmly. Nevertheless he hated the lieutenant, and he resolved that on some future occasion he would take much trouble to arrange a stinging social revenge upon that grinning jackanapes. It did not occur to him until later that he was now going to battle mainly because at a previous time a certain man had smiled.

IV

The road curved round the base of a little hill, and on this hill a battery of mountain guns was leisurely shelling something unseen. In the lee of the height the mules, contented under their heavy saddles, were quietly browsing the long grass. Peza ascended the hill by a slanting path. He felt his heart beat swiftly; once at the top of the hill he would be obliged to look this phenomenon in the face. He hurried, with a mysterious idea of preventing by this strategy the battle from making his appearance a signal for some tremendous renewal. This vague thought seemed logical at the time. Certainly this living thing had knowledge of his coming. He endowed it with the intelligence of a barbaric deity. And so he hurried; he wished to surprise war, this terrible emperor, when it was growling on its throne. The ferocious

251

and horrible sovereign was not to be allowed to make the arrival a pretext for some fit of smoky rage and blood. In this half-lull, Peza had distinctly the sense of stealing upon the battle unawares.

The soldiers watching the mules did not seem to be impressed by anything august. Two of them sat side by side and talked comfortably; another lay flat upon his back staring dreamily at the sky; another cursed a mule for certain refractions. Despite their uniforms, their bandoliers and rifles, they were dwelling in the peace of hostlers. However, the long shells were whooping from time to time over the brow of the hill, and swirling in almost straight lines toward the vale of trees, flowers, and grass. Peza, hearing and seeing the shells, and seeing the pensive guardians of the mules, felt reassured. They were accepting the condition of war as easily as an old sailor accepts the chair behind the counter of a tobacco-shop. Or, it was merely that the farm-boy had gone to sea, and he had adjusted himself to the circumstances immediately, and with only the usual first misadventures in conduct. Peza was proud and ashamed that he was not of them, these stupid peasants, who, throughout the world, hold potentates on their thrones, make statesmen illustrious, provide generals with lasting victories, all with ignorance, indifference, or half-witted hatred, moving the world with the strength of their arms and getting their heads knocked together in the name of God, the king, or the Stock Exchange; immortal, dreaming, hopeless asses who surrender their reason to the care of a shining puppet, and persuade some toy to carry their lives in his purse. Peza mentally abased himself before them, and wished to stir them with furious kicks.

As his eyes ranged above the rim of the plateau, he saw a group of artillery officers talking busily. They turned at once and regarded his ascent. A moment later a row of infantry soldiers in a trench beyond the little guns all faced him. Peza bowed to the officers. He understood at the time that he had made a good and cool bow, and he wondered at it, for his breath was coming in gasps, he was stifling from sheer excitement. He felt like a tipsy man trying to conceal his muscular uncertainty from the people in the street. But the officers did not display any knowledge. They bowed. Behind them Peza saw the plain, glittering green, with three lines of black marked upon it heavily. The front of the first of these lines was frothy with smoke. To the left of this hill was a craggy mountain, from which came a continual dull rattle of musketry. Its summit was ringed with the white smoke. The black lines on the plain slowly moved. The shells that came from there passed overhead with the sound of great birds frantically flapping their wings. Peza thought of the first sight of the sea during a storm. He seemed to feel against his face the wind that races over the tops of cold and tumultuous billows.

He heard a voice afar off—"Sir, what would you?" He turned, and saw the dapper captain of the battery standing beside him. Only a moment had elapsed. "Pardon me, sir," said Peza, bowing again. The officer was evidently reserving his bows; he scanned the new-comer attentively. "Are you a correspondent?" he asked. Peza produced a card. "Yes, I came as a correspondent," he replied, "but now, sir, I have other thoughts. I wish to help. You see? I wish to help."

"What do you mean?" said the captain. "Are you a Greek? Do you wish to fight?"

"Yes, I am a Greek. I wish to fight." Peza's voice surprised him by coming from his lips in even and deliberate tones. He thought with gratification that he was behaving rather well. Another shell travelling from some unknown point on the plain whirled close and furiously in the air, pursuing an apparently horizontal course as if it were never going to touch the earth. The dark shape swished across the sky.

"Ah," cried the captain, now smiling, "I am not sure that we will be able to accommodate you with a fierce affair here just at this time, but——" He walked gaily to and fro behind the guns with Peza, pointing out to him the lines of the Greeks, and describing his opinion of the general plan of defence. He wore the air of an amiable host. Other officers questioned Peza in regard to the politics of the war. The king, the ministry, Germany, England, Russia, all these huge words were continually upon their tongues. "And the people in Athens? Were they——" Amid this vivacious babble Peza, seated upon an ammunition box, kept his glance high, watching the appearance of shell after shell. These officers were like men who had been lost for days in the forest.

They were thirsty for any scrap of news. Nevertheless, one of them would occasionally dispute their informant courteously. What would Servia have to say to that? No, no, France and Russia could never allow it. Peza was elated. The shells killed no one; war was not so bad. He was simply having coffee in the smoking-room of some embassy where reverberate the names of nations.

A rumour had passed along the motley line of privates in the trench. The new arrival with the clean white helmet was a famous English cavalry officer come to assist the army with his counsel. They stared at the figure of him, surrounded by officers. Peza, gaining sense of the glances and whispers, felt that his coming was an event.

Later, he resolved that he could with temerity do something finer. He contemplated the mountain where the Greek infantry was engaged, and announced leisurely to the captain of the battery that he thought presently of going in that direction and getting into the fight. He re-affirmed the sentiments of a patriot. The captain seemed surprised. "Oh, there will be fighting here at this knoll in a few minutes," he said orientally. "That will be sufficient? You had better stay with us. Besides, I have been ordered to resume fire." The officers all tried to dissuade him from departing. It was really not worth the trouble. The battery would begin again directly. Then it would be amusing for him.

Peza felt that he was wandering with his protestations of high patriotism through a desert of sensible men. These officers gave no heed to his exalted declarations. They seemed too jaded. They were fighting the men who were fighting them. Palaver of the particular kind had subsided before their intense pre-occupation in war as a craft. Moreover, many men had talked in that manner and only talked.

Peza believed at first that they were treating him delicately. They were considerate of his inexperience. War had turned out to be such a gentle business that Peza concluded he could scorn this idea. He bade them a heroic farewell despite their objections.

However, when he reflected upon their ways afterward, he saw dimly that they were actuated principally by some universal childish desire for a spectator of their fine things. They were going into action, and they wished to be seen at war, precise and fearless.

V

Climbing slowly to the high infantry position, Peza was amazed to meet a soldier whose jaw had been half shot away, and who was being helped down the sheep track by two tearful comrades. The man's breast was drenched with blood, and from a cloth which he held to the wound drops were splashing wildly upon the stones of the path. He gazed at Peza for a moment. It was a mystic gaze, which Peza withstood with difficulty. He was exchanging looks with a spectre; all aspect of the man was somehow gone from this victim. As Peza went on, one of the unwounded soldiers loudly shouted to him to return and assist in this tragic march. But even Peza's fingers revolted; he was afraid of the spectre; he would not have dared to touch it. He was surely craven in the movement of refusal he made to them. He scrambled hastily on up the path. He was running away.

At the top of the hill he came immediately upon a part of the line that was in action. Another battery of mountain guns was here firing at the streaks of black on the plain. There were trenches filled with men lining parts of the crest, and near the base were other trenches, all crashing away mightily. The plain stretched as far as the eye can see, and from where silver mist ended this emerald ocean of grass, a great ridge of snow-topped mountains poised against a fleckless blue sky. Two knolls, green and yellow with grain, sat on the prairie confronting the dark hills of the Greek position. Between them were the lines of the enemy. A row of trees, a village, a stretch of road, showed faintly on this great canvas, this tremendous picture, but men, the Turkish battalions, were emphasized startlingly upon it. The ranks of troops between the knolls and the Greek position were as black as ink.

The first line of course was muffled in smoke, but at the rear of it battalions crawled up and to and fro plainer than beetles on a plate. Peza had never understood that masses of men were so declarative, so unmistakable, as if nature makes every arrangement to give information of the coming and the presence of destruction, the end, oblivion. The firing was full, complete, a roar of cataracts, and this pealing of connected volleys was adjusted to the grandeur of the far-off range of snowy mountains. Peza, breathless, pale, felt that he had been set upon a pillar and was surveying mankind, the world. In the meantime dust had got in his eye. He took his handkerchief and mechanically administered to it.

An officer with a double stripe of purple on his trousers paced in the rear of the battery of howitzers. He waved a little cane. Sometimes he paused in his promenade to study the field through his glasses. "A fine scene, sir," he cried airily, upon the approach of Peza. It was like a blow in the chest to the wide-eyed volunteer. It revealed to him a point of view. "Yes, sir, it is a fine scene," he answered. They spoke in French. "I am happy to be able to entertain monsieur with a little practice," continued the officer. "I am firing upon that mass of troops you see there a little to the right. They are probably forming for another attack." Peza smiled; here again appeared manners, manners erect by the side of death.

The right-flank gun of the battery thundered; there was a belch of fire and smoke; the shell flung swiftly and afar was known only to the ear in which rang a broadening hooting wake of sound. The howitzer had thrown itself backward convulsively, and lay with its wheels moving in the air as a squad of men rushed toward it. And later, it seemed as if each little gun had made the supreme effort of its being in each particular shot. They roared with voices far too loud, and the thunderous effort caused a gun to bound as in a dying convulsion. And then occasionally one was hurled with wheels in air. These shuddering howitzers presented an appearance of so many cowards always longing to bolt to the rear, but being implacably held to their business by this throng of soldiers who ran in squads to drag them up again to their obligation. The guns were herded and cajoled and bullied interminably. One by one, in relentless program, they were dragged forward to contribute a profound vibration of steel and wood, a flash and a roar, to the important happiness of man.

The adjacent infantry celebrated a good shot with smiles and an outburst of gleeful talk.

"Look, sir," cried an officer to Peza. Thin smoke was drifting lazily before Peza, and dodging impatiently he brought his eyes to bear upon that part of the plain indicated by the officer's finger. The enemy's infantry was advancing to attack. From the black lines had come forth an inky mass which was shaped much like a human tongue. It advanced slowly, casually, without apparent spirit, but with an insolent confidence that was like a proclamation of the inevitable.

The impetuous part was all played by the defensive side. Officers called, men plucked each other by the sleeve; there were shouts, motions, all eyes were turned upon the inky mass which was flowing toward the base of the hills, heavily, languorously, as oily and thick as one of the streams that ooze through a swamp.

Peza was chattering a question at every one. In the way, pushed aside, or in the way again, he continued to repeat it. "Can they take the position? Can they take the position? Can they take the position?" He was apparently addressing an assemblage of deaf men. Every eye was busy watching every hand. The soldiers did not even seem to see the interesting stranger in the white helmet who was crying out so feverishly.

Finally, however, the hurried captain of the battery espied him and heeded his question. "No, sir! no, sir! It is impossible," he shouted angrily. His manner seemed to denote that if he had sufficient time he would have completely insulted Peza. The latter swallowed the crumb of news without regard to the coating of scorn, and, waving his hand in adieu, he began to run along the crest of the hill toward the part of the Greek line against which the attack was directed.

VI

Peza, as he ran along the crest of the mountain, believed that his action was receiving the wrathful attention of the hosts of the foe. To him then it was incredible foolhardiness thus to call to himself the stares of thousands of hateful eyes. He was like a lad induced by playmates to commit some indiscretion in a cathedral. He was abashed; perhaps he even blushed as he ran. It seemed to him that the whole solemn ceremony of war had paused during this commission. So he scrambled wildly over the rocks in his haste to end the embarrassing ordeal. When he came among the crowning rifle-pits filled with eager soldiers he wanted to yell with joy. None noticed him save a young officer of infantry, who said—"Sir, what do you want?" It was obvious that people had devoted some attention to their own affairs.

Peza asserted, in Greek, that he wished above everything to battle for the fatherland. The officer nodded; with a smile he pointed to some dead men covered with blankets, from which were thrust upturned dusty shoes.

"Yes, I know, I know," cried Peza. He thought the officer was poetically alluding to the danger.

"No," said the officer at once. "I mean cartridges—a bandolier. Take a bandolier from one of them."

Peza went cautiously toward a body. He moved a hand toward the corner of a blanket. There he hesitated, stuck, as if his arm had turned to plaster. Hearing a rustle behind him he spun quickly. Three soldiers of the close rank in the trench were regarding him. The officer came again and tapped him on the shoulder. "Have you any tobacco?" Peza looked at him in bewilderment. His hand was still extended toward the blanket which covered the dead soldier. "Yes," he said, "I have some tobacco." He gave the officer his pouch. As if in compensation, the other directed a soldier to strip the bandolier from the corpse. Peza, having crossed the long cartridge belt on his breast, felt that the dead man had flung his two arms around him.

A soldier with a polite nod and smile gave Peza a rifle, a relic of another dead man. Thus, he felt, besides the clutch of a corpse about his neck, that the rifle was as inhumanly horrible as a snake that lives in a tomb. He heard at his ear something that was in effect like the voices of those two dead men, their low voices speaking to him of bloody death, mutilation. The bandolier gripped him tighter; he wished to raise his hands to his throat like a man who is choking. The rifle was clammy; upon his palms he felt the movement of the sluggish currents of a serpent's life; it was crawling and frightful.

258

All about him were these peasants, with their interested countenances, gibbering of the fight. From time to time a soldier cried out in semi-humorous lamentations descriptive of his thirst. One bearded man sat munching a great bit of hard bread. Fat, greasy, squat, he was like an idol made of tallow. Peza felt dimly that there was a distinction between this man and a young student who could write sonnets and play the piano quite well. This old blockhead was coolly gnawing at the bread, while he, Peza, was being throttled by a dead man's arms.

He looked behind him, and saw that a head by some chance had been uncovered from its blanket. Two liquid-like eyes were staring into his face. The head was turned a little sideways as if to get better opportunity for the scrutiny. Peza could feel himself blanch; he was being drawn and drawn by these dead men slowly, firmly down as to some mystic chamber under the earth where they could walk, dreadful figures, swollen and blood-marked. He was bidden; they had commanded him; he was going, going, going.

When the man in the new white helmet bolted for the rear, many of the soldiers in the trench thought that he had been struck, but those who had been nearest to him knew better. Otherwise they would have heard the silken sliding tender noise of the bullet and the thud of its impact. They bawled after him curses, and also outbursts of self-congratulation and vanity. Despite the prominence of the cowardly part, they were enabled to see in this exhibition a fine comment upon their own fortitude. The other soldiers thought that Peza had been wounded somewhere in the neck, because as he ran he was tearing madly at the bandolier, the dead man's arms. The soldier with the bread paused in his eating and cynically remarked upon the speed of the runaway.

An officer's voice was suddenly heard calling out the calculation of the distance to the enemy, the readjustment of the sights. There was a stirring rattle along the line. The men turned their eyes to the front. Other trenches beneath them to the right were already heavily in action. The smoke was lifting toward the blue sky. The soldier with the bread placed it carefully on a bit of paper beside him as he turned to kneel in the trench.

VII

In the late afternoon, the child ceased his play on the mountain with his flocks and his dogs. Part of the battle had whirled very near to the base of his hill, and the noise was great. Sometimes he could see fantastic smoky shapes which resembled the curious figures in foam which one sees on the slant of a rough sea. The plain indeed was etched in white circles and whirligigs like the slope of a colossal wave. The child took seat on a stone and contemplated the fight. He was beginning to be astonished; he had never before seen cattle herded with such uproar. Lines of flame flashed out here and there. It was mystery.

Finally, without any preliminary indication, he began to weep. If the men struggling on the plain had had time and greater vision, they could have seen this strange tiny figure seated on a boulder, surveying them while the tears streamed. It was as simple as some powerful symbol.

As the magic clear light of day amid the mountains dimmed the distances, and the plain shone as a pallid blue cloth marked by the red threads of the firing, the child arose and moved off to the unwelcoming door of his home. He called softly for his mother, and complained of his hunger in the familiar formula. The pearl-coloured cow, grinding her jaws thoughtfully, stared at him with her large eyes. The peaceful gloom of evening was slowly draping the hills.

The child heard a rattle of loose stones on the hillside, and facing the sound, saw a moment later a man drag himself up to the crest of the hill and fall panting. Forgetting his mother and his hunger, filled with calm interest, the child walked forward and stood over the heaving form. His eyes too were now large and inscrutably wise and sad like those of the animal in the house.

After a silence he spoke inquiringly. "Are you a man?"

Peza rolled over quickly and gazed up into the fearless cherubic countenance. He did not attempt to reply. He breathed as if life was about to leave his body. He was covered with dust; his face had been cut in some way, and his cheek was ribboned with blood. All the spick of his former appearance had vanished in a general dishevelment, in which he resembled a creature that had been flung to and fro, up and down, by cliffs and prairies during an earthquake. He rolled his eye glassily at the child.

They remained thus until the child repeated his words. "Are you a man?"

Peza gasped in the manner of a fish. Palsied, windless, and abject, he confronted the primitive courage, the sovereign child, the brother of the mountains, the sky and the sea, and he knew that the definition of his misery could be written on a grass-blade.

Part II. Midnight Sketches

AN EXPERIMENT IN MISERY

(From the Press, New York.)

It was late at night, and a fine rain was swirling softly down, causing the pavements to glisten with hue of steel and blue and yellow in the rays of the innumerable lights. A youth was trudging slowly, without enthusiasm, with his hands buried deep in his trouser's pockets, towards the down-town places where beds can be hired for coppers. He was clothed in an aged and tattered suit, and his derby was a marvel of dust-covered crown and torn rim. He was going forth to eat as the wanderer may eat, and sleep as the homeless sleep. By the time he had reached City Hall Park he was so completely plastered with yells of "bum" and "hobo," and with various unholy epithets that small boys had applied to him at intervals, that he was in a state of the most profound dejection. The sifting rain saturated the old velvet collar of his overcoat, and as the wet cloth pressed against his neck, he felt that there no longer could be pleasure in life. He looked about him searching for an outcast of highest degree that they too might share miseries, but the lights threw a quivering glare over rows and circles of deserted benches that glistened damply, showing patches of wet sod behind them. It seemed that their usual freights had fled on this night to better things. There were only squads of well-dressed Brooklyn people who swarmed towards the bridge.

The young man loitered about for a time and then went shuffling off down Park Row. In the sudden descent in style of the dress of the crowd he felt relief, and as if he were at last in his own country. He began to see tatters that matched his tatters. In Chatham Square there were aimless men strewn in front of saloons and lodging-houses, standing sadly, patiently, reminding one vaguely of the attitudes of chickens in a storm. He aligned himself with these men, and turned slowly to occupy himself with the flowing life of the great street.

Through the mists of the cold and storming night, the cable cars went in silent procession, great affairs shining with red and brass, moving with formidable power, calm and irresistible, dangerful and gloomy, breaking silence only by the loud fierce cry of the gong. Two rivers of people swarmed along the side walks, spattered with black mud, which made each shoe leave a scar-like impression. Overhead elevated trains with a shrill grinding of the wheels stopped at the station, which upon its leg-like pillars seemed to resemble some monstrous kind of crab squatting over the street. The quick fat puffings of the engines could be heard. Down an alley there were sombre curtains of purple and black, on which street lamps dully glittered like embroidered flowers.

A saloon stood with a voracious air on a corner. A sign leaning against the front of the door-post announced "Free hot soup to-night!" The swing doors, snapping to and fro like ravenous lips, made gratified smacks as the saloon gorged itself with plump men, eating with astounding and endless appetite, smiling in some indescribable manner as the men came from all directions like sacrifices to a heathenish superstition.

Caught by the delectable sign the young man allowed himself to be swallowed. A bar-tender placed a schooner of dark and portentous beer on the bar. Its monumental form up-reared until the froth a-top was above the crown of the young man's brown derby.

"Soup over there, gents," said the bar-tender affably. A little yellow man in rags and the youth grasped their schooners and went with speed toward a lunch counter, where a man with oily but imposing whiskers ladled genially from a kettle until he had furnished his two mendicants with a soup that was steaming hot, and in which there were little floating suggestions of chicken. The young man, sipping his broth, felt the cordiality expressed by the warmth of the mixture, and he beamed at the man with oily but imposing whiskers, who was presiding like a priest behind an altar. "Have some more, gents?" he inquired of the two sorry figures before him. The little yellow man accepted with a swift gesture, but the youth shook his head and went out, following a man whose wondrous seediness promised that he would have a knowledge of cheap lodging-houses.

On the side-walk he accosted the seedy man. "Say, do you know a cheap place to sleep?"

The other hesitated for a time gazing sideways. Finally he nodded in the direction of the street, "I sleep up there," he said, "when I've got the price."

"How much?"

"Ten cents."

The young man shook his head dolefully. "That's too rich for me."

At that moment there approached the two a reeling man in strange garments. His head was a fuddle of bushy hair and whiskers, from which his eyes peered with a guilty slant. In a close scrutiny it was possible to distinguish the cruel lines of a mouth which looked as if its lips had just closed with satisfaction over some tender and piteous morsel. He appeared like an assassin steeped in crimes performed awkwardly.

But at this time his voice was tuned to the coaxing key of an affectionate puppy. He looked at the men with wheedling eyes, and began to sing a little melody for charity.

"Say, gents, can't yeh give a poor feller a couple of cents t' git a bed. I got five, and I gits anudder two I gits me a bed. Now, on th' square, gents, can't yeh jest gimme two cents t' git a bed? Now, yeh know how a respecter'ble gentlem'n feels when he's down on his luck, an' I——"

The seedy man, staring with imperturbable countenance at a train which clattered overhead, interrupted in an expressionless voice—"Ah, go t' h—!"

But the youth spoke to the prayerful assassin in tones of astonishment and inquiry. "Say, you must be crazy! Why don't yeh strike somebody that looks as if they had money?"

The assassin, tottering about on his uncertain legs, and at intervals brushing imaginary obstacles from before his nose, entered into a long explanation of the psychology of the situation. It was so profound that it was unintelligible.

When he had exhausted the subject, the young man said to him—

"Let's see th' five cents."

The assassin wore an expression of drunken woe at this sentence, filled with suspicion of him. With a deeply pained air he began to fumble in his clothing, his red hands trembling. Presently he announced in a voice of bitter grief, as if he had been betrayed—"There's on'y four."

"Four," said the young man thoughtfully. "Well, look-a-here, I'm a stranger here, an' if ye'll steer me to your cheap joint I'll find the other three."

The assassin's countenance became instantly radiant with joy. His whiskers quivered with the wealth of his alleged emotions. He seized the young man's hand in a transport of delight and friendliness.

"B' Gawd," he cried, "if ye'll do that, b' Gawd, I'd say yeh was a damned good fellow, I would, an' I'd remember yeh all m' life, I would, b' Gawd, an' if I ever got a chance I'd return the compliment"—he spoke with drunken dignity,—"b' Gawd, I'd treat yeh white, I would, an' I'd allus remember yeh."

The young man drew back, looking at the assassin coldly. "Oh, that's all right," he said. "You show me th' joint—that's all you've got t' do."

The assassin, gesticulating gratitude, led the young man along a dark street. Finally he stopped before a little dusty door. He raised his hand impressively. "Look-a-here," he said, and there was a thrill of deep and ancient wisdom upon his face, "I've brought yeh here, an' that's my part, ain't it? If th' place don't suit yeh, yeh needn't git mad at me, need yeh? There won't be no bad feelin', will there?"

"No," said the young man.

The assassin waved his arm tragically, and led the march up the steep stairway. On the way the young man furnished the assassin with three pennies. At the top a man with benevolent spectacles looked at them through a hole in a board. He collected their money, wrote some names on a register, and speedily was leading the two men along a gloom-shrouded corridor.

Shortly after the beginning of this journey the young man felt his liver turn white, for from the dark and secret places of the building there suddenly came to his nostrils strange and unspeakable odours, that assailed him like malignant diseases with wings. They seemed to be from human bodies closely packed in dens; the exhalations from a hundred pairs of reeking lips; the fumes from a thousand bygone debauches; the expression of a thousand present miseries.

A man, naked save for a little snuff-coloured undershirt, was parading sleepily along the corridor. He rubbed his eyes, and, giving vent to a prodigious yawn, demanded to be told the time.

"Half-past one."

The man yawned again. He opened a door, and for a moment his form was outlined against a black, opaque interior. To this door came the three men, and as it was again opened the unholy odours rushed out like fiends, so that the young man was obliged to struggle as against an overpowering wind.

It was some time before the youth's eyes were good in the intense gloom within, but the man with benevolent spectacles led him skilfully, pausing but a moment to deposit the limp assassin upon a cot. He took the youth to a cot that lay tranquilly by the window, and showing him a tall locker for clothes that stood near the head with the ominous air of a tombstone, left him.

The youth sat on his cot and peered about him. There was a gas-jet in a distant part of the room, that burned a small flickering orange-hued flame. It caused vast masses of tumbled shadows in all parts of the place, save where, immediately about it, there was a little grey haze. As the young man's eyes became used to the darkness, he could see upon the cots that thickly littered the floor the forms of men sprawled out, lying in death-like silence, or heaving and snoring with tremendous effort, like stabbed fish.

The youth locked his derby and his shoes in the mummy case near him, and then lay down with an old and familiar coat around his shoulders. A blanket he handed gingerly, drawing it over part of the coat. The cot was covered with leather, and as cold as melting snow. The youth was obliged to shiver for some time on this affair, which was like a slab. Presently, however, his chill gave him peace, and during this period of leisure from it he turned his head to stare at his friend the assassin, whom he could dimly discern where he lay sprawled on a cot in the abandon of a man filled with drink. He was snoring with incredible vigour. His wet hair and beard dimly glistened, and his inflamed nose shone with subdued lustre like a red light in a fog.

Within reach of the youth's hand was one who lay with yellow breast and shoulders bare to the cold drafts. One arm hung over the side of the cot, and the fingers lay full length upon the wet cement floor of the room. Beneath the inky brows could be seen the eyes of the man exposed by the partly opened lids. To the youth it seemed that he and this corpse-like being were exchanging a prolonged stare, and that the other threatened with his eyes. He drew back watching his neighbour from the shadows of his blanket edge. The man did not move once through the night, but lay in this stillness as of death like a body stretched out expectant of the surgeon's knife.

And all through the room could be seen the tawny hues of naked flesh, limbs thrust into the darkness, projecting beyond the cots; upreared knees, arms hanging long and thin over the cot edges. For the most part they were statuesque, carven, dead. With the curious lockers standing all about like tombstones, there was a strange effect of a graveyard where bodies were merely flung.

Yet occasionally could be seen limbs wildly tossing in fantastic nightmare gestures, accompanied by guttural cries, grunts, oaths. And there was one fellow off in a gloomy corner, who in his dreams was oppressed by some frightful calamity, for of a sudden he began to utter long wails that went almost like yells from a hound, echoing wailfully and weird through this chill place of tombstones where men lay like the dead.

The sound in its high piercing beginnings, that dwindled to final melancholy moans, expressed a red and grim tragedy of the unfathomable possibilities of the man's dreams. But to the youth these were not merely the shrieks of a vision-pierced man: they were an utterance of the meaning of the room and its occupants. It was to him the protest of the wretch who feels the touch of the imperturbable granite wheels, and who then cries with an impersonal eloquence, with a strength not from him, giving voice to the wail of a whole section, a class, a people. This, weaving into the young man's brain, and mingling with his views of the vast and sombre shadows that, like mighty black fingers, curled around the naked bodies, made the young man so that he did not sleep, but lay carving the biographies for these men from his meagre experience. At times the fellow in the corner howled in a writhing agony of his imaginations.

Finally a long lance-point of grey light shot through the dusty panes of the window. Without, the young man could see roofs drearily white in the dawning. The point of light yellowed and grew brighter, until the golden rays of the morning sun came in bravely and strong. They touched with radiant colour the form of a small fat man, who snored in stuttering fashion. His round and shiny bald head glowed suddenly with the valour of a decoration. He sat up, blinked at the sun, swore fretfully, and pulled his blanket over the ornamental splendours of his head.

The youth contentedly watched this rout of the shadows before the bright spears of the sun, and presently he slumbered. When he awoke he heard the voice of the assassin raised in valiant curses. Putting up his head, he perceived his comrade seated on the side of the cot engaged in scratching his neck with long finger-nails that rasped like files.

"Hully Jee, dis is a new breed. They've got can-openers on their feet." He continued in a violent tirade.

The young man hastily unlocked his closet and took out his shoes and hat. As he sat on the side of the cot lacing his shoes, he glanced about and saw that daylight had made the room comparatively common-place and uninteresting. The men, whose faces seemed stolid, serene or absent, were engaged in dressing, while a great crackle of bantering conversation arose.

A few were parading in unconcerned nakedness. Here and there were men of brawn, whose skins shone clear and ruddy. They took splendid poses, standing massively like chiefs. When they had dressed in their ungainly garments there was an extraordinary change. They then showed bumps and deficiencies of all kinds.

There were others who exhibited many deformities. Shoulders were slanting, humped, pulled this way and pulled that way. And notable among these latter men was the little fat man, who had refused to allow his head to be glorified. His pudgy form, builded like a pear, bustled to and fro, while he swore in fish-wife fashion. It appeared that some article of his apparel had vanished.

The young man attired speedily, and went to his friend the assassin. At first the latter looked dazed at the sight of the youth. This face seemed to be appealing to him through the cloud wastes of his memory. He scratched his neck and reflected. At last he grinned, a broad smile gradually spreading until his countenance was a round illumination. "Hello, Willie," he cried cheerily.

"Hello," said the young man. "Are yeh ready t' fly?"

"Sure." The assassin tied his shoe carefully with some twine and came ambling.

When he reached the street the young man experienced no sudden relief from unholy atmospheres. He had forgotten all about them, and had been breathing naturally, and with no sensation of discomfort or distress.

He was thinking of these things as he walked along the street, when he was suddenly startled by feeling the assassin's hand, trembling with excitement, clutching his arm, and when the assassin spoke, his voice went into quavers from a supreme agitation.

"I'll be hully, bloomin' blowed if there wasn't a feller with a nightshirt on up there in that joint."

The youth was bewildered for a moment, but presently he turned to smile indulgently at the assassin's humour.

"Oh, you're a d——d liar," he merely said.

Whereupon the assassin began to gesture extravagantly, and take oath by strange gods. He frantically placed himself at the mercy of remarkable fates if his tale were not true.

"Yes, he did! I cross m'heart thousan' times!" he protested, and at the moment his eyes were large with amazement, his mouth wrinkled in unnatural glee.

"Yessir! A nightshirt! A hully white nightshirt!"

"You lie!"

"No, sir! I hope ter die b'fore I kin git anudder ball if there wasn't a jay wid a hully, bloomin' white nightshirt!"

His face was filled with the infinite wonder of it. "A hully white nightshirt," he continually repeated.

The young man saw the dark entrance to a basement restaurant. There was a sign which read "No mystery about our hash!" and there were other age-stained and world-battered legends which told him that the place was within his means. He stopped before it and spoke to the assassin. "I guess I'll git somethin' t' eat."

At this the assassin, for some reason, appeared to be quite embarrassed. He gazed at the seductive front of the eating place for a moment. Then he started slowly up the street. "Well, good-bye, Willie," he said bravely.

For an instant the youth studied the departing figure. Then he called out, "Hol' on a minnet." As they came together he spoke in a certain fierce way, as if he feared that the other would think him to be charitable. "Look-a-here, if yeh wanta git some breakfas' I'll lend yeh three cents t' do it with. But say, look-a-here, you've gota git out an' hustle. I ain't goin' t' support yeh, or I'll go broke b'fore night. I ain't no millionaire."

"I take me oath, Willie," said the assassin earnestly, "th' on'y thing I really needs is a ball. Me t'roat feels like a fryin'-pan. But as I can't get a ball, why, th' next bes' thing is breakfast, an' if yeh do that for me, b' Gawd, I say yeh was th' whitest lad I ever see."

They spent a few moments in dexterous exchanges of phrases, in which they each protested that the other was, as the assassin had originally said, "a respecter'ble gentlem'n." And they concluded with mutual assurances

270

that they were the souls of intelligence and virtue. Then they went into the restaurant.

There was a long counter, dimly lighted from hidden sources. Two or three men in soiled white aprons rushed here and there.

The youth bought a bowl of coffee for two cents and a roll for one cent. The assassin purchased the same. The bowls were webbed with brown seams, and the tin spoons wore an air of having emerged from the first pyramid. Upon them were black moss-like encrustations of age, and they were bent and scarred from the attacks of long-forgotten teeth. But over their repast the wanderers waxed warm and mellow. The assassin grew affable as the hot mixture went soothingly down his parched throat, and the young man felt courage flow in his veins.

Memories began to throng in on the assassin, and he brought forth long tales, intricate, incoherent, delivered with a chattering swiftness as from an old woman. "—— great job out'n Orange. Boss keep yeh hustlin' though all time. I was there three days, and then I went an' ask 'im t' lend me a dollar. 'G-g-go ter the devil,' he ses, an' I lose me job."

"South no good. Damn niggers work for twenty-five an' thirty cents a day. Run white man out. Good grub though. Easy livin'."

"Yas; useter work little in Toledo, raftin' logs. Make two or three dollars er day in the spring. Lived high. Cold as ice though in the winter."

"I was raised in northern N'York. O-o-oh, yeh jest oughto live there. No beer ner whisky though, way off in the woods. But all th' good hot grub yeh can eat. B' Gawd, I hung around there long as I could till th' ol' man fired me. 'Git t' hell outa here, yeh wuthless skunk, git t' hell outa here, an' go die,' he ses. 'You're a hell of a father,' I ses, 'you are,' an' I quit 'im."

As they were passing from the dim eating place, they encountered an old man who was trying to steal forth with a tiny package of food, but a tall man with an indomitable moustache stood dragon fashion, barring the way of escape. They heard the old man raise a plaintive protest. "Ah, you always want to know what I take out, and you never see that I usually bring a package in here from my place of business."

As the wanderers trudged slowly along Park Row, the assassin began to expand and grow blithe. "B' Gawd, we've been livin' like kings," he said, smacking appreciative lips.

"Look out, or we'll have t' pay fer it t'night," said the youth with gloomy warning.

But the assassin refused to turn his gaze toward the future. He went with a limping step, into which he injected a suggestion of lamblike gambols. His mouth was wreathed in a red grin.

In the City Hall Park the two wanderers sat down in the little circle of benches sanctified by traditions of their class. They huddled in their old garments, slumbrously conscious of the march of the hours which for them had no meaning.

The people of the street hurrying hither and thither made a blend of black figures changing yet frieze-like. They walked in their good clothes as upon important missions, giving no gaze to the two wanderers seated upon the benches. They expressed to the young man his infinite distance from all that he valued. Social position, comfort, the pleasures of living, were unconquerable kingdoms. He felt a sudden awe.

And in the background a multitude of buildings, of pitiless hues and sternly high, were to him emblematic of a nation forcing its regal head into the clouds, throwing no downward glances; in the sublimity of its aspirations ignoring the wretches who may flounder at its feet. The roar of the city in his ear was to him the confusion of strange tongues, babbling heedlessly; it was the clink of coin, the voice of the city's hopes which were to him no hopes.

He confessed himself an outcast, and his eyes from under the lowered rim of his hat began to glance guiltily, wearing the criminal expression that comes with certain convictions.

THE MEN IN THE STORM

The blizzard began to swirl great clouds of snow along the streets, sweeping it down from the roofs, and up from the pavements, until the faces of pedestrians tingled and burned as from a thousand needle-prickings. Those on the walks huddled their necks closely in the collars of their coats, and went along stooping like a race of aged people. The drivers of vehicles hurried their horses furiously on their way. They were made more cruel by the exposure of their position, aloft on high seats. The street cars, bound up town, went slowly, the horses slipping and straining in the spongy brown mass that lay between the rails. The drivers, muffled to the eyes, stood erect, facing the wind, models of grim philosophy. Overhead trains rumbled and roared, and the dark structure of the elevated railroad, stretching over the avenue, dripped little streams and drops of water upon the mud and snow beneath.

All the clatter of the street was softened by the masses that lay upon the cobbles, until, even to one who looked from a window, it became important music, a melody of life made necessary to the ear by the dreariness of the pitiless beat and sweep of the storm. Occasionally one could see black figures of men busily shovelling the white drifts from the walks. The sounds from their labour created new recollections of rural experiences which every man manages to have in a measure. Later, the immense windows of the shops became aglow with light, throwing great beams of orange and yellow upon the pavement. They were infinitely cheerful, yet in a way they accentuated the force and discomfort of the storm, and gave a meaning to the pace of the people and the vehicles, scores of pedestrians and drivers, wretched with cold faces, necks and feet, speeding for scores of unknown doors and entrances, scattering to an infinite variety of shelters, to places which the imagination made warm with the familiar colours of home.

There was an absolute expression of hot dinners in the pace of the people. If one dared to speculate upon the destination of those who came trooping, he lost himself in a maze of social calculation; he might fling a handful of sand and attempt to follow the flight of each particular grain. But as to the suggestion of hot dinners, he was in firm lines of thought, for it was upon every hurrying face. It is a matter of tradition; it is from the tales of childhood. It comes forth with every storm.

However, in a certain part of a dark west-side street, there was a collection of men to whom these things were as if they were not. In this street was located a charitable house, where for five cents the homeless of the city could get a bed at night, and in the morning coffee and bread.

During the afternoon of the storm, the whirling snows acted as drivers, as men with whips, and at half-past three the walk before the closed doors of the house was covered with wanderers of the street, waiting. For some distance on either side of the place they could be seen lurking in the doorways and behind projecting parts of buildings, gathering in close bunches in an effort to get warm. A covered wagon drawn up near the curb sheltered a dozen of them. Under the stairs that led to the elevated railway station, there were six or eight, their hands stuffed deep in their pockets, their shoulders stooped, jiggling their feet. Others always could be seen coming, a strange procession, some slouching along with the characteristic hopeless gait of professional strays, some coming with hesitating steps, wearing the air of men to whom this sort of thing was new.

It was an afternoon of incredible length. The snow, blowing in twisting clouds, sought out the men in their meagre hiding-places, and skilfully beat in among them, drenching their persons with showers of fine stinging flakes. They crowded together, muttering, and fumbling in their pockets to get their red inflamed wrists covered by the cloth.

New-comers usually halted at one end of the groups and addressed a question, perhaps much as a matter of form, "Is it open yet?"

Those who had been waiting inclined to take the questioner seriously and became contemptuous. "No; do yeh think we'd be standin' here?"

The gathering swelled in numbers steadily and persistently. One could always see them coming, trudging slowly through the storm.

Finally, the little snow plains in the street began to assume a leaden hue from the shadows of evening. The buildings upreared gloomily save where various windows became brilliant figures of light, that made shimmers and splashes of yellow on the snow. A street lamp on the curb struggled to illuminate, but it was reduced to impotent blindness by the swift gusts of sleet crusting its panes.

In this half-darkness, the men began to come from their shelter places and mass in front of the doors of charity. They were of all types, but the nationalities were mostly American, German, and Irish. Many were strong, healthy, clear-skinned fellows, with that stamp of countenance which is not frequently seen upon seekers after charity. There were men of undoubted patience, industry, and temperance, who, in time of ill-fortune, do not habitually turn to rail at the state of society, snarling at the arrogance of the rich, and bemoaning the cowardice of the poor, but who at these times are apt to wear a sudden and singular meekness, as if they saw the world's progress marching from them, and were trying to perceive where they had failed, what they had lacked, to be thus vanquished in the race. Then there were others of the shifting, Bowery element, who were used to paying ten cents for a place to sleep, but who now came here because it was cheaper.

But they were all mixed in one mass so thoroughly that one could not have discerned the different elements, but for the fact that the labouring men, for the most part, remained silent and impassive in the blizzard, their eyes fixed on the windows of the house, statues of patience.

The sidewalk soon became completely blocked by the bodies of the men. They pressed close to one another like sheep in a winter's gale, keeping one another warm by the heat of their bodies. The snow came down upon this compressed group of men until, directly from above, it might have appeared like a heap of snow-covered merchandise, if it were not for the fact that the crowd swayed gently with a unanimous, rhythmical motion. It was wonderful to see how the snow lay upon the heads and shoulders of these men, in little ridges an inch thick perhaps in places, the flakes steadily adding drop and drop, precisely as they fall upon the unresisting grass of the fields. The feet of the men were all wet and cold, and the wish to warm them accounted for the slow, gentle, rhythmical motion. Occasionally some man whose ear or nose tingled acutely from the cold winds would wriggle down until his head was protected by the shoulders of his companions.

There was a continuous murmuring discussion as to the probability of the doors being speedily opened. They persistently lifted their eyes towards the windows. One could hear little combats of opinion.

"There's a light in th' winder!"

"Naw; it's a reflection f'm across th' way."

"Well, didn't I see 'em light it?"

"You did?"

"I did!"

"Well, then, that settles it!"

As the time approached when they expected to be allowed to enter, the men crowded to the doors in an unspeakable crush, jamming and wedging in a way that it seemed would crack bones. They surged heavily against the building in a powerful wave of pushing shoulders. Once a rumour flitted among all the tossing heads.

"They can't open th' door! Th' fellers er smack up agin 'em."

Then a dull roar of rage came from the men on the outskirts; but all the time they strained and pushed until it appeared to be impossible for those that they cried out against to do anything but be crushed into pulp.

"Ah, git away f'm th' door!"

"Git outa that!"

"Throw 'em out!"

"Kill 'em!"

"Say, fellers, now, what th' 'ell? G've 'em a chance t' open th' door!"

"Yeh dam pigs, give 'em a chance t' open th' door!"

Men in the outskirts of the crowd occasionally yelled when a boot-heel of one of trampling feet crushed on their freezing extremities.

"Git off me feet, yeh clumsy tarrier!"

"Say, don't stand on me feet! Walk on th' ground!"

A man near the doors suddenly shouted—"O-o-oh! Le' me out—le' me out!" And another, a man of infinite valour, once twisted his head so as to half face those who were pushing behind him. "Quit yer shovin', yeh"—and he delivered a volley of the most powerful and singular invective, straight into the faces of the men behind him. It was as if he was hammering the noses of them with curses of triple brass. His face, red with rage, could be seen upon it, an expression of sublime disregard of consequences. But nobody cared to reply to his imprecations; it was too cold. Many of them snickered, and all continued to push.

In occasional pauses of the crowd's movement the men had opportunities to make jokes; usually grim things, and no doubt very uncouth. Nevertheless, they were notable—one does not expect to find the quality of humour in a heap of old clothes under a snow-drift.

The winds seemed to grow fiercer as time wore on. Some of the gusts of snow that came down on the close collection of heads, cut like knives and needles, and the men huddled, and swore, not like dark assassins, but in a sort of American fashion, grimly and desperately, it is true, but yet with a wondrous under-effect, indefinable and mystic, as if there was some kind of humour in this catastrophe, in this situation in a night of snow-laden winds.

Once the window of the huge dry-goods shop across the street furnished material for a few moments of forgetfulness. In the brilliantly-lighted space appeared the figure of a man. He was rather stout and very well clothed. His beard was fashioned charmingly after that of the Prince of Wales. He stood in an attitude of magnificent reflection. He slowly stroked his moustache with a certain grandeur of manner, and looked down at the snow-encrusted mob. From below, there was denoted a supreme complacence in him. It seemed that the sight operated inversely, and enabled him to more clearly regard his own delightful environment.

One of the mob chanced to turn his head, and perceived the figure in the window. "Hello, lookit 'is whiskers," he said genially.

Many of the men turned then, and a shout went up. They called to him in all strange keys. They addressed him in every manner, from familiar and cordial greetings, to carefully-worded advice concerning changes in his personal appearance. The man presently fled, and the mob chuckled ferociously, like ogres who had just devoured something.

They turned then to serious business. Often they addressed the stolid front of the house.

"Oh, let us in fer Gawd's sake!"

"Let us in, or we'll all drop dead!"

"Say, what's th' use o' keepin' us poor Indians out in th' cold?"

And always some one was saying, "Keep off my feet."

The crushing of the crowd grew terrific toward the last. The men, in keen pain from the blasts, began almost to fight. With the pitiless whirl of snow upon them, the battle for shelter was going to the strong. It became known that the basement door at the foot of a little steep flight of stairs was the one to be opened, and they jostled and heaved in this direction like labouring fiends. One could hear them panting and groaning in their fierce exertion.

Usually some one in the front ranks was protesting to those in the rear—"O-o-ow! Oh, say now, fellers, let up, will yeh? Do yeh wanta kill somebody!"

A policeman arrived and went into the midst of them, scolding and be-rating, occasionally threatening, but using no force but that of his hands and shoulders against these men who were only struggling to get in out of the storm. His decisive tones rang out sharply—"Stop that pushin' back there! Come, boys, don't push! Stop that! Here you, quit yer shovin'! Cheese that!"

When the door below was opened, a thick stream of men forced a way down the stairs, which were of an extraordinary narrowness, and seemed only wide enough for one at a time. Yet they somehow went down almost three abreast. It was a difficult and painful operation. The crowd was like a turbulent water forcing itself through one tiny outlet. The men in the rear, excited by the success of the others, made frantic exertions, for it seemed that this large band would more than fill the quarters, and that many would be left upon the pavements. It would be disastrous to be of the last, and accordingly men with the snow biting their faces, writhed and twisted with their might. One expected that from the tremendous pressure, the narrow passage to the basement door would be so choked and clogged with human limbs and bodies that movement would be impossible. Once indeed the crowd was forced to stop, and a cry went along that a man had been injured at the foot of the stairs. But presently the slow movement began again, and the policeman fought at the top of the flight to ease the pressure of those that were going down.

A reddish light from a window fell upon the faces of the men, when they, in turn, arrived at the last three steps, and were about to enter. One could then note a change of expression that had come over their features. As they stood thus upon the threshold of their hopes, they looked suddenly contented and complacent. The fire had passed from their eyes and the snarl had vanished from their lips. The very force of the crowd in the rear, which had previously vexed them, was regarded from another point of view, for it now made it inevitable that they should go through the little doors into the place that was cheery and warm with light.

The tossing crowd on the sidewalk grew smaller and smaller. The snow beat with merciless persistence upon the bowed heads of those who waited. The wind drove it up from the pavements in frantic forms of winding white, and it seethed in circles about the huddled forms passing in one by one, three by three, out of the storm.

THE DUEL THAT WAS NOT FOUGHT

Patsy Tulligan was not as wise as seven owls, but his courage could throw a shadow as long as the steeple of a cathedral. There were men on Cherry Street who had whipped him five times, but they all knew that Patsy would be as ready for the sixth time as if nothing had happened.

Once he and two friends had been away up on Eighth Avenue, far out of their country, and upon their return journey that evening they stopped frequently in saloons until they were as independent of their surroundings as eagles, and cared much less about thirty days on Blackwell's.

On Lower Sixth Avenue they paused in a saloon where there was a good deal of lamp-glare and polished wood to be seen from the outside, and within, the mellow light shone on much furbished brass and more polished wood. It was a better saloon than they were in the habit of seeing, but they did not mind it. They sat down at one of the little tables that were in a row parallel to the bar and ordered beer. They blinked stolidly at the decorations, the bartender, and the other customers. When anything transpired they discussed it with dazzling frankness, and what they said of it was as free as air to the other people in the place.

At midnight there were few people in the saloon. Patsy and his friends still sat drinking. Two well-dressed men were at another table, smoking cigars slowly and swinging back in their chairs. They occupied themselves with themselves in the usual manner, never betraying by a wink of an eyelid that they knew that other folk existed. At another table directly behind Patsy and his companions was a slim little Cuban, with miraculously small feet and hands, and with a youthful touch of down upon his lip. As he lifted his cigarette from time to time his little finger was bended in dainty fashion, and there was a green flash when a huge emerald ring caught the light. The bartender came often with his little brass tray. Occasionally Patsy and his two friends quarrelled.

Once this little Cuban happened to make some slight noise and Patsy turned his head to observe him. Then Patsy made a careless and rather loud comment to his two friends. He used a word which is no more than passing the time of day down in Cherry Street, but to the Cuban it was a dagger-point. There was a harsh scraping sound as a chair was pushed swiftly back.

The little Cuban was upon his feet. His eyes were shining with a rage that flashed there like sparks as he glared at Patsy. His olive face had turned a shade of grey from his anger. Withal his chest was thrust out in portentous dignity, and his hand, still grasping his wine-glass, was cool and steady, the little finger still bended, the great emerald gleaming upon it. The others, motionless, stared at him.

"Sir," he began ceremoniously. He spoke gravely and in a slow way, his tone coming in a marvel of self-possessed cadences from between those lips which quivered with wrath. "You have insult me. You are a dog, a hound, a cur. I spit upon you. I must have some of your blood."

Patsy looked at him over his shoulder.

"What's th' matter wi' che?" he demanded. He did not quite understand the words of this little man who glared at him steadily, but he knew that it was something about fighting. He snarled with the readiness of his class and heaved his shoulders contemptuously. "Ah, what's eatin' yeh? Take a walk! You h'ain't got nothin' t' do with me, have yeh? Well, den, go sit on yerself."

And his companions leaned back valorously in their chairs, and scrutinized this slim young fellow who was addressing Patsy.

"What's de little Dago chewin' about?"

"He wants t' scrap!"

"What!"

The Cuban listened with apparent composure. It was only when they laughed that his body cringed as if he was receiving lashes. Presently he put down his glass and walked over to their table. He proceeded always with the most impressive deliberation.

281

"Sir," he began again. "You have insult me. I must have s-s-satisfac-shone. I must have your body upon the point of my sword. In my country you would already be dead. I must have s-s-satisfac-shone."

Patsy had looked at the Cuban with a trifle of bewilderment. But at last his face began to grow dark with belligerency, his mouth curve in that wide sneer with which he would confront an angel of darkness. He arose suddenly in his seat and came towards the little Cuban. He was going to be impressive too.

"Say, young feller, if yeh go shootin' off fer face at me, I'll wipe d' joint wid yeh. What'cher gaffin' about, hey? Are yeh givin' me er jolly? Say, if yeh pick me up fer a cinch, I'll fool yeh. Dat's what! Don't take me fer no dead easy mug." And as he glowered at the little Cuban, he ended his oration with one eloquent word, "Nit!"

The bar-tender nervously polished his bar with a towel, and kept his eyes fastened upon the men. Occasionally he became transfixed with interest, leaning forward with one hand upon the edge of the bar and the other holding the towel grabbed in a lump, as if he had been turned into bronze when in the very act of polishing.

The Cuban did not move when Patsy came toward him and delivered his oration. At its conclusion he turned his livid face toward where, above him, Patsy was swaggering and heaving his shoulders in a consummate display of bravery and readiness. The Cuban, in his clear, tense tones, spoke one word. It was the bitter insult. It seemed to fairly spin from his lips and crackle in the air like breaking glass.

Every man save the little Cuban made an electric movement. Patsy roared a black oath and thrust himself forward until he towered almost directly above the other man. His fists were doubled into knots of bone and hard flesh. The Cuban had raised a steady finger.

"If you touch me wis your hand, I will keel you."

The two well-dressed men had come swiftly, uttering protesting cries. They suddenly intervened in this second of time in which Patsy had sprung forward and the Cuban had uttered his threat. The four men were now a tossing, arguing, violent group, one well-dressed man lecturing the Cuban, and the other holding off Patsy, who was now wild with rage, loudly repeating the Cuban's threat, and manoeuvring and struggling to get at him for revenge's sake.

The bar-tender, feverishly scouring away with his towel, and at times pacing to and fro with nervous and excited tread, shouted out—

"Say, for heaven's sake, don't fight in here. If yeh wanta fight, go out in the street and fight all yeh please. But don't fight in here."

Patsy knew only one thing, and this he kept repeating—

"Well, he wants t' scrap! I didn't begin dis! He wants t' scrap."

The well-dressed man confronting him continually replied—

"Oh, well, now, look here, he's only a lad. He don't know what he's doing. He's crazy mad. You wouldn't slug a kid like that."

Patsy and his aroused companions, who cursed and growled, were persistent with their argument. "Well, he wants t' scrap!" The whole affair was as plain as daylight when one saw this great fact. The interference and intolerable discussion brought the three of them forward, battleful and fierce.

"What's eatin' you, anyhow?" they demanded. "Dis ain't your business, is it? What business you got shootin' off your face?"

The other peacemaker was trying to restrain the little Cuban, who had grown shrill and violent.

"If he touch me wis his hand I will keel him. We must fight like gentlemen or else I keel him when he touch me wis his hand."

The man who was fending off Patsy comprehended these sentences that were screamed behind his back, and he explained to Patsy—

"But he wants to fight you with swords. With swords, you know."

The Cuban, dodging around the peacemakers, yelled in Patsy's face—

"Ah, if I could get you before me wis my sword! Ah! Ah! A-a-ah!" Patsy made a furious blow with a swift fist, but the peacemakers bucked against his body suddenly like football players.

Patsy was greatly puzzled. He continued doggedly to try to get near enough to the Cuban to punch him. To these attempts the Cuban replied savagely—

"If you touch me wis your hand, I will cut your heart in two piece."

At last Patsy said—"Well, if he's so dead stuck on fightin' wid swords, I'll fight 'im. Soitenly! I'll fight 'im." All this palaver had evidently tired him, and he now puffed out his lips with the air of a man who is willing to submit to any conditions if he can only bring on the row soon enough. He swaggered, "I'll fight 'im wid swords. Let 'im bring on his swords, an' I'll fight 'im 'til he's ready t' quit."

The two well-dressed men grinned. "Why, look here," they said to Patsy, "he'd punch you full of holes. Why, he's a fencer. You can't fight him with swords. He'd kill you in 'bout a minute."

"Well, I'll giv' 'im a go at it, anyhow," said Patsy, stout-hearted and resolute. "I'll giv' 'im a go at it, anyhow, an' I'll stay wid 'im long as I kin."

As for the Cuban, his lithe little body was quivering in an ecstasy of the muscles. His face radiant with a savage joy, he fastened his glance upon Patsy, his eyes gleaming with a gloating, murderous light. A most unspeakable, animal-like rage was in his expression.

"Ah! ah! He will fight me! Ah!" He bended unconsciously in the posture of a fencer. He had all the quick, springy movements of a skilful swordsman. "Ah, the b-r-r-rute! The b-r-r-rute! I will stick him like a pig!"

The two peacemakers, still grinning broadly, were having a great time with Patsy.

"Why, you infernal idiot, this man would slice you all up. You better jump off the bridge if you want to commit suicide. You wouldn't stand a ghost of a chance to live ten seconds."

Patsy was as unshaken as granite. "Well, if he wants t' fight wid swords, he'll get it. I'll giv' 'im a go at it, anyhow."

One man said—"Well, have you got a sword? Do you know what a sword is? Have you got a sword?"

"No, I ain't got none," said Patsy honestly, "but I kin git one." Then he added valiantly—"An' quick too."

The two men laughed. "Why, can't you understand it would be sure death to fight a sword duel with this fellow?"

"Dat's all right! See? I know me own business. If he wants t' fight one of dees d—n duels, I'm in it, understan'?"

"Have you ever fought one, you fool?"

"No, I ain't. But I will fight one, dough! I ain't no muff. If he want t' fight a duel, by Gawd, I'm wid 'im! D'yeh understan' dat!" Patsy cocked his hat and swaggered. He was getting very serious.

The little Cuban burst out—"Ah, come on, sirs: come on! We can take cab. Ah, you big cow, I will stick you, I will stick you. Ah, you will look very beautiful, very beautiful. Ah, come on, sirs. We will stop at hotel—my hotel. I there have weapons."

"Yeh will, will yeh? Yeh bloomin' little black Dago," cried Patsy in hoarse and maddened reply to the personal part of the Cuban's speech. He stepped forward. "Git yer d—n swords," he commanded. "Git yer swords. Git 'em quick! I'll fight wi' che! I'll fight wid anyting, too! See? I'll fight yeh wid a knife an' fork if yeh say so! I'll fight yer standin' up er sittin' down!" Patsy delivered this intense oration with sweeping, intensely emphatic gestures, his hands stretched out eloquently, his jaw thrust forward, his eyes glaring.

"Ah," cried the little Cuban joyously. "Ah, you are in very pretty temper. Ah, how I will cut your heart in two piece, my dear, d-e-a-r friend." His eyes, too, shone like carbuncles, with a swift, changing glitter, always fastened upon Patsy's face.

The two peacemakers were perspiring and in despair. One of them blurted out—

"Well, I'll be blamed if this ain't the most ridiculous thing I ever saw."

The other said—"For ten dollars I'd be tempted to let these two infernal blockheads have their duel."

Patsy was strutting to and fro, and conferring grandly with his friends.

"He took me for a muff. He tought he was goin' t' bluff me out, talkin' 'bout swords. He'll get fooled." He addressed the Cuban—"You're a fine little dirty picter of a scrapper, ain' che? I'll chew yez up, dat's what I will."

There began then some rapid action. The patience of well-dressed men is not an eternal thing. It began to look as if it would at last be a fight with six corners to it. The faces of the men were shining red with anger. They jostled each other defiantly, and almost every one blazed out at three or four of the others. The bar-tender had given up protesting. He swore for a time, and banged his glasses. Then he jumped the bar and ran out of the saloon, cursing sullenly.

When he came back with a policeman, Patsy and the Cuban were preparing to depart together. Patsy was delivering his last oration—

"I'll fight yer wid swords! Sure I will! Come ahead, Dago! I'll fight yeh anywheres wid anyting! We'll have a large, juicy scrap, an' don't yeh forget dat! I'm right wid yez. I ain't no muff! I scrap wid a man jest as soon as he ses scrap, an' if yeh wanta scrap, I'm yer kitten. Understan' dat?"

The policeman said sharply—"Come, now; what's all this?" He had a distinctly business air.

The little Cuban stepped forward calmly. "It is none of your business."

The policeman flushed to his ears. "What?"

One well-dressed man touched the other on the sleeve. "Here's the time to skip," he whispered. They halted a block away from the saloon and watched the policeman pull the Cuban through the door. There was a minute of scuffle on the sidewalk, and into this deserted street at midnight fifty people appeared at once as if from the sky to watch it.

At last the three Cherry Hill men came from the saloon, and swaggered with all their old valour toward the peacemakers.

"Ah," said Patsy to them, "he was so hot talkin' about this duel business, but I would a-given 'im a great scrap, an' don't yeh forgit it."

For Patsy was not as wise as seven owls, but his courage could throw a shadow as long as the steeple of a cathedral.

AN OMINOUS BABY

A baby was wandering in a strange country. He was a tattered child with a frowsled wealth of yellow hair. His dress, of a checked stuff, was soiled, and showed the marks of many conflicts, like the chain-shirt of a warrior. His sun-tanned knees shone above wrinkled stockings, which he pulled up occasionally with an impatient movement when they entangled his feet. From a gaping shoe there appeared an array of tiny toes.

He was toddling along an avenue between rows of stolid brown houses. He went slowly, with a look of absorbed interest on his small flushed face. His blue eyes stared curiously. Carriages went with a musical rumble over the smooth asphalt. A man with a chrysanthemum was going up steps. Two nursery maids chatted as they walked slowly, while their charges hobnobbed amiably between perambulators. A truck wagon roared thunderously in the distance.

The child from the poor district made his way along the brown street filled with dull grey shadows. High up, near the roofs, glancing sun-rays changed cornices to blazing gold and silvered the fronts of windows. The wandering baby stopped and stared at the two children laughing and playing in their carriages among the heaps of rugs and cushions. He braced his legs apart in an attitude of earnest attention. His lower jaw fell, and disclosed his small, even teeth. As they moved on, he followed the carriages with awe in his face as if contemplating a pageant. Once one of the babies, with twittering laughter, shook a gorgeous rattle at him. He smiled jovially in return.

Finally a nursery maid ceased conversation and, turning, made a gesture of annoyance.

"Go 'way, little boy," she said to him. "Go 'way. You're all dirty."

He gazed at her with infant tranquillity for a moment, and then went slowly off dragging behind him a bit of rope he had acquired in another street. He continued to investigate the new scenes. The people and houses struck him with interest as would flowers and trees. Passengers had to avoid the small, absorbed figure in the middle of the sidewalk. They glanced at the intent baby face covered with scratches and dust as with scars and with powder smoke.

After a time, the wanderer discovered upon the pavement a pretty child in fine clothes playing with a toy. It was a tiny fire-engine, painted brilliantly in crimson and gold. The wheels rattled as its small owner dragged it uproariously about by means of a string. The babe with his bit of rope trailing behind him paused and regarded the child and the toy. For a long while he remained motionless, save for his eyes, which followed all movements of the glittering thing. The owner paid no attention to the spectator, but continued his joyous imitations of phases of the career of a fire-engine. His gleeful baby laugh rang against the calm fronts of the houses. After a little the wandering baby began quietly to sidle nearer. His bit of rope, now forgotten, dropped at his feet. He removed his eyes from the toy and glanced expectantly at the other child.

"Say," he breathed softly.

The owner of the toy was running down the walk at top speed. His tongue was clanging like a bell and his legs were galloping. He did not look around at the coaxing call from the small tattered figure on the curb.

The wandering baby approached still nearer, and presently spoke again.

"Say," he murmured, "le' me play wif it?"

The other child interrupted some shrill tootings. He bended his head and spoke disdainfully over his shoulder.

"No," he said.

The wanderer retreated to the curb. He failed to notice the bit of rope, once treasured. His eyes followed as before the winding course of the engine, and his tender mouth twitched.

"Say," he ventured at last, "is dat yours?"

"Yes," said the other, tilting his round chin. He drew his property suddenly behind him as if it were menaced. "Yes," he repeated, "it's mine."

"Well, le' me play wif it?" said the wandering baby, with a trembling note of desire in his voice.

"No," cried the pretty child with determined lips. "It's mine. My ma-ma buyed it."

"Well, tan't I play wif it?" His voice was a sob. He stretched forth little covetous hands.

"No," the pretty child continued to repeat. "No, it's mine."

"Well, I want to play wif it," wailed the other. A sudden fierce frown mantled his baby face. He clenched his fat hands and advanced with a formidable gesture. He looked some wee battler in a war.

"It's mine! It's mine," cried the pretty child, his voice in the treble of outraged rights.

"I want it," roared the wanderer.

"It's mine! It's mine!"

"I want it!"

"It's mine!"

The pretty child retreated to the fence, and there paused at bay. He protected his property with outstretched arms. The small vandal made a charge. There was a short scuffle at the fence. Each grasped the string to the toy and tugged. Their faces were wrinkled with baby rage, the verge of tears. Finally, the child in tatters gave a supreme tug and wrenched the string from the other's hands. He set off rapidly down the street, bearing the toy in his arms. He was weeping with the air of a wronged one who has at last succeeded in achieving his rights. The other baby was squalling lustily. He seemed quite helpless. He rung his chubby hands and railed.

After the small barbarian had got some distance away, he paused and regarded his booty. His little form curved with pride. A soft, gleeful smile loomed through the storm of tears. With great care he prepared the toy for travelling. He stopped a moment on a corner and gazed at the pretty child, whose small figure was quivering with sobs. As the latter began to show signs of beginning pursuit, the little vandal turned and vanished down a dark side street as into a cavern.

A GREAT MISTAKE

An Italian kept a fruit-stand on a corner where he had good aim at the people who came down from the elevated station, and at those who went along two thronged streets. He sat most of the day in a backless chair that was placed strategically.

There was a babe living hard by, up five flights of stairs, who regarded this Italian as a tremendous being. The babe had investigated this fruit-stand. It had thrilled him as few things he had met with in his travels had thrilled him. The sweets of the world had laid there in dazzling rows, tumbled in luxurious heaps. When he gazed at this Italian seated amid such splendid treasures, his lower lip hung low and his eyes, raised to the vendor's face, were filled with deep respect, worship, as if he saw omnipotence.

The babe came often to this corner. He hovered about the stand and watched each detail of the business. He was fascinated by the tranquillity of the vendor, the majesty of power and possession. At times he was so engrossed in his contemplation that people, hurrying, had to use care to avoid bumping him down.

He had never ventured very near to the stand. It was his habit to hang warily about the curb. Even there he resembled a babe who looks unbidden at a feast of gods.

One day, however, as the baby was thus staring, the vendor arose, and going along the front of the stand, began to polish oranges with a red pocket handkerchief. The breathless spectator moved across the side walk until his small face almost touched the vendor's sleeve. His fingers were gripped in a fold of his dress.

At last, the Italian finished with the oranges and returned to his chair. He drew a newspaper printed in his language from behind a bunch of bananas. He settled himself in a comfortable position, and began to glare savagely at the print. The babe was left face to face with the massed joys of the world. For a time he was a simple worshipper at this golden shrine. Then tumultuous desires began to shake him. His dreams were of conquest. His lips moved. Presently into his head there came a little plan. He sidled nearer, throwing swift and cunning glances at the Italian. He strove to maintain his conventional manner, but the whole plot was written upon his countenance.

At last he had come near enough to touch the fruit. From the tattered skirt came slowly his small dirty hand. His eyes were still fixed upon the vendor. His features were set, save for the under lip, which had a faint fluttering movement. The hand went forward.

Elevated trains thundered to the station and the stairway poured people upon the sidewalks. There was a deep sea roar from feet and wheels going ceaselessly. None seemed to perceive the babe engaged in a great venture.

The Italian turned his paper. Sudden panic smote the babe. His hand dropped, and he gave vent to a cry of dismay. He remained for a moment staring at the vendor. There was evidently a great debate in his mind. His infant intellect had defined this Italian. The latter was undoubtedly a man who would eat babes that provoked him. And the alarm in the babe when this monarch had turned his newspaper brought vividly before him the consequences if he were detected. But at this moment the vendor gave a blissful grunt, and tilting his chair against a wall, closed his eyes. His paper dropped unheeded.

The babe ceased his scrutiny and again raised his hand. It was moved with supreme caution toward the fruit. The fingers were bent, claw-like, in the manner of great heart-shaking greed. Once he stopped and chattered convulsively, because the vendor moved in his sleep. The babe, with his eyes still upon the Italian, again put forth his hand, and the rapacious fingers closed over a round bulb.

And it was written that the Italian should at this moment open his eyes. He glared at the babe a fierce question. Thereupon the babe thrust the round bulb behind him, and with a face expressive of the deepest guilt, began a wild but elaborate series of gestures declaring his innocence. The Italian howled. He sprang to his feet, and with three steps overtook the babe. He whirled him fiercely, and took from the little fingers a lemon.

AN ELOQUENCE OF GRIEF

The windows were high and saintly, of the shape that is found in churches. From time to time a policeman at the door spoke sharply to some incoming person. "Take your hat off!" He displayed in his voice the horror of a priest when the sanctity of a chapel is defied or forgotten. The court-room was crowded with people who sloped back comfortably in their chairs, regarding with undeviating glances the procession and its attendant and guardian policemen that moved slowly inside the spear-topped railing. All persons connected with a case went close to the magistrate's desk before a word was spoken in the matter, and then their voices were toned to the ordinary talking strength. The crowd in the court-room could not hear a sentence; they could merely see shifting figures, men that gestured quietly, women that sometimes raised an eager eloquent arm. They could not always see the judge, although they were able to estimate his location by the tall stands surmounted by white globes that were at either hand of him. And so those who had come for curiosity's sweet sake wore an air of being in wait for a cry of anguish, some loud painful protestation that would bring the proper thrill to their jaded, world-weary nerves—wires that refused to vibrate for ordinary affairs.

Inside the railing the court officers shuffled the various groups with speed and skill; and behind the desk the magistrate patiently toiled his way through mazes of wonderful testimony.

In a corner of this space, devoted to those who had business before the judge, an officer in plain clothes stood with a girl that wept constantly. None seemed to notice the girl, and there was no reason why she should be noticed, if the curious in the body of the court-room were not interested in the devastation which tears bring upon some complexions. Her tears seemed to burn like acid, and they left fierce pink marks on her face. Occasionally the girl looked across the room, where two well-dressed young women and a man stood waiting with the serenity of people who are not concerned as to the interior fittings of a jail.

The business of the court progressed, and presently the girl, the officer, and the well-dressed contingent stood before the judge. Thereupon two lawyers engaged in some preliminary fire-wheels, which were endured generally in silence. The girl, it appeared, was accused of stealing fifty dollars' worth of silk clothing from the room of one of the well-dressed women. She had been a servant in the house.

In a clear way, and with none of the ferocity that an accuser often exhibits in a police-court, calmly and moderately, the two young women gave their testimony. Behind them stood their escort, always mute. His part, evidently, was to furnish the dignity, and he furnished it heavily, almost massively.

When they had finished, the girl told her part. She had full, almost Afric, lips, and they had turned quite white. The lawyer for the others asked some questions, which he did—be it said, in passing—with the air of a man throwing flower-pots at a stone house.

It was a short case and soon finished. At the end of it the judge said that, considering the evidence, he would have to commit the girl for trial. Instantly the quick-eyed court officer began to clear the way for the next case. The well-dressed women and their escort turned one way and the girl turned another, toward a door with an austere arch leading into a stone-paved passage. Then it was that a great cry rang through the court-room, the cry of this girl who believed that she was lost.

The loungers, many of them, underwent a spasmodic movement as if they had been knived. The court officers rallied quickly. The girl fell back opportunely for the arms of one of them, and her wild heels clicked twice on the floor. "I am innocent! Oh, I am innocent!"

People pity those who need none, and the guilty sob alone; but innocent or guilty, this girl's scream described such a profound depth of woe—it was so graphic of grief, that it slit with a dagger's sweep the curtain of commonplace, and disclosed the gloom-shrouded spectre that sat in the young girl's heart so plainly, in so universal a tone of the mind, that a man heard expressed some far-off midnight terror of his own thought.

The cries died away down the stone-paved passage. A patrol-man leaned one arm composedly on the railing, and down below him stood an aged, almost toothless wanderer, tottering and grinning.

"Plase, yer honer," said the old man as the time arrived for him to speak, "if ye'll lave me go this time, I've niver been dhrunk befoor, sir."

A court officer lifted his hand to hide a smile.

THE AUCTION

Some said that Ferguson gave up sailoring because he was tired of the sea. Some said that it was because he loved a woman. In truth it was because he was tired of the sea and because he loved a woman.

He saw the woman once, and immediately she became for him the symbol of all things unconnected with the sea. He did not trouble to look again at the grey old goddess, the muttering slave of the moon. Her splendours, her treacheries, her smiles, her rages, her vanities, were no longer on his mind. He took heels after a little human being, and the woman made his thought spin at all times like a top; whereas the ocean had only made him think when he was on watch.

He developed a grin for the power of the sea, and, in derision, he wanted to sell the red and green parrot which had sailed four voyages with him. The woman, however, had a sentiment concerning the bird's plumage, and she commanded Ferguson to keep it in order, as it happened, that she might forget to put food in its cage.

The parrot did not attend the wedding. It stayed at home and blasphemed at a stock of furniture, bought on the installment plan, and arrayed for the reception of the bride and groom.

As a sailor, Ferguson had suffered the acute hankering for port; and being now always in port, he tried to force life to become an endless picnic. He was not an example of diligent and peaceful citizenship. Ablution became difficult in the little apartment, because Ferguson kept the wash-basin filled with ice and bottles of beer: and so, finally, the dealer in second-hand furniture agreed to auction the household goods on commission. Owing to an exceedingly liberal definition of a term, the parrot and cage were included. "On the level?" cried the parrot, "On the level? On the level? On the level?"

On the way to the sale, Ferguson's wife spoke hopefully. "You can't tell, Jim," she said. "Perhaps some of 'em will get to biddin', and we might get almost as much as we paid for the things."

The auction room was in a cellar. It was crowded with people and with house furniture; so that as the auctioneer's assistant moved from one piece to another he caused a great shuffling. There was an astounding number of old women in curious bonnets. The rickety stairway was thronged with men who wished to smoke and be free from the old women. Two lamps made all the faces appear yellow as parchment. Incidentally they could impart a lustre of value to very poor furniture.

The auctioneer was a fat, shrewd-looking individual, who seemed also to be a great bully. The assistant was the most imperturbable of beings, moving with the dignity of an image on rollers. As the Fergusons forced their way down the stair-way, the assistant roared: "Number twenty-one!"

"Number twenty-one!" cried the auctioneer. "Number twenty-one! A fine new handsome bureau! Two dollars? Two dollars is bid! Two and a half! Two and a half! Three? Three is bid. Four! Four dollars! A fine new handsome bureau at four dollars! Four dollars! Four dollars! F-o-u-r d-o-l-l-a-r-s! Sold at four dollars."

"On the level?" cried the parrot, muffled somewhere among furniture and carpets. "On the level? On the level?" Every one tittered.

Mrs. Ferguson had turned pale, and gripped her husband's arm. "Jim! Did you hear? The bureau—four dollars—"

Ferguson glowered at her with the swift brutality of a man afraid of a scene. "Shut up, can't you!"

Mrs. Ferguson took a seat upon the steps; and hidden there by the thick ranks of men, she began to softly sob. Through her tears appeared the yellowish mist of the lamplight, streaming about the monstrous shadows of the spectators. From time to time these latter whispered eagerly: "See, that went cheap!" In fact when anything was bought at a particularly low price, a murmur of admiration arose for the successful bidder.

The bedstead was sold for two dollars, the mattresses and springs for one dollar and sixty cents. This figure seemed to go through the woman's heart. There was derision in the sound of it. She bowed her head in her hands. "Oh, God, a dollar-sixty! Oh, God, a dollar-sixty!"

The parrot was evidently under heaps of carpet, but the dauntless bird still raised the cry, "On the level?"

Some of the men near Mrs. Ferguson moved timidly away upon hearing her low sobs. They perfectly understood that a woman in tears is formidable.

The shrill voice went like a hammer, beat and beat, upon the woman's heart. An odour of varnish, of the dust of old carpets, assailed her and seemed to possess a sinister meaning. The golden haze from the two lamps was an atmosphere of shame, sorrow, greed. But it was when the parrot called that a terror of the place and of the eyes of the people arose in her so strongly that she could not have lifted her head any more than if her neck had been of iron.

At last came the parrot's turn. The assistant fumbled until he found the ring of the cage, and the bird was drawn into view. It adjusted its feathers calmly and cast a rolling wicked eye over the crowd.

"Oh, the good ship Sarah sailed the seas,

And the wind it blew all day—"

This was the part of a ballad which Ferguson had tried to teach it. With a singular audacity and scorn, the parrot bawled these lines at the auctioneer as if it considered them to bear some particular insult.

The throng in the cellar burst into laughter. The auctioneer attempted to start the bidding, and the parrot interrupted with a repetition of the lines. It swaggered to and fro on its perch, and gazed at the faces of the crowd, with so much rowdy understanding and derision that even the auctioneer could not confront it. The auction was brought to a halt; a wild hilarity developed, and every one gave jeering advice.

Ferguson looked down at his wife and groaned. She had cowered against the wall, hiding her face. He touched her shoulder and she arose. They sneaked softly up the stairs with heads bowed.

Out in the street, Ferguson gripped his fists and said: "Oh, but wouldn't I like to strangle it!"

His wife cried in a voice of wild grief: "It—it m—made us a laughing-stock in—in front of all that crowd!"

For the auctioning of their household goods, the sale of their home—this financial calamity lost its power in the presence of the social shame contained in a crowd's laughter.

THE PACE OF YOUTH

I

Stimson stood in a corner and glowered. He was a fierce man and had indomitable whiskers, albeit he was very small.

"That young tarrier," he whispered to himself. "He wants to quit makin' eyes at Lizzie. This is too much of a good thing. First thing you know, he'll get fired."

His brow creased in a frown, he strode over to the huge open doors and looked at a sign. "Stimson's Mammoth Merry-Go-Round," it read, and the glory of it was great. Stimson stood and contemplated the sign. It was an enormous affair; the letters were as large as men. The glow of it, the grandeur of it was very apparent to Stimson. At the end of his contemplation, he shook his head thoughtfully, determinedly. "No, no," he muttered. "This is too much of a good thing. First thing you know, he'll get fired."

A soft booming sound of surf, mingled with the cries of bathers, came from the beach. There was a vista of sand and sky and sea that drew to a mystic point far away in the northward. In the mighty angle, a girl in a red dress was crawling slowly like some kind of a spider on the fabric of nature. A few flags hung lazily above where the bath-houses were marshalled in compact squares. Upon the edge of the sea stood a ship with its shadowy sails painted dimly upon the sky, and high overhead in the still, sun-shot air a great hawk swung and drifted slowly.

Within the Merry-Go-Round there was a whirling circle of ornamental lions, giraffes, camels, ponies, goats, glittering with varnish and metal that caught swift reflections from windows high above them. With stiff wooden legs, they swept on in a never-ending race, while a great orchestrion clamoured in wild speed. The summer sunlight sprinkled its gold upon the garnet canopies carried by the tireless racers and upon all the devices of decoration that made Stimson's machine magnificent and famous. A host of laughing children bestrode the animals, bending forward like charging cavalrymen, and shaking reins and whooping in glee. At intervals they leaned out perilously to clutch at iron rings that were tendered to them by a long wooden arm. At the intense moment before the swift grab for the rings one could see their little nervous bodies quiver with eagerness; the laughter rang shrill and excited. Down in the long rows of benches, crowds of people sat watching the game, while occasionally a father might arise and go near to shout encouragement, cautionary commands, or applause at his flying offspring. Frequently mothers called out: "Be careful, Georgie!" The orchestrion bellowed and thundered on its platform, filling the ears with its long monotonous song. Over in a corner, a man in a white apron and behind a counter roared above the tumult: "Pop corn! Pop corn!"

A young man stood upon a small, raised platform, erected in a manner of a pulpit, and just without the line of the circling figures. It was his duty to manipulate the wooden arm and affix the rings. When all were gone into the hands of the triumphant children, he held forth a basket, into which they returned all save the coveted brass one, which meant another ride free and made the holder very illustrious. The young man stood all day upon his narrow platform, affixing rings or holding forth the basket. He was a sort of general squire in these lists of childhood. He was very busy.

And yet Stimson, the astute, had noticed that the young man frequently found time to twist about on his platform and smile at a girl who shyly sold tickets behind a silvered netting. This, indeed, was the great reason of Stimson's glowering. The young man upon the raised platform had no manner of licence to smile at the girl behind the silvered netting. It was a most gigantic insolence. Stimson was amazed at it. "By Jiminy," he said to himself again, "that fellow is smiling at my daughter." Even in this tone of great wrath it could be discerned that Stimson was filled with wonder that any youth should dare smile at the daughter in the presence of the august father.

Often the dark-eyed girl peered between the shining wires, and, upon being detected by the young man, she usually turned her head away quickly to prove to him that she was not interested. At other times, however, her eyes seemed filled with a tender fear lest he should fall from that exceedingly dangerous platform. As for the young man, it was plain that these glances filled him with valour, and he stood carelessly upon his perch, as if he deemed it of no consequence that he might fall from it. In all the complexities of his daily life and duties he found opportunity to gaze ardently at the vision behind the netting.

This silent courtship was conducted over the heads of the crowd who thronged about the bright machine. The swift eloquent glances of the young man went noiselessly and unseen with their message. There had finally become established between the two in this manner a subtle understanding and companionship. They communicated accurately all that they felt. The boy told his love, his reverence, his hope in the changes of the future. The girl told him that she loved him, that she did not love him, that she did not know if she loved him, that she loved him. Sometimes a little sign saying "cashier" in gold letters, and hanging upon the silvered netting, got directly in range and interfered with the tender message.

The love affair had not continued without anger, unhappiness, despair. The girl had once smiled brightly upon a youth who came to buy some tickets for his little sister, and the young man upon the platform observing this smile had been filled with gloomy rage. He stood like a dark statue of vengeance upon his pedestal and thrust out the basket to the children with a gesture that was full of scorn for their hollow happiness, for their insecure and temporary joy. For five hours he did not once look at the girl when she was looking at him. He was going to crush her with his indifference; he was going to demonstrate that he had never been serious. However, when he narrowly observed her in secret he discovered that she seemed more blythe than was usual with her. When he found that his apparent indifference had not crushed her he suffered greatly. She did not love him, he concluded. If she had loved him she would have been crushed. For two days he lived a miserable existence upon his high perch. He consoled himself by thinking of how unhappy he was, and by swift, furtive glances at the loved face. At any rate he was in her presence, and he could get a good view from his perch when there was no interference by the little sign: "Cashier."

But suddenly, swiftly, these clouds vanished, and under the imperial blue sky of the restored confidence they dwelt in peace, a peace that was satisfaction, a peace that, like a babe, put its trust in the treachery of the future. This confidence endured until the next day, when she, for an unknown cause, suddenly refused to look at him. Mechanically he continued his task, his brain dazed, a tortured victim of doubt, fear, suspicion. With his eyes he supplicated her to telegraph an explanation. She replied with a stony glance that froze his blood. There was a great difference in their respective reasons for becoming angry. His were always foolish, but apparent, plain as the moon. Hers were subtle, feminine, as incomprehensible as the stars, as mysterious as the shadows at night.

They fell and soared, and soared and fell in this manner until they knew that to live without each other would be a wandering in deserts. They had grown so intent upon the uncertainties, the variations, the guessings of their affair that the world had become but a huge immaterial background. In time of peace their smiles were soft and prayerful, caresses confided to the air. In time of war, their youthful hearts, capable of profound agony, were wrung by the intricate emotions of doubt. They were the victims of the dread angel of affectionate speculation that forces the brain endlessly on roads that lead nowhere.

At night, the problem of whether she loved him confronted the young man like a spectre, looming as high as a hill and telling him not to delude himself. Upon the following day, this battle of the night displayed itself in the renewed fervour of his glances and in their increased number. Whenever he thought he could detect that she too was suffering, he felt a thrill of joy.

But there came a time when the young man looked back upon these contortions with contempt. He believed then that he had imagined his pain. This came about when the redoubtable Stimson marched forward to participate.

"This has got to stop," Stimson had said to himself, as he stood and watched them. They had grown careless of the light world that clattered about them; they were become so engrossed in their personal drama that the language of their eyes was almost as obvious as gestures. And Stimson, through his keenness, his wonderful, infallible penetration, suddenly came into possession of these obvious facts. "Well, of all the nerves," he said, regarding with a new interest the young man upon the perch.

He was a resolute man. He never hesitated to grapple with a crisis. He decided to overturn everything at once, for, although small, he was very fierce and impetuous. He resolved to crush this dreaming.

He strode over to the silvered netting. "Say, you want to quit your everlasting grinning at that idiot," he said, grimly.

The girl cast down her eyes and made a little heap of quarters into a stack. She was unable to withstand the terrible scrutiny of her small and fierce father.

Stimson turned from his daughter and went to a spot beneath the platform. He fixed his eyes upon the young man and said—

"I've been speakin' to Lizzie. You better attend strictly to your own business or there'll be a new man here next week." It was as if he had blazed away with a shot-gun. The young man reeled upon his perch. At last he in a measure regained his composure and managed to stammer: "A—all right, sir." He knew that denials would be futile with the terrible Stimson. He agitatedly began to rattle the rings in the basket, and pretend that he was obliged to count them or inspect them in some way. He, too, was unable to face the great Stimson.

For a moment, Stimson stood in fine satisfaction and gloated over the effect of his threat.

"I've fixed them," he said complacently, and went out to smoke a cigar and revel in himself. Through his mind went the proud reflection that people who came in contact with his granite will usually ended in quick and abject submission.

II

One evening, a week after Stimson had indulged in the proud reflection that people who came in contact with his granite will usually ended in quick and abject submission, a young feminine friend of the girl behind the silvered netting came to her there and asked her to walk on the beach after "Stimson's Mammoth Merry-Go-Round" was closed for the night. The girl assented with a nod.

The young man upon the perch holding the rings saw this nod and judged its meaning. Into his mind came an idea of defeating the watchfulness of the redoubtable Stimson.

When the Merry-Go-Round was closed and the two girls started for the beach, he wandered off aimlessly in another direction, but he kept them in view, and as soon as he was assured that he had escaped the vigilance of Stimson, he followed them.

The electric lights on the beach made a broad band of tremoring light, extending parallel to the sea, and upon the wide walk there slowly paraded a great crowd, intermingling, intertwining, sometimes colliding. In the darkness stretched the vast purple expanse of the ocean, and the deep indigo sky above was peopled with yellow stars. Occasionally out upon the water a whirling mass of froth suddenly flashed into view, like a great ghostly robe appearing, and then vanished, leaving the sea in its darkness, from whence came those bass tones of the water's unknown emotion. A wind, cool, reminiscent of the wave wastes, made the women hold their wraps about their throats, and caused the men to grip the rims of their straw hats. It carried the noise of the band in the pavilion in gusts. Sometimes people unable to hear the music, glanced up at the pavilion and were reassured upon beholding the distant leader still gesticulating and bobbing, and the other members of the band with their lips glued to their instruments. High in the sky soared an unassuming moon, faintly silver.

For a time the young man was afraid to approach the two girls; he followed them at a distance and called himself a coward. At last, however, he saw them stop on the outer edge of the crowd and stand silently listening to the voices of the sea. When he came to where they stood, he was trembling in his agitation. They had not seen him.

"Lizzie," he began. "I——"

The girl wheeled instantly and put her hand to her throat.

"Oh, Frank, how you frightened me," she said—inevitably.

"Well, you know I—I——" he stuttered.

But the other girl was one of those beings who are born to attend at tragedies. She had for love a reverence, an admiration that was greater the more that she contemplated the fact that she knew nothing of it. This couple, with their emotions, awed her and made her humbly wish that she might be destined to be of some service to them. She was very homely.

When the young man faltered before them, she, in her sympathy, actually over-estimated the crisis, and felt that he might fall dying at their feet. Shyly, but with courage, she marched to the rescue.

"Won't you come and walk on the beach with us?" she said.

The young woman gave her a glance of deep gratitude which was not without the patronage which a man in his condition naturally feels for one who pities it. The three walked on.

Finally, the being who was born to attend at this tragedy, said that she wished to sit down and gaze at the sea, alone.

They politely urged her to walk on with them, but she was obstinate. She wished to gaze at the sea, alone. The young man swore to himself that he would be her friend until he died.

And so the two young lovers went on without her. They turned once to look at her.

"Jennie's awful nice," said the girl.

"You bet she is," replied the young man, ardently.

They were silent for a little time.

At last the girl said—

"You were angry at me yesterday."

"No, I wasn't."

"Yes, you were, too. You wouldn't look at me once all day."

"No, I wasn't angry. I was only putting on."

Though she had, of course, known it, this confession seemed to make her very indignant. She flashed a resentful glance at him.

"Oh, were you, indeed?" she said with a great air.

For a few minutes she was so haughty with him that he loved her to madness. And directly this poem, which stuck at his lips, came forth lamely in fragments.

When they walked back toward the other girl and saw the patience of her attitude, their hearts swelled in a patronizing and secondary tenderness for her.

They were very happy. If they had been miserable they would have charged this fairy scene of the night with a criminal heartlessness; but as they were joyous, they vaguely wondered how the purple sea, the yellow stars, the changing crowds under the electric lights could be so phlegmatic and stolid.

They walked home by the lake-side way, and out upon the water those gay paper lanterns, flashing, fleeting, and careering, sang to them, sang a chorus of red and violet, and green and gold; a song of mystic bands of the future.

One day, when business paused during a dull sultry afternoon, Stimson went up town. Upon his return, he found that the popcorn man, from his stand over in a corner, was keeping an eye upon the cashier's cage, and that nobody at all was attending to the wooden arm and the iron rings. He strode forward like a sergeant of grenadiers.

"Where in thunder is Lizzie?" he demanded, a cloud of rage in his eyes.

The popcorn man, although associated long with Stimson, had never got over being dazed.

"They've—they've—gone round to th'—th'—house," he said with difficulty, as if he had just been stunned.

"Whose house?" snapped Stimson.

"Your—your house, I 'spose," said the popcorn man.

Stimson marched round to his home. Kingly denunciations surged, already formulated, to the tip of his tongue, and he bided the moment when his anger could fall upon the heads of that pair of children. He found his wife convulsive and in tears.

"Where's Lizzie?"

And then she burst forth—"Oh—John—John-they've run away, I know they have. They drove by here not three minutes ago. They must have done it on purpose to bid me good-bye, for Lizzie waved her hand sad-like; and then, before I could get out to ask where they were going or what, Frank whipped up the horse."

Stimson gave vent to a dreadful roar.

"Get my revolver—get a hack—get my revolver, do you hear—what the devil——" His voice became incoherent.

He had always ordered his wife about as if she were a battalion of infantry, and despite her misery, the training of years forced her to spring mechanically to obey; but suddenly she turned to him with a shrill appeal.

"Oh, John—not—the—revolver."

"Confound it, let go of me," he roared again, and shook her from him.

He ran hatless upon the street. There were a multitude of hacks at the summer resort, but it was ages to him before he could find one. Then he charged it like a bull.

"Uptown," he yelled, as he tumbled into the rear seat.

The hackman thought of severed arteries. His galloping horse distanced a large number of citizens who had been running to find what caused such contortions by the little hatless man.

It chanced as the bouncing hack went along near the lake, Stimson gazed across the calm grey expanse and recognized a colour in a bonnet and a pose of a head. A buggy was travelling along a highway that led to Sorington. Stimson bellowed—"There—there—there they are—in that buggy."

The hackman became inspired with the full knowledge of the situation. He struck a delirious blow with the whip. His mouth expanded in a grin of excitement and joy. It came to pass that this old vehicle, with its drowsy horse and its dusty-eyed and tranquil driver, seemed suddenly to awaken, to become animated and fleet. The horse ceased to ruminate on his state, his air of reflection vanished. He became intent upon his aged legs and spread them in quaint and ridiculous devices for speed. The driver, his eyes shining, sat critically in his seat. He watched each motion of this rattling machine down before him. He resembled an engineer. He used the whip with judgment and deliberation as the engineer would have used coal or oil. The horse clacked swiftly upon the macadam, the wheels hummed, the body of the vehicle wheezed and groaned.

Stimson, in the rear seat, was erect in that impassive attitude that comes sometimes to the furious man when he is obliged to leave the battle to others. Frequently, however, the tempest in his breast came to his face and he howled—

"Go it—go it—you're gaining; pound 'im! Thump the life out of 'im; hit 'im hard, you fool." His hand grasped the rod that supported the carriage top, and it was clenched so that the nails were faintly blue.

Ahead, that other carriage had been flying with speed, as from realization of the menace in the rear. It bowled away rapidly, drawn by the eager spirit of a young and modern horse. Stimson could see the buggy-top bobbing, bobbing. That little pane, like an eye, was a derision to him. Once he leaned forward and bawled angry sentences. He began to feel impotent; his whole expedition was a tottering of an old man upon a trail of birds. A sense of age made him choke again with wrath. That other vehicle, that was youth, with youth's pace; it was swift-flying with the hope of dreams. He began to comprehend those two children ahead of him, and he knew a sudden and strange awe, because he understood the power of their young blood, the power to fly strongly into the future and feel and hope again, even at that time when his bones must be laid in the earth. The dust rose easily from the hot road and stifled the nostrils of Stimson.

The highway vanished far away in a point with a suggestion of intolerable length. The other vehicle was becoming so small that Stimson could no longer see the derisive eye.

At last the hackman drew rein to his horse and turned to look at Stimson.

"No use, I guess," he said.

Stimson made a gesture of acquiescence, rage, despair. As the hackman turned his dripping horse about, Stimson sank back with the astonishment and grief of a man who has been defied by the universe. He had been in a great perspiration, and now his bald head felt cool and uncomfortable. He put up his hand with a sudden recollection that he had forgotten his hat.

At last he made a gesture. It meant that at any rate he was not responsible.

A DETAIL

The tiny old lady in the black dress and curious little black bonnet had at first seemed alarmed at the sound made by her feet upon the stone pavements. But later she forgot about it, for she suddenly came into the tempest of the Sixth Avenue shopping district, where from the streams of people and vehicles went up a roar like that from headlong mountain torrents.

She seemed then like a chip that catches, recoils, turns and wheels, a reluctant thing in the clutch of the impetuous river. She hesitated, faltered, debated with herself. Frequently she seemed about to address people; then of a sudden she would evidently lose her courage. Meanwhile the torrent jostled her, swung her this and that way.

At last, however, she saw two young women gazing in at a shop-window. They were well-dressed girls; they wore gowns with enormous sleeves that made them look like full-rigged ships with all sails set. They seemed to have plenty of time; they leisurely scanned the goods in the window. Other people had made the tiny old woman much afraid because obviously they were speeding to keep such tremendously important engagements. She went close to the girls and peered in at the same window. She watched them furtively for a time. Then finally she said—

"Excuse me!"

The girls looked down at this old face with its two large eyes turned towards them.

"Excuse me, can you tell me where I can get any work?"

For an instant the two girls stared. Then they seemed about to exchange a smile, but, at the last moment, they checked it. The tiny old lady's eyes were upon them. She was quaintly serious, silently expectant. She made one marvel that in that face the wrinkles showed no trace of experience, knowledge; they were simply little, soft, innocent creases. As for her glance, it had the trustfulness of ignorance and the candour of babyhood.

"I want to get something to do, because I need the money," she continued since, in their astonishment, they had not replied to her first question. "Of course I'm not strong and I couldn't do very much, but I can sew well; and in a house where there was a good many men folks, I could do all the mending. Do you know any place where they would like me to come?"

The young women did then exchange a smile, but it was a subtle tender smile, the edge of personal grief.

"Well, no, madame," hesitatingly said one of them at last; "I don't think I know any one."

A shade passed over the tiny old lady's face, a shadow of the wing of disappointment.

"Don't you?" she said, with a little struggle to be brave, in her voice.

Then the girl hastily continued—"But if you will give me your address, I may find some one, and if I do, I will surely let you know of it."

The tiny old lady dictated her address, bending over to watch the girl write on a visiting card with a little silver pencil. Then she said—

"I thank you very much." She bowed to them, smiling, and went on down the avenue.

As for the two girls, they walked to the curb and watched this aged figure, small and frail, in its black gown and curious black bonnet. At last, the crowd, the innumerable wagons, intermingling and changing with uproar and riot, suddenly engulfed it.

About Author

Stephen Crane (November 1, 1871 – June 5, 1900) was an American poet, novelist, and short story writer. Prolific throughout his short life, he wrote notable works in the Realist tradition as well as early examples of American Naturalism and Impressionism. He is recognized by modern critics as one of the most innovative writers of his generation.

The ninth surviving child of Methodist parents, Crane began writing at the age of four and had published several articles by the age of 16. Having little interest in university studies though he was active in a fraternity, he left Syracuse University in 1891 to work as a reporter and writer. Crane's first novel was the 1893 Bowery tale Maggie: A Girl of the Streets, generally considered by critics to be the first work of American literary Naturalism. He won international acclaim in 1895 for his Civil War novel The Red Badge of Courage, which he wrote without having any battle experience.

In 1896, Crane endured a highly publicized scandal after appearing as a witness in the trial of a suspected prostitute, an acquaintance named Dora Clark. Late that year he accepted an offer to travel to Cuba as a war correspondent. As he waited in Jacksonville, Florida for passage, he met Cora Taylor, with whom he began a lasting relationship. En route to Cuba, Crane's vessel the SS Commodore sank off the coast of Florida, leaving him and others adrift for 30 hours in a dinghy. Crane described the ordeal in "The Open Boat". During the final years of his life, he covered conflicts in Greece (accompanied by Cora, recognized as the first woman war correspondent) and later lived in England with her. He was befriended by writers such as Joseph Conrad and H. G. Wells. Plagued by financial difficulties and ill health, Crane died of tuberculosis in a Black Forest sanatorium in Germany at the age of 28.

At the time of his death, Crane was considered an important figure in American literature. After he was nearly forgotten for two decades, critics revived interest in his life and work. Crane's writing is characterized by vivid intensity, distinctive dialects, and irony. Common themes involve fear, spiritual crises and social isolation. Although recognized primarily for The Red Badge of Courage, which has become an American classic, Crane is also known for his poetry, journalism, and short stories such as "The Open Boat", "The Blue Hotel", "The Bride Comes to Yellow Sky", and The Monster. His writing made a deep impression on 20th-century writers, most prominent among them Ernest Hemingway, and is thought to have inspired the Modernists and the Imagists.

Biography

Early years

Stephen Crane was born on November 1, 1871, in Newark, New Jersey, to Jonathan Townley Crane, a minister in the Methodist Episcopal church, and Mary Helen Peck Crane, daughter of a clergyman, George Peck. He was the fourteenth and last child born to the couple. At 45, Helen Crane had suffered the early deaths of her previous four children, each of whom died within one year of birth. Nicknamed "Stevie" by the family, he joined eight surviving brothers and sisters—Mary Helen, George Peck, Jonathan Townley, William Howe, Agnes Elizabeth, Edmund Byran, Wilbur Fiske, and Luther.

The Cranes were descended from Jaspar Crane, a founder of New Haven Colony, who had migrated there from England in 1639. Stephen was named for a putative founder of Elizabethtown, New Jersey, who had, according to family tradition, come from England or Wales in 1665, as well as his great-great-grandfather Stephen Crane (1709–1780), a Revolutionary War patriot who served as New Jersey delegate to the First Continental Congress in Philadelphia. Crane later wrote that his father, Dr. Crane, "was a great, fine, simple mind," who had written numerous tracts on theology. Although his mother was a popular spokeswoman for the Woman's Christian Temperance Union and a highly religious woman, Crane wrote that he did not believe "she was as narrow as most of her friends or family." The young Stephen was raised primarily by his sister Agnes, who was 15 years his senior. The family moved to Port Jervis, New York, in 1876, where Dr. Crane became the pastor of Drew Methodist Church, a position that he retained until his death.

As a child, Stephen was often sickly and afflicted by constant colds.

When the boy was almost two, his father wrote in his diary that his youngest son became "so sick that we are anxious about him." Despite his fragile nature, Crane was an intelligent child who taught himself to read before the age of four. His first known inquiry, recorded by his father, dealt with writing; at the age of three, while imitating his brother Townley's writing, he asked his mother, "how do you spell O?" In December 1879, Crane wrote a poem about wanting a dog for Christmas. Entitled "I'd Rather Have –", it is his first surviving poem. Stephen was not regularly enrolled in school until January 1880, but he had no difficulty in completing two grades in six weeks. Recalling this feat, he wrote that it "sounds like the lie of a fond mother at a teaparty, but I do remember that I got ahead very fast and that father was very pleased with me."

Dr. Crane died on February 16, 1880, at the age of 60; Stephen was eight years old. Some 1,400 people mourned Dr. Crane at his funeral, more than double the size of his congregation. After her husband's death, Mrs. Crane moved to Roseville, near Newark, leaving Stephen in the care of his older brother Edmund, with whom the young boy lived with cousins in Sussex County. He next lived with his brother William, a lawyer, in Port Jervis for several years.

His older sister Helen took him to Asbury Park to be with their brother Townley and his wife, Fannie. Townley was a professional journalist; he headed the Long Branch department of both the New-York Tribune and the Associated Press, and also served as editor of the Asbury Park Shore Press. Agnes, another Crane sister, joined the siblings in New Jersey. She took a position at Asbury Park's intermediate school and moved in with Helen to care for the young Stephen.

Within a couple of years, the Crane family suffered more losses. First, Townley and his wife lost their two young children. His wife Fannie died of Bright's disease in November 1883. Agnes Crane became ill and died on June 10, 1884, of meningitis at the age of 28.

Schooling

Crane wrote his first known story, "Uncle Jake and the Bell Handle", when he was 14. In late 1885, he enrolled at Pennington Seminary, a ministry-focused coeducational boarding school 7 miles (11 km) north of Trenton. His father had been principal there from 1849 to 1858. Soon after her youngest son left for school, Mrs. Crane began suffering what the Asbury Park Shore Press reported as "a temporary aberration of the mind." She had apparently recovered by early 1886, but later that year, her son, 23-year-old Luther Crane, died after falling in front of an oncoming train while working as a flagman for the Erie Railroad. It was the fourth death in six years among Stephen's immediate family.

After two years, Crane left Pennington for Claverack College, a quasi-military school. He later looked back on his time at Claverack as "the happiest period of my life although I was not aware of it." A classmate remembered him as a highly literate but erratic student, lucky to pass examinations in math and science, and yet "far in advance of his fellow students in his knowledge of History and Literature", his favorite subjects. While he held an impressive record on the drill field and baseball diamond, Crane generally did not excel in the classroom. Not having a middle name, as was customary among other students, he took to signing his name "Stephen T. Crane" in order "to win recognition as a regular fellow". Crane was seen as friendly, but also moody and rebellious. He sometimes skipped class in order to play baseball, a game in which he starred as catcher. He was also greatly interested in the school's military training program. He rose rapidly in the ranks of the student battalion. One classmate described him as "indeed physically attractive without being handsome", but he was aloof, reserved and not generally popular at Claverack. Although academically weak, Crane gained experience at Claverack that provided background (and likely some anecdotes from the Civil War veterans on the staff) that proved useful when he came to write The Red Badge of Courage.

In mid-1888, Crane became his brother Townley's assistant at a New Jersey shore news bureau, working there every summer until 1892. Crane's first publication under his byline was an article on the explorer Henry M. Stanley's famous quest to find the Scottish missionary David Livingstone in Africa. It appeared in the February 1890 Claverack College Vidette. Within a few months, Crane was persuaded by his family to forgo a military career and transfer to Lafayette College in Easton, Pennsylvania, in order to pursue a mining engineering degree. He registered at Lafayette on September 12, and promptly became involved in extracurricular activities; he took up baseball again and joined the largest fraternity, Delta Upsilon. He also joined both rival literary societies, named for (George) Washington and (Benjamin) Franklin. Crane infrequently attended classes and ended the semester with grades for four of the seven courses he had taken.

After one semester, Crane transferred to Syracuse University, where he enrolled as a non-degree candidate in the College of Liberal Arts. He roomed in the Delta Upsilon fraternity house and joined the baseball team. Attending just one class (English Literature) during the middle trimester, he remained in residence while taking no courses in the third semester.

Concentrating on his writing, Crane began to experiment with tone and style while trying out different subjects. He published his fictional story, "Great Bugs of Onondaga," simultaneously in the Syracuse Daily Standard and the New York Tribune. Declaring college "a waste of time", Crane decided to become a full-time writer and reporter. He attended a Delta Upsilon chapter meeting on June 12, 1891, but shortly afterward left college for good.

Full-time writer

In the summer of 1891, Crane often camped with friends in the nearby area of Sullivan County, New York, where his brother Edmund occupied a house obtained as part of their brother William's Hartwood Club (Association) land dealings. He used this area as the geographic setting for several short stories, which were posthumously published in a collection under the title Stephen Crane: Sullivan County Tales and Sketches. Crane showed two of these works to Tribune editor Willis Fletcher Johnson, a friend of the family, who accepted them for the publication. "Hunting Wild Dogs" and "The Last of the Mohicans" were the first of fourteen unsigned Sullivan County sketches and tales that were published in the Tribune between February and July 1892. Crane also showed Johnson an early draft of his first novel, Maggie: A Girl of the Streets.

Later that summer, Crane met and befriended author Hamlin Garland, who had been lecturing locally on American literature and the expressive arts; on August 17 he gave a talk on novelist William Dean Howells, which Crane wrote up for the Tribune. Garland became a mentor for and champion of the young writer, whose intellectual honesty impressed him. Their relationship suffered in later years, however, because Garland disapproved of Crane's alleged immorality, related to his living with a woman married to another man.

Stephen moved into his brother Edmund's house in Lakeview, a suburb of Paterson, New Jersey, in the fall of 1891. From here he made frequent trips into New York City, writing and reporting particularly on its impoverished tenement districts. Crane focused particularly on The Bowery, a small and once prosperous neighborhood in the southern part of Manhattan. After the Civil War, Bowery shops and mansions had given way to saloons, dance halls, brothels and flophouses, all of which Crane frequented. He later said he did so for research. He was attracted to the human nature found in the slums, considering it "open and plain, with nothing hidden". Believing nothing honest and unsentimental had been written about the Bowery, Crane became determined to do so himself; this was the setting of his first novel. On December 7, 1891, Crane's mother died at the age of 64, and the 20-year-old appointed Edmund as his guardian.

Despite being frail, undernourished and suffering from a hacking cough, which did not prevent him from smoking cigarettes, in the spring of 1892 Crane began a romance with Lily Brandon Munroe, a married woman who was estranged from her husband. Although Munroe later said Crane "was not a handsome man", she admired his "remarkable almond-shaped gray eyes." He begged her to elope with him, but her family opposed the match because Crane lacked money and prospects, and she declined. Their last meeting likely occurred in April 1898, when he again asked her to run away with him and she again refused.

Between July 2 and September 11, 1892, Crane published at least ten news reports on Asbury Park affairs. Although a Tribune colleague stated that Crane "was not highly distinguished above any other boy of twenty who had gained a reputation for saying and writing bright things," that summer his reporting took on a more skeptical, hypocrisy-deflating tone. A storm of controversy erupted over a report he wrote on the Junior Order of United American Mechanics' American Day Parade, entitled "Parades and Entertainments". Published on August 21, the report juxtaposes the "bronzed, slope-shouldered, uncouth" marching men "begrimed with dust" and the spectators dressed in "summer gowns, lace parasols, tennis trousers, straw hats and indifferent smiles". Believing they were being ridiculed, some JOUAM marchers were outraged and wrote to the editor. The owner of the Tribune, Whitelaw Reid, was that year's Republican vice-presidential candidate, and this likely increased the sensitivity of the paper's management to the issue. Although Townley wrote a piece for the Asbury Park Daily Press in his brother's defense, the Tribune quickly apologized to its readers, calling Stephen Crane's piece "a bit of random correspondence, passed inadvertently by the copy editor". Hamlin Garland and biographer John Barry attested that Crane told them he had been dismissed by the Tribune, although Willis Fletcher Johnson later denied this. The paper did not publish any of Crane's work after 1892.

> Such an assemblage of the spraddle-legged men of the middle class, whose hands were bent and shoulders stooped from delving and constructing, had never appeared to an Asbury Park summer crowd, and the latter was vaguely amused.

> — Stephen Crane, account of the JOUAM parade as it appeared in the Tribune.

Life in New York

Crane struggled to make a living as a free-lance writer, contributing sketches and feature articles to various New York newspapers. In October 1892, he moved into a rooming house in Manhattan whose boarders were a group of medical students. During this time, he expanded or entirely reworked Maggie: A Girl of the Streets, which is about a girl who "blossoms in a mud-puddle" and becomes a pitiful victim of circumstance. In the winter of 1893, Crane took the manuscript of Maggie to Richard Watson Gilder, who rejected it for publication in The Century Magazine.

Crane decided to publish it privately, with money he had inherited from his mother. The novel was published in late February or early March 1893 by a small printing shop that usually printed medical books and religious tracts. The typewritten title page for the Library of Congress copyright application read simply: "A Girl of the Streets, / A Story of New York. / —By—/Stephen Crane." The name "Maggie" was added to the title later. Crane used the pseudonym "Johnston Smith" for the novel's initial publication, later telling friend and artist Corwin Knapp Linson that the nom de plume was the "commonest name I could think of. I had an editor friend named Johnson, and put in the "t", and no one could find me in the mob of Smiths." Hamlin Garland reviewed the work in the June 1893 issue of The Arena, calling it "the most truthful and unhackneyed study of the slums I have yet read, fragment though it is." Despite this early praise, Crane became depressed and destitute from having spent $869 for 1,100 copies of a novel that did not sell; he ended up giving a hundred copies away. He would later remember "how I looked forward to publication and pictured the sensation I thought it would make. It fell flat. Nobody seemed to notice it or care for it... Poor Maggie! She was one of my first loves."

In March 1893, Crane spent hours lounging in Linson's studio while having his portrait painted. He became fascinated with issues of the Century that were largely devoted to famous battles and military leaders from the Civil War. Frustrated with the dryly written stories, Crane stated, "I wonder that some of those fellows don't tell how they felt in those scraps. They spout enough of what they did, but they're as emotionless as rocks." Crane returned to these magazines during subsequent visits to Linson's studio, and eventually the idea of writing a war novel overtook him. He would later state that he "had been unconsciously working the detail of the story out through most of his boyhood" and had imagined "war stories ever since he was out of knickerbockers." This novel would ultimately become The Red Badge of Courage.

A river, amber-tinted in the shadow of its banks, purled at the army's feet; and at night, when the stream had become of a sorrowful blackness, one could see across it the red, eyelike gleam of hostile campfires set in the low brows of distant hills.

— Stephen Crane, The Red Badge of Courage

From the beginning, Crane wished to show how it felt to be in a war by writing "a psychological portrayal of fear." Conceiving his story from the point of view of a young private who is at first filled with boyish dreams of the glory of war and then quickly becomes disillusioned by war's reality, Crane borrowed the private's surname, "Fleming", from his sister-in-law's maiden name. He later said that the first paragraphs came to him with "every word in place, every comma, every period fixed." Working mostly nights, he wrote from around midnight until four or five in the morning. Because he could not afford a typewriter, he wrote carefully in ink on legal-sized paper, seldom crossing through or interlining a word. If he did change something, he would rewrite the whole page.

While working on his second novel, Crane remained prolific, concentrating on publishing stories to stave off poverty; "An Experiment in Misery", based on Crane's experiences in the Bowery, was printed by the New York Press. He also wrote five or six poems a day. In early 1894, he showed some of his poems or "lines" as he called them, to Hamlin Garland, who said he read "some thirty in all" with "growing wonder." Although Garland and William Dean Howells encouraged him to submit his poetry for publication, Crane's free verse was too unconventional for most. After brief wrangling between poet and publisher, Copeland & Day accepted Crane's first book of poems, The Black Riders and Other Lines, although it would not be published until after The Red Badge of Courage. He received a 10 percent royalty and the publisher assured him that the book would be in a form "more severely classic than any book ever yet issued in America."

In the spring of 1894, Crane offered the finished manuscript of The Red Badge of Courage to McClure's Magazine, which had become the foremost magazine for Civil War literature. While McClure's delayed giving him an answer on his novel, they offered him an assignment writing about the Pennsylvania coal mines. "In the Depths of a Coal Mine", a story with pictures by Linson, was syndicated by McClure's in a number of newspapers, heavily edited. Crane was reportedly disgusted by the cuts, asking Linson: "Why the hell did they send me up there then? Do they want the public to think the coal mines gilded ball-rooms with the miners eating ice-cream in boiled shirt-fronts?"

Sources report that following an encounter with a male prostitute that spring, Crane began a novel on the subject entitled Flowers of Asphalt, which he later abandoned. The manuscript has never been recovered.

After discovering that McClure's could not afford to pay him, Crane took his war novel to Irving Bacheller of the Bacheller-Johnson Newspaper Syndicate, which agreed to publish The Red Badge of Courage in serial form. Between the third and the ninth of December 1894, The Red Badge of Courage was published in some half-dozen newspapers in the United States. Although it was greatly cut for syndication, Bacheller attested to its causing a stir, saying "its quality [was] immediately felt and recognized." The lead editorial in the Philadelphia Press of December 7 said that Crane "is a new name now and unknown, but everybody will be talking about him if he goes on as he has begun".

Travels and fame

At the end of January 1895, Crane left on what he called "a very long and circuitous newspaper trip" to the west. While writing feature articles for the Bacheller syndicate, he traveled to Saint Louis, Missouri, Nebraska, New Orleans, Galveston, Texas and then Mexico City. Irving Bacheller would later state that he "sent Crane to Mexico for new color", which the author found in the form of Mexican slum life. Whereas he found the lower class in New York pitiful, he was impressed by the "superiority" of the Mexican peasants' contentment and "even refuse[d] to pity them."

Returning to New York five months later, Crane joined the Lantern (alternately spelled "Lanthom" or "Lanthorne") Club organized by a group of young writers and journalists. The Club, located on the roof of an old house on William Street near the Brooklyn Bridge, served as a drinking establishment of sorts and was decorated to look like a ship's cabin. There Crane ate one good meal a day, although friends were troubled by his "constant smoking, too much coffee, lack of food and poor teeth", as Nelson Greene put it. Living in near-poverty and greatly anticipating the publication of his books, Crane began work on two more novels: The Third Violet and George's Mother.

The Black Riders was published by Copeland & Day shortly before his return to New York in May, but it received mostly criticism, if not abuse, for the poems' unconventional style and use of free verse. A piece in the Bookman called Crane "the Aubrey Beardsley of poetry," and a commentator from the Chicago Daily Inter-Ocean stated that "there is not a line of poetry from the opening to the closing page. Whitman's Leaves of Grass were luminous in comparison. Poetic lunacy would be a better name for the book." In June, the New York Tribune dismissed the book as "so much trash." Crane was pleased that the book was "making some stir".

In contrast to the reception for Crane's poetry, The Red Badge of Courage was welcomed with acclaim after its publication by Appleton in September 1895. For the next four months, the book was in the top six on various bestseller lists around the country. It arrived on the literary scene "like a flash of lightning out of a clear winter sky", according to H. L. Mencken, who was about 15 at the time. The novel also became popular in Britain; Joseph Conrad, a future friend of Crane, wrote that the novel "detonated... with the impact and force of a twelve-inch shell charged with a very high explosive." Appleton published two, possibly three, printings in 1895 and as many as eleven more in 1896. Although some critics considered the work overly graphic and profane, it was widely heralded for its realistic portrayal of war and unique writing style. The Detroit Free Press declared that The Red Badge would give readers "so vivid a picture of the emotions and the horrors of the battlefield that you will pray your eyes may never look upon the reality."

Wanting to capitalize on the success of The Red Badge, McClure Syndicate offered Crane a contract to write a series on Civil War battlefields. Because it was a wish of his to "visit the battlefield—which I was to describe—at the time of year when it was fought", Crane agreed to take the assignment. Visiting battlefields in Northern Virginia, including Fredericksburg, he would later produce five more Civil War tales: "Three Miraculous Soldiers",

"The Veteran", "An Indiana Campaign", "An Episode of War" and The Little Regiment.

Scandal

At the age of 24, Crane, who was reveling in his success, became involved in a highly publicized case involving a suspected prostitute named Dora Clark. At 2 a.m. on September 16, 1896, he escorted two chorus girls and Clark from New York City's Broadway Garden, a popular "resort" where he had interviewed the women for a series he was writing. As Crane saw one woman safely to a streetcar, a plainclothes policeman named Charles Becker arrested the other two for solicitation; Crane was threatened with arrest when he tried to interfere. One of the women was released after Crane confirmed her erroneous claim that she was his wife, but Clark was charged and taken to the precinct. Against the advice of the arresting sergeant, Crane made a statement confirming Dora Clark's innocence, stating that "I only know that while with me she acted respectably, and that the policeman's charge was false." On the basis of Crane's testimony, Clark was discharged. The media seized upon the story; news spread to Philadelphia, Boston and beyond, with papers focusing on Crane's courage. The Stephen Crane story, as it became known, soon became a source for ridicule; the Chicago Dispatch in particular quipped that "Stephen Crane is respectfully informed that association with women in scarlet is not necessarily a 'Red Badge of Courage' ".

A couple of weeks after her trial, Clark pressed charges of false arrest against the officer who had arrested her. The next day, the officer physically attacked Clark in the presence of witnesses for having brought charges against him. Crane, who initially went briefly to Philadelphia to escape the pressure of publicity, returned to New York to give testimony at Becker's trial despite advice given to him from Theodore Roosevelt, who was Police Commissioner at the time and a new acquaintance of Crane. The defense targeted Crane: police raided his apartment and interviewed people who knew him, trying to find incriminating evidence in order to lessen the effect of his testimony. A vigorous cross-examination took place that sought to portray Crane as a man of dubious morals; while the prosecution proved that he frequented brothels, Crane claimed this was merely for research purposes. After the trial ended on

October 16, the arresting officer was exonerated, and Crane's reputation was ruined.

Cora Taylor and the Commodore shipwreck

> None of them knew the color of the sky. Their eyes glanced level and were fastened upon the waves that swept toward them. These waves were of the hue of slate, save for the tops, which were of foaming white, and all of the men knew the colors of the sea.
>
> — Stephen Crane, "The Open Boat"

Given $700 in Spanish gold by the Bacheller-Johnson syndicate to work as a war correspondent in Cuba as the Spanish–American War was pending, the 25-year-old Crane left New York on November 27, 1896, on a train bound for Jacksonville, Florida. Upon arrival in Jacksonville, he registered at the St. James Hotel under the alias of Samuel Carleton to maintain anonymity while seeking passage to Cuba. While waiting for a boat, he toured the city and visited the local brothels. Within days he met 31-year-old Cora Taylor, proprietor of the downtown bawdy house Hotel de Dream. Born into a respectable Boston family, Taylor (whose legal name was Cora Ethel Stewart) had already had two brief marriages; her first husband, Vinton Murphy, divorced her on grounds of adultery. In 1889, she had married British Captain Donald William Stewart. She left him in 1892 for another man, but was still legally married. By the time Crane arrived, Taylor had been in Jacksonville for two years. She lived a bohemian lifestyle, owned a hotel of assignation, and was a well-known and respected local figure. The two spent much time together while Crane awaited his departure. He was finally cleared to leave for the Cuban port of Cienfuegos on New Year's Eve aboard the SS Commodore.

The ship sailed from Jacksonville with 27 or 28 men and a cargo of supplies and ammunition for the Cuban rebels. On the St. Johns River and less than 2 miles (3.2 km) from Jacksonville, Commodore struck a sandbar in a dense fog and damaged its hull. Although towed off the sandbar the following day, it was beached again in Mayport and again damaged. A leak began in the boiler room that evening and, as a result of malfunctioning water

327

pumps, the ship came to a standstill about 16 miles (26 km) from Mosquito Inlet. As the ship took on more water, Crane described the engine room as resembling "a scene at this time taken from the middle kitchen of hades." Commodore's lifeboats were lowered in the early hours of the morning on January 2, 1897 and the ship ultimately sank at 7 a.m. Crane was one of the last to leave the ship in a 10-foot (3.0 m) dinghy. In an ordeal that he recounted in the short story "The Open Boat", Crane and three other men (including the ship's Captain) foundered off the coast of Florida for a day and a half before trying to land the dinghy at Daytona Beach. The small boat overturned in the surf, forcing the exhausted men to swim to shore; one of them died. Having lost the gold given to him for his journey, Crane wired Cora Taylor for help. She traveled to Daytona and returned to Jacksonville with Crane the next day, only four days after he had left on the Commodore.

The disaster was reported on the front pages of newspapers across the country. Rumors that the ship had been sabotaged were widely circulated but never substantiated. Portrayed favorably and heroically by the press, Crane emerged from the ordeal with his reputation enhanced, if not restored, after the battering he had received in the Dora Clark affair. Meanwhile, Crane's affair with Taylor blossomed.

Three seasons of archaeological investigation were conducted in 2002-04 to examine and document the exposed remains of a wreck near Ponce Inlet, FL conjectured to be that of the SS Commodore. The collected data, and other accumulated evidence, finally substantiated the identification of the Commodore beyond a reasonable doubt.

Greco-Turkish War

Despite contentment in Jacksonville and the need for rest after his ordeal, Crane became restless. He left Jacksonville on January 11 for New York City, where he applied for a passport to Cuba, Mexico and the West Indies. Spending three weeks in New York, he completed "The Open Boat" and periodically visited Port Jervis to see family. By this time, however, blockades had formed along the Florida coast as tensions rose with Spain, and Crane concluded that he would never be able to travel to Cuba. He sold "The Open

Boat" to Scribner's for $300 in early March. Determined to work as a war correspondent, Crane signed on with William Randolph Hearst's New York Journal to cover the impending Greco-Turkish conflict. He brought along Taylor, who had sold the Hotel de Dream in order to follow him.

On March 20, they sailed first to England, where Crane was warmly received. They arrived in Athens in early April; between April 17 (when Turkey declared war on Greece) and April 22, Crane wrote his first published report of the war, "An Impression of the 'Concert' ". When he left for Epirus in the northwest, Taylor remained in Athens, where she became the Greek war's first woman war correspondent. She wrote under the pseudonym "Imogene Carter" for the New York Journal, a job that Crane had secured for her. They wrote frequently, traveling throughout the country separately and together. The first large battle that Crane witnessed was the Turks' assault on General Constantine Smolenski's Greek forces at Velestino. Crane wrote, "It is a great thing to survey the army of the enemy. Just where and how it takes hold upon the heart is difficult of description." During this battle, Crane encountered "a fat waddling puppy" that he immediately claimed, dubbing it "Velestino, the Journal dog". Greece and Turkey signed an armistice on May 20, ending the 30-day war; Crane and Taylor left Greece for England, taking two Greek brothers as servants and Velestino the dog with them.

Spanish–American War

After staying in Limpsfield, Surrey, for a few days, Crane and Taylor settled in Ravensbrook, a plain brick villa in Oxted. Referring to themselves as Mr. and Mrs. Crane, the couple lived openly in England, but Crane concealed the relationship from his friends and family in the United States. Admired in England, Crane thought himself attacked back home: "There seem so many of them in America who want to kill, bury and forget me purely out of unkindness and envy and—my unworthiness, if you choose", he wrote. Velestino the dog sickened and died soon after their arrival in England, on August 1. Crane, who had a great love for dogs, wrote an emotional letter to a friend an hour after the dog's death, stating that "for eleven days we fought death for him, thinking nothing of anything but his life." The Limpsfield-Oxted area was home to members of the socialist Fabian

Society and a magnet for writers such as Edmund Gosse, Ford Madox Ford and Edward Garnett. Crane also met the Polish-born novelist Joseph Conrad in October 1897, with whom he would have what Crane called a "warm and endless friendship".

Although Crane was confident among peers, strong negative reviews of the recently published The Third Violet were causing his literary reputation to dwindle. Reviewers were also highly critical of Crane's war letters, deeming them self-centered. Although The Red Badge of Courage had by this time gone through fourteen printings in the United States and six in England, Crane was running out of money. To survive financially, he worked at a feverish pitch, writing prolifically for both the English and the American markets. He wrote in quick succession stories such as The Monster, "The Bride Comes to Yellow Sky", "Death and the Child" and "The Blue Hotel". Crane began to attach price tags to his new works of fiction, hoping that "The Bride", for example, would fetch $175.

As 1897 ended, Crane's money crisis worsened. Amy Leslie, a reporter from Chicago and a former lover, sued him for $550. The New York Times reported that Leslie gave him $800 in November 1896 but that he'd repaid only a quarter of the sum. In February he was summoned to answer Leslie's claim. The claim was apparently settled out of court, because no record of adjudication exists. Meanwhile, Crane felt "heavy with troubles" and "chased to the wall" by expenses. He confided to his agent that he was $2,000 in debt but that he would "beat it" with more literary output.

Soon after the USS Maine exploded in Havana Harbor on February 15, 1898, under suspicious circumstances, Crane was offered a £60 advance by Blackwood's Magazine for articles "from the seat of war in the event of a war breaking out" between the United States and Spain. His health was failing, and it is believed that signs of his pulmonary tuberculosis, which he may have contracted in childhood, became apparent. With almost no money coming in from his finished stories, Crane accepted the assignment and left Oxted for New York. Taylor and the rest of the household stayed behind to fend off local creditors. Crane applied for a passport and left New York for Key West two days before Congress declared war. While the war idled, he interviewed people and produced occasional copy.

In early June, he observed the establishment of an American base in Cuba when Marines seized Guantánamo Bay. He went ashore with the Marines, planning "to gather impressions and write them as the spirit moved." Although he wrote honestly about his fear in battle, others observed his calmness and composure. He would later recall "this prolonged tragedy of the night" in the war tale "Marines Signaling Under Fire at Guantanamo". After showing a willingness to serve during fighting at Cuzco, Cuba, by carrying messages to company commanders, Crane was officially cited for his "material aid during the action".

He continued to report upon various battles and the worsening military conditions and praised Theodore Roosevelt's Rough Riders, despite past tensions with the Commissioner. In early July, Crane was sent to the United States for medical treatment for a high fever. He was diagnosed with yellow fever, then malaria. Upon arrival in Old Point Comfort, Virginia, he spent a few weeks resting in a hotel. Although Crane had filed more than twenty dispatches in the three months he had covered the war, the World's business manager believed that the paper had not received its money's worth and fired him. In retaliation, Crane signed with Hearst's New York Journal with the wish to return to Cuba. He traveled first to Puerto Rico and then to Havana. In September, rumors began to spread that Crane, who was working anonymously, had either been killed or disappeared. He sporadically sent out dispatches and stories; he wrote about the mood in Havana, the crowded city sidewalks, and other topics, but he was soon desperate for money again. Taylor, left alone in England, was also penniless. She became frantic with worry over her lover's whereabouts; they were not in direct communication until the end of the year. Crane left Havana and arrived in England on January 11, 1899.

Death

Rent on Ravensbrook had not been paid for a year. Upon returning to England, Crane secured a solicitor to act as guarantor for their debts, after which Crane and Taylor relocated to Brede Place. This manor in Sussex, which dated to the 14th century and had neither electricity nor indoor plumbing, was offered to them by friends at a modest rent. The relocation appeared to give hope to Crane, but his money problems continued. Deciding that he could no longer afford to write for American publications, he concentrated on publishing in English magazines.

Crane pushed himself to write feverishly during the first months at Brede; he told his publisher that he was "doing more work now than I have at any other period in my life". His health worsened, and by late 1899 he was asking friends about health resorts. The Monster and Other Stories was in production and War Is Kind, his second collection of poems, was published in the United States in May. None of his books after The Red Badge of Courage had sold well, and he bought a typewriter to spur output. Active Service, a novella based on Crane's correspondence experience, was published in October. The New York Times reviewer questioned "whether the author of 'Active Service' himself really sees anything remarkable in his newspapery hero."

In December, the couple held an elaborate Christmas party at Brede, attended by Conrad, Henry James, H. G. Wells and other friends; it lasted several days. On December 29 Crane suffered a severe pulmonary hemorrhage. In January 1900 he'd recovered sufficiently to work on a new novel, The O'Ruddy, completing 25 of the 33 chapters. Plans were made for him to travel as a correspondent to Gibraltar to write sketches from Saint Helena, the site of a Boer prison, but at the end of March and in early April he suffered two more hemorrhages. Taylor took over most of Crane's correspondence while he was ill, writing to friends for monetary aid. The couple planned to travel on the continent, but Conrad, upon visiting Crane for the last time, remarked that his friend's "wasted face was enough to tell me that it was the most forlorn of all hopes."

On May 28, the couple arrived at Badenweiler, Germany, a health spa on the edge of the Black Forest. Despite his weakened condition, Crane continued to dictate fragmentary episodes for the completion of The O'Ruddy. He died on June 5, 1900, at the age of 28. In his will he left everything to Taylor, who took his body to New Jersey for burial. Crane was interred in Evergreen Cemetery in what is now Hillside, New Jersey.

Fiction and poetry

Style and technique

Stephen Crane's fiction is typically categorized as representative of Naturalism, American realism, Impressionism or a mixture of the three. Critic Sergio Perosa, for example, wrote in his essay, "Stephen Crane fra naturalismo e impressionismo," that the work presents a "symbiosis" of Naturalistic ideals and Impressionistic methods. When asked whether or not he would write an autobiography in 1896, Crane responded that he "dare not say that I am honest. I merely say that I am as nearly honest as a weak mental machinery will allow." Similarities between the stylistic techniques in Crane's writing and Impressionist painting—including the use of color and chiaroscuro—are often cited to support the theory that Crane was not only an Impressionist but also influenced by the movement. H. G. Wells remarked upon "the great influence of the studio" on Crane's work, quoting a passage from The Red Badge of Courage as an example: "At nightfall the column broke into regimental pieces, and the fragments went into the fields to camp. Tents sprang up like strange plants. Camp fires, like red, peculiar blossoms, dotted the night.... From this little distance the many fires, with the black forms of men passing to and fro before the crimson rays, made weird and satanic effects." Although no direct evidence exists that Crane formulated a precise theory of his craft, he vehemently rejected sentimentality, asserting that "a story should be logical in its action and faithful to character. Truth to life itself was the only test, the greatest artists were the simplest, and simple because they were true."

Poet and biographer John Berryman suggested that there were three basic variations, or "norms", of Crane's narrative style. The first, being "flexible, swift, abrupt and nervous", is best exemplified in The Red Badge of Courage, while the second ("supple majesty") is believed to relate to "The Open Boat", and the third ("much more closed, circumstantial and 'normal' in feeling and syntax") to later works such as The Monster. Crane's work, however, cannot be determined by style solely on chronology. Not only does his fiction not take place in any particular region with similar characters, but it varies from serious in tone to reportorial writing and light fiction. Crane's writing, both fiction and nonfiction, is consistently driven by immediacy and is at once concentrated, vivid and intense. The novels and short stories contain poetic characteristics such as shorthand prose, suggestibility, shifts in perspective and ellipses between and within sentences. Similarly, omission plays a large part in Crane's work; the names of his protagonists are not commonly used and sometimes they are not named at all.

Crane was often criticized by early reviewers for his frequent incorporation of everyday speech into dialogue, mimicking the regional accents of his characters with colloquial stylization. This is apparent in his first novel, in which Crane ignored the romantic, sentimental approach of slum fiction; he instead concentrated on the cruelty and sordid aspects of poverty, expressed by the brashness of the Bowery's crude dialect and profanity, which he used lavishly. The distinct dialect of his Bowery characters is apparent at the beginning of the text; the title character admonishes her brother saying: "Yeh knows it puts mudder out when yes comes home half dead, an' it's like we'll all get a poundin'."

Major themes

Crane's work is often thematically driven by Naturalistic and Realistic concerns, including ideals versus realities, spiritual crises and fear. These themes are particularly evident in Crane's first three novels, Maggie: A Girl of the Streets, The Red Badge of Courage and George's Mother. The three main characters search for a way to make their dreams come true, but ultimately suffer from crises of identity. Crane was fascinated by war and death, as well as fire, disfigurement, fear and courage, all of which inspired him to write many works based on these concepts. In The Red Badge of Courage, the main character both longs for the heroics of battle but ultimately fears it, demonstrating the dichotomy of courage and cowardice. He experiences the threat of death, misery and a loss of self.

Extreme isolation from society and community is also apparent in Crane's work. During the most intense battle scenes in The Red Badge of Courage, for example, the story's focus is mainly "on the inner responses of a self unaware of others". In "The Open Boat", "An Experiment in Misery" and other stories, Crane uses light, motion and color to express degrees of epistemological uncertainty. Similar to other Naturalistic writers, Crane scrutinizes the position of man, who has been isolated not only from society, but also from God and nature. "The Open Boat", for example, distances itself from Romantic optimism and affirmation of man's place in the world by concentrating on the characters' isolation.

While he lived, Stephen Crane was denominated by critical readers a realist, a naturalist, an impressionist, symbolist, Symboliste, expressionist and ironist; his posthumous life was enriched by critics who read him as nihilistic, existentialist, a neo-Romantic, a sentimentalist, protomodernist, pointilliste, visionist, imagist and, by his most recent biographer, a "bleak naturalist." At midcentury he was a "predisciple of the New Criticism"; by its end he was "a proto-deconstructionist anti-artist hero" who had "leapfrogged modernism, landing on postmodernist ground." Or, as Sergio Perosa wrote in 1964, "The critic wanders in a labyrinth of possibilities, which every new turn taken by Crane's fiction seems to explode or deny."

One undeniable fact about Crane's work, as Anthony Splendora noted in 2015, is that Death haunts it; like a threatening eclipse it overshadows his best efforts, each of which features the signal demise of a main character. Allegorically, "The Blue Hotel," at the pinnacle of the short story form, may even be an autothanatography, the author's intentional exteriorization or objectification, in this case for the purpose of purgation, of his own impending death. Crane's "Swede" in that story can be taken, following current psychoanalytical theory, as a surrogative, sacrificial victim, ritually to be purged.

Transcending this "dark circumstance of composition," Crane had a particular telos and impetus for his creation: beyond the tautologies that all art is alterity and to some formal extent mimesis, Crane sought and obviously found "a form of catharsis" in writing. This view accounts for his uniqueness, especially as operative through his notorious "disgust" with his family's religion, their "vacuous, futile psalm-singing". His favorite book, for example, was Mark Twain's Life on the Mississippi, in which God is mentioned only twice—once as irony and once as "a swindle." Not only did Crane call out God specifically with the lines "Well then I hate thee / righteous image" in "The Black Riders" (1895), but even his most hopeful tropes, such as the "comradeship" of his "Open Boat" survivors, make no mention of deity, specifying only "indifferent nature." His antitheism is most evident in his characterization of the human race as "lice clinging to a space-lost bulb," a climax-nearing speech in "The Blue Hotel," Ch. VI. It is possible that Crane utilized religion's formal psychic space, now suddenly available resulting from the recent "Death of God", as a milieu for his compensatory art.

Novels

Beginning with the publication of Maggie: A Girl of the Streets in 1893, Crane was recognized by critics mainly as a novelist. Maggie was initially rejected by numerous publishers because of its atypical and true-to-life depictions of class warfare, which clashed with the sentimental tales of that time. Rather than focusing on the very rich or middle class, the novel's characters are lower-class denizens of New York's Bowery. The main character, Maggie, descends into prostitution after being led astray by her lover. Although the novel's plot is simple, its dramatic mood, quick pace and portrayal of Bowery life have made it memorable. Maggie is not merely an account of slum life, but also represents eternal symbols. In his first draft, Crane did not give his characters proper names. Instead, they were identified by epithets: Maggie, for example, was the girl who "blossomed in a mud-puddle" and Pete, her seducer, was a "knight". The novel is dominated by bitter irony and anger, as well as destructive morality and treacherous sentiment. Critics would later call the novel "the first dark flower of American Naturalism" for its distinctive elements of naturalistic fiction.

Written thirty years after the end of the Civil War and before Crane had any experience of battle, The Red Badge of Courage was innovative stylistically as well as psychologically. Often described as a war novel, it focuses less on battle and more on the main character's psyche and his reactions and responses in war. It is believed that Crane based the fictional battle in the novel on that of Chancellorsville; he may also have interviewed veterans of the 124th New York Volunteer Infantry Regiment, commonly known as the Orange Blossoms, in Port Jervis, New York. Told in a third-person limited point of view, it reflects the private experience of Henry Fleming, a young soldier who flees from combat. The Red Badge of Courage is notable in its vivid descriptions and well-cadenced prose, both of which help create suspense within the story. Similarly, by substituting epithets for characters' names ("the youth", "the tattered soldier"), Crane injects an allegorical quality into his work, making his characters point to a specific characteristic of man. Like Crane's first novel, The Red Badge of Courage has a deeply ironic tone which increases in severity as the novel progresses. The title of the work is ironic; Henry wishes "that he, too, had a wound, a red badge of courage", echoing a wish to have been wounded in battle. The wound he does receive (from the rifle butt of a fleeing Union soldier) is not a badge of courage but a badge of shame.

The novel expresses a strong connection between humankind and nature, a frequent and prominent concern in Crane's fiction and poetry throughout his career. Whereas contemporary writers (Ralph Waldo Emerson, Nathaniel Hawthorne, Henry David Thoreau) focused on a sympathetic bond on the two elements, Crane wrote from the perspective that human consciousness distanced humans from nature. In The Red Badge of Courage, this distance is paired with a great number of references to animals, and men with animalistic characteristics: people "howl", "squawk", "growl", or "snarl".

Since the resurgence of Crane's popularity in the 1920s, The Red Badge of Courage has been deemed a major American text. The novel has been anthologized numerous times, including in the 1942 collection Men at War: The Best War Stories of All Time, edited by Ernest Hemingway. In the introduction, Hemingway wrote that the novel "is one of the finest books of our literature, and I include it entire because it is all as much of a piece as a great poem is."

Crane's later novels have not received as much critical praise. After the success of The Red Badge of Courage, Crane wrote another tale set in the Bowery. George's Mother is less allegorical and more personal than his two previous novels, and it focuses on the conflict between a church-going, temperance-adhering woman (thought to be based on Crane's mother) and her single remaining offspring, who is a naive dreamer. Critical response to the novel was mixed. The Third Violet, a romance that he wrote quickly after publishing The Red Badge of Courage, is typically considered as Crane's attempt to appeal to popular audiences. Crane considered it a "quiet little story." Although it contained autobiographical details, the characters have been deemed inauthentic and stereotypical. Crane's second to last novel, Active Service, revolves around the Greco-Turkish War of 1897, with which the author was familiar. Although noted for its satirical take on the melodramatic and highly passionate works that were popular of the nineteenth century, the novel was not successful. It is generally accepted by critics that Crane's work suffered at this point due to the speed which he wrote in order to meet his high expenses. His last novel, a suspenseful and picaresque work entitled The O'Ruddy, was finished posthumously by Robert Barr and published in 1903.

Short fiction

Crane wrote many different types of fictional pieces while indiscriminately applying to them terms such as "story", "tale" and "sketch". For this reason, critics have found clear-cut classification of Crane's work problematic. While "The Open Boat" and "The Bride Comes to Yellow Sky" are often considered short stories, others are variously identified.

In an 1896 interview with Herbert P. Williams, a reporter for the Boston Herald, Crane said that he did "not find that short stories are utterly different in character from other fiction. It seems to me that short stories are the easiest things we write." During his brief literary career, he wrote more than a hundred short stories and fictional sketches. Crane's early fiction was based in camping expeditions in his teen years; these stories eventually became known as The Sullivan County Tales and Sketches. He considered these "sketches", which are mostly humorous and not of the same caliber of work as his later fiction, to be "articles of many kinds," in that they are part fiction and part journalism.

The subject matter for his stories varied extensively. His early New York City sketches and Bowery tales accurately described the results of industrialization, immigration and the growth of cities and their slums. His collection of six short stories, The Little Regiment, covered familiar ground with the American Civil War, a subject for which he became famous with The Red Badge of Courage. Although similar to Crane's noted novel, The Little Regiment was believed to lack vigor and originality. Realizing the limitations of these tales, Crane wrote: "I have invented the sum of my invention with regard to war and this story keeps me in internal despair."

The Open Boat and Other Tales of Adventure (1898) contains thirteen short stories that deal with three periods in Crane's life: his Asbury Park boyhood, his trip to the West and Mexico in 1895, and his Cuban adventure in 1897. This collection was well received and included several of his most critically successful works. His 1899 collection, The Monster and Other Stories, was similarly well received.

Two posthumously published collections were not as successful. In August 1900 The Whilomville Stories were published, a collection of thirteen stories that Crane wrote during the last year of his life. The work deals almost exclusively with boyhood, and the stories are drawn from events occurring in Port Jervis, where Crane lived from the age of six to eleven. Focusing on small-town America, the stories tend toward sentimentality, but remain perceptive of the lives of children. Wounds in the Rain, published in September 1900, contains fictional tales based on Crane's reports for the World and the Journal during the Spanish–American War. These stories, which Crane wrote while desperately ill, include "The Price of the Harness" and "The Lone Charge of William B. Perkins" and are dramatic, ironic and sometimes humorous.

Despite Crane's prolific output, only four stories--"The Open Boat", "The Blue Hotel", "The Bride Comes to Yellow Sky", and The Monster— have received extensive attention from scholars. H. G. Wells considered "The Open Boat" to be "beyond all question, the crown of all his work", and it is one of the most frequently discussed of Crane's works.

Poetry

Many red devils ran from my heart

And out upon the page.

They were so tiny

The pen could mash them.

And many struggled in the ink.

It was strange

To write in this red muck

Of things from my heart.

— Stephen Crane

Crane's poems, which he preferred to call "lines", are typically not given as much scholarly attention as his fiction; no anthology contained Crane's verse until 1926. Although it is not certain when Crane began to write poetry seriously, he once said that his overall poetic aim was "to give my ideas of life as a whole, so far as I know it". The poetic style used in both of his books of poetry, The Black Riders and Other Lines and War is Kind, was unconventional for the time in that it was written in free verse without rhyme, meter, or even titles for individual works. They are typically short in length; although several poems, such as "Do not weep, maiden, for war is kind", use stanzas and refrains, most do not. Crane also differed from his peers and poets of later generations in that his work contains allegory, dialectic and narrative situations.

Critic Ruth Miller claimed that Crane wrote "an intellectual poetry rather than a poetry that evokes feeling, a poetry that stimulates the mind rather than arouses the heart". In the most complexly organized poems, the significance of the states of mind or feelings is ambiguous, but Crane's poems tend to affirm certain elemental attitudes, beliefs, opinions and stances toward God, man and the universe. The Black Riders in particular is essentially a dramatic concept and the poems provide continuity within the dramatic structure. There is also a dramatic interplay in which there is frequently a major voice reporting an incident seen ("In the desert / I saw a creature, naked, bestial") or experienced ("A learned man came to me once"). The second voice or additional voices represent a point of view which is revealed to be inferior; when these clash, a dominant attitude emerges.

340

Legacy

In four years, Crane published five novels, two volumes of poetry, three short story collections, two books of war stories, and numerous works of short fiction and reporting. Today he is mainly remembered for The Red Badge of Courage, which is regarded as an American classic. The novel has been adapted several times for the screen, including John Huston's 1951 version. By the time of his death, Crane had become one of the best known writers of his generation. His eccentric lifestyle, frequent newspaper reporting, association with other famous authors, and expatriate status made him somewhat of an international celebrity. Although most stories about his life tended toward the romantic, rumors about his alleged drug use and alcoholism persisted long after his death.

By the early 1920s, Crane and his work were nearly forgotten. It was not until Thomas Beer published his biography in 1923, which was followed by editor Wilson Follett's The Work of Stephen Crane (1925–1927), that Crane's writing came to the attention of a scholarly audience. Crane's reputation was then enhanced by faithful support from writer friends such as Joseph Conrad, H. G. Wells and Ford Madox Ford, all of whom either published recollections or commented upon their time with Crane. John Berryman's 1950 biography of Crane further established him as an important American author. Since 1951 there has been a steady outpouring of articles, monographs and reprints in Crane scholarship.

Today, Crane is considered one of the most innovative writers of the 1890s. His peers, including Conrad and James, as well as later writers such as Robert Frost, Ezra Pound and Willa Cather, hailed Crane as one of the finest creative spirits of his time. His work was described by Wells as "the first expression of the opening mind of a new period, or, at least, the early emphatic phase of a new initiative." Wells said that "beyond dispute", Crane was "the best writer of our generation, and his untimely death was an irreparable loss to our literature." Conrad wrote that Crane was an "artist" and "a seer with a gift for rendering the significant on the surface of things and with an incomparable insight into primitive emotions". Crane's work has proved inspirational for future writers; not only have scholars drawn similarities between Hemingway's A Farewell to Arms and The Red Badge of Courage, but Crane's fiction is thought to have been an important inspiration for Hemingway and his fellow Modernists. In 1936, Hemingway wrote in The Green Hills of Africa that "The good writers are Henry James, Stephen Crane, and Mark Twain. That's not the order they're good in. There is no order for good writers." Crane's poetry is thought to have been a precursor to the Imagist movement, and his short fiction has also influenced American literature. "The Open Boat", "The Blue Hotel", The Monster and "The Bride Comes to Yellow Sky" are generally considered by critics to be examples of Crane's best work.

Several institutions and places have endeavored to keep Crane's legacy alive. Badenweiler and the house where he died became something of a tourist attraction for its fleeting association with the American author; Alexander Woollcott attested to the fact that, long after Crane's death, tourists would be directed to the room where he died. Columbia University Rare Book and Manuscript Library has a collection of Crane and Taylor's personal correspondence dating from 1895 to 1908. Near his brother Edmund's Sullivan County home in New York, where Crane stayed for a short time, a pond is named after him. The Stephen Crane House in Asbury Park, New Jersey, where the author lived with his siblings for nine years, is operated as a museum dedicated to his life and work. Syracuse University has an annual Stephen Crane Lecture Series which is sponsored by the Dikaia Foundation.

Columbia University purchased much of the Stephen Crane materials held by Cora Crane at her death. The Crane Collection is one of the largest in the nation of his materials. Columbia University had an exhibit: 'The Tall Swift Shadow of a Ship at Night': Stephen and Cora Crane, November 2, 1995 through February 16, 1996, about the lives of the couple, featuring letters and other documents and memorabilia. (Source : Wikipedia)

NOTABLE WORKS

NOVELS

Maggie: A Girl of the Streets, 1893.

The Red Badge of Courage, 1895.

George's Mother, 1896.

The Third Violet, 1897.

Active Service, 1899.

Crane, Stephen and Robert Barr. The O'Ruddy, 1903.

The Black Riders and Other Lines, 1895.

The Open Boat and Other Tales of Adventure, 1898

War is Kind, 1899

The Monster and Other Stories, 1899

Wounds in the Rain, 1900

Great Battles of the World, 1901

The O'Ruddy, 1903

SHORT STORY COLLECTIONS

The Little Regiment and Other Episodes from the American Civil War, 1896.

The Open Boat and Other Tales of Adventure, 1898.

The Monster and Other Stories, 1899.

Whilomville Stories, 1900.

Wounds in the Rain: War Stories, 1900.

Great Battles of the World, 1901.

The Monster,1901.

Last Words, 1902.

POETRY COLLECTIONS

The Black Riders and Other Lines, 1895.

War is Kind, 1899.

UNFINISHED WORKS

Sources report that following an encounter with a male prostitute in the spring of 1894, Crane began a novel on the subject entitled Flowers of Asphalt. He reportedly abandoned the project and the manuscript has never been recovered.

CPSIA information can be obtained
at www.ICGtesting.com
Printed in the USA
LVHW052054261020
669863LV00017B/284

9 781662 722387